Artists in Crime

"ARTISTS IN CRIME is Miss Marsh's best
...Her touch is light, without lapsing into the
facetious; her characterization excellent; her
plot neat and precise."
—*Nicholas Blake*, SPECTATOR

"A genuinely absorbing detective story."
—THE NEW YORK TIMES

ARTISTS IN CRIME

NGAIO MARSH

A JOVE BOOK

Requests for permission to make copies of any part of the work should be mailed to: Permissions, Jove Publications, Inc., 200 Madison Avenue, New York, NY 10016

Back-cover photograph by Mannering and Associates Ltd.

First Jove edition published January 1980

10 9 8 7 6 5 4 3 2

Printed in the United States of America

Jove books are published by Jove Publications, Inc.
200 Madison Avenue, New York, NY 10016

For Phyllis and John

Contents

The Characters in the Tale

CHIEF DETECTIVE-INSPECTOR RODERICK ALLEYN, C.I.D.

MISS VAN MAES, the success of the ship.

AGATHA TROY, R.A., of Tatler's End House, Bossicote, Bucks. Painter.

KATTI BOSTOCK, well-known painter of plumbers and negro musicians.

NIGEL BATHGATE, journalist.

LADY ALLEYN, of Danes Lodge, Bossicote, Bucks; mother of Chief Detective-Inspector Alleyn.

CEDRIC MALMSLEY, a student with a beard.

GARCIA, a sculptor.

SONIA GLUCK, a model.

FRANCIS ORMERIN, a student from Paris.

PHILLIDA LEE, a student from the Slade.

WATT HATCHETT, a student from Australia.

THE HON. BASIL PILGRIM, a student from the nobility.

VALMAI SEACLIFF, a student with sex-appeal.

SUPERINTENDENT BLACKMAN, of the Buckingham Constabulary Force.

DETECTIVE-INSPECTOR FOX, C.I.D.

DETECTIVE-SERGEANT BAILEY, C.I.D., a fingerprint expert.

DETECTIVE-SERGEANT THOMPSON, C.I.D., a photographic expert.

DR. AMPTHILL, police surgeon at Bossicote, Bucks.

P.C. SLIGO, of Bossicote Police Force.

A CHARLADY

BOBBIE O'DAWNE, a lady of the Ensemble.

AN ESTATE AGENT

TED MCCULLY, foreman at a car depot.

DR. CURTIS, police surgeon, C.I.D.

CAPTAIN PASCOE, of Boxover.

HIS SERVANT

CHAPTER I

Prologue at Sea

Alleyn leant over the deck-rail, looking at the wet brown wharf and the upturned faces of the people. In a minute or two now they would slide away, lose significance, and become a vague memory. "We called at Suva." He had a sudden desire to run a mental ring round the scene beneath him, to isolate it, and make it clear for ever in his mind. Idly at first, and then with absurd concentration, he began to memorise, starting with a detail. The tall Fijian with dyed hair. The hair was vivid magenta against the arsenic green of a pile of fresh bananas. He trapped and held the pattern of it. Then the brown face beneath, with liquid blue half-tones reflected from the water, then the oily dark torso, foreshortened, the white loincloth, and the sharp legs. The design made by the feet on wet planks. It became a race. How much of the scene could he fix in his memory before the ship sailed? The sound, too—he must get that—the firm slap of bare feet on wet boards, the languid murmur of voices and the snatches of song drifting from a group of native girls near those clumps of fierce magenta coral. The smell must not be forgotten— frangipanni, coco-nut oil, and sodden wood. He widened his circle, taking in more figures—the Indian woman in the shrill pink sari, sitting by the green bananas; wet roofs on the wharf and damp roads wandering aimlessly towards mangrove swamps and darkened hills. Those hills, sharply purple at their base, lost outline behind a sulky company of clouds, to jag out, fantastically peaked, against a motionless and sombre sky. The clouds themselves were indigo at the edges, heavy with the ominous depression of unshed rain. The darkness of everything and the violence of colour—it was a pattern of wet brown, acid green, magenta and indigo. The round voices of the Fijians, loud and deep, as though they spoke through resounding tubes, pierced the moist air and made it vibrant.

Everything shifted a little, stepped back a pace. The ship had parted from the wharf. Already the picture was remote, the sounds would soon fade out. Alleyn shut his eyes and found the whole impression vivid under the closed lids. When he opened them the space between vessel and land had widened. He no longer wanted to look at the wharf, and turned away.

"And am I *hart*?" the success of the ship was saying to a group of young men. "Oh baby! I'll say I've left hoff a stone back there in that one-eyed lil' burg. Hart! Phoo!"

The young men laughed adoringly.

"It's hotter than this in Honolulu!" teased one of the young men.

"Maybe. But it's not so enervating."

"Very hot spot, Honolulu!"

"Oh boy!" chanted the success, rolling her eyes and sketching a Hawaiian movement with her hips. "You wait a while till I show you round the lil' old home town. Gee, that label on my grips certainly looks good to me." She saw Alleyn. "Hello, hello, look who's here! Come right over and join the party."

Alleyn strolled over. Ever since they sailed from Auckland he had been uneasily aware of a certain warmth in the technique of the success where he was concerned. He supposed it was rather one up to him with all these youngsters in hot pursuit. At this stage of speculation he invariably pulled a fastidious face and thought ruefully: "Lord, lord, the vanity of the male forties." But she was very lovely, and the thought of her almost lent a little glamour to the possible expectation of the weary routine of a shipboard flirtation.

"Look at him!" cried the success. "Isn't he the cutest thing! That quiet English stuff certainly makes one great big appeal with this baby. And does he flash the keep-clear signal! Boys, I'll take you right into my confidence. Listen! This Mr. Alleyn is my big flop. I don't mean a thing to him."

"She really is rather awful," thought Alleyn, and he said: "Ah, Miss Van Maes, you don't know a coward when you see one."

"Meaning?"

"I—I really don't know," mumbled Alleyn hurriedly.

"Hullo, we're going through the barrier," said one of the youths.

They all turned to the deck-rail. The sea wrapped itself

sluggishly about the thin rib of the reef and fell away on either side in an enervated pother of small breakers. Over Fiji the rain still hung in ponderable clouds. The deep purple of the islands was lit by desultory patches of livid sunshine, banana-green, sultry, but without iridescence. The ship passed through the fangs of the reef.

Alleyn slipped away, walked aft, and climbed the companion-way to the boat deck. Nobody about up there, the passengers in their shoregoing clothes were still collected on the main deck. He filled his pipe meditatively, staring back towards Fiji. It was pleasant up there. Peaceful.

"Damn!" said a female voice. "Damn, damn, damn! Oh *blast!*"

Startled, Alleyn looked up. Sitting on the canvas cover of one of the boats was a woman. She seemed to be dabbing at something. She stood up and he saw that she wore a pair of exceedingly grubby flannel trousers, and a short grey overall. In her hand was a long brush. Her face was disfigured by a smudge of green paint, and her short hair stood up in a worried shock, as though she had run her hands through it. She was very thin and dark. She scrambled to the bows of the boat and Alleyn was able to see what she had been at. A small canvas was propped up in the lid of an open paint-box. Alleyn drew in his breath sharply. It was as if his deliberately cultivated memory of the wharf at Suva had been simplified and made articulate. The sketch was an almost painfully explicit statement of the feeling of that scene. It was painted very directly with crisp, nervous touches. The pattern of blue-pinks and sharp greens fell across it like the linked syllables of a perfect phrase. It was very simply done, but to Alleyn it was profoundly satisfying—an expression of an emotion, rather than a record of a visual impression.

The painter, an unlit cigarette between her lips, stared dispassionately at her work. She rummaged in her trouser pockets, found nothing but a handkerchief that had been used as a paint-rag, and ran her fingers through her hair.

"Blast!" she repeated, and took the unlit cigarette from her lips.

"Match?" said Alleyn.

She started, lost her balance, and sat down abruptly. "How long have you been there?" she demanded ungraciously.

"Only just come. I—I haven't been spying. May I give you a match?"

"Oh—thanks. Chuck up the box, would you?" She lit her cigarette, eyeing him over the top of her long thin hands, and then turned to look again at her work.

"It is exceedingly good, isn't it?" said Alleyn.

She hunched up one shoulder as if his voice was a piercing draught in her ear, muttered something, and crawled back to her work. She picked up her palette and began mixing a streak of colour with her knife.

"You're not going to do anything more to it?" said Alleyn involuntarily.

She turned her head and stared at him.

"Why not?"

"Because it's perfect—you'll hurt it. I say, please forgive me. Frightful impertinence. I do apologise."

"Oh, don't be ridiculous," she said impatiently, and screwed up her eyes to peer at the canvas.

"I merely thought——" began Alleyn.

"I had an idea," said the painter, "that if I worked up here on this hideously uncomfortable perch, I might possibly have the place to myself for a bit."

"You shall," said Alleyn, and bowed to her profile. He tried to remember if he had ever before been quite so pointedly snubbed by a total stranger. Only, he reflected, by persons he was obliged to interview in the excution of his duties as an officer of Scotland Yard. On those occasions he persisted. On this an apologetic exit seemed to be clearly indicated. He walked to the top of the companion-way, and then paused.

"But if you do anything more, you'll be a criminal. The thing's perfect. Even I can see that, and I——"

"'Don't know anything about it, but I *do* know what I like,'" quoted the lady savagely.

"I was not about to produce that particular bromide," said Alleyn mildly.

For the first time since he had spoken to her, she gave him her full attention. A rather charming grin lifted the corners of her mouth.

"All right," she said, "I'm being objectionable. My turn to apologise. I thought at first you were one of the 'don't put me in it' sort of onlookers."

"Heaven forbid!"

"I wasn't going to do too much," she went on, actually as if she had turned suddenly shy. "It's just that figure in the foreground—I left it too late. Worked for an hour before we sailed. There should be a repetition of the blueish grey there,

4

but I can't remember——" She paused, worried.

"But there was!" exclaimed Alleyn. "The reflection off the water up the inside of the thighs. Don't you remember?"

"Golly—you're right," she said. "Here—wait a bit."

She picked up a thin brush, broke it through the colour, held it poised for a second, and then laid a delicate touch on the canvas. "That?"

"Yes," cried Alleyn excitedly. "That's done it. Now you can stop."

"All right, all right. I didn't realise you were a painting bloke."

"I'm not. It's simply insufferable cheek."

She began to pack up her box.

"Well, I must say you're very observant for a layman. Good memory."

"Not really," said Alleyn. "It's synthetic."

"You mean you've trained your eye?"

"I've had to try to do so, certainly."

"Why?"

"Part of my job. Let me take that box for you."

"Oh—thank you. Mind the lid—it's a bit painty. Pity to spoil those lovely trousers. Will you take the sketch?"

"Do you want a hand down?" offered Alleyn.

"I can manage, thank you," she said gruffly, and clambered down to the deck.

Alleyn had propped the canvas against the rail and now stood looking at it. She joined him, eyeing it with the disinterested stare of the painter.

"Why!" murmured Alleyn suddenly. "Why, you must be Agatha Troy."

"That's me."

"Good Lord, what a self-sufficient fathead I've been."

"Why?" said Agatha Troy. "You were all right. Very useful."

"Thank you," said Alleyn humbly. "I saw your one-man show a year ago in London."

"Did you?" she said without interest.

"I should have guessed at once. Isn't there a sort of relationship between this painting and the 'In the Stadium'?"

"Yes." She moved her eyebrows quickly. "That's quite true. The arrangement's much the same—radiating lines and a spotted pattern. Same feeling. Well, I'd better go down to my cabin and unpack."

"You joined the ship at Suva?"

"Yes. I noticed this subject from the main deck. Things shove themselves at you like that sometimes. I dumped my luggage, changed, and came up."

She slung her box over her shoulder and picked up the sketch.

"Can I——?" said Alleyn diffidently.

"No, thanks."

She stood for a moment staring back towards Fiji. Her hands gripped the shoulder-straps of her paintbox. The light breeze whipped back her short dark hair, revealing the contour of the skull and the delicate bones of the face. The temples were slightly hollow, the cheek-bones showed, the dark-blue eyes were deep-set under the thin ridge of the brows. The sun caught the olive skin with its smudge of green paint, and gave it warmth. There was a kind of spare gallantry about her. She turned quickly before he had time to look away and their gaze met.

Alleyn was immediately conscious of a clarification of his emotions. As she stood before him, her face slowly reddening under his gaze, she seemed oddly familiar. He felt that he already knew her next movement, and the next inflexion of her clear, rather cold voice. It was a little as though he had thought of her a great deal, but never met her before. These impressions held him transfixed, for how long he never knew, while he still kept his eyes on hers. Then something clicked in his mind, and he realised that he had stared her out of countenance. The blush had mounted painfully to the roots of her hair and she had turned away.

"I'm sorry," said Alleyn steadily. "I'm afraid I was looking at the green smudge on your cheek."

She scrubbed at her face with the cuff of her smock.

"I'll go down," she said, and picked up the sketch.

He stood aside, but she had to pass close to him, and again he was vividly aware of her, still with the same odd sense of surprised familiarity. She smelt of turpentine and paint, he noticed.

"Well—good evening," she said vaguely.

Alleyn laughed a little.

"Good evening, madam."

She started off down the ladder, moving sideways and holding the wet sketch out over the hand-rail. He turned away and lit a cigarette. Suddenly a terrific rumpus broke out on the deck below. The hot cheap reek of frangipanni blossoms drifted up, and with it the voice of the success of the ship.

"Oh, pardon me. Come right down. Gangway, fellows. Oh say, pardon me, but have you been making a picture? Can I have a peek? I'm just crazy about sketching. Look, boys—isn't that cute? The wharf! My, my, it's a shame you haven't been able to finish it, isn't it? It would have been swell! Look, boys, it's the wharf. Maybe a snapshot would help. We'll surely have to watch our step with an artist on board. Say, let's get acquainted. We've been celebrating and we feel fine. Meet the mob. I'm Virginia Van Maes."

"My name's Troy," said a voice that Alleyn could scarcely recognise. A series of elaborate introductions followed.

"Well, Miss Troy, I was going to tell you how Caley Burt painted my portrait in Noo York. You've heard of Caley Burt? I guess he's one of the most exclusive portraitists in America. Well, it seems he was just crazy to take my picture——"

The anecdote was a long one. Agatha Troy remained silent throughout.

"Well, when he was through—and say, did I get tired of that dress?—it was one big success. Poppa bought it, and it's in our reception-hall at Honolulu. Some of the crowd say it doesn't just flatter, but it looks good to me. I don't pretend to know a whole lot about art, Miss Troy, but I know what I like."

"Quite," said Agatha Troy. "Look here, I think I'd better get down to my cabin. I haven't unpacked yet. If you'll excuse me——"

"Why, certainly. We'll be seeing you. Say, have you seen that guy Alleyn around?"

"I'm afraid I don't know——"

"He's tall and thin, and I'll say he's good-looking. And he is British? Gee! I'm crazy about him. I got a little gamble with these boys, I'll have him doing figure eights trying to dope out when the petting-party gets started."

"I've kissed good-bye to my money," one of the youths said.

"Listen to him, will you, Miss Troy? But we certainly saw Mr. Alleyn around this way a while back."

"He went up to the boat deck," said a youth.

"Oh," said Miss Troy clearly. "That man! Yes, he's up there now."

"Atta-boy!"

"Whoopee!"

7

"Oh damn!" said Alleyn softly.

And the next thing that happened was Miss Van Maes showing him how she'd made a real Honolulu *lei* out of Fijian frangipanni, and asking him to come down with the crowd for a drink.

"Has this party gone cuckoo or something? We're three rounds behind the clock. C'm on!"

"Virginia," said a youth, "you're tight."

"What the hell! Is it my day to be sober? You coming, Mr. Alleyn?"

"Thank you so much," said Alleyn, "but if you'll believe it, I'm a non-drinker at the moment. Doctor's orders."

"Aw, be funny!"

"Fact, I assure you."

"Mr. Alleyn's thinking of the lady with the picture," said a youth.

"What—her? With her face all mussed in green paint. Mr. Alleyn's not screwy yet, is he? Gee, I'll say a woman's got no self-respect to go around that way in public. Did you get a look at that smock? And the picture! Well, I had to be polite and say it was cute, but it's nobody's big sorrow she didn't finish it. The wharf at Suva! Seems I struck it lucky, but what it's meant for's just anyone's guess. C'm on, Mr. Strong-Silent-Sleuth, put me out of my agony and say she don't mean one thing to you."

"Miss Van Maes," said Alleyn, "do you know that you make me feel very middle-aged and inexpressibly foolish? I haven't got the smallest idea what the right answer is to any one of your questions."

"Maybe I could teach you. Maybe I could teach you a whole lot of fun, honey."

"You're very kind, but, do you know, I'm afraid I'm past the receptive age."

She widened her enormous eyes. The mascaraed lashes stuck out round them like black toothpicks. Her ash-fair hair was swept back from her very lovely face into a cluster of disciplined and shining curls. She had the unhuman good looks of a film star. Undoubtedly she was rather tight.

"Well," she said, "my bet with the boys is still good. Twenty-five'll get anybody fifty you kiss me before we hit Honolulu. And I don't mean maybe."

"I should be very much honoured——"

"Yeah? And I don't mean the get-by-the-censor stuff, either. No, sir!"

She stared at him, and upon her normally blank and beautiful face there dawned a look of doubt.

"Say," she said, "you're not going to tell me you got a yen for that woman?"

"I don't know what a yen is," Alleyn said, "but I've got nothing at all for Miss Troy, and I can assure you she has got even less than that for me."

CHAPTER II

Five Letters

From Miss Agatha Troy to her friend, Miss Katti Bostock, the well-known painter of plumbers, miners and negro musicians:

S.S. *Niagara*,
August 1st.

Dear Katti,

I am breaking this journey at Quebec, so you'll get this letter about a fortnight before I get home. I'm glad everything is fixed up for next term. It's a bore in some ways having to teach, but now I've reached the giddy heights of picking and choosing I don't find it nearly so irksome. Damn' good of you to do all the arranging for me. If you can, get the servants into the house by Sept. 1st—I get back on the 3rd—they ought to have everything fixed up by the 10th, when we start classes. Your air-mail reached Suva the day we sailed. Yes, book Sonia Gluck for model. The little swine's beautiful and knows how to pose as long as she behaves herself. You yourself might do a big nude for the Group Show on the 16th or thereabouts. You paint well from the nude and I think you shouldn't remain wedded to your plumbers—your stuff will get static if you don't look out. I don't think I told you who is coming next term. Here is the list:

(1) Francis Ormerin. He's painting in Paris at the moment, but says the lot at Malaquin's has come all over surrealist and he can't see it and doesn't want to. Says he's depressed about his work or something.

(2) Valmai Seacliff. That's the girl that did those dabby Rex Whistlerish posters for the Board of Trade. She says she wants to do some solid work from the model. Quite true, she does; but I rather fancy she's on the hunt.

(3) Basil Pilgrim. If I'm not mistaken, Basil is Valmai's

quarry. He's an Hon., you know, and the old Lord Pilgrim is doddering to the grave. He's the "Peer that became a Primitive Methodist" a few years ago—you remember. The papers were full of it. He comes to light with the odd spot of hell-fire on the subject of birth-control, every now and then. Basil's got six elder sisters, and Lady Pilgrim died when he was born, so we don't know what she thought about it. I hardly think Valmai Seacliff will please the old gentleman. Basil's painting nearly drove him into the Salvation Army, I fancy.

(4) Watt Hatchett. This is new blood. He's an Australian youth I found working in Suva. Very promising stuff. Simplified form and swinging lines. He's as keen as mustard, and was practically living on bananas and cheek when I ran into him. His voice is like the crashing together of old tin cans, and he can talk of nothing but his work, his enthusiasms, and his dislikes. I'm afraid he'll get on their nerves and they may put him on the defensive. Still, his work is good.

(5) Cedric Malmsley. He's got a job illustrating some *de luxe* edition of medieval romances, and wants to get down to it with a model handy. It ought to work in all right. I told him to get in touch with you. I hear he's grown a blond beard that parts in the middle and wears sandals—Cedric, not the beard.

(6) Wolf Garcia. I had a letter from Garcia. No money, but a commission to do Comedy and Tragedy in marble for the new cinema in Westminster, so will I let him stay with me and do the clay model? No stamp on the envelope and written in conte chalk on lavatory paper. He will probably turn up long before you get this letter. Let him use the studio, will you, but look out, if you've got Sonia there. Garcia's got the use of someone's studio in London after the 20th, and hopes to have a cast ready by then, so it won't be for long. Now don't bully me, Katti. You know the creature is really—Heaven save the mark—a genius; and the others all pay me through the nose, so I can afford to carry a couple of deadheads. Yes, you're quite right. Hatchett *is* the other.

(7) One Phillida Lee. Just left the Slade. Rich father. She sent me some of her stuff and a rather gushing little request to work under me "because she has always longed," etc. etc. I wrote back asking the earth in fees and she snapped at it.

(8) You, bless you. I've told them all to fix up with you. Malmsley, Ormerin and Pilgrim can have the dormitory; Garcia one attic, and Hatchett the other. You have the yellow room as usual, and put Valmai Seacliff and the Lee child in the

blue. The great thing is to segregate Garcia. You know what he is, and I won't have that sort of thing—it's too muddly. On second thoughts it might be better to put him in the studio and the model in the attic. I rather think they were living together in London. By the way, I'm going to do a portrait of Valmai Seacliff. It'll do for Burlington House and the Salon, drat them. She'll be good enough to paint in the slap-up grand manner.

I'm scratching this off in the writing-room on my first night out from Suva. Did a small thing looking down in the wharf before we sailed. Came off rather well. I was interrupted by a man whom I thought was a fool, and who turned out to be intelligent, so I felt the fool. There's an American ex-cinema actress running about this ship half tight. She looks like one of their magazine covers and behaves like the wrath of God. The man seems to be her property, so perhaps he is a fool, after all.

If anything amusing happens, I'll add to this. It's been an interesting holiday, and I'm glad I did it. Your letters have been grand. Splendid the work goes on so well. I look forward to seeing it. Think about a nude for the Group. You don't want to be called the Plumber's Queen.

Later. We get into Vancouver to-morrow. It's been a peaceful trip since Honolulu, where the Ship's Belle left us. Before that it was rather hellish. Unfortunately someone had the number of *The Palette* that ran a special supplement of my show. The Belle got hold of it and decided I must be a real artist after all. When she saw the reproduction of the Royal portrait she laid her ears back and settled down to a steady pursuit. Wouldn't it be just wonderful if I did a portrait of her before we got to Honolulu? Her poppa would be tickled to death. She changed her clothes six times a day and struck a new attitude whenever she caught my eye. I had to pretend I'd got neuritis in my hand, which was a curse, as I rather wanted to do a head of one of the other passengers—a very paintable subject with plenty of good bone. However, I got down to it after Honolulu. The subject is a detective and looks like a grandee. Sounds like it, too—very old-world and chivalrous and so on. Damn! that looks like a cheap sneer, and it's not meant to. I'm rather on the defensive about this sleuth—I was so filthily rude to him, and he took it like a gent and made me feel like a bounder. Very awkward. The head is fairly successful.

Well, Katti, old lady, we meet on the 3rd. I'll come straight to Tatler's End. Best Love.

Your ever,
Troy.

P.S.—Perhaps you'd better give Garcia a shakedown in the studio and lock him in. We'll hope he'll have gone by the 20th.

Katti Bostock to Agatha Troy.

Tatler's End House,
Bossicote,
Bucks.
August 14th.

Dear Troy,

You are a gump to collect these bloodsuckers. Yes, I know Garcia is damn' good at sculping, but he's a nasty little animal, and thinks everyone else is born to keep him. God knows how much he's got out of you already. All right, I'll shut him up in the studio, but if he's after Sonia or anyone else, he'll crawl out by the ventilator. And if you imagine you'll get rid of him before the 20th, you're wandering. And who in the name of Bacchus is this Australian blight? You're paying his fare Home, of course. Well, I suppose I can't talk, as you've given me the run of your house for twelve months. It's been a godsend, and I've done my best work here. Been working on a thing of two negro saxophonists, worm's-eye view of, with cylindrical background. Not bad, I fancy. It's finished now. I've started on a big thing, using that little devil Sonia Gluck. It's a standing pose and she's behaving abominably, blast her! However, she agreed to come next term for the usual exorbitant fee, as soon as she heard Garcia and Pilgrim were to be in the class. Malmsley arrived to-day. The beard is there all right, and looks like the Isle of Patmos gone decadent. He's full of the book-illustration job, and showed me some of the sketches—quite good. I've met Pilgrim several times, and like him and his work. I hear he's always to be seen with the Seacliff blight, so I suppose she's after the title. That girl's a nymphomaniac, and a successful one at that. Funny this "It" stuff. I've never inspired a thought that wasn't respectable, and yet I get on with men all right. You're different. They'd fall for you if you'd let them, only you're so unprovocative they never know where they are, and end by taking you at your own valuation. The Seacliff and Pilgrim arrive to-morrow. I've seen Miss Phillida Lee. She's very would-be Slade. Wears hand-printed clothes with high necks, and shudders and burbles alternately. She comes on the 9th, and so does Ormerin, who writes from Paris and sounds very depressed. Nice bloke. I don't know whether it's struck you what a rum brew the class will be this term. It's impossible to keep Sonia in her place, wherever a model's place may be. Garcia, if he's here, will either be in full cry after her, which will be unpleasant, or else sick of her, which will be worse. Valmai Seacliff will naturally expect every male on the premises to be hot on her trail, and if that comes off, Sonia will get the pip. Perhaps with Basil Pilgrim on the tapis, the Seacliff will be less catholic, but I doubt it. Oh, well, you know your own business best, and I suppose will float through on the good old recipe of not noticing. You are such a bloody aristocrat. Your capacity for ignoring the unpleasant is a bit irritating to a plebeian like myself.

The servants are all right. The two Hipkins and Sadie Welsh from the village. They only tolerate me and are thrilled over your return. So am I, actually. I want your advice over the big thing of Sonia, and I'm longing to see your own stuff. You say don't forward any more letters, so I won't. Your allusions to a detective are quite incomprehensible, but if he interrupted you in your work, you had every right to bite his head off. What had you been up to, anyway?

Well, so long until the 3rd.

Katti.

PS.—Garcia has just sent a case of clay and a lot of material—carriage forward, *of course*—so I suppose I may expect to be honoured with his company any time now. We'll probably get a bill for the clay.

PPS.—Plumber's Queen yourself.

PPPS.—The bill for Garcia's material has come.

Chief Detective-Inspector Roderick Alleyn, C.I.D., to Mr. Nigel Bathgate, journalist.

S.S. *Niagara* (At Sea).
August 6th

Dear Bathgate,

How is it with Benedict, the married man? I was extremely sorry to be away for the wedding, and thought of you both on

14

my mountain vastness in New Zealand. What a perfect place that would have been for a honeymoon. A primitive but friendly back-country pub, a lovely lake, tall mountains and nothing else for fifty miles. But I suppose you and your Angela were fashionably on the Riviera or somewhere. You're a lucky young devil, and I wish you both all the happiness in the world, and send you my blessing. I'm glad my offering met with Mrs. Angela's approval.

We get to Vancouver in no time now, and leave the same day on the C.P.R. Most of the passengers are going on. I am breaking my journey at Quebec, a place I have always wanted to see. That will still give me fifteen days in England before I climb back into the saddle. My mother expects me to spend a fortnight with her, and if I may, I'll come on to you about the 21st?

The passengers on this ship are much like all passengers on all ships. Sea voyages seem to act as rather searching reagents on character. The essential components appear in alarming isolation. There is the usual ship's belle, this time a perfectly terrific American cinema lady who throws me into a fever of diffidence and alarm, but who exhibits the close-up type of loveliness to the nth degree of unreality. There is the usual sprinkling of pleasant globe-trotters, bounders, and avid women. The most interesting person is Miss Agatha Troy, the painter. Do you remember her one-man show? She has done a miraculous painting of the wharf at Suva. I long to ask what the price will be, but am prevented by the circumstances of her not liking me very much. She bridles like a hedgehog (yes, they do) whenever I approach her, and as I don't believe I suffer from any of those things in the strip advertisements, I'm rather at a loss to know why. Natural antipathy, perhaps. I don't share it. Oddly enough, she suddenly asked me in a very gruff standoffish voice if she might paint my head. I've never been took a likeness of before—it's a rum sensation when they get to the eyes; such a searching impersonal sort of glare they give you. She even comes close sometimes and peers into the pupils. Rather humiliating, it is. I try to return a stare every bit as impersonal, and find it tricky. The painting seems to me to be quite brilliant, but alarming.

Fox has written regularly. He seems to have done damn' well over that arson case. I rather dread getting back into the groove, but suppose it won't be so bad when it comes. Hope I don't have to start off with anything big—if Mrs. Angela thinks of putting rat's-bane in your Ovaltine, ask her to do it out of my division.

I look forward to seeing you both, my dear Bathgate, and send you my salutations the most distinguished.

Yours ever,
Roderick Alleyn.

Chief Detective-Inspector Alleyn to Lady Alleyn, Danes Lodge, Bossicote, Bucks.

C.P.R.
August 15th.

My Dearest Mamma,
Your letter found me at Vancouver. Yes, please—I should like to come straight to you. We arrive at Liverpool on the 7th, and I'll make for Bucks as fast as may be. The garden sounds very attractive, but don't go doing too much yourself, bless you. No, darling, I did not lose my heart in the Antipodes. Would you have been delighted to welcome a strapping black Fijian lady? I might have got one to regard me with favour at Suva, perhaps, but they smell of coco-nut oil, which you would not have found particularly delicious. I expect if I ever do get it in the neck, she'll think me no end of a dull dog and turn icy. Talking of Suva, which I was not, do you know of a place called Tatler's End House, somewhere near Bossicote? Agatha Troy, who painted that picture we both liked so much, lives there. She joined this ship at Suva, and did a lovely thing of the wharf. Look here, mamma, if ever a Virginia Van Maes writes and asks you to receive her, you must be away, or suffering from smallpox. She's an American beauty who looks people up in Kelly's and collects scalps. She looked me up and—Heaven knows why—she seemed inclined to collect ours. It's the title, I suppose. Talking of titles, how's the blasted Baronet? She was on to him like a shot. "Gee, Mr. Alleyn, I never knew your detective force was recruited from your aristocracy. I'm crazy to know if this Sir George Alleyn is your only brother." You see? She threatens to come to England and has already said she's sure you must be the cutest old-world mother. She's quite capable of muscling in on the strength of being my dearest girl-friend. So you look out, darling. I've told her you're a horrid woman, but I don't think she cares. You'll be sixty-five on or about the day this arrives.

In thirty years I shall be nearly ten years older than you are now, and you'll still be trying to bully me. Do you remember how I found out your real age on your thirty-fifth birthday? My first really good bit of investigation, nasty little tick that I was. Well, little mum, don't flirt with the vicar, and be sure to have the red carpet out on the 7th.

Your dutiful and devoted son,
Roderick.

PS.—Miss Troy has done a sketch of your son which he will purchase for your birthday if it's not too expensive.

From Lady Alleyn, Danes Lodge, Bossicote, to Chief Detective-Inspector Alleyn, Chateau Frontenac, Quebec.

Dear Roderick,

Your ingenuous little letter reached me on my birthday, and I was delighted to receive it. Thank you, my dear. It will be a great joy to have you for nearly a fortnight, greedily to myself. I trust I am *not* one of those avaricious mammas—clutch, clutch, clutch—which, after all, is only a form of cluck, cluck, cluck.

It will be delightful to have a Troy version of you, and I hope it was not too expensive—if it was, perhaps you would let me join you, my dear. I should like to do that, but have no doubt you will ruin yourself and lie to your mother about the price. I shall call on Miss Troy, not only because you obviously wish me to do so, but because I have always liked her work, and should be pleased to meet her, as your Van Maes would say. George is with his family in Scotland. He talks of standing for Parliament, but I am afraid he will only make a fool of himself, poor dear. It's a pity he hasn't got your brains. I have bought a hand-loom and am also breeding Alsatians. I hope the bitch—Tunbridge Tessa—does not take a dislike to you. She is very sweet really. I always feel, darling, that you should not have left the Foreign Office, but at the same time, I am a great believer in everybody doing what he wants to, and I *do* enjoy hearing about your cases.

Until the 7th, my dearest son.

Your loving
Mother.

PS.—I have just discovered the whereabouts of Miss

Troy's house, Tatler's End. It is only two miles out of Bossicote, and a nice old place. Apparently she takes students there. My spies tell me a Miss Bostock has been living in it during Miss Troy's absence. She returns on the 3rd. How old is she?

CHAPTER III

Class Assemblies

On the 10th of September at ten o'clock in the morning, Agatha Troy opened the door in the eastward wall of her house and stepped out into the garden. It was a sunny morning with a tang of autumn about it, a bland, mellow morning. Somewhere in the garden a fire had been lit, and an aromatic trace of smouldering brushwood threaded the air. There was not a breath of wind.

"Autumn!" muttered Troy. "And back to work again. Damn! I'm getting older." She paused for a moment to light a cigarette, and then she set off towards the studio, down on the old tennis court. Troy had built this studio when she inherited Tatler's End House from her father. It was a solid square of decent stone with top lighting, and a single window facing south on a narrow lane. It stood rather lower than the house, and about a minute's walk away from it. It was screened pleasantly with oaks and lilac bushes. Troy strode down the twisty path between the lilac bushes and pushed open the studio door. From beyond the heavy wooden screen inside the entrance she heard the voices of her class. She was out of patience with her class. "I've been too long away," she thought. She knew so exactly how each of them would look, how their work would take shape, how the studio would smell of oil colour, turpentine, and fixative, how Sonia, the model, would complain of the heat, the draught, the pose, the cold, and the heat again. Katti would stump backwards and forwards before her easel, probably with one shoe squeaking. Ormerin would sigh, Valmai Seacliff would attitudinise, and Garcia, wrestling with clay by the south window, would whistle between his teeth.

"Oh, well," said Troy, and marched round the screen.

Yes, there it all was, just as she expected, the throne shoved against the left-hand wall, the easels with fresh white canvases, the roaring gas heater, and the class. They had all come down to the studio after breakfast and, with the exception of Garcia and Malmsley, waited for her to pose the model. Malmsley was already at work; the drawings were spread out on a table. He wore, she noticed with displeasure, a sea-green overall. "To go with the beard, I suppose," thought Troy. Garcia was in the south window, glooming at the clay sketch of Comedy and Tragedy. Sonia, the model, wrapped in a white kimono, stood beside him. Katti Bostock, planted squarely in the centre of the room before a large black canvas, set her enormous palette. The rest of the class, Ormerin, Phillida Lee, Watt Hatchett and Basil Pilgrim, were grouped round Valmai Seacliff.

Troy walked over to Malmsley's table and looked over his shoulder at the drawings.

"What's that?"

"That's the thing I was talking about," explained Malmsley. His voice was high-pitched and rather querulous. "It's the third tale in the series. The female has been murdered by her lover's wife. She's lying on a wooden bench, impaled on a dagger. The wife jammed the dagger through the bench from underneath, and when the lover pressed her down—you see? The knife is hidden by the drape. It seems a little far-fetched, I must say. Surely it would show. The wretched publisher man insists on having this one."

"It needn't show if the drape is suspended a little," said Troy. "From the back of the bench, for instance. Then as she falls down she would carry the drape with her. Anyway, the probabilities are none of your business. You're not going a 'before and after,' like a strip advertisement, are you?"

"I can't get the pose," said Malmsley languidly. "I want to treat it rather elaborately. Deliberately mannered."

"Well, you can't go in for the fancy touches until you've got the flesh and blood to work from. That pose will do us as well as another, I dare say. I'll try it. You'd better make a separate drawing as a study."

"Yes, I suppose I had," drawled Malmsley. "Thanks most frightfully."

"Of course," Valmai Seacliff was saying, "I went down rather well in Italy. The Italians go mad when they see a good blonde. They used to murmur when I passed them in the streets. 'Bella' and 'Bellissima.' It was rather fun."

"Is that Italian?" asked Katti morosely, of her flake-white.

"It means beautiful, darling," answered Miss Seacliff.

"Oh hell!" said Sonia, the model.

"Well," said Troy loudly, "I'll set the pose."

They all turned to watch her. She stepped on the throne, which was the usual dais on wheels, and began to arrange a seat for the model. She threw a cerise cushion down, and then, from a chest by the wall she got a long blue length of silk. One end of this drape she threw across the cushion and pinned, the other she gathered carefully in her hands, drew round to one side, and then pinned the folds to the floor of the dais.

"Now, Sonia," she said. "Something like this."

Keeping away from the drape, Troy knelt and then slid sideways into a twisted recumbent pose on the floor. The right hip was raised, the left took the weight of the pose. The torso was turned upwards from the waist so that both shoulders touched the boards. Sonia, noticing the twist, grimaced disagreeably.

"Get into it," said Troy, and stood up. "Only you lie across the drape with your head on the cushion. Lie on your left side, first."

Sonia slid out of the white kimono. She was a most beautiful little creature, long-legged, delicately formed and sharp-breasted. Her black hair was drawn tightly back from the suave forehead. The bony structure of her face was sharply defined, and suggested a Slavonic mask.

"You little devil, you've been sunbathing," said Troy. "Look at those patches."

"Well, they don't like nudism at Bournemouth," said Sonia.

She lay across the drape on her left side, her head on the cerise cushion. Troy pushed her right shoulder over until it touched the floor. The drape was pressed down by the shoulders and broke into uneven blue folds about the body.

"That's your pose, Malmsley," said Troy. "Try it from where you are."

She walked round the studio, eyeing the model.

"It's pretty good from everywhere," she said. "Right! Get going, everybody." She glanced at her watch. "You can hold that for forty minutes, Sonia."

"It's a terrible pose, Miss Troy," grumbled Sonia. "All twisted like this."

"Nonsense," said Troy briskly.

The class began to settle itself.

Since each member of Troy's little community played a

part in the tragedy that followed ten days later, it may be well to look a little more closely at them.

Katti Bostock's work is known to everyone who is at all interested in modern painting. At the time of which I am writing she was painting very solidly and smoothly, using a heavy outline and a simplified method of dealing with form. She painted large figure compositions, usually with artisans as subjects. Her "Foreman Fitter" had been the picture of the year at the Royal Academy, and had set all the die-hards by the ears. Katti herself was a short, stocky, dark-haired individual with an air of having no nonsense about her. She was devoted to Troy in a grumbling sort of way, lived at Tatler's End House most of the year, but was not actually a member of the class.

Valmai Seacliff was thin, blonde, and very, very pretty. She was the type that certain modern novelists write about with an enthusiasm which they attempt to disguise as satirical detachment. Her parents were well-to-do and her work was clever. You have heard Katti describe Valmai as a nymphomaniac and will be able to draw your own conclusions about the justness of this criticism.

Phillida Lee was eighteen, plump, and naturally gushing. Two years of Slade austerity had not altogether damped her enthusiasms, but when she remembered to shudder, she shuddered.

Watt Hatchett, Troy's Australian protégé, was a short and extremely swarthy youth, who looked like a dago in an American talking picture. He came from one of the less reputable streets of Sydney and was astoundingly simple, cocksure, egotistical and enthusiastic. He seemed to have no aesthetic perceptions of any description, so that his un-doubted talent appeared to be a sort of parasite, flowering astonishingly on an unpromising and stunted stump.

Cedric Malmsley we have noticed already. Nothing further need be said about him at this stage of the narrative.

The Hon. Basil Pilgrim, son of the incredible Primitive Methodist peer, was a pleasant-looking young man of twenty-three, whose work was sincere, able, but still rather tentative. His father, regarding all art schools as hot-beds of vice and depravity, had only consented to Basil becoming a pupil of Troy's because her parents had been landed gentry of Lord Pilgrim's acquaintance, and because Troy herself had once painted a picture of a revivalist meeting. Her somewhat ironical treatment of this subject had not struck Lord Pilgrim, who was, in many ways, a remarkably stupid old man.

Francis Ormerin was a slight and delicate-looking Frenchman who worked in charcoal and wash. His drawings of the nude were remarkable for their beauty of line, and for a certain emphatic use of accent. He was a nervous, over-sensitive creature, subject to fits of profound depression, due, said Troy, to his digestion.

And lastly Garcia, whose first name—Wolf—was remembered by nobody. Garcia, who preserved on his pale jaws a static ten days' growth of dark stubble which never developed into a beard, whose clothes consisted of a pair of dirty grey trousers, a limp shirt, and an unspeakable raincoat. Garcia, with his shock of unkempt brown hair, his dark impertinent eyes, his beautiful hands, and his complete unscrupulousness. Two years ago he had presented himself one morning at the door of Troy's studio in London. He had carried there a self-portrait in clay, wrapped about with wet and dirty cloths. He walked past her into the studio and unwrapped the clay head. Troy and Garcia stood looking at it in silence. Then she asked him his name and what he wanted. He told her—"Garcia"—and he wanted to go on modelling, but had no money. Troy talked about the head, gave him twenty pounds, and never really got rid of him. He used to turn up, sometimes inconveniently, always with something to show her. In everything but clay he was quite inarticulate. It was as if he had been allowed only one medium of expression, but that an abnormally eloquent one. He was dirty, completely devoid of ordinary scruples, interested in nothing but his work. Troy helped him, and by and by people began to talk about his modelling. He began to work in stone. He was asked to exhibit with the New Phoenix Group, was given occasional commissions. He never had any money, and to most people he was entirely without charm, but to some women he was irresistible, and of this he took full advantage.

It was to Garcia that Troy went after she had set the pose. The others shifted their easels about, skirmishing for positions. Troy looked at Garcia's sketch in clay of the "Comedy and Tragedy" for the new cinema in Westminster. He had stood it on a high stool in the south window. It was modelled on a little wooden platform with four wheels, a substitute he had made for the usual turntable. The two figures rose from a cylindrical base. Comedy was nude, but

Tragedy wore an angular robe. Above their heads they held the conventional masks. The general composition suggested flames. The form was greatly simplified. The face of Comedy, beneath the grinning mask, was grave, but upon the face of Tragedy Garcia had pressed a faint smile.

He stood scowling while Troy looked at his work.

"Well," said Troy, "it's all right."

"I thought of——" He stopped short, and with his thumb suggested dragging the drape across the feet of Comedy.

"I wouldn't," said Troy. "Break the line up. But I've told you I know nothing about this stuff. I'm a painter. Why did you come and plant yourself here, may I ask?"

"Thought you wouldn't mind." His voice was muffled and faintly Cockney. "I'll be clearing out in a fortnight. I wanted somewhere to work."

"So you said in your extraordinary note. Are you broke?"

"Yes."

"Where are you going in a fortnight?"

"London. I've got a room to work in."

"Where is it?"

"Somewhere in the East End, I think. It's an old warehouse. I know a bloke who got them to let me use it. He's going to let me have the address. I'll go for a week's holiday somewhere before I begin work in London. I'll cast this thing there and then start on the sculping."

"Who's going to pay for the stone?"

"They'll advance me enough for that."

"I see. It's coming along very well. Now attend to me, Garcia." Troy lowered her voice. "While you're here you've got to behave yourself. You know what I mean?"

"No."

"Yes, you do. No nonsense with women. You and Sonia seem to be sitting in each other's pockets. Have you been living together?"

"When you're hungry," said Garcia, "you eat."

"Well, this isn't a restaurant and you'll please remember that. You understand? I noticed you making some sort of advance to Seacliff yesterday. That won't do, either. I won't have any bogus Bohemianism, or free love, or mere promiscuity at Tatler's End. It shocks the servants, and it's messy. All right?"

"O.K.," said Garcia with a grin.

"The pose has altered," said Katti Bostock from the middle of the studio.

24

"Yeah, that's right," said Watt Hatchett. The others looked coldly at him. His Sydney accent was so broad as to be almost comic. One wondered if he could be doing it on purpose. It was not the custom at Troy's for new people to speak until they were spoken to. Watt was quite unaware of this and Troy, who hated rows, felt uneasy about him. He was so innocently impossible. She went to Katti's easel and looked from the bold drawing in black paint to the model. Then she went up to the throne and shoved Sonia's right shoulder down.

"Keep it on the floor."

"It's a swine of a pose, Miss Troy."

"Well, stick it a bit longer."

Troy began to go round the work, beginning with Ormerin on the extreme left.

"Bit tied up, isn't it?" she said after a minute's silence.

"She is never for one moment still," complained Ormerin. "The foot moves, the shoulders are in a fidget continually. It is impossible for me to work—impossible."

"Start again. The pose is right now. Get it down directly. You can do it."

"My work has been abominable since three months or more. All this surrealism at Malaquin's. I cannot feel like that and yet I cannot prevent myself from attempting it when I am there. That is why I return to you. I am in a muddle."

"Try a little ordinary study for a bit. Don't worry about style. It'll come. Take a new stretcher and make a simple statement." She moved to Valmai Seacliff and looked at the flowing lines so easily laid down. Seacliff moved back, contriving to touch Ormerin's shoulder. He stopped working at once and whispered in her ear.

"I can understand French, Ormerin," said Troy casually, still contemplating Seacliff's canvas. "This is going quite well, Seacliff. I suppose the elongation of the legs is deliberate?"

"Yes, I see her like that. Long and slinky. They say people always paint like themselves. Don't they?"

"Do they?" said Troy. "I shouldn't let it become a habit."

She moved on to Katti, who creaked back from her canvas. One of her shoes did squeak. Troy discussed the placing of the figure and then went on to Watt Hatchett. Hatchett had already begun to use solid paint, and was piling pure colour on his canvas.

"You don't usually start off like this, do you?"

"Naow, that's right, I don't, but I thought I'd give it a pop."

"Was that, by any chance, because you could see Miss

Bostock working in that manner?" asked Troy, not too unkindly. Hatchett grinned and shuffled his feet. "You stick to your own ways for a bit," advised Troy. "You're a beginner still, you know. Don't try to acquire a manner till you've got a little more method. Is that foot too big or too small?"

"Too small."

"Should that space there be wider or longer?"

"Longer."

"Make it so."

"Good oh, Miss Troy. Think that bit of colour there's all right?" asked Hatchett, regarding it complacently.

"It's perfectly good colour, but don't choke the pores of your canvas up with paint till you've got the big things settled. Correct your drawing and scrape it down."

"Yeah, but she wriggles all the time. It's a fair nark. Look where the shoulder has shifted. See?"

"Has the pose altered?" inquired Troy at large.

"Naow!" said Sonia with vindictive mimicry.

"It's shifted a whole lot," asserted Hatchett aggressively. "I bet you anything you like——"

"Wait a moment," said Troy.

"It's moved a little," said Katti Bostock.

Troy sighed.

"Rest!" she said. "No! Wait a minute."

She took a stick of chalk from her overall pocket and ran it round the model wherever she touched the throne. The position of both legs, one flank, one hip, and one shoulder were thus traced on the boards. The blue drape was beneath the rest of the figure.

"Now you can get up."

Sonia sat up with an ostentatious show of discomfort, reached out her hand for the kimono and shrugged herself into it. Troy pulled the drape out taut from the cushion to the floor.

"It'll have to go down each time with the figure," she told the class.

"As it does in the little romance," drawled Malmsley.

"Yes, it's quite feasible," agreed Valmai Seacliff. "We could try it. There's that Chinese knife in the lumber-room. May we get it, Miss Troy?"

"If you like," said Troy.

"It doesn't really matter," said Malmsley languidly, getting to his feet.

"Where is it, Miss Seacliff?" asked Hatchett eagerly.

"On the top shelf in the lumber-room."

Hatchett went into an enormous cupboard by the window, and after a minute or two returned with a long, thin-bladed knife. He went up to Malmsley's table and looked over his shoulder at the typescript. Malmsley moved away ostentatiously.

"Aw yeah, I get it," said Hatchett. "What a corker! Swell way of murdering somebody, wouldn't it be?" He licked his thumb and turned the page.

"I've taken a certain amount of trouble to keep those papers clean," remarked Malmsely to no one in particular.

"Don't be so damned precious, Malmsley," snapped Troy. "Here, give me the knife, Hatchett, and don't touch other people's tools in the studio. It's not done."

"Good oh, Miss Troy."

Pilgrim, Ormerin, Hatchett and Vaimai Seacliff began a discussion about the possibility of using the knife in the manner suggested by Malmsley's illustration. Phillida Lee joined in.

"Where would the knife enter the body?" asked Seacliff.

"Just here," said Pilgrim, putting his hand on her back and keeping it there. "Behind your heart, Valmai."

She turned her head and looked at him through half-closed eyes. Hatchett stared at her, Malmsely smiled curiously. Pilgrim had turned rather white.

"Can you feel it beating?" asked Seacliff softly.

"If I move my hand—here."

"Oh, come off it," said the model violently. She walked over to Garcia. "I don't believe you could kill anybody like that. Do you, Garcia?"

Garcia grunted unintelligibly. He, too, was staring at Valmai Seacliff.

"How would he know where to put the dagger?" demanded Katti Bostock suddenly. She drew a streak of background colour across her canvas.

"Can't we try it out?" asked Hatchett.

"If you like," said Troy. "Mark the throne before you move it."

Basil Pilgrim chalked the position of the throne on the floor, and then he and Ormerin tipped it up. The rest of the class looked on with gathering interest. By following the chalked-out line on the throne they could see the spot where the heart would come, and after a little experiment found the plot of this spot on the underneath surface of the throne.

"Now, you see," said Ormerin, "the jealous wife would drive the knife through from underneath."

"Incidentally taking the edge off," said Basil Pilgrim.

"You could force it through the crack between the boards," said Garcia suddenly, from the window.

"How? It'd fall out when she was shoved down."

"No, it wouldn't. Look here."

"Don't break the knife and don't damage the throne," said Troy.

"I get you," said Hatchett eagerly. "The dagger's wider at the base. The boards would press on it. You'd have to hammer it through. Look, I'll bet you it could be done. There you are, I'll betcher."

"Not interested, I'm afraid," said Malmsley.

"Let's try," said Pilgrim. "May we, Troy?"

"Oh, do let's," cried Phillida Lee. She caught up her enthusiasm with an apologetic glance at Malmsley. "I adore bloodshed," she added with a painstaking nonchalance.

"The underneath of the throne's absolutely filthy," complained Malmsley.

"Pity if you spoiled your nice green pinny," jeered Sonia. Valmai Seacliff laughed.

"I don't propose to do so," said Malmsley. "Garcia can if he likes."

"Go on," said Hackett. "Give it a pop. I betcher five bob it'll work. Fair dinkum."

"What does that mean?" asked Seacliff. "You must teach me the language, Hatchett."

"Too right I will," said Hatchett with enthusiasm. "I'll make a dinkum Aussie out of you."

"God forbid," said Malmsley. Sonia giggled.

"Don't you like Australians?" Hatchett asked her aggressively.

"Not particularly."

"Well, I'll tell you one thing. Models at the school I went to in Sydney knew how to hold a pose for longer than ten minutes."

"You don't seem to have taken advantage of it, judging by your drawing."

"And they didn't get saucy with the students."

"Perhaps they weren't all like you."

"Sonia," said Troy, "that will do. If you boys are going to

make your experiment, you'd better hurry up. We start again in five minutes."

In the boards of the throne they found a crack that passed through the right spot. Hatchett slid the thin tip of the knife into it from underneath and shoved. By tapping the hilt of the dagger with an easel ledge, he forced the widening blade upwards through the crack. Then he let the throne back on to the floor. The blade projected wickedly through the blue chalk cross that marked the plot of Sonia's heart on the throne. Basil Pilgrim took the drape, laid it across the cushion, pulled it in taut folds down to the throne, and pinned it there.

"You see, the point of the knife is lower than the top of the cushion," he said. "It doesn't show under the drape."

"What did I tell you?" said Hatchett.

Garcia strolled over and joined the group.

"Go into your pose, Sonia," he said with a grin.

Sonia shuddered.

"Don't," she said.

"I wonder if the tip would show under the left breast," murmured Malmsley. "Rather amusing to have it in the drawing. With a cast shadow and a thin trickle of blood. Keep the whole thing black and white except for the little scarlet thread. After all, it is melodrama."

"Evidently," grunted Garcia.

"The point of suspension for the drape would have to be higher," said Troy. "It must be higher than the tip of the blade. You could do it. If your story was a modern detective novel, Malmsley, you could do a drawing of the knife as it is now."

Malmsley smiled and began to sketch on the edge of his paper. Valmai Seacliff leant over him, her hands on his shoulders. Hatchett, Ormerin and Pilgrim stood round her, Pilgrim with his arm across her shoulder. Phillida Lee hovered on the outskirts of the little group. Troy, looking vaguely round the studio, said to herself that her worst forebodings were likely to be realised. Watt Hatchett was already at loggerheads with Malmsley and the model. Valmai was at her Cleopatra game, and there was Sonia in a corner with Garcia. Something in their faces caught Troy's attention. What the devil were they up to? Garcia's eyes were on the group round Malmsley. A curious smile lifted one corner of his mouth, and on Sonia's face, turned to him, the smile was reflected.

"You'll have to get that thing out now, Hatchett," said Troy.

It took a lot of working and tugging to do this, but at last the knife was pulled out, the throne put back, and Sonia, with many complaints, took the pose again.

"Over more on the right shoulder," said Katti Bostock.

Troy thrust the shoulder down. The drape fell into folds round the figure.

"Ow!" said Sonia.

"That is when the dagger goes in," said Malmsley.

"Don't—you'll make me sick," said Sonia.

Garcia gave a little chuckle.

"Right through the ribs and coming out under the left breast," murmured Malmsley.

"Shut up!"

"Spitted like a little chicken."

Sonia raised her head.

"I wouldn't be too damn' funny, Mr. Malmsley," she said. "Where do you get your ideas from, I wonder? Books? Or pictures?"

Malmsley's brush slipped from his fingers to the paper, leaving a trace of paint. He looked fixedly at Sonia, and then began to dab his drawing with a sponge. Sonia laughed.

"For God's sake," said Katti Bostock, "let's get the pose."

"Quiet!" said Troy, and was obeyed. She set the pose, referring to the canvases. "Now get down to it, all of you. The Phoenix Group Show opens on the 16th. I suppose most of us want to go up to London for it. Very well, I'll give the servants a holiday that week-end, and we'll start work again on Monday."

"If this thing goes decently," said Katti, "I want to put it in for the Group. It it's not done, it'll do for B. House next year."

"I take it," said Troy, "you'll all want to go up for the Group's private view?"

"I don't," said Garcia. "I'll be pushing off for my holiday about then."

"What about us?" asked Valmai Seacliff of Basil Pilgrim.

"What do you think, darling?"

"'Us'?" said Troy. "'Darling'? What's all this?"

"We may as well tell them, Basil," said Valmai sweetly. "Don't faint, anybody We got engaged last night."

CHAPTER IV

Case for Mr. Alleyn

Lady Alleyn knelt back on her gardening-mat and looked up at her son.

"I think we have done enough weeding for to-day, darling. You bustle off with that barrow-load and then we'll go indoors and have a glass of sherry and a chat. We've earned it."

Chief Detective-Inspector Alleyn obediently trundled off down the path, tipped his barrow-load on the smudge fire, mopped his brow and went indoors for a bath. Half an hour later he joined his mother in the drawing-room.

"Come up to the fire, darling. There's the sherry. It's a bottle of the very precious for our last evening."

"Ma'am," said Alleyn, "you are the perfect woman."

"No, only the perfect mamma. I flatter myself I am a *very* good parent. You look charming in a dinner jacket, Roderick. I wish your brother had some of your finish. George always looks a little too hearty."

"I like George," said Alleyn.

"I quite like him, too," agreed their mother.

"This is really a superlative wine. I wish it wasn't our last night, though. Three days with the Bathgates, and then my desk, my telephone, the smell of the Yard, and old Fox beaming from ear to ear, bless him. Ah well, I expect I shall quite enjoy it once I'm there."

"Roderick," said Lady Alleyn, "why wouldn't you come to Tatler's End House with me?"

"For the very good reason, little mum, that I should not have been welcomed."

"How do you know?"

"Miss Troy doesn't like me."

"Nonsense! She's a very intelligent young woman."

"Darling!"

"The day I called I suggested she should dine with us while you were here. She accepted."

"And put us off when the time came."

"My dear man, she had a perfectly good excuse."

"Naturally," said Alleyn. "She is, as you say, a very intelligent young woman."

Lady Alleyn looked at a portrait head that hung over the mantelpiece.

"She can't dislike you very much, my dear. That picture gives the lie to your theory."

"Aesthetic appreciation of a paintable object has nothing to do with personal preferences."

"Bosh! Don't talk pretentious nonsense about things you don't understand."

Alleyn grinned.

"I think you are being self-conscious and silly," continued Lady Alleyn grandly.

"It's the lady that you should be cross about, not me."

"I'm not cross, Roderick. Give yourself another glass of sherry. No, not for me."

"Anyway," said Alleyn, "I'm glad you like the portrait."

"Did you see much of her in Quebec?"

"Very little, darling. We bowed to each other at mealtimes and had a series of stilted conversations in the lounge. On the last evening she was there I took her to the play."

"Was that a success?"

"No. We were very polite to each other."

"Ha!" said Lady Alleyn.

"Mamma," said Alleyn, "you know I *am* a detective." He paused, smiling at her. "You look divine when you blush," he added.

"Well, Roderick, I shan't deny that I would like to see you married."

"She wouldn't dream of having me, you know. Put the idea out of your head, little mum. I very much doubt if I shall ever have another stilted conversation with Miss Agatha Troy."

The head parlourmaid came in.

"A telephone call from London for Mr. Roderick, m'lady."

"From London?" asked Alleyn. "Oh Lord, Clibborn, why didn't you say I was dead?"

Clibborn smiled the tolerant smile of a well-trained servant, and opened the door.

"Excuse me, please, mamma," said Alleyn, and went to the telephone.

As he unhooked the receiver, Alleyn experienced the little

prick of foreboding that so often accompanies an unexpected long-distance call. It was the smallest anticipatory thrill and was succeeded at once by the unhappy reflection that probably Scotland Yard was already on his track. He was not at all surprised when a familiar voice said:

"Mr. Alleyn?"

"That's me. Is it you, Watkins?"

"Yes, sir. Very pleasant to hear your voice again. The Assistant Commissioner would like to speak to you, Mr. Alleyn."

"Right!"

"Hullo, Mr. Alleyn?" said a new voice.

"Hullo, sir."

"You can go, Watkins." A pause, and then: "How are you, Rory?"

"Very fit, thanks, sir."

"Ready for work?"

"Yes. Oh, rather!"

"Well now, look here. How do you feel about slipping into the saddle three days before you're due? There's a case cropped up a few miles from where you are, and the local people have called us in. It would save time and help the department if you could take over for us."

"Certainly, sir," said Alleyn, with a sinking heart. "When?"

"Now. It's a homicide case. Take the details. Address, Tatler's End House."

"*What!* I beg your pardon, sir. Yes?"

"A woman's been stabbed. Do you know the place, by any chance?"

"Yes, sir."

"Thrrree minutes."

"Extend the call, please. Are you there, Rory?"

"Yes," said Alleyn. He noticed suddenly that the receiver was clammy.

"It belongs to the artist, Miss Agatha Troy."

"I know."

"You'll get the information from the local super—Blackman—who's there now. The model has been killed, and it looks like murder."

"I—can't—hear."

"The victim is an artist's model. I'll send Fox down with the other people and your usual kit. Much obliged. Sorry to drag you back before Monday."

"That's all right, sir."

"Splendid. I'll expect your report. Nice to see you again. Good-bye."

"Good-bye, sir."

Alleyn went back to the drawing-room.

"Well?" began his mother. She looked up at him, and in a moment was at his side. "What's the matter, old man?"

"Nothing, ma'am. It was the Yard. They want me to take a case near here. It's at Tatler's End House."

"But what is it?"

"Murder, it seems."

"Roderick!"

"No, no. I thought that, too, for a moment. It's the model. I'll have to go at once. May I have the car?"

"Of course, darling." She pressed a bell-push, and when Clibborn came, said: "Mr. Roderick's overcoat at once, Clibborn, and tell French to bring the car round quickly." When Clibborn had gone she put her hand on Alleyn's. "Please tell Miss Troy that if she would like to come to me——"

"Yes, darling. Thank you. But I must see what it's all about first. It's a case."

"Well, you won't include Agatha Troy among your suspects, I hope?"

"If there's a question of that," said Alleyn, "I'll leave the service. Good night. Don't sit up. I may be late."

Clibborn came in with his overcoat.

"Finish your sherry," ordered his mother. He drank it obediently. "And, Roderick, look in at my room, however late it is."

He bowed, kissed her lightly, and went out to the car.

It was a cold evening with a hint of frost on the air. Alleyn dismissed the chauffeur and drove himself at breakneck speed towards Tatler's End House. On the way, three vivid little pictures appeared, one after another, in his mind. The wharf at Suva. Agatha Troy, in her old smock and grey bags, staring out over the sea while the wind whipped the short hair back from her face. Agatha Troy saying good-bye at night on the edge of the St. Lawrence.

The headlights shone on rhododendrons and tree-trunks, and then on a closed gate and the figure of a constable. A torch flashed on Alleyn's face.

"Excuse me, sir——"

"All right. Chief Detective-Inspector Alleyn from the Yard."

The man saluted.

"They're expecting you, sir."

The gate swung open, and Alleyn slipped in his clutch. It was a long winding drive, and it seemed an age before he pulled up before a lighted door. A second constable met him and showed him into a pleasant hall where a large fire burned.

"I'll tell the superintendent you've arrived, sir," said the man, but as he spoke, a door on Alleyn's left opened and a stout man with a scarlet face came out.

"Hullo, hullo! This is very nice. Haven't seen you for ages."

"Not for ages," said Alleyn. They shook hands. Blackman had been superintendent at Bossicote for six years, and he and Alleyn were old acquaintances. "I hope I haven't been too long."

"You've been very quick indeed, Mr. Alleyn. We only rang the Yard half an hour ago. They told us you were staying with her ladyship. Come in here, will you?"

He led the way into a charming little drawing-room with pale-grey walls and cerise-and-lemon-striped curtains.

"How much did they tell from the Yard?"

"Only that a model had been knifed."

"Yes. Very peculiar business. I don't mind telling you I'd have liked to tackle it myself, but we've got our hands full with a big burglary case over at Ranald's Cross, and I'm short-staffed just now. So the chief constable thought, all things considered, and you being so handy, it'd better be the Yard. He's just gone. Sit down, and I'll give you the story before we look at the body and so on. That suit you?"

"Admirably," said Alleyn.

Blackman opened a fat pocket-book, settled his chins, and began.

"This property, Tatler's End house, is owned and occupied by Miss Agatha Troy, R.A., who returned here after a year's absence abroad, on September 3rd. During her absence the house was occupied by a Miss Katti Bostock, another painter. Miss Troy arranged by letter to take eight resident pupils from September to December, and all of these were already staying in the house when she arrived. There was also a Sonia Gluck, spinster, aged twenty-two, an artist's model, engaged by Miss Bostock for the coming term. The classes began officially on the 10th, but they had all been more or less working together since the 3rd. From the 10th to Friday the 16th they worked from the model every morning in the studio. On the 16th, three days ago, the class disbanded for the week-end, in order that members might attend a function in London. The servants were given Friday night off, and went to a cinema in Baxtonbridge. One student, Wolf Garcia, no permanent address, remained alone in the studio. The house was closed. Garcia is believed to have left on Saturday the 17th, the day before yesterday. Miss Troy returned on Saturday at midday and found Garcia had gone. The others came back on Sunday, yesterday, by car, and by the evening bus. This morning, September 19th, the class reassembled in the studio, which is a detached building situated about a hundred yards to the south-east of the rear eastward corner of the house. Here's the sketch plan of the house and studio," said the superintendent in a more normal voice. "And here's another of the studio interior."

"Splendid," said Alleyn, and spread them out before him on a small table. Mr. Blackman coughed and took up the burden of his recital.

"At ten-thirty the class, with the exception of Garcia, who, as we have seen, had left, was ready to begin work. Miss Troy had given instructions that they were to start without her. This is her usual practice, except on the occasions when a new pose is to be set. The model lay down to resume the pose which she had been taking since Septembebr 10th. It was a recumbent position on her back. She lay half on a piece of silk material and half on the bare boards of the dais known as the model's 'throne.' The model was undraped. She lay first of all on her right side. One of the students, Miss Valmai Seacliff, of No. 8 Partington Mews, W.C.4, approached the model, placed her hands on Gluck's shoulders and thrust the left shoulder firmly over and down. This was the usual procedure. Gluck cried out 'Don't!' as if in pain, but as she habitually objected to the pose, Miss Seacliff paid no attention, shifted her hands to the model's chest, and pressed down. Gluck made another sound, described by Miss Seacliff as a moan, and seemed to jerk and then relax. Miss Seacliff then said: "Oh, don't be such a fool, Sonia" and was about to rise from her stooping posture when she noticed that Gluck was in an abnormal condition. She called for the others to come. Miss Katti Bostock, followed by two students, Mr. Watt Hatchett, an Australian, and Mr. Francis Ormerin, a Frenchman, approached the throne. Hatchett said: 'She's taken a fit.' Miss Bostock said: 'Get out of the way.' She examined the body. She states that the eyelids fluttered and the limbs jerked slightly. Miss Bostock attempted to raise Gluck. She placed her hand behind the shoulders and pulled. There was a certain amount of resistance, but after a few seconds the body came up suddenly. Miss Seacliff cried out loudly that there was blood on the blue silk drape. Mr. Ormerin said: 'Mong dew, the knife!'"

Mr. Blackman cleared his throat and turned a page.

"It was then seen that a thin triangular blade protruded vertically through the drape. It appeared to be the blade of some sort of dagger that had been driven through a crack in the dais from underneath. It has not been moved. It seems that later on, when Miss Troy arrived, she stopped anybody from touching the dais as soon as she saw what had occurred. On examining Gluck a wound was discovered in the back somewhere about the position of the fourth rib and about three inches to the left of the spine. There was an effusion of blood. The blade was stained with blood. Miss Bostock attempted to staunch the wound with rag. At this point Miss Troy arrived, and immediately sent Mr. Basil Pilgrim, another student, to ring up the doctor. Dr. Ampthill arrived ten minutes later and found life was extinct. Miss Troy states that Gluck died a few minutes after she—Miss Troy—arrived at the studio. Gluck made no statement before she died."

Mr. Blackman closed his note-book, and laid it on the table.

"That's just from notes," he said modestly. "I haven't got it down in a ship-shape report yet."

"It is sufficiently clear," said Alleyn. "You might have been giving it to a jury."

An expression of solemn complacency settled down among the superintendent's chins.

"Well," he said, "we haven't had a great deal of time. It's a curious business. We've taken statements from all this crowd, except, of course, the man called Garcia. He's gone, and we haven't got a line on him. That looks a bit funny on the face of it, but it seems he said he'd be leaving for a hiking trip on Saturday morning, and is due to turn up at some place in London in about a week's time. He left his baggage to be forwarded to this London address, and it had all gone when Miss Troy returned on Saturday about three o'clock. We're trying to get on the carrier that called for it, but haven't got hold of anybody yet. It was all in the studio. It seems Garcia slept in the studio and had his gear there. I've got into touch with the police stations for fifty miles round and asked them to look out for this Garcia. Here's the description of him: Height—about five-foot nine; sallow complexion, dark eyes, very thin. Thick dark hair, rather long. Usually dressed in old grey flannel trousers and a raincoat. Does not wear a hat. Probably carrying a ruck-sack containing painting materials. It seems he does a bit of sketching as well as sculping. We got that in the course of the statements made by the rest of this crowd. Will you look at the statements before you see anybody?"

Alleyn thought for a moment.

"I'll see Miss Troy first," he said. "I have met her before."

"Have you, really? I suppose with her ladyship being as you might say a neighbour——"

"The acquaintance is very slight," said Alleyn. "What about the doctors?"

"I said I'd let Ampthill know as soon as you came. He is the police surgeon. He heads the list in the directory, so Mr. Pilgrim rang him first."

"Very handy. Well, Mr. Blackman, if you wouldn't mind getting hold of him while I see Miss Troy——"

"Right."

"Fox and Co. ought to be here soon. We'll go and look at the scene of action when they arrive. Where is Miss Troy?"

"In the study. I'll take you there. It's across the hall."

"Don't bother—I'll find my way."

"Right you are—I'll ring the doctor and join you there. I've got the rest of the class penned up in the dining-room with a P.C. on duty. They're a rum lot and no mistake," said Blackman, leading the way into the hall. "Real artistic freaks. You know. There's the library door. See you in a minute."

Alleyn crossed the hall, tapped on the door, and walked in.

It was a long room with a fireplace at the far end. The only light there was made by the flicker of flames on the book-lined walls. Coming out of the brightly lit hall, he was at first unable to see clearly and stood for a moment inside the door.

"Yes?" said a quick voice from the shadows. "Who is it? Do you want me?"

A slim, dark shape, outlined by a waveri..g halo of light, rose from a chair by the fire.

"It's me," said Alleyn. "Roderick Alleyn."

"You!"

"I'm sorry to come in unannounced. I thought perhaps you would rather——"

"But—yes, please come in."

The figure moved forward a little and held out a hand. Alleyn said apologetically:

"I'm coming as fast as I can. It's rather dark."

"Oh!" There was a moment's pause, a movement, and then a shaded lamp came to life and he saw her clearly. She wore a long plain dress of a material that absorbed the light and gave off none. She looked taller than his remembrance of her. Her face was white under the short black hair. Alleyn took her hand, held it lightly for a second, and then moved to the fire.

"It was kind of you to come," said Troy.

"No, it wasn't. I'm here on duty."

She stiffened at once.

"I'm sorry. That was stupid of me."

"If I was not a policeman," Alleyn said, "I think I should still have come. You could have brought about a repetition of our first meeting and sent me about my business."

"Must you always remind me of my ill manners?"

"That was not the big idea. Your manners did not seem ill to me. May we sit down, please?"

"Do."

They sat in front of the fire.

"Well," said Troy, "get your note-book."

Alleyn felt in the inside pocket of his dinner jacket.

"It's still there," he said. "The last time I used it was in New Zealand. Here we are. Have you had any dinner, by the way?"

"What's that got to do with it?"

"Come, come," said Alleyn "you mustn't turn into a hostile witness before there's anything to be hostile about."

"Don't be facetious. Oh damn! Rude again. Yes, thank you, I toyed with a chunk of athletic hen."

"Good! A glass of port wouldn't do you any harm. Don't offer me any, please: I'm not supposed to drink on duty, unless it's with a sinister purpose. I suppose this affair has shaken you up a bit?"

Troy waited for a moment and then she said: "I'm terrified of dead people."

"I know," said Alleyn. "I was, at first. Before the war. Even now they are not quite a commonplace to me."

"She was a silly little creature. More like a beautiful animal than a reasonable human. But to see her suddenly, like that—everything emptied away. She looked faintly astonished—that was all."

"It's so often like that. Astonished, but sort of knowing. Are there any relatives to be informed?"

"I haven't the faintest idea. She lived alone—officially."

"We'll have to try and find out."

"What do you want me to do now?" asked Troy.

"I want you to bring this girl to life for me. I know the circumstances surrounding her death—the immediate circumstances—and as soon as my men get here from London, I'll look at the studio. In the meantime I'd like to know if any possible explanation for this business has occurred to you. I must thank you for having kept the place untouched. Not many people think like that on these occasions."

"I've no explanation, reasonable or fantastic, but there's one thing you ought to know at once. I told the class they were not to speak of it to the police. I knew they'd all give excited and exaggerated accounts of it, and thought it better that the first statement should come from me."

"I see."

"I'll make that statement now."

"An official statement?" asked Alleyn lightly.

"If you like. When you move the throne you will find that a dagger has been driven through the boards from underneath."

"Shall we?"

"Yes. You don't say 'How do you know?'"

"Well, I expect you're going on to that, aren't you?"

"Yes. On the 10th, the first morning when I set this pose, I arranged it to look as if the figure had been murdered in exactly this way. Cedric Malmsley, one of my students, was doing a book illustration of a similar incident." She paused for a moment, looking into the fire. "During the rest they began arguing about the possibilities of committing a crime in this way. Hatchett, another student, got a knife that is in the junk-room, and shoved it through from underneath. Ormerin helped him. The throne was roughly knocked up for me in the village and the boards have warped apart. The blade is much narrower at the tip than at the hilt. The tip went through easily, but he hammered at the hilt to force it right up. The boards gripped the wider end. You will see all that when you look at it."

"Yes." Alleyn made a note in his book and waited.

"The drape was arranged to hide the knife and it all looked quite convincing. Sonia was—she was quite—frightened. Hatchett pulled the knife out—it needed some doing—and we put everything straight again."

"What happened to the knife?"

"Let me see. I think Hatchett put it away."

"From a practical point of view, how could you be sure that the knife would come through at exactly the right place to do what it has done?"

"The position of the figure is chalked on the floor. When she took her pose, Sonia fitted her right hip and leg into the chalk-marks, and then slid down until the whole of her right side was on the floor. One of the students would move her until she was inside the marks. Then she let her torso go over until her left shoulder touched the floor. The left hip was off the ground. I could draw it for you."

Alleyn opened his note-book at a clean page and handed it to her with his pencil. Troy swept a dozen lines down and gave it back to him.

"Wonderful!" said Alleyn, "to be able to do that—so easily."

"I'm not likely to forget that pose," said Troy dryly.

"What about the drape? Didn't that cover the chalk-marks?"

"Only in places. It fell from a suspension-point on the cushion to the floor. As she went down, she carried it with her. The accidental folds that came that way were more interesting than any laboured arrangement. When the students made their experiment they found the place where the heart would be, quite easily, inside the trace on the floor. The crack passed through this point. Hatchett put a pencil through the crack and they marked the position on the under-side of the throne."

"Is there any possibility that they repeated this performance for some reason on Friday and forgot to withdraw the dagger?"

"I thought of that at once, naturally. I asked them. I begged them to tell me." Troy moved her long hands restlessly. "Anything," she said, "anything rather than the thought of one of them deliberately—there's no reason. I—I can't bear to think of it. As if a beastly unclean thing was in one of their minds, behind all of us. And then, suddenly, crawled out and did this."

He heard her draw in her breath sharply. She turned her head away.

Alleyn swore softly.

"Oh, don't pay any attention to me," said Troy impatiently. "I'm all right. About Friday. We had the morning class as usual from ten o'clock to twelve-thirty, with that pose. We all lunched at one. Then we went up to London. The private view of the Phoenix Group Show was on Friday night, and several of us had things in it. Valmai Seacliff and Basil Pilgrim, who are engaged to be married, left in his two-seater immediately after lunch. Neither of them was going to the private view. They were going to his people's place, to break the engagement news, I imagine. Katti Bostock and I left in my car at about half-past two. Hatchett, Phillida Lee and Ormerin caught the three o'clock bus. Malmsley wanted to do some work, so he stayed behind until six, went up in the six-fifteen bus and joined us later at the show. I believe Phillida Lee and Hatchett had a meal together and went to a show. She took him to her aunt's house in London for the week-end, I fancy."

"And the model?"

"Caught the two-thirty bus. I don't know where she went or what she did. She came back with Malmsley, Ormerin, Katti Bostock, Hatchett and Phillida Lee by yesterday evening's bus."

"When Friday's class broke up, did you all leave the studio together and come up to the house?"

"I—let me think for a moment. No, I can't remember; but usually we come up in dribbles. Some of them go on working, and they have to clean up their palettes and so on. Wait a second. Katti and I came up together before the others. That's all I can tell you."

"Would the studio be locked before you went to London?"

"No." Troy turned her head and looked squarely at him.

"Why not?" asked Alleyn.

"Because of Garcia."

"Blackman told me about Garcia. He stayed behind, didn't he?"

"Yes."

"Alone?"

"Yes," said Troy unhappily. "Quite alone."

There was a tap at the door. It opened and Blackman appeared, silhouetted against the brightly lit hall.

"The doctor's here, Mr. Alleyn, and I think the car from London is just arriving."

"Right," said Alleyn. "I'll come."

Blackman moved away. Alleyn rose and looked down at Troy in her arm-chair.

"Perhaps I may see you again before I go?"

"I'll be in here or with the others in the dining-room. It's a bit grim sitting round there under the eye of the village constable."

"I hope it won't be for very long," said Alleyn.

Troy suddenly held out her hand.

"I'm glad it's you," she said.

They shook hands.

"I'll try to be as inoffensive as possible," Alleyn told her. "Good-bye for the moment."

CHAPTER V

Routine

When Alleyn returned to the hall he found it full of men. The Scotland Yard officials had arrived, and with their appearance the case, for the first time, seemed to take on a familiar complexion. The year he had spent away from England clicked back into the past at the sight of those familiar overcoated and bowler-hatted figures with their cases and photographic impedimenta. There, beaming at him, solid, large, the epitome of horse-sense, was old Fox.

"Very nice indeed to have you with us again, sir."

"Fox, you old devil, how are you?"

And there, looking three degrees less morose, was Detective-Sergeant Bailey, and behind him Detective-Sergeant Thompson. A gruff chorus began:

"Very nice indeed——"

A great shaking of hands, while Superintendent Blackman looked on amicably, and then a small, clean, bald man came forward. Blackman introduced him.

"Inspector Alleyn, this is Dr. Ampthill, our divisional surgeon."

"How d'you do, Mr. Alleyn? Understand you want to see me. Sorry if I've kept you waiting."

"I've not long arrived," said Alleyn. "Let's have a look at the scene of action, shall we?"

Blackman led the way down the hall to a side passage at the end of which there was a door. Blackman unlocked it and ushered them through. They were in the garden. The smell of box borders came up from their feet. It was very dark.

"Shall I lead the way?" suggested Blackman.

A long pencil of light from a torch picked up a section of flagged path. They tramped along in single file. Tree-trunks started up out of the darkness, leaves brushed Alleyn's cheek. Presently a rectangle of deeper dark loomed up.

Blackman said: "You there, Sligo?"

"Yes, sir," said a voice close by.

There was a jangle of keys, the sound of a door opening.

"Wait till I find the light switch," said Blackman. "Here we are."

The lights went up. They walked round the wooden screen inside the door, and found themselves in the studio.

Alleyn's first impression was of a reek of paint and turpentine, and of a brilliant and localised glare. Troy had installed a high-powered lamp over the throne. This lamp was half shaded, so that it cast all its light on the throne, rather as the lamp above an operating-table is concentrated on the patient. Blackman had only turned on one switch, so the rest of the studio was in darkness. The effect at the moment could scarcely have been more theatrical. The blue drape, sprawled across the throne, was so brilliant that it hurt the eyes. The folds fell sharply from the cushion into a flattened mass. In the middle, stupidly irrelevant, was a spike. It cast a thin shadow irregularly across the folds of the drape. On the margin of this picture, disappearing abruptly into shadow, was a white mound.

"The drapery and the knife haven't been touched since the victim died," explained Blackman. "Of course, they disarranged the stuff a bit when they hauled her up."

"Of course," said Alleyn. He walked over to the throne and examined the blade of the knife. It was rather like an oversized packing-needle, sharp, three-edged, and greatly tapered towards the point. It was stained a rusty brown. At the base, where it pierced the drape, there was the same discoloration, and in one or two of the folds small puddles of blood had seeped through the material and dried. Alleyn glanced at Dr. Ampthill.

"I suppose there would be an effusion of blood when they pulled her off the knife?"

"Oh yes, yes. The bleeding would probably continue until death. I understand that beyond lifting her away from the knife, they did not move her until she died. When I arrived the body was where it is now."

He turned to the sheeted mound that lay half inside the circle of light.

"Shall I?"

"Yes, please," said Alleyn.

Dr. Ampthill drew away the white sheet.

Troy had folded Sonia's hands over her naked breast. The shadow cut sharply across the wrists so that the lower half of the torso was lost. The shoulders, hands and head were violently lit. The lips were parted rigidly, showing the teeth. The eyes were only half closed. The plucked brows were raised as if in astonishment.

"Rigor mortis is well established," said the doctor. "She was apprently a healthy woman, and this place was well heated. The gas fire was not turned off until some time after she died. She has been dead eleven hours."

"Have you examined the wound, Dr. Ampthill?"

"Superficially. The knife-blade was not absolutely vertical, evidently. It passed between the fourth and fifth ribs, and no doubt pierced the heart."

"Let us have a look at the wound."

Alleyn slid his long hands under the rigid body and turned it on its side. The patches of sunburn showed clearly on the back. About three inches to the left of the spine was a dark puncture. It looked very small and neat in spite of the traces of blood that surrounded it.

"Ah, yes," said Alleyn. "As you say. We had better have a photograph of this. Bailey, you go over the body for prints. You'd better tackle the drape, and the knife, and the top surface of the throne. Not likely to prove very useful, I'm afraid, but do your best."

While Thompson set up his camera, Alleyn turned up the working-lamps and browsed about the studio. Fox joined him.

"Funny sort of case, sir," said Fox. "Romantic."

"Good heavens, Fox, what a macabre idea of romance you've got."

"Well, sensational," amended Fox. "The papers will make a big thing of it. We'll have them all down in hordes before the night's over."

"That reminds me—I must send a wire to the Bathgates. I'm due there to-morrow. To business, Brer Fox. Here we have the studio as it was when the class assembled this morning. Paint set out on the pallettes, you see. Canvases on all the easels. We've got seven versions of the pose."

"Very useful, I dare say," conceded Fox. "Or, at any rate, the ones that look like something human may come in handy. That affair over on your left looks more like a set of worms than a naked female. I suppose it *is* meant for the deceased, isn't it?"

"I think so," said Alleyn. "The artist is probably a surrealist or a vorticist or something." He inspected the canvas and the paint-table in front of it.

"Here we are. The name's on the paint-box. Phillida Lee. It is a rum bit of work, Fox, no doubt of it. This big thing next door is more in our line. Very solid and simple."

He pointed to Katti Bostock's enormous canvas.

"Bold," said Fox. He put on his spectacles and stared blankly at the picture.

"You get the posture of the figure very well there," said Alleyn.

They moved to Cedric Malmsley's table.

"This, I think, must be the illustrator," continued Alleyn. "Yes—here's the drawing for the story."

"Good God!" exclaimed Fox, greatly scandalised. "He's made a picture of the girl after she was killed."

"No, no. That was the original idea for the pose. He's merely added the dagger and the dead look. Here's the portfolio with all the drawings. H'm, very volup. and Beardsley, with a slap of modern thrown in. Hullo!" Alleyn had turned to a delicate watercolour in which three medieval figures mowed a charming field against a background of hayricks, pollard willows, and a turreted palace. "That's rum!" muttered Alleyn.

"What's up, Mr. Alleyn?"

"It looks oddly familiar. One half of the old brain functioning a fraction ahead of the other, perhaps. Or perhaps not. No matter. Look here, Brer Fox, I think before we go any farther I'd better tell you as much as I know about the case." And Alleyn repeated the gist of Blackman's report and of his conversation with Troy. "This, you see," he ended, "is the illustration for the story. It was to prove the possibility of murdering someone in this manner that they made the experiment with the dagger, ten days ago."

"I see," said Fox. "Well, somebody's proved it now all right, haven't they?"

"Yes," agreed Alleyn. "It is proved—literally, up to the hilt."

"Cuh!" said Fox solemnly.

"Malmsley has represented the dagger as protruding under the left breast, you see. I suppose he thought he'd add the extra touch of what *you'd* call romance, Brer Fox. The scarlet thread of gore is rather effective in a meretricious sort of way. Good Lord, this is a queer show and no mistake."

"Here's what I call a pretty picture, now," said Fox approvingly. He had moved in front of Valmai Seacliff's canvas. Seacliff had used a flowing, suave line. The figure was exaggeratedly slender, the colour scheme a light sequence of blues and pinks.

"Very elegant," said Fox.

"A little too elegant," said Alleyn. "Hullo! Look at this."

Across Francis Ormerin's water-colour drawing ran an ugly streak of dirty blue, ending in a blob that had run down the paper. The drawing was ruined.

"Had an accident, seemingly."

"Perhaps. This student's stool is overturned, you'll notice, Fox. Some of the water in his paint-pot has slopped over and one of his brushes is on the floor."

Alleyn picked up the brush and dabbed it on the china palette. A half-dry smudge of dirty blue showed.

"I see him or her preparing to flood a little of this colour on the drawing. He receives a shock, his hand jerks sideways and the brush streaks across the paper. He jumps up, overturning his stool and jolting the table. He drops the brush on the floor. Look, Fox. There are signs of the same sort of disturbance everywhere. Notice the handful of brushes on the table in front of the big canvas—I think that must be Katti Bostock's—I remember her work. Those brushes have been put down suddenly on the palette. The handles are messed in paint. Look at this very orderly array of tubes and brushes over here. This student has dropped a tube of blue paint and then trodden on it. Here are traces leading to the throne. It's a man's shoe, don't you think? He's tramped about all over the place, leaving a blue painty trail. The modern lady—Miss Lee—has overturned a bottle of turpentine, and it's run into her paint-box. There are even signs of disturbance on the illustrator's table. He has put a wet brush down on the very clean typescript. The place is like a first lesson in detection."

"But beyond telling us they all got a start when the affair occurred, it doesn't appear to lead us anywhere," said Fox.

"Not on the face of it." He turned back to Seacliff's canvas and examined it with placid approval.

"You seem very taken with Miss Seacliff's effort," said Alleyn.

"Eh?" Fox transferred his attention sharply to Alleyn. "Now then, sir, how do you make out the name of this artist?"

"Rather prettily, Fox. This is the only outfit that is quite in order. Very neat everything is, you'll notice. Tidy box, clean brushes laid down carefully by the palette, fresh paint-rag all ready to use. I make a long guess that it belongs to Valmai Seacliff, because Miss Seacliff was with the model when she got her quietus. There is no reason why Miss Seacliff's paraphernalia should show signs of disturbance. In a sense, Miss Seacliff killed Sonia Gluck. She pressed her naked body down on the knife. Not a very pleasant reflection for Miss Seacliff now, unless she happens to be a murderess. Yes, I think this painting is hers."

"Very neat bit of reasoning, chief. Lor', here's a mess." Fox bent over Watt Hatchett's open box. It overflowed with half-used tubes of oil-colour, many of them without caps. A glutinous mess to which all sorts of odds and ends adhered spread over the trays and brushes. Cigarette-butts, matches, bits of charcoal, were mixed up with fragments of leaves and twigs, and filthy scraps of rag.

"This looks like chronic muck," said Fox.

"It does, indeed." From the sticky depths of a tin tray Alleyn picked out a fragment of a dried leaf and smelt it.

"Blue gum," he said. "This will be the Australian, I suppose. Funny. He must have collected that leaf sketching in the bush, half the world away. I know this youth. He joined our ship with Miss Troy at Suva. Travelled second at her expense."

"Fancy that," said Fox placidly. "Then you know this Miss Troy, sir?"

"Yes. Now you see, even he appears to have put his hand down on his palette. He'd hardly do that in normal moments."

"We've finished, sir," said the photographic expert.

"Right."

Alleyn went over to the throne. The body lay as it was when he first saw it. He looked at it thoughtfully, remembering what Troy had said: "I'm always frightened of dead people."

"She was very lovely," said Alleyn gently. He covered the body again. "Carry her over to that couch. It's a divan-bed, I fancy. She can be taken away now. You'll do the post-mortem to-morrow, I suppose, Dr. Ampthill?"

"First thing," said the doctor briskly. "The mortuary car is outside in the lane now. This studio is built into the brick wall that divides the garden from the lane. I thought it would save a lot of trouble and difficulty if we opened that window, backed the car up to it, and lifted the stretcher through."

"Over there?"

Alleyn walked over to the window in the south wall. He stooped and inspected the floor.

"This is where the modeling fellow, Garcia, did his stuff. Bits of clay all over the place. His work must have stood on the tall stool here, well in the light. Wait a moment."

He flashed his pocket-torch along the sill. It was scored by several cross-scratches.

"Someone else has had your idea, Dr. Ampthill," said Alleyn. He pulled a pair of gloves from his overcoat pocket, put them on, and opened the window. The light from the studio shone on the white body of a mortuary van drawn up in the lane outside. The air smelt cold and dank. Alleyn shone his torch on the ground under the window-sill. He could see clearly the print of car tyres in the soft ground under the window.

"Look here, Mr. Blackman."

Blackman joined him.

"Yes," he said. "Someone's backed a car across the lane under the window. Miss Troy says the carrier must have called for this Mr. Garcia's stuff on Saturday morning. The maids say nobody came to the house about it. Well now, suppose Garcia left instructions for them to come straight to this window? Eh? How about that? He'd help them put the stuff through the window on to the van and then push off himself to wherever he was going."

"On his walking tour," finished Alleyn. "You're probably right. Look here, if you don't mind, I think we'll take the stretcher out through the door and along the path. Perhaps there's a door in the wall somewhere. Is there?"

"Well, the garage yard is not far off. We could take it through the yard into the lane, and the van could go along and meet them there."

"I think it would be better."

Blackman called through the window.

"Hullo there! Drive along to the back entrance and send the stretcher in from there. Keep over on the far side of the lane."

"O.K., super," said a cheerful voice.

"Sligo, you go along and show the way."

The constable at the door disappeared, and in a minute or two returned with two men and a stretcher. They carried Sonia's body out into the night.

"Well, I'll push off," said Dr. Ampthill.

"I'd like to get away, too, if you'll let me off, Mr. Alleyn," said Blackman. "I'm expecting a report at the station on this other case. Two of my chaps are down with flu and I'm rushed off my feet. I needn't say we'll do everything we can. Use the station whenever you want to."

"Thank you so much. I'll worry you as little as possible. Good night."

The door slammed and the voices died away in the distance. Alleyn turned to Fox, Bailey and Thompson.

"The old team."

"That's right, sir," said Bailey. "Suits us all right."

"Well," said Alleyn, "it's always suited me. Let's get on with it. You've got your photographs and prints. Now we'll up-end the throne. Everything's marked, so we can get it back. Let me take a final look at the drape. Yes. You see, Fox, it fell taut from the cushion to the floor, above the point of the knife. Nobody would dream of disturbing it, I imagine. As soon as Miss Seacliff pressed the model over, the drape went with her, pulling away the drawing-pin that held it to the boards. That's all clear enough. Over with the throne."

They turned the dais on its side. The light shone through the cracks in the roughly built platform. From the widest of these cracks projected the hilt of the dagger. It was a solid-looking round handle, bound with tarnished wire and protected by a crossbar guard. One side of the guard actually dug into the platform. The other just cleared it. The triangular blade had bitten into the edges of the planks. The end of the hilt was shiny.

"It's been hammered home at a slight angle, so that the blade would be at right-angles to the inclined plane of the body. It's an ingenious, dirty, deliberated bit of work, this. Prints, please, Bailey, and a photograph. Go over the whole of the under-surface. You won't get anything, I'm afraid."

While Bailey and Thompson worked, Alleyn continued his tour of the room. He pulled back the cover of the divan and saw an unmade bed beneath it. "Bad mark for Mr. Garcia." Numbers of stretched canvases stood with their faces to the wall. Alleyn began to inspect them. He thought he recognised a large picture of a trapeze artiste in pink tights and spangles as the work of Katti Bostock. That round, high-cheeked face was the one he had seen dead a few minutes ago. The head and shoulders had been scraped down with a knife. He turned another big canvas round and exclaimed softly.

"What's up, sir?" asked Fox.

"Look."

It was a portrait of a girl in a green velvet dress. She stood, very erect, against a white wall. The dress fell in austere folds about the feet. It was most simply done. The hands looked as though they had been put down with twelve direct touches. The form of the girl shone through the heavy dress, in great beauty. It was painted with a kind of quiet thoughtfulness.

But across the head where the paint was wet, someone had scrubbed a rag, and scratched with red paint an idiotic semblance of a face with a moustache.

"Lor'," said Fox, "is that a modern idea, too, sir?"

"I hardly think so," murmured Alleyn. "Good God, Fox, what a perfectly filthy thing to do. Don't you see, somebody's wiped away the face while the paint was wet, and then daubed this abortion on top of the smudge. Look at the lines of paint—you can see a kind of violence in them. The brush has been thrust savagely at the canvas so that the tip has spread. It's as if a nasty child had done it in a fit of temper. A stupid child."

"I wonder who painted the picture, sir. If it's a portrait of this girl Sonia Gluck, it looks as if there's been a bit of spite at work. By gum, it'd be a rum go if the murderer did it."

"I don't think this was Sonia," said Alleyn. "There's a smudge of blonde hair left. Sonia Gluck was dark. As for the painter——" He paused. "I don't think there's much doubt about that. The painter was Agatha Troy."

"You can pick the style, can you?"

"Yes."

With a swift movement Alleyn turned the canvas to the wall. He lit a cigarette and squatted on his heels.

"Let us take what used to be called a 'lunar' at the case. In a little while I must start interviewing people, but I'd like you fellows to get as clear an idea as possible of the case as we know it. At the moment we haven't got so much as a smell of motive. Very well. Eight students, the model, and Miss Troy have used this studio every morning from Saturday the 10th until last Friday, the 16th. On Friday they used it until twelve-thirty, came away in dribbles, lunched at the house, and then, at different intervals, all went away with the exception of Wolf Garcia, a bloke who models and sculps. He stayed behind, saying that he would be gone when they returned on Sunday. The studio was not locked at any time, unless by Garcia, who slept in it. They reopened this morning with this tragedy. Garcia and his belongings had gone. That's all. Any prints, Bailey?"

"There's a good many blue smears round the edge, sir, but it's unplaned wood underneath, and we can't do much with it. It looks a bit as if someone had mopped it up with a painty rag."

"There's a chunk of paint-rag on the floor there. Is it dusty?"

"Yes, thick with it."

"Possibly it was used for mopping up. Have a go at it."

Alleyn began to prowl round the back of the throne.

"Hullo! More grist for the mill." He pointed to a strip of wood lying in a corner of the studio. "Covered with indentations. It's the ledge off an easel. That's what was used for hammering. Take it next, Bailey. Let's find an easel without a ledge. Detecting is so simple when you only know how. Mr. Hatchett has no ledge on his easel—therefore Mr. Hatchett is a murderer. Q.E.D. This man is clever. Oh, lawks-a-mussy-me, I suppose I'd better start off on the statements. How goes it, Bailey?"

"This paint-rag's a mucky bit of stuff," grumbled Bailey. "It's been used for dusting all right. You can see the smudges on the platform. Same colour. I thought I might get a print off some of the smears of paint on the rag. They're still tacky in places. Yes, here's something. I'll take this rag back and have a go at it, sir."

"Right. Now the ledge."

Bailey used his insufflator on the strip of wood.

"No," he said, after a minute or two. "It's clean."

"All right. We'll leave the studio to these two now, Fox. Try to get us as full a record of footprints as you can, Bailey. Go over the whole show. I can't tell you what to look out for. Just do your stuff. And, by the way, I want photographs of the area round the window and the tyre-prints outside. You'd better take a cast of them and look out for any other manifestations round about them. If you come across any keys, try them for prints. Lock the place up when you've done. Good sleuthing."

Fox and Alleyn returned to the house.

"Well, Brer Fox," said Alleyn on the way, "how goes it with everybody?"

"The Yard's still in the same old place, sir. Pretty busy lately."

"What a life! Fox, I think I'll see Miss Valmai Seacliff first.

On the face of it she's a principal witness."

"What about Miss Troy, sir?" asked Fox.

Alleyn's voice came quietly out of the darkness:

"I've seen her. Just before you came."

"What sort of a lady is she?"

"I like her," said Alleyn. "Mind the step. Here's the side door. I suppose we can use it. Hullo! Look here, Fox."

He paused, his hand on Fox's arm. They were close by a window. The curtains had been carelessly drawn and a wide band of light streamed through the gap. Alleyn stood a little to one side of this light and looked into the room. Fox joined him. They saw a long refectory table at which eight people sat. In the background, half in shadow, loomed the figure of a uniformed constable. Seven of the people round the table appeared to listen to the eighth, who was Agatha Troy. The lamplight was full on her face. Her lips moved rapidly and incisively; she looked from one attentive face to the other. No sound of her voice came to Alleyn and Fox, but it was easy to see that she spoke with urgency. She stopped abruptly and looked round the table as if she expected a reply. The focus of attention shifted. Seven faces were turned towards a thin, languid-looking young man with a blond beard. He seemed to utter a single sentence, and at once a stocky woman with black straight hair cut in a bang, sprang to her feet to answer him angrily. Troy spoke again. Then nobody moved. They all sat staring at the table.

"Come on," whispered Alleyn.

He opened the side door and went along the passage to a door on the left. He tapped on this door. The policeman answered it.

"All right," said Alleyn quietly, and walked straight in, followed by Fox and the constable. The eight faces round the table turned like automatons.

"Please forgive me for barging in like this," said Alleyn to Troy.

"It's all right," said Troy. "This is the class. We were talking—about Sonia." She looked round the table. "This is Mr. Roderick Alleyn," she said.

"Good evening," said Alleyn generally. "Please don't move. If you don't mind, I think Inspector Fox and I will join you for a moment. I shall have to ask you all the usual sort of things, you know, and we may as well get it over. May we bring up a couple of chairs?"

Basil Pilgrim jumped up and brought a chair to the head of the table.

"Don't worry about me, sir," said Fox. "I'll just sit over here, thank you."

He settled himself in a chair by the sideboard. Alleyn sat at the head of the table, and placed his notebook before him.

"The usual thing," he said, looking pleasantly round the table, "is to interview people severally. I think I shall depart from routine for once and see if we can't work together. I have got your names here, but I don't know which of you is which. I'll just read them through, and if you don't mind——"

He glanced at his notes.

"Reminiscent of a roll-call, I'm afraid, but here goes. Miss Bostock?"

"Here," said Katti Bostock.

"Thank you. Mr. Hatchett?"

"That's me."

"Miss Phillida Lee?"

Miss Lee made a plaintive murmuring sound. Malmsley said: "Yes." Pilgrim said: "Here." Valmai Seacliff merely turned her head and smiled.

"That's that," said Alleyn. "Now then. Before we begin I must tell you that in my opinion there is very little doubt that Miss Sonia Gluck has been deliberately done to death. Murdered."

They seemed to go very still.

"Now, as you all must realise, she was killed by precisely the means which you discussed and worked out among yourselves ten days ago. The first question I have to put to you is this. Has any one of you discussed the experiment with the dagger outside this class? I want you to think very carefully. You have been scattered during the week-end, and it is possible, indeed very likely, that you may have talked about the pose, the model, and the experiment with the knife. This is extremely important, and I ask you to give me a deliberated answer."

He waited for quite a minute.

"I take it that none of you have spoken of this matter, then," said Alleyn.

Cedric Malmsley, leaning back in his chair, said: "Just a moment."

"Yes, Mr. Malmsley?"

"I don't know, I'm sure, if it's of any interest," drawled

55

Malmsley, "but Garcia and I talked about it on Friday afternoon."

"After the others had gone up to London?"

"Oh, yes. I went down to the studio, you see, after lunch. I did some work there. Garcia was messing about with his stuff. He's usually rather sour when he's working, but on Friday he babbled away like the brook."

"What about?"

"Oh," said Malmsley vaguely, "women and things. He's drearily keen on women, you know. Tediously over-sexed." He turned to the others. "Did you know he and Sonia were living together in London?"

"I always said they were," said Valmai Seacliff.

"Well, my sweet, it seems you were right."

"I told you, Seacliff, didn't I?" began Phillida Lee excitedly. "You remember?"

"Yes. But I thought so long before that."

"Did you pursue this topic?" asked Alleyn.

"Oh, no, we talked about you, Seacliff."

"About me?"

"Yes. We discussed your engagement, and your virtue and so on."

"Very charming of you," said Basil Pilgrim angrily.

"Oh, we agreed that you were damned lucky and so on. Garcia turned all knowing, and said——"

"Is this necessary?" demanded Pilgrim, of Alleyn.

"Not at the moment, I think," said Alleyn. "How did you come to discuss the experiment with the dagger, Mr. Malmsley?"

"Oh, that was when we talked about Sonia. Garcia looked at my drawing and asked me if I'd ever felt like killing my mistress just for the horror of doing it."

CHAPTER VI

Sidelights on Sonia

"And was that all?" inquired Alleyn, after a rather deadly little pause.

"Oh, yes," said Cedric Malmsley, and lit a cigarette. "I just thought I'd better mention it."

"Thank you. It was just as well. Did he say anything else that could possibly have a bearing on this affair?"

"I don't think so. Oh, he did say Sonia wanted him to marry her. Then he began talking about Seacliff, you know."

"Couple of snotty little bounders," grunted Katti Bostock unexpectedly.

"Oh, I don't think so," said Malmsley, with an air of sweet reasonableness. "Seacliff likes being discussed, don't you, my angel? She knows she's simply lousy with It."

"Don't be offensive, please, Malmsley," said Pilgrim dangerously.

"Good heavens! Why so sour? I thought you'd like to know we appreciated her."

"That will do, Malmsley," said Troy very quietly.

Alleyn said: "When did you leave the studio on Friday afternoon, Mr. Malmsley?"

"At five. I kept an eye on the time because I had to bathe and change and catch the six o'clock bus."

"You left Mr. Garcia still working?"

"Yes. He said he wanted to pack up the clay miniature ready to send it up to London the next morning."

"He didn't begin to pack it while you were there?"

"Well, he got me to help him carry in a zinc-lined case from the junk-room. He said it would do quite well."

"He would," said Troy grimly. "I paid fifteen shillings for that case."

"How would it be managed?" asked Alleyn. "Surely a clay model is a ticklish thing to transport?"

"He'd wrap masses of damp cloths round it," explained Troy.

"How about lifting it? Wouldn't it be very heavy?"

"Oh, he'd thought all that out," said Malmsley, yawning horribly. "We put the case on a tall stool in the window with the open end sideways, beside the tall stool he worked on. The thing was on a platform with wheels. He just had to wheel it into the case and fill the case with packing."

"How about getting it into the van?"

"Dear me. Isn't this all rather tedious?"

"Extremely. A concise answer would enable us to move on to a more interesting narrative."

Troy gave an odd little snort of laughter.

"Well, Mr. Malmsley?" said Alleyn.

"Garcia said the lorry would back into the window from the lane outside. The sill is only a bit higher than the stools. He said they'd be able to drag the case on to the sill and get it in the lorry."

"Did he say anything about arranging for the lorry?"

"He asked me if there was a man in the village," said Troy. "I told him Burridge would do it."

The policeman at the door gave a deprecatory cough.

"Hullo!" said Alleyn, slewing round in his chair. "Thought of something?"

"The super asked Burridges if they done it, sir, and they says no."

"Right. Thank you. Now, Mr. Malmsley, did you get any idea when Mr. Garcia proposed to put the case on board the lorry?"

"He said early next morning—Saturday."

"I see. There was no other mention of Miss Gluck, the pose, or Mr. Garcia's subsequent plans?"

"No."

"He didn't tell you where the clay model was to be delivered?"

"No. He just said he'd got the loan of a disused warehouse in London."

"He told me he was going on a sketching-tramp for a week before he started work," said Valmai Seacliff.

"To me also, he said this." Francis Ormerin leant forward, glancing nervously at Alleyn. "He said he wished to paint landscape for a little before beginning this big work."

"He painted?" asked Alleyn.

"Oh, yes," said Troy. "Sculping was his long suit, but he

painted and etched a bit as well."

"Very interesting stuff," said Katti Bostock.

"Drearily representational though, you must own," murmured Malmsley.

"I don't agree," said Ormerin.

"Good God!" exclaimed Basil Pilgrim, "we're not here to discuss aesthetics."

"Does anyone here," Alleyn cut in firmly, "know who lent this warehouse to Garcia, where it was, when he proposed to go there, or in what direction he has supposedly walked away?"

Silence.

"He is possibly the most uncommunicative young man in England," said Troy suddenly.

"It would seem so, indeed," agreed Alleyn.

"There's this, though," added Troy. "He told me the name of the man who commissioned the 'Comedy and Tragedy.' It's Charleston, and I think he's secretary to the board of the New Palace Theatre, Westminster. Is that any help?"

"It may be a lot of help."

"Do you think Garcia murdered Sonia?" asked Malmsley vaguely. "I must say I don't."

"The next point is this," said Alleyn, exactly as though Malmsley had not spoken. "I want to arrive at the order in which you all left the studio on Friday at midday. I believe Miss Troy and Miss Bostock came away together as soon as the model got down. Any objection to that?"

There were none apparently.

"Well, who came next?"

"I—I think I did," said Phillida Lee, "and I think I ought to tell you about an *extraordinary* thing that I heard Garcia say to Sonia one day——"

"Thank you so much, Miss Lee. I'll come to that later, if I may. At the moment we're talking about the order in which you left the studio on Friday at noon. You followed Miss Troy and Miss Bostock?"

"Yes," said Miss Lee restlessly.

"Good. Are you sure of that, Miss Lee?"

"Yes. I mean I know I did because I was absolutely *exhausted*. It always takes it out of me most *frightfully* when I paint. It simply drains every *ounce* of my energy. I even forget to *breathe*."

"That must be most uncomfortable," said Alleyn gravely.

"You came out to breathe, perhaps?"

"Yes. I mean I felt I must get away from it all. So I simply put down my brushes and walked out. Miss Troy and Bostock were just ahead of me."

"You went straight to the house?"

"Yes, I think so. Yes, I did."

"Yeah, that's right," said Watt Hatchett loudly. "You came straight up here because I was just after you, see? I saw you through the dining-room window. This window here, Mr. Alleyn. That's right, Miss Lee. You went up to the sideboard and began eating something."

"I—I don't remember that," said Miss Lee in a high voice. She darted an unfriendly glance at Hatchett.

"Well," said Alleyn briskly, "that leaves Miss Seacliff, Messrs. Ormerin, Pilgrim, Malmsley and Garcia, and the model. Who came next?"

"We all did—except Garcia and Sonia," said Valmai Seacliff. "Sonia hadn't dressed. I remember I went into the junk-room and washed my brushes under the tap. Ormerin and Malmsley and Basil followed me there."

She spoke with a slight hesitation, the merest shadow of a stutter, and with a markedly falling inflexion. She had a trick of uttering the last words of a phrase on an indrawn breath. Everything she looked and did, Alleyn felt, was the result of a carefully concealed deliberation. She managed now to convey the impression that men followed her inevitably, wherever she went.

"They were in the way," she went on. "I told them to go. Then I finished washing my brushes and came up to the house."

"Garcia was in the junk-room, too, I think," said Ormerin.

"Oh, yes," agreed Seacliff softly. "He came in, as soon as you'd gone. He would, you know. Sonia was glaring through the door—furious, of course." Her voice died away and was caught up on that small gasp. She looked through her eyelashes at Alleyn. "I walked up to the house with the other three."

"That is so," agreed Ormerin.

"Leaving Mr. Garcia and the model in the studio?" asked Alleyn.

"I suppose so."

"Yes," said Pilgrim.

"You say the model was furious, Miss Seacliff," said Alleyn. "Why was that?"

"Oh, because Garcia was making passes at me in the junk-room. Nothing much. He can't help himself—Garcia."

"I see," said Alleyn politely. "Now, please. Did any of you revisit the studio before you went up to London?"

"I did," said Ormerin.

"At what time?"

"Immediately after lunch. I wished to look again at my work. I was very troubled about my work. Everything was difficult. The model——" He stopped short.

"Yes?"

"Never for a second was she still. It was impossible. Impossible! I believe that she did it deliberately."

"She's dead now," said Phillida Lee, on muted strings. "Poor little Sonia."

"Spare us the *nil nisi* touch, for God's sake," begged Malmsley.

"Did you all notice the model's restlessness?"

"You bet!" said Watt Hatchett. "She was saucy, that's what she was. Seemed to have got hold of the idea she amounted to something. She gave me a pain in the neck, dinkum, always slinging off about Aussie."

"'Aussie,'" groaned Malmsley. "'Ausie,' 'Tassie,' 'a goodee,' 'a badee.' Pray spare me these bloody abbreviations."

"Look, Mr. Malmsley, I'd sooner talk plain honest Australian than make a noise like I'd got a fish-bone stuck in me gullet. Aussie'll do me. And one other thing, too. If you walked down Bondi beach with that half-chewed mouthful of hay sprouting out of your dial, they'd phone the Zoo something was missing."

"Hatchett," said Troy. "Pipe down."

"Good oh, Miss Troy."

"I gather," said Alleyn mildly, "that you didn't altogether like the model?"

"Who, me? Too right I didn't. I'm sorry the poor kid's coughed out. Gosh, I reckon it's a fair cow, but just the same she gave me a pain in the neck. I asked her one day had she got fleas or something, the way she was twitching. And did she go crook!" Hatchett uttered a raucous yelp of laughter. Malmsley shuddered.

"Thank you, Mr. Hatchett," said Alleyn firmly. "The next point I want to raise is this. Have there been any definite quarrels with the model? Any scenes, any rows between Miss Gluck and somebody else?"

He looked round the table. Everyone seemed disconcerted. There was a sudden feeling of tension. Alleyn waited. After a silence of perhaps a minute, Katti Bostock said slowly:

"I suppose you might say there were a good many scenes."

"You had one with her yourself, Bostock," said Malmsley. "I did."

"What was that about, Miss Bostock?"

"Same thing. Wriggling. I'm doing—I was doing a big thing. I wanted to finish it in time for the Group Show. It opened last Friday. She was to give me separate sittings—out of class, you know. She seemed to have the devil in her. Fidgeting, going out when I wanted her. Complaining. Drove me dotty. I didn't get the thing finished, of course."

"Was that the trapeze-artiste picture?" asked Alleyn.

Katti Bostock scowled.

"I dislike people looking at my things before they're finished."

"I'm sorry; it is beastly, I know," said Alleyn. "But, you see, we've got to do our nosing round."

"I suppose you have. Well"—she laughed shortly—"it'll never be finished now."

"It wouldn't have been finished anyway, though, would it?" asked Phillida Lee. "I meant I heard you tell her you hated the sight of her, and she could go to the devil."

"What d'you mean?" demanded Katti Bostock harshly. "You were not there when I was working."

"I happened to come in on Thursday afternoon. I only got inside the door, and you were having such a *frightful* row I beetled off again."

"You'd no business to hang about and eavesdrop," said Miss Bostock. Her broad face was dull crimson; she leant forward, scowling.

"There's no need to lose your temper with *me*," squeaked Miss Lee. "I didn't eavesdrop. I simply walked in. You couldn't see me because of the screen inside the door, and anyway, you were in such a *seething* rage you wouldn't have noticed the Angel Gabriel himself."

"For Heaven's sake let's keep our sense of proportion," said Troy. "The poor little wretch was infuriating, and we've all lost our tempers with her again and again." She looked at Alleyn. "Really, you might say each of us has felt like murdering her at some time or another."

"Yes, Miss Troy," said Phillida Lee, still staring at Katti Bostock, "but we haven't all said so, have we?"

"My God——"

"Katti," said Troy. "Please!"

"She's practically suggesting that——"

"No, no," said Ormerin. "Let us, as Troy says, keep our sense of proportion. If exasperation could have stabbed this girl, any one of us might be a murderer. But whichever one of us *did*——"

"I don't see why it need be one of us," objected Valmai Seacliff placidly.

"Nor I," drawled Malmsley. "The cook may have taken a dislike to her and crawled down to the studio with murder in her heart."

"Are we meant to laugh at that?" asked Hatchett.

"It is perfectly clearly to be seen," Ormerin said loudly, "what is the view of the police. This gentleman, Mr. Alleyn, who is so quiet and so polite, who waits in silence for us to make fools of ourselves—he knows as each of us must know in his heart that the murderer of this girl was present in the studio on the morning we made the experiment with the dagger. That declares itself. There is no big motive that sticks out like a bundle in a haystack, so Mr. Alleyn sits and says nothing and hears much. And we—we talk."

"Mr. Ormerin," said Alleyn, "you draw up the blinds on my technique, and leave it blinking foolishly in the light of day. I see that I may be silent no longer."

"Ah-ah-ah! It is as I have said." Ormerin wagged his head sideways, shrugged up his shoulders and threw himself back in his chair. "But as for this murder—it is the *crime passionnel*, depend upon it. The girl was very highly sexed."

"That doesn't necessarily lead to homicide," Alleyn pointed out, with a smile.

"She was jealous," said Ormerin; "she was yellow with jealousy and chagrin. Every time Garcia looks at Seacliff she suffers as if she is ill. And when Pilgrim announces that he is affianced with Seacliff, again Sonia feels as if a knife is twisted inside her."

"That's absolute bosh," said Basil Pilgrim violently. "You don't know what you are talking about, Ormerin."

"Do I not? She was avid for men, that little one."

"Dear me," murmured Malmsley, "this all sounds very Montmartre."

"She certainly was a hot little dame," said Hatchett.

"It was apparent," added Ormerin. "And when a more compelling—a more *troublante*—woman arrived, she became quite frantic. Because Seacliff——"

"Will you keep Valmai's name out of this?" shouted Pilgrim.

"Basil, darling, how divinely county you are," said Valmai Seacliff. "I know she was jealous of me. We all know she was. And she obviously was very attracted to you, my sweet."

"This conversation," said Troy, "seems slightly demented. All this, if it was true, might mean that Sonia would feel like killing Valmai or Pilgrim or Garcia, but why should anybody kill her?"

"Closely reasoned," murmured Alleyn. Troy threw a suspicious glance at him.

"It is true, is it not," insisted Ormerin, "that you suspect one of us?"

"Or Garcia," said Katti Bostock.

"Yes, there's always the little tripe-hound," agreed Seacliff.

"And the servants," added Malmsley.

"Very well," amended Ormerin, still talking to Alleyn. "You suspect one of this party, or Garcia, or—if you will—the servants."

"An inside job," said Hatchett, proud of the phrase.

"Oh, yes," said Alleyn. "I do rather suspect one of you—or Mr. Garcia—or the servants. But it's early days yet. I am capable of almost limitless suspicion. At the moment I am going to tighten up this round-table conference." He looked at Hatchett. "How long have you been working without a tray on your easel?"

"Eh? What d'you mean?" Hatchett sounded startled.

"It's not very difficult. How long is it since you had a ledge on your easel?"

"Haven't I got one now?"

"No."

"Oh yeah! That's right. I took it off to hammer the dagger into the throne."

"What!" screamed Phillida Lee. "Oh, I see."

"On the day of the experiment?" asked Alleyn.

"That's right."

"And it's been kicking about on the floor ever since?"

"I suppose so. Half a tick, though—has it? Naow—it hasn't, either. I've had a ledge all right. I stuck my dipper on it. Look, I had a ledge on me easel Fridee after lunch."

"*After* lunch," said Alleyn.

"Yeah, I remember now. I ran down some time after lunch to have a look at the thing I'd been painting. I met you coming away, Ormerin, didn't I?"

"Yes. I only looked at my work and felt sick and came away."

"Yeah. Well, when I got there I thought I'd play round with the wet paint, see? Well, I'd just had a smack at it when I heard Ormerin singing out the old bus went past the corner on the main road in ten minutes. Well, I remember now; I jammed my brush into my dipper so's it wouldn't go hard, and then beat it. But the dipper was on the ledge all right."

"And was the ledge there this morning?"

"You're right. It wasn't. And it wasn't there Sundee night either."

"Sunday night?" said Alleyn sharply.

"That's right. After we got back, see? I ran down to the studio just after tea."

"After tea? But I thought you didn't come back until——" Alleyn looked at his notes. "Until six-thirty."

"That's correct, Mr. Alleyn. We finished tea at half-past eight, about."

"The gentleman is talking of the evening meal, Inspector," said Malmsley. "They dine at noon in the Antipodes, I understand."

"Aw go and chase yourself," invited Hatchett. "I went down to the studio at about eight-thirty, Inspector. 'After dinnah' if you've got enlarged tonsils. 'After tea' if you're normal."

"Did you get in?"

"Too right. She was locked, but the key's left on a nail, and I opened her up and had a look-see at my picture. Gosh, it looked all right, too, Miss Troy, by artificial light. Have you seen it by lamplight, Miss Troy?"

"No," said Troy. "Don't wander."

"Good oh, Miss Troy."

"Well," said Alleyn, "you went into the studio, and put the lights up, and looked at your work. Did you look at the throne?"

"Er—yes. Yes, I did. I was wondering if I'd paint a bit of the drape, and I had a look, and it was all straightened out. Like it always is before she gets down into the pose. Stretched tight from the cushion to the floor. If I had a pencil I could show you——"

"Thank you, I think I follow."

"Good oh, then. Well, I wondered if I'd try and fix it like as if the model was laying on it. I'd an idea that I might get it right if I lay down myself in the pose. Cripes!" exclaimed Hatchett, turning paper-white. "If I'd a-done that would I have got a knife in me slats? Cripey, Mr. Alleyn, do you reckon that dagger was sticking up under the drape on Sundee evening?"

"Possibly."

"What a cow!" whispered Hatchett.

"However, you didn't arrange yourself on the drape. Why not?"

"Well, because Miss Troy won't let anybody touch the throne without she says they can, and I thought she'd go crook if I did."

"Correct?" asked Alleyn, with a smile at Troy.

"Certainly. It's the rule of the studio. Otherwise the drapes would get bundled about, and the chalked positions rubbed off."

"Yeah, but listen, Miss Troy. Mr. Alleyn, listen. I've just remembered something."

"Come on, then," said Alleyn.

"Gee, I reckon this is important," continued Hatchett excitedly. "Look, when I went down to the studio just before we all went to catch the bus on Fridee, the drape was all squashed down, just as it had been when the model got up."

"You're sure of that?"

"I'm certain. I'll swear to it."

"Did you notice the drape on your brief visit to the studio after lunch, Mr. Ormerin?"

"Yes," said Ormerin excitedly. "Now you ask I remember well. I looked at my work, and then automatically I looked at the throne as though the model was still there. And I got the small tiny shock one receives at the sight of that which one does not expect. Then I looked at my treatment of the drape and back to the drape itself. It was as Hatchett describes—crumpled and creased by the weight of her body, just as when she arose at midday."

"Here!" exclaimed Hatchett. "See what that means? It means——"

"It is pregnant with signification, I'm sure, Mr. Hatchett," said Alleyn. Hatchett was silent. Alleyn looked at his notes and continued: "I understand that Miss Troy and Miss Bostock left by car. So did Miss Seacliff and Mr. Pilgrim. Then came the bus party at three o'clock. Miss Lee, Mr. Ormerin, Mr. Hatchett, and the model. It seems," said Alleyn very deliberately, "that at a few minutes before three when Mr. Hatchett left to catch the bus, the drape was still flat and crushed on the floor." He paused, contemplating Cedric Malmsley. "What did you do after the others had gone?"

Malmsley lit a cigarette and took his time over it.

"Oh," he said at last, "I wandered down to the studio."

"When?"

"Immediately after lunch."

"Did you look at the drape on the throne?"

"I believe I did."

"How was it then?"

"Quite well, I imagine. Just like a drape on a throne."

"Mr. Malmsley," said Alleyn, "I advise you not to be too amusing. I am investigating a murder. Was the drape still flat?"

"Yes."

"How long did you stay in the studio?"

"I've told you. Until five."

"Alone with Mr. Garcia?"

"I've told you. Alone with Garcia."

"Did either of you leave the studio during the afternoon?"

"Yes."

"Who?"

"Garcia."

"Do you know why?"

"I imagine it was to pay a visit to the usual offices."

"How long was he away?"

"Dear me, I don't know. Perhaps eight or ten minutes."

"When he worked, did he face the window?"

"I believe so."

"With his back to the room?"

"Naturally."

"Did you look at the drape before you left?"

"I don't think so."

"Did you touch the drape, Mr. Malmsley?"

"No."

"Who scrawled that appalling defacement on Miss Troy's painting of a girl in green?"

There was an uneasy silence, broken at last by Troy.

"You mean my portrait of Miss Seacliff. Sonia did that."

"The model?" exclaimed Alleyn.

"I believe so. I said we have all felt like murdering her. That was my motive, Mr. Alleyn."

CHAPTER VII

Alibi for Troy

Alleyn lifted a hand as if in protest. He checked himself and, after a moment's pause, went on with his customary air of polite diffidence.

"The model defaced your painting. Why did she do this?"

"Because she was livid with *me*," said Valmai Seacliff. "You see, it was rather a marvelous painting. Troy was going to exhibit it. Sonia hated that. Besides, Basil wanted to buy it."

"When did she commit this—outrage?" asked Alleyn.

"A week ago," said Troy. "Miss Seacliff gave me the final sitting last Monday morning. The class came down to the studio to see the thing. Sonia came too. She'd been in a pretty foul frame of mind for some days. It's perfectly true what they all say. She was an extraordinary little animal and, as Ormerin has told you, extremely jealous. They all talked about the portrait. She was left outside the circle. Then Pilgrim asked me if he might buy it before it went away. Perhaps I should tell you that I have also done a portrait of Sonia which has been sold. Sonia took that as a sort of personal slight on her beauty. It's hard to believe, but she did. She seemed to think I'd painted Miss Seacliff because I was dissatisfied with her own charms as a model. Then, when they all came down and looked at the thing and liked it, and Pilgrim said he wanted it, I suppose that upset her still more. Several of these people said in front of her, they thought the thing of Miss Seacliff was the best portrait I have done."

"It was all worms and gallwood to her," said Ormerin.

"Well," Troy went on, "we came away, and I suppose she stayed behind. When I went down to the studio later on that day, I found—" she caught her breath—"I found—what you saw."

"Did you tackle her?"

"Not at first. I—felt sick. You see, once in a painter's

lifetime he, or she, does something that's extra."

"I know."

"Something that they look at afterwards and say to themselves: 'How did the stumbling ninny that is me, do this?' It happened with the head in Valmai's portrait. So when I saw—I just felt sick."

"Bloody little swine," said Miss Bostock.

"Oh, well," said Troy, "I did tackle her that evening. She admitted she'd done it. She said all sorts of things about Valmai and Pilgrim, and indeed everybody in the class. She stormed and howled."

"You didn't sack her?" asked Alleyn.

"I felt like it, of course. But I couldn't quite do that. You see, they'd all got going on these other things, and there was Katti's big thing, too. I think she was honestly sorry she'd done it. She really rather liked me. She simply went through life doing the first thing that came into her head. This business had been done in a blind fury with Valmai. She only thought of me afterwards. She fetched up by having hysterics and offering to pose for nothing for the rest of her life." Troy smiled crookedly. "The stable-door idea," she said.

"Basil and I were frightfully upset," said Valmai Seacliff. "Weren't we, Basil?"

Alleyn looked to see how Pilgrim would take this remark. He thought that for a moment he saw a look of reluctant surprise.

"Darling!" said Pilgrim, "of course we were." And then in his eyes appeared the reflection of her beauty, and he stared at her with the solemn alarm of a man very deeply in love.

"Were there any more upheavals after this?" asked Alleyn after a pause.

"Not exactly," answered Troy. "She was chastened a bit. The others let her see that they thought she'd—she'd——"

"I went crook at her," announced Hatchett. "I told her I reckoned she was ——"

"Pipe down, Hatchett."

"Good-oh, Miss Troy."

"We were all livid," said Katti Bostock hotly. "I could have mur——" She stopped short. "Well, there you are, you see," she said doggedly. "I could have murdered her but I didn't. She knew how I felt, and she took it out in the sittings she gave me."

"It was sacrilege," squeaked Phillida Lee. "That exquisite

thing. To see it with that obscene——"

"Shut up, Lee, for God's sake," said Katti Bostock.

"Oddly enough," murmured Malmsley, "Garcia seemed to take it as heavily as anybody. Worse if anything. Do you know, he was actually ill, Troy? I found him in the garden, a most distressing sight."

"How extraordinary!" said Valmai Seacliff vaguely. "I always thought he was entirely without emotion. Oh, but of course——"

"Of course—what?" asked Alleyn.

"Well, it *was* a portrait of me, wasn't it? I attracted him *tremendously* in the physical sense. I suppose that was why he was sick."

"Oh, bilge and bosh!" said Katti Bostock.

"Think so?" said Seacliff quite amiably.

"Can any of you tell me on what sort of footing the model and Mr. Garcia were during the last week?" asked Alleyn.

"Well, I told you she'd been his mistress," said Malmsley. "He said that himself during Friday afternoon."

"Not while they were here, I hope," said Troy. "I told him I wouldn't have anything like that."

"He said so. He was very pained and hurt at your attitude, I gathered."

"Well, I *know* there was something going on, anyway," said Phillida Lee, with a triumphant squeak. "I've been waiting to tell the superintendent this, but you were all so busy talking, I didn't get a *chance*. I know Sonia wanted him to marry her."

"Why, Miss Lee?"

"Well, they were always whispering together, and I went to the studio one day, about a week ago, I think, and there they were having a session—I mean, they were talking—nothing else."

"You seem to have had a good many lucky dips in the studio, Lee," said Katti Bostock. "What did you overhear this time?"

"You needn't be so acid. It may turn out a mercy I *did* hear them. Mayn't it, Superintendent?" She appealed to Alleyn.

"I haven't risen to superintendent heights, Miss Lee. But please do tell me what you heard."

"As a matter of fact, it wasn't *very* much, but it was exciting. Garcia said: 'All right—on Friday night, then.' And Sonia said: 'Yes, if it's possible.' Then there was quite a long pause and she said: 'I won't stand for any funny business with *her*, you know.' And Garcia said: 'Who?' and she said—I'm sorry, Mr. Alleyn—but she said: 'The Seacliff bitch, of course.'" Miss Lee turned pink. "I *am* sorry, Mr. Alleyn."

"Miss Seacliff will understand the exigencies of a verbatim report," said Alleyn with the faintest possible twinkle.

"Oh, I've heard all about it. She knew what he was up to, of course," said Valmai Seacliff. She produced a lipstick and mirror and, with absorbed attention, made up her lovely mouth.

"Why didn't you tell me the swine was pestering you?" Pilgrim asked her.

"My sweet—I could manage Garcia perfectly well," said Seacliff with a little chuckle.

"Anything more, Miss Lee?" asked Alleyn.

"Well, yes. Sonia suddenly began to cry and say Garcia ought to marry her. He said nothing. She said something about Friday evening again, and she said if he let her down after that she'd go to Troy and tell her the whole story. Garcia just said—Mr. Alleyn, he just sort of *grunted* it, but honestly it sounded *frightful*. Truly. And she didn't say another *thing*. I think she was *terrified*—really!"

"But you haven't told us what he did say, you know."

"Well, he said: 'If you don't shut up and leave me to get on with my work, I'll bloody well stop your mouth for keeps. Do what I tell you. Get out!' *There!*" ended Miss Lee triumphantly.

"Have you discussed this incident with anyone else?"

"I told Seacliff, in confidence."

"I advised her to regard it as nobody's business but theirs," said Seacliff.

"Well—I thought *somebody* ought to know."

"I said," added Seacliff, "that if she still felt all repressed and congested, she could tell Troy."

"Did you follow this excellent advice, Miss Lee?"

"No—I didn't—because—well, because I thought—I mean——"

"I have rather sharp views on gossip," said Troy dryly. "And even sharper views on listening-in. Possibly she realised this." She stared coldly at Miss Lee, who turned very pink indeed.

"How did this incident terminate?" asked Alleyn.

"Well, I made a bangy sort of noise with the door to show I

was there, and they stopped. And I *didn't* eavesdrop, Miss Troy, truly. I just rooted to the ground with *horror*. It all sounded so *sinister*. And *now* see what's happened!"

Troy looked up at Alleyn. Suddenly she grinned, and Alleyn felt a sort of thump in his chest. "Oh God," he thought urgently, "what am I going to do about this? I didn't *want* to lose my heart." He looked away quickly.

"Are there any other incidents of any sort that might have some bearing on this tragedy?" he asked at large.

Nobody answered.

"Then I shall ask you all to stay in here for a little while longer. I want to see each of you separately, before we close down to-night. Miss Troy, will you allow us to use a separate room as a temporary office? I am sorry to give so much trouble."

"Certainly," said Troy. "I'll show you——"

She led the way to the door and went into the hall without waiting for them. Alleyn and Fox followed, leaving the local man behind. When the door had shut behind them Alleyn said to Fox:

"Get through to the Yard, Fox. We'll have to warn all stations about Garcia. If he's tramping, he can't have walked so far in three days. If he's bolted, he may be anywhere by now. I'll try and get hold of a photograph. We'd better broadcast, I think. Make sure nobody's listening when you telephone. Tell them to get in touch with the city. We must find this warehouse. Then see the maids. Ask if they know anything at all about the studio on Friday night and Saturday morning. Come along to the drawing-room when you've finished, will you?"

"Right, sir. I'll just ask this P.C. where the telephone hangs out."

Fox turned back, and Alleyn moved on to the end of the hall, where Troy waited in a pool of light that came from the library.

"In here," she said.

"Thank you."

She was turning away as Alleyn said:

"May I keep you a moment?"

He stood aside for her to go through the door. They returned to the fire. Troy got a couple of logs from the wood basket.

"Let me do that," Alleyn said.

"It's all right."

She pitched the logs on the fire and dusted her hands.

"There are cigarettes on that table, Mr. Alleyn. Will you have one?"

He lit her cigarette and his own and they sat down.

"What now?" asked Troy.

"I want you to tell me exactly what you did from the time you left the studio on Friday at noon until the class assembled this morning."

"An alibi?"

"Yes."

"Do you think for a moment," said Troy, in a level voice, "that I might have killed this girl?"

"Not for a moment," answered Alleyn.

"I suppose I shouldn't have asked you that. I'm sorry. Shall I begin with the time I got up to the house?"

"Yes, please," said Alleyn.

He thought she was very stiff with him and supposed she resented the very sight of himself and everything he stood for. It did not occur to Alleyn that his refusal to answer that friendly grin had sent up all Troy's defences. Where women were concerned he was, perhaps, unusually intelligent and intuitive, but the whole of this case is coloured by his extraordinary wrong-headedness over Troy's attitude towards himself. He afterwards told Nigel Bathgate that he was quite unable to bring Troy into focus with the case. To Troy it seemed that he treated her with an official detachment that was a direct refusal to acknowledge any former friendliness. She told herself, with a sick feeling of shame, that she had probably thought she pursued him in the ship. He had consented to sit to her, with a secret conviction that she hoped it might lead to a flirtation. "Or," thought Troy, deliberately jabbing at the nerve, "he probably decided I was fishing for a sale."

Now, on this first evening at Tatler's End House, they treated each other to displays of frigid courtesy. Troy, summoning her wits, began an account of her week-end activities.

"I came up to the house, washed, changed and lunched. After lunch, as far as I remember, Katti and I sat in here and smoked. Then we went round to the garage, got the car, and drove up to our club in London. It's the United Arts. We got there about four o'clock, had tea with some people we ran into in the club, shopped for an hour afterwards, and got back to the club about six, I should think. I bathed, changed and met Katti in the lounge. We had a cocktail and then dined with the Arthur Jayneses. It was a party of six. He's president of the Phoenix Group. From there we all went to the private view. We supped at the Hungaria with the Jayneses. I got back to the club somewhere round two o'clock. On Saturday I had my hair done at Cattcherly's in Bond Street. Katti and I had another look at the show. I lunched early at the Ritz with a man called John Bellasca. Then I picked Katti up at the club and we got back here about three."

"Did you go down to the studio?"

"Yes. I went there to collect my sketch-box. I wanted to see what materials I had and tidy it up. I was going to work out of doors on Sunday. I brought the box in here and spent the afternoon at different tidying jobs. After that Katti and I went for a walk to look for a subject. We dined out. I asked when we got here on Saturday if Garcia had gone, and the maids told me he hadn't been in to breakfast or lunch, so I supposed he had pushed off at daybreak. They had sent his dinner down to the studio the night before—Friday night. It was easier than having it up here. He sleeps in the studio, you know."

"Why was that?"

"It was advisable. I didn't want him in the house. You've heard what he's like with women."

"I see. On Saturday were you long in the studio?"

"No. I simply got my sketch-box. I was painting out of doors."

"Anyone go in with you?"

"No."

"Did you notice the drape?"

Troy leant forward, her cropped head between two clenched fists.

"That's what I've been trying to remember ever since Hatchett said it was stretched out when he saw it on Sunday.

"Give me a moment. I went straight to my cupboard behind the door and got out my sketching gear. I had a look in the box and found there was no turpentine in the bottle, so I took it to the junk-room and filled it up. Then I came back to the studio and—yes, yes!"

"You've remembered it?"

"Yes. I—I must tell you I hadn't screwed myself up to looking at the portrait of Seacliff again. Not since I first saw

74

what Sonia had done to it. I just turned it face to the wall behind the throne. Well, I saw it when I came out of the junk-room, and I thought: 'I can't go on cutting it dead. It can't stand there for ever, giving me queasy horrors whenever I catch sight of it.' So I began to walk towards it, and I got as far as the edge of the throne, and I remember now quite clearly I walked carefully round the drape, so as not to disturb it, and I noticed, without noticing, don't you know, that the silk was in position—stretched straight from the cushion and pinned to the floor of the throne. You may have noticed that it was caught with a safety-pin to the top of the cushion. That was to prevent it slipping off when she lay down on it. It was fixed lightly to the floor with a drawing-pin that flew out when the drape took her weight. The whole idea was to get the accidental swill of the silk round the figure. It was stretched out like that when I saw it."

"I needn't tell you the significance of this," said Alleyn, slowly. "You are absolutely certain the drape was in position?"

"Yes. I'd swear to it."

"And did you look at the portrait of Miss Seacliff?"

Troy turned her face away from him.

"No," she said gruffly, "I funked it. Poor sort of business, wasn't it?" She laughed shortly.

Alleyn made a quick movement, stopped himself, and said: "I don't think so. Did either of you go down to the studio at any time during yesterday, do you know?"

"I don't know. I don't think so. I didn't, and Katti had an article to do for *The Palette* and was writing in the library all day. She's got a series of articles on the Italian primitives running in *The Palette*. You'd better ask her about yesterday."

"I will. To return to your own movements. You went out to paint in the garden?"

"Yes. At eleven o'clock. The Bossicote church bell had just stopped. I worked till about two o'clock and came in for a late lunch. After lunch I cleaned up my brushes at the house. I hadn't gone to the studio. Katti and I had a good glare at my sketch, and then she read over her article and began to type it. I sat in here, working out an idea for a decorative panel on odd bits of paper. Seacliff and Pilgrim arrived in his car for tea at five, and the others came by the six o'clock bus."

"Sonia Gluck with them?"

"Yes."

"Did you all spend the evening together?"

"The class has a sort of common-room at the back of the house. In my grandfather's day it was really a kind of ballroom, but when my father lost most of his money, part of the house was shut up, including this place. I had a lot of odds and ends of furniture put into it and let them use it. It's behind the dining-room, at the end of an odd little passage. They all went in there after dinner on Sunday—yesterday—evening. I looked in for a little while."

"They were all there?"

"I think so. Pilgrim and Seacliff wandered out through the french window into the garden. I suppose they wanted to enjoy the amenities of betrothal."

Alleyn laughed unexpectedly. He had a very pleasant laugh.

"What's the matter?" asked Troy.

"'The amenities of betrothal,'" quoted Alleyn.

"Well, what's wrong with that?"

"Such a grand little phrase!"

For a moment there was no constraint between them. They looked at each other as if they were old friends.

"Well," said Troy, "they came back looking very smug and complacent and self-conscious, and all the others were rather funny about it. Except Sonia, who looked like thunder. It's quite true, what Seacliff says. Sonia, you see, was the main attraction last year, as far as the men-students were concerned. She used to hold a sort of court in the rest-times and fancied herself as a Bohemian siren, poor little idiot. Then Seacliff came and wiped her eye. She was beside herself with chagrin. You've seen what Seacliff is like. She doesn't exactly disguise the fact that she is attractive to men, does she? Katti says she's a successful nymphomaniac."

"Pilgrim seems an honest-to-God sort of fellow."

"He's a nice fellow, Pilgrim."

"Do you approve of the engagement?"

"No, I don't. I think she's after his title."

"You don't mean to say he's a son of the Methodist peer?"

"Yes, he is. And the Methodist peer may leave us for crowns and harps any moment now. The old gentlemen's failing."

"I see."

"As a matter of fact——" Troy hesitated.

"Yes?"

"I don't know that it matters."

"Please, tell me anything you can think of."

"You may attach too much importance to it."

"We are warned against that at the Yard, you know."

"I beg your pardon," said Troy stiffly. "I was merely going to say that I thought Basil Pilgrim had been worried about something since his engagement."

"Have you any idea what it was?"

"I thought at first it might have been his father's illness, but somehow I don't think it was that."

"Perhaps he has already regretted his choice. The trapped feeling."

"I don't think so," said Troy still more stiffly. "I fancy it was something to do with Sonia."

"With the model?"

"I simply meant that I thought he felt uncomfortable about Sonia. She was always uttering little jeers about engaged couples. I think they made Pilgrim feel uncomfortable."

"Do you imagine there has ever been anything between Pilgrim and Sonia Gluck?"

"I have no idea," said Troy.

There was a tap on the door, and Fox came in.

"I got through, sir. They'll get busy at once. The men have finished in the studio."

"Ask them to wait. I'll see them in a minute."

"Have you finished with me?" asked Troy, standing up.

"Yes, thank you, Miss Troy," said Alleyn formally. "If you wouldn't mind giving us the names and addresses of the people you met in London, I should be very grateful. You see, we are obliged to check all statements of this sort."

"I quite understand," answered Troy coldly.

She gave the names and addresses of her host and hostess, of the people she met in the club, and of the man who took her to lunch—John Bellasca, 44, Little Belgrave Street.

"The club porter may be useful," she said, "his name's Jackson. He may have noticed my goings out and comings in. I remember that I asked him the time, and got him to call taxis. The sort of things people do when they wish to establish alibis, I understand."

"They occasionally do them at normal times, I believe," said Alleyn. "Thank you, Miss Troy. I won't bother you any more for the moment. Do you mind joining the others until we have finished this business?"

77

"Not at all," answered Troy with extreme grandeur. "Please use this room as much as you like. Good evening, good evening."

"Good evening, miss," said Fox.

Troy made an impressive exit.

CHAPTER VIII

Sidelights on Garcia

"The lady seems a bit upset," said Fox mildly, when Troy had gone.

"I irritate the lady," answered Alleyn.

"*You* do, sir? I always think you've got a very pleasant way with female witnesses. Sort of informal and at the same time very polite."

"Thank you, Fox," said Alleyn wryly.

"Learn anything useful, sir?"

"She says the drape was in the second position on Saturday afternoon."

"Stretched out straight?"

"Yes."

"Well," said Fox, "if she's telling the truth, it looks as though the knife was fixed up between the time this Mr. Malmsley walked out on Friday afternoon and the time Miss Troy looked in on Saturday. That's if Malmsley was telling the truth when he said the drape was crumpled and flat on Friday afternoon. It all points one way, chief, doesn't it?"

"It does, Brer Fox, it does."

"The Yard's getting straight on to chasing up this Mr. Garcia. I've rung all the stations round this district and asked them to make inquiries. I got a pretty fair description of him from the cook, and Bailey found a couple of photographs of the whole crowd in the studio. Here's one of them."

He thrust a massive hand inside his pocket and produced a half-plate group of Troy and her class. It had been taken in the garden.

"There's the model, Fox. Look!"

Fox gravely put on his spectacles and contemplated the photograph.

"Yes, that's the girl," he said. "She looks merry, doesn't she, sir?"

"Yes," said Alleyn slowly. "Very merry."

"That'll be this Garcia, then," Fox continued. He pointed a stubby finger at a figure on the outside of the group. Alleyn took out a lens and held it over the photograph. Up leaped a thin, unshaven face, with an untidy lock of dark hair falling across the forehead. The eyes were set rather close and the brows met above the thin nose. The lips were unexpectedly full. Garcia had scowled straight into the camera. Alleyn gave Fox the lens.

"Yes," said Fox, after a look through it, "we'll have enlargements done at once. Bailey's got the other. He says it will enlarge very nicely."

"He looks a pretty good specimen of a wild man," said Alleyn.

"If Malmsley and Miss Troy are telling the truth," said Fox, who had a way of making sure of his remarks, "he's a murderer. Of course, the motive's not much of an affair as far as we've got."

"Well, I don't know, Brer Fox. It looks as though the girl was badgering him to marry her. It's possible the P.M. may offer the usual explanation for that sort of thing."

"In the family way?" Fox took off his spectacles and stared blandly at his chief. "Yes. That's so. What did you make of that statement of Mr. Malmsley's about Garcia being ill in the garden after he saw the defaced likeness? That seems a queer sort of thing to me. It wasn't as if he'd done the photo."

"The painting, Fox," corrected Alleyn. "One doesn't call inspired works of art photographs, you know. Yes, that was rather a rum touch, wasn't it? You heard Miss Seacliff's theory. Garcia is infatuated with her and was all upheaved by the sight of her defaced loveliness."

"Far-fetched," said Fox.

"I'm inclined to agree with you. But it might be an explanation of his murdering Sonia Gluck when he realised she had done it. He might have thought to himself: 'This looks like a more than usually hellish fury from the woman scorned—what am I in for?' and decided to get rid of her. There's a second possibility which will seem even more farfetched to you, I expect. To me it seems conceivable that Garcia's aesthetic nerves were lacerated by the outrage on a lovely piece of painting. Miss Troy says the portrait of Valmai Seacliff was the best thing she has ever done." Alleyn's voice deepened and was not quite steady. "That means it was a really great work. I think, Fox, that if I had seen that painted head and known it for a superlatively beautiful thing, and then seen it again with that beastly defacement—I believe I might have sicked my immortal soul up into the nearest flower-bed. I also believe that I would have felt remarkably like murder."

"Is that so, sir?" said Fox stolidly. "But you wouldn't have done murder, though, however much you felt like it."

"I'd have felt *damn'* like it," muttered Alleyn. He walked restlessly about the room. "The secret of Garcia's reaction," he said, "lies behind this." He wagged the photograph at Fox. "Behind that very odd-looking head. I wish we knew more about Garcia. We'll have to go hunting for his history, Brer Fox. Records of violence and so on. I wonder if there are any. Suppose he turns up quite innocently to do his 'Comedy and Tragedy' in his London warehouse?"

"That'll look as if either Malmsley or Miss Troy was a liar, sir, won't it? I must say I wouldn't put Mr. Malmsley down as a very dependable sort of gentleman. A bit cheeky in an arty sort of fashion."

Alleyn smiled.

"Fox, what a neat description of him! Admirable! No, unless Malmsley is lying, the knife was hammered through and the drape stretched out after they had all gone on Friday. And if Miss Troy found it stretched out on Saturday afternoon, then the thing was done before then."

"If," said Fox. And after a moment's silence Alleyn replied: "'If'—of course."

"You might say Miss Troy had the strongest motive, sir, as far as the portrait is concerned."

There was a longer pause.

"Do you think it at all likely that she is a murderess?" said Alleyn from the fireplace. "A very deliberate murderess, Fox. The outrage to the portrait was committed a week before the murder."

"I must say I don't think so, sir. Very unlikely indeed, I'd say. This Garcia seems the likeliest proposition on the face of it. What did you make of Miss Phillida Lee's statement, now? The conversation she overheard. Looks as though Garcia and the deceased were making an assignation for Friday night, doesn't it? Suppose she came back to the studio on Friday night in order that they should resume intimacy?"

"Yes, I know."

"He seems to have actually threatened her, if the young lady can be depended upon."

"Miss Seacliff didn't contradict the account, and you must remember that extraordinary little party, Phillida Lee,

81

confided the fruits of her nosy-parkering to Miss Seacliff long before the tragedy. I think we may take it that Garcia and Sonia Gluck had a pretty good dust-up on the lines indicated by the gushing Lee. You took notes in the dining-room, of course. Turn up her report of the quarrel, will you?"

Fox produced a very smug-looking note-book, put on his spectacles, and turned up a page.

"'Garcia——'" he read slowly from his shorthand notes. "'All right. On Friday night then.' Sonia Gluck: 'Yes, if it's possible.' Then later Gluck said: 'I won't stand for any funny business with her, you know.' Garcia said: 'Who?' and Gluck answered: 'The Seacliff bitch, of course.' Sonia Gluck said Garcia ought to marry her. He did not reply. She threatened to go to Miss Troy with the whole story if he let her down. He said: 'If you don't shut up and leave me to get on with my work, I'll bloody well stop your mouth for keeps.' That's the conversation, sir."

"Yes. We'll have to get hold of something about Friday night. Damn it all, the studio is built into the wall, and the window opens on the lane. Surely to Heaven someone must have passed by that evening and heard voices if Garcia had the girl in the place with him."

"And how did he get his stuff away on Friday night or Saturday morning? They've tried all the carriers for miles around."

"I know, Brer Fox, I know. Well, on we go. We've got to get all these people's time-tables from Friday noon till Sunday evening. What about Bailey? I'd better see him first, I suppose."

Bailey came in with his usual air of mulish displeasure and reported that they had finished in the studio. They had gone over everything for prints, had photographed the scratched window-sill, measured and photographed the car's prints and footprints in the lane, and taken casts of them. They had found the key of the studio hanging on a nail outside the door. It was smothered in prints. Under the pillow was an empty whisky bottle. On the window-sill one set of prints occurred many times, and seemed to be superimposed on most of the others. He had found traces of clay with these prints, and with those on the bottle.

"Those will be Garcia's" said Alleyn. "He worked in the window."

In the junk-room Bailey had found a mass of jars, brushes,

bottles of turpentine and oil, costumes, lengths of materials, a spear, an old cutlass, and several shallow dishes that smelt of nitric acid. There was also what Bailey described as "as sort of mangle affair with a whale of a heavy chunk of metal and a couple of rollers."

"An etching press," said Alleyn.

"There's a couple of stains on the floor of the junk-room," continued Bailey. "Look like nitric-acid-stains. They're new. I can't find any nitric acid anywhere, though. I've looked in all the bottles and jars."

"Um!" said Alleyn, and made a note of it.

"There's one other thing," said Bailey. He opened a bag he had brought in with him, and out of it he took a small box which he handed to Alleyn.

"Hullo," said Alleyn. "This is the *bon-bouche*, is it?"

He opened the little box and held it under the lamp. Inside was a flattened greenish-grey pellet.

"Clay," said Alleyn. "Where was it?"

"In the folds of that silk stuff that was rigged on the platform," said Bailey, staring morosely at his boots.

"I see," said Alleyn softly. "Look here, Fox."

Fox joined him. They could both see quite clearly that the flattened surface of the pellet was delicately scrolled by minute holes and swirling lines.

"A nice print," said Fox, "only half there, but very sharp what there is."

"If the prints on the sill are Garcia's," said Bailey, "that's Garcia's, too."

There was a silence.

"Well," said Alleyn at last, "that's what you call a fat little treasure-trove, Bailey."

"I reckon it must have dropped off his overall when he was stretching that stuff above the point of the knife, sir. That's what I reckon."

"Yes. It's possible."

"He must have used gloves for the job. There are one or two smudges about the show that look like glove-marks, and I think one of them's got a trace of the clay. We've photographed the whole outfit."

"You've done rather well, Bailey."

"Anything more, sir?"

"Yes, I'm afraid there is. I want you to find the deceased's room and go over it. I don't think we should let that wait any longer. One of the maids will show you where it is. Come and get me if anything startling crops up."

"Very good, Mr. Alleyn."

"And when that's done, you can push off if you want to. You've left a man on guard, I suppose?"

"Yes, sir. One of these local chaps. Getting a great kick out of it."

"Guileless fellow. Away you go, Bailey. I'll see you later on."

"O.K., sir."

"Nitric acid?" ruminated Fox, when Bailey had gone.

"I think it's the acid they used for etching. I must ask Miss Troy about it."

"Looks as if all we've got to do is to find Garcia, don't it, sir?"

"It do, Fox. But for the love of Mike don't let's be too sure of ourselves."

"That bit of clay, you know, sir—how could it have got there by rights? He'd no business up on the model's throne now, had he?"

"No."

"And according to Malmsley's story, the drape must have been fixed when the rest of them had gone up to London."

"Yes. We'll have to trace 'em in London just the same. Have to get on to these others now. Go and take a dip in the dining-room, Fox, and see what the fairies will send us in the way of a witness."

Fox went off sedately and returned with Katti Bostock. She came in looking very four-square and sensible. Her short and stocky person was clad in corduroy trousers, a red shirt and a brown jacket. Her straight black hair hung round her ears in a Cromwellian cut with a determined bang across her wide forehead. She was made up in a rather slapdash sort of manner. Her face was principally remarkable for its exceedingly heavy eyebrows.

Alleyn pushed forward a chair and she slumped herself down on it. Fox went quietly to the desk and prepeared to make a shorthand report. Alleyn sat opposite Katti.

"I'm sorry to bother you again, Miss Bostock," he said. "We've got a good deal of tidying up to do, as you may imagine. First of all, is nitric acid used in the studio for anything?"

"Etching," said Katti. "Why?"

"We've found stains in the junk-room that looked like it. Where is it kept?"

"In a bottle on the top shelf. It's marked with a red cross."

"We couldn't find it."

"It was filled up on Friday, and put on the top shelf. Must be there."

"I see. Right. Now I just want to check everybody's movements from lunch-time on Friday. In your case it would be a simple matter. I believe you spent most of your time in London with Miss Troy?" He opened his note-book and put it on the arms of his chair.

"Yes," he said. "I see you both went to your club, changed and dined with Sir Arthur and Lady Jaynes at Eaton Square. From there you went to the private view of the Phoenix Group Show, and supped at the Hungaria. That right?"

"Yes. Quite correct."

"You stayed at the club. What time did you get back from the Hungaria on Friday night?"

"Saturday morning," corrected Katti. "I left with the Jayneses about twelve-thirty. They drove me to the club. Troy stayed on with John Bellasca and was swept out with the dust whenever they closed."

"You met again at breakfast?"

"Yes. We separated during the morning and met again at the show. I lunched with some people I ran into there— Graham Barnes and his wife—he's the water-colour bloke. Then Troy and I met at the club and came home. She lunched with John Bellasca."

"Yes. That's all very straightforward. I'll have to ask Sir Arthur Jaynes or someone to confirm it. The usual game, you know."

"That's all right," said Katti. "You want to find out whether either of us had time to sneak back here and set a death-trap for that little fool Sonia, don't you?"

"That's the sort of idea," agreed Alleyn with a smile. "I know Sir Arthur slightly. Would you like me to say you've lost a pearl necklace and want to trace it, or——"

"Good Lord, no. Tell him the facts of the business. Do I look like pearls? And John will fix up Troy's alibi for her. He'll probably come down at ninety miles an hour to say he did it himself if you're not careful." Katti chuckled and lit a cigarette.

"I see." said Alleyn. And into his thoughts came the picture of Troy as she had sat before the fire with her cropped head between her long hands. There had been no ring on those hands.

"When you got back to the club after you left the Hungaria, did anyone see you?"

"The night porter let me in. I don't remember anyone else."

"Was your room near Miss Troy's?"

"Next door."

"Did you hear her return?"

"No. She says she tapped on the door, but I must have been asleep. The maid came in at seven with my tea, but I'd have had time to go out, get Troy's car and drive down here and back, between twelve-thirty and seven, you know."

"True," said Alleyn. "Did you?"

"No."

"Well—we'll have to do our best with night porters, garage attendants, and petrol consumption."

"Wish you luck," said Katti.

"Thank you, Miss Bostock. You got back here for lunch, I understand. How did you spend the afternoon?"

"Dishing up bilge for *The Palette*. I was in here."

"Did you at any time go to the studio?"

"No."

"Was Miss Troy with you on Saturday afternoon?"

"She was in and out. Let's see. She spent a good time turning out that desk over there and burning old papers. Then she tidied her sketching-kit. We had tea in here. After tea we went out to look at a place across the fields where Troy thought of doing a sketch. We dined out with some people at Bossicote—the Haworths—and got home about eleven."

"Thank you. Sunday?"

"I was at my article for *The Pallette* all day. Troy painted in the morning and came in here in the afternoon. The others were all back for dinner."

"Did you hear the model say anything about her own movements during the week-end?"

"No. Don't think so. I fancy she said she was going to London."

"You engaged her for this term before Miss Troy returned, didn't you?"

"Yes."

"How did you get hold of her?"

"Through Graham Barnes. He gave me her address."

"Have you got it?"

"Oh Lord, where was it? Somewhere in Battersea, I think. Battersea Bridge Gardens. That's it. I've got it written down somewhere. I'll try and find it for you."

"I wish you would. It would save us one item in a loathsome itinerary of dull jobs. Now, about this business with the model and your picture. The trapeze-artiste subject, I mean. Did she pose for you again after the day when there was the trouble described by Miss Phillida Lee?"

Again that dull crimson stained the broad face. Katti's thick eyebrows came together and her lips protruded in a sort of angry pout.

"That miserable little worm Lee! I told Troy she was a fool to take her, fees or no fees. The girl's bogus. She went to the Slade and was no doubt made to feel entirely extraneous. She tries to talk 'Slade' when she remembers, but the original nice-girl gush oozes out all over the place. She sweats suburbia from every pore. She deliberately sneaked in and listened to what I had to say."

"To the model?"

"Yes. Little drip!"

"It was true, then, that you did have a difference with Sonia?"

"If I did, that doesn't mean I killed her."

"Of course it doesn't. But I should be glad of an answer, Miss Bostock."

"She was playing up, and I ticked her off. She knew I wanted to finish the thing for the Group Show, and she deliberately set out to make work impossible. I scraped the head down four times, and now the canvas is unworkable—the tooth has gone completely. Troy is always too easy with the models. She spoils them. I gave the little brute hell because she needed it."

"And did she pose again for you?"

"No. I've told you the thing was dead."

"How did she misbehave? Just fidgeting?"

Katti leant forward, her square hands on her knees. Alleyn noticed that she was shaking a little, like an angry terrier.

"I'd got the head laid in broadly—I wanted to draw it together with a dry brush and then complete it. I wanted to keep it very simple and round, the drawing of the mouth was giving me trouble. I told her not to move—she had a damnable trick of biting her lip. Every time I looked at her she gave a sort of sneering smirk. As if she knew it wasn't going well. I mixed a touch of cadmium red for the underlip. Just as

I was going to lay it down she grimaced. I cursed her. She didn't say anything. I pulled myself together to put the brush on the canvas and looked at her. She stuck her foul little tongue out."

"And that tore it to shreds, I imagine?"

"It did. I said everything I'd been trying not to say for the past fortnight. I let go."

"Not surprising. It must have been unspeakably maddening. Why, do you suppose, was she so set on making things impossible?"

"She deliberately baited me," said Katti, under her breath.

"But why?"

"Why? Because I'd treated her as if she was a model. Because I expected to get some return for the excessive wages Troy was giving her. I engaged her, and I managed things till Troy came back. Sonia resented that. Always hinting that I wasn't her boss and so on."

"That was all?"

"Yes."

"I see. You say her wages were excessively generous. What was she paid?"

"Four pounds a week and her keep. She'd spun Troy some tale about doctor's bills, and Troy, as usual, believed the sad story and stumped up. She's anybody's mark for sponging. It's so damned immoral to let people get away with that sort of thing. It's no good talking to Troy. Street-beggars see her coming a mile away. She's got two dead-heads here now."

"Really? Which two?"

"Garcia, of course. She's been shelling out money to Garcia for ages. And now there's this Austrialian wildman Hatchett. She says she makes the others pay through the nose, but Lord knows if she ever gets the money. She's hopeless," said Katti, with an air of exasperated affection.

"Would you call this a good photograph of Mr. Garcia?" asked Alleyn suddenly. He held out the group. Katti took it and glowered at it.

"Yes, it's very like him," she said. "That thing was taken last year during the summer classes. Yes—that's Garcia all right."

"He was here as Miss Troy's guest then, I suppose?"

"Oh Lord, yes. Garcia never pays for anything. He's got no sort of decency where money is concerned. No conscience at all."

"No aesthetic conscience?"

"Um!" said Katti. "I wouldn't say that. No—his work's the

only thing he is honest about, and he's passionately sincere there."

"I wish you'd give me a clear idea of him, Miss Bostock. Will you?"

"Not much of a hand at that sort of thing," growled Katti, "but I'll have a shot. He's a dark, dirty, weird-looking fellow. Very paintable head. Plenty of bone. You think he murdered the model, don't you?"

"I don't know who murdered the model."

"Well, I think he did. It's just the sort of thing he would do. He's absolutely ruthless and as cold-blooded as a flat-fish. He asked Malmsley if he ever felt like murdering his mistress, didn't he?"

"So Mr. Malmsley told us."

"I'll bet it's true. If Sonia interfered with his work and put him off his stride, and he couldn't get rid of her any other way, he'd get rid of her that way. She may have refused to give him any more money."

"Did she give him money?"

"I think so. Ormerin says she was keeping him last year. He wouldn't have the slightest qualms about taking it. Garcia just looks upon money as something you've got to have to keep you going. How you get it is of no importance. He could have got a well-paid job with a monumental firm. Troy got on to it for him. When he saw the tombstones with angels and open Bibles he said something indecent and walked out. He was practically starving that time," said Katti, half to herself, and with a sort of reluctant admiration, "but he wouldn't haul his flag down."

"You think the model was really attached to him?"

Katti took another cigarette and Alleyn lit it for her.

"I don't know," she said. "I'm not up in the tender passion. I've got an idea that she'd switched over to Basil Pilgrim, but whether it was to try and make Garcia jealous or because she'd fallen for Pilgrim is another matter. She was obviously livid with Seacliff. But then Garcia had begun to hang round Seacliff."

"Dear me," said Alleyn, "what a labyrinth of untidy emotions."

"You may say so," agreed Katti. She hitched herself out of her chair. "Have you finished with me, Mr. Alleyn?"

"Yes, do you know, I think I have. We shall have a statement in longhand for you to look at and sign, if you will, later on."

She glared at Fox. "Is that what he's been up to?"

"Yes."

"Pah!"

"It's only to establish your movements. Of course, if you don't want to sign it——"

"Who said I didn't? Let me wait till I see it."

"That's the idea, miss," said Fox, looking benignly at her over the top of his spectacles.

"Will you show Miss Bostock out, please, Fox?"

"Thank you, I know my way about this house," said Katti with a prickly laugh. She stumped off to the door. Fox closed it gently behind her.

"Rather a tricky sort of lady, that," he said.

"She is a bit. Never mind. She gave us some sidelights on Garcia."

"She did that all right."

There was a rap on the door and one of the local men looked in.

"Excuse me, sir, but there's a gentlemen out here says he wants to see you very particular."

"What's his name?"

"He just said you'd be very glad indeed to see him, sir. He never gave a name."

"Is he a journalist?" asked Alleyn sharply. "If he is, I shall be very glad indeed to kick him out. We're too busy for the Press just now."

"Well, sir, he didn't say he was a reporter. He said—er—er—er——"

"What?"

"His words was, sir, that you'd scream the place down with loud cries of gladness when you clapped eyes on him."

"That's no way to ask to see the chief," said Fox. "You ought to know that."

"Go and ask him to give his name," said Alleyn.

The policeman retired.

Fox eyed Alleyn excitedly.

"By gum, sir, you don't think it may be this Garcia? By all accounts he's eccentric enough to send in a message like that."

"No," said Alleyn, as the door opened. "I rather fancy I recognize the style. I rather fancy, Fox, that an old and persistent friend of ours has got in first on the news."

"Unerring as ever, Mr. Alleyn," said a voice from the hall, and Nigel Bathgate walked into the room.

CHAPTER IX

Phillida Lee and Wait Hatchett

"Where the devil did you spring from?" asked Alleyn.
Nigel advanced with a shameless grin.

> "'Where did I come from, 'Specky dear?
> The blue sky opened and I am here!'"

"Hullo, Fox!"

"Good evening, Mr. Bathgate," said Fox.

"I suppose you've talked to my mamma on the telephone,"
said Alleyn as they shook hands.

"There now," returned Nigel, "aren't you wonderful,
Inspector? Yes, Lady Alleyn rang me up to say you'd been
sooled on to the trail before your time, and she thought the
odds were you'd forget to let us know you couldn't come and
stay with us."

"So you instantly motored twenty miles in not much more
than as many minutes in order to tell me how sorry you were?"

"That's it," said Nigel cheerfully. "You read me like a book.
Angela sends her fondest love. She'd have come too only she's
not feeling quite up to long drives just now."

He sat down in one of the largest chairs.

"Don't let me interrupt," he said. "You can give me the
story later on. I've got enough to go on with from the local
cop. I'll ring up the office presently and give them the
headlines. Your mother—divine woman—has asked me to
stay."

"Has my mother gone out of her mind?" asked Alleyn of
nobody in particular.

"Come, come, Inspector," reasoned Nigel, with a trace of
nervousness in his eye, "you know you're delighted to have
me."

"There's not the smallest excuse for your bluffing your way

in, you know. I've a damn' good mind to have you chucked out."

"Don't do that. I'll take everything down in shorthand and nobody will see me if I turn the chair round. Fox will then be able to fix the stammering witnesses with a basilisk glare. All will go like clock-work. All right?"

"All right. It's quite irregular, but you occasionally have your uses. Go into the corner there."

Nigel hurried into a shadowy corner, turned a high armchair with its back to the room and dived into it.

"'I am invisible,'" he said. "'And I shall overhear their conference,' The Bard."

"I'll deal with you later," said Alleyn grimly. "Tell them to send another of these people along, Fox."

When Fox had gone Nigel asked hoarsely from the armchair if Alleyn had enjoyed himself in New Zealand.

"Yes," said Alleyn.

"Funny you getting a case there," ventured Nigel. "Rather a busman's holiday, wasn't it?"

"I enjoyed it. Nobody interfered and the reporters were very well-behaved."

"Oh," said Nigel.

There was a short silence broken by Nigel.

"Did you have a slap-and-tickle with the American lady on the boat deck?"

"I did not."

"Oh! Funny coincidence about Agatha Troy. I mean she was in the same ship, wasn't she? Lady Alleyn tells me the portrait is quite miraculously like you."

"Don't prattle," said Alleyn. "Have you turned into a gossip hound?"

"No. I say!"

"What!"

"Angela's started a baby."

"So I gathered, and so no doubt Fox also gathered, from your opening remarks."

"I'm so thrilled I could yell it in the teeth of the whole police force."

Alleyn smiled to himself.

"Is she all right?" he asked.

"She's not sick in the mornings any more. We want you to be a godfather. Will you, Alleyn?"

"I should be charmed."

"Alleyn!"

"What?"

"You might tell me a bit about this case. Somebody's murdered the model, haven't they?"

"Quite possibly."

"How?"

"Stuck a knife through the throne so that when she took the pose——"

"She sat on it?"

"Don't be an ass. She lay on it and was stabbed to the heart, poor little fool!"

"Who's the prime suspect?"

"A bloke called Garcia, who has been her lover, was heard to threaten her, has possibly got tired of her, and has probably been living on her money."

"Is he here?"

"No. He's gone on a walking tour to Lord knows where, and is expected to turn up at an unknown warehouse in London in the vaguely near future, to execute a marble statue of 'Comedy and Tragedy' for a talkie house."

"D'you think he's bolted?"

"I don't know. He seems to be one of those incredible and unpleasant people with strict aesthetic standards, and no moral ones. He appears to be a genius. Now shut up. Here comes another of his fellow-students."

Fox came in with Phillida Lee.

Alleyn, who had only met her across the dining-room table was rather surprised to see how small she was. She wore a dull red dress covered in a hand-painted design. It was, he realised, deliberately unfashionable and very deliberately interesting. Miss Lee's hair was parted down the centre and dragged back from her forehead with such passionate determination that the corners of her eyes had attempted to follow it. Her face, if left to itself, would have been round and eager, but the austerities of the Slade school had superimposed upon it a careful expression of detachment. When she spoke one heard a faint undercurrent of the Midlands. Alleyn asked her to sit down. She perched on the edge of a chair and stared fixedly at him.

"Well, Miss Lee," Alleyn began in his best official manner, "we shan't keep you very long. I just want to have an idea of your movements during the week-end."

"How ghastly!" said Miss Lee.

"But why?"

"I don't know. It's all so terrible. I feel I'll never be quite the same again. The *shock*. Of course, I ought to try and sublimate it, I suppose, but it's so difficult."

"I shouldn't try to do anything but be common-sensical if I were you," said Alleyn.

"But I thought they used psycho methods in the police!"

"At all events we don't need to apply them to the matter in hand. You left Tatler's End House on Friday afternoon by the three o'clock bus?"

"Yes."

"With Mr. Ormerin and Mr. Watt Hatchett?"

"Yes," agreed Miss Lee, looking self-conscious and maidenly.

"What did you do when you got to London?"

"We all had tea at The Flat Hat in Vincent Square."

"And then?"

"Ormerin suggested we should go to an exhibition of poster-work at the Westminster. We did go, and met some people we knew."

"Their names, please, Miss Lee."

She gave him the names of half a dozen people and the addresses of two.

"When did you leave the Westminster Art School?"

"I don't know. About six, I should think. Ormerin had a date somewhere. Hatchett and I had dinner together at a Lyons. He took me. Then we went to the show at the Vortex Theatre."

"That's in Maida Vale, isn't it?"

"Yes. I'm a subscriber and I had tickets. They were doing a play by Michael Sasha. It's called *Angle of Incidence*. It's *frightfully* thrilling and absolutely new. All about three county council labourers in a sewer. Of course," added Miss Lee, adopting a more mature manner, "the Vortex is purely experimental."

"So it would seem. Did you speak to anyone while you were there?"

"Oh yes. We talked to Sasha himself, and to Lionel Shand who did the decor. I know both of them."

"Can you give me their addresses?"

Miss Lee was vague on this point, but said that care of the Vortex would always find them. Patiently led by Alleyn she gave a full account of her week-end. She had stayed with an aunt in the Fulham Road, and had spent most of her time in this aunt's company. She had also seen a great deal of Watt Hatchett, it seemed, and had gone to a picture with him on Saturday night.

"Only I *do* hope you won't have to ask auntie anything, Inspector Alleyn, because you see she pays my fees with Miss Troy, and if she thought the *police* were after me she'd very likely turn sour, and then I wouldn't be able to go on painting. And that," added Miss Lee with every appearance of sincerity, "would be the most frightful tragedy."

"It shall be averted if possible," said Alleyn gravely, and got the name and address of the aunt.

"Now then, Miss Lee, about those two conversations, you overheard——"

"I don't want to be called as a witness," began Miss Lee in a hurry.

"Possibly not. On the other hand you must realise that in a serious case—and this is a very serious case—personal objections of this sort cannot be allowed to stand in the way of police investigation."

"But I didn't mean you to think that because Bostock flew into a blind rage with Sonia she was capable of *murdering* her."

"Nor do I think so. It appears that half the class flew into rages at different times, and for much the same reason."

"I didn't! I never had a row with her. Ask the others. I got on all right with her. I was sorry for her."

"Why?"

"Because Garcia was so beastly to her. Oh, I do think he was *foul*! If you'd *heard* him that time!"

"I wish very much that I had."

"When he said he'd shut her mouth for keeps—I mean it's the sort of thing you might think he'd say without meaning it, but he sounded as if he did mean it. He spoke so softly in a kind of drawl. I thought he was going to do it *then*. I was *terrified*. Truly! That's why I banged the door and walked in."

"About the scrap of conversation you overheard—did you get the impression that they planned to meet on Friday night?"

"It sounded like that. Sonia said: 'If it's possible.' I think that's what she meant. I think she meant to come back and bed down with Garcia for the night while no one was here."

"To *what*, Miss Lee?"

"Well—you know—to spend the night with him."

"What did they do when you appeared?"

"Garcia just stared at me. He's got a beastly sort of way of looking at you. As if you were an animal. I was awfully scared he'd guessed I'd overheard them, but I saw in a minute that he hadn't. I said: 'Hullo, you two, what are you up to? Having a woo or something?' I don't know how I managed it but I did. And he said: 'No, just a little chat.' He turned away and began working at his thing. Sonia just walked out. She looked *ghastly*, Mr. Alleyn, honestly. She always made up pretty heavily except when we were painting the head, but even under her make-up I could see she was absolutely *bleached*. Oh, Mr. Alleyn, I do believe he did it, I do, *actually*."

"You tell me you were on quite good terms with the model. Did she ever say anything that had any bearing on her relationship with Mr. Garcia?"

Phillida Lee settled herself more comfortably in her chair. She was beginning to enjoy herself.

"Well, of course, ever since this morning, I've been thinking of everything I can remember. I didn't talk much to her until I'd been here for a bit. As a matter of fact the others were so frightfully superior that I didn't get a chance to talk to *anybody* at first."

Her round face turned pink, and suddenly Alleyn felt a little sorry for her.

"It's always a bit difficult, settling down among new people," he said.

"Yes, I dare say it is, but if the new people just do their best to make you feel they don't want you, it's worse than that. That was why I left the Slade, really, Mr. Alleyn. The instructors just used to come round once in a blue moon and look at one's things and sigh. And the students never even seemed to see one, and if they did they looked as if one smelt. And at first this place was just as bad, though of course Miss Troy's *marvellous*. Malmsley was at the Slade, and he's *typical*. Seacliff's worse. Anyway, Seacliff never *sees* another female, much less speaks to her. And all the men just beetle round Seacliff and never give anyone else a *thought*. It was a *bit* better after she said she was engaged to Pilgrim. Sonia felt like I did about Seacliff, and we talked about her a bit—and—well, we sort of sympathised about her." The thin voice with its faint echo of the Midlands went on and on.

Alleyn, listening, could see the two of them, Phillida Lee,

sore and lonely, God knew how angry and miserable, taking comfort in mutual abuse of Valmai Seacliff.

"So you made friends?" he asked.

"Sort of. Yes, we did. I'm not one to look down my nose at a girl because she's a model. I'm a communist, anyway. Sonia was furious about Seacliff. She called her awful names—all beginning with B, you know. She said somebody ought to tell Pilgrim what Seacliff was like. She—she—said——"

Miss Lee stopped abruptly.

"Yes?"

"I don't know whether I ought to—I mean—I like Pilgrim awfully and—well, I *mean*——"

"Is it something that the model said about Miss Seacliff?" said Alleyn.

"About *her!* Ooo no! I wouldn't mind what anybody said about *her.* But I don't believe it was true about Pilgrim. I don't think he was *ever* attracted to Sonia. I think she just made it up."

"Made what up, Miss Lee? Did she suggest there had been anything like a romance between herself and Mr. Pilgrim?"

"Well, if you can call it romance. I mean she said—I mean, it was only *once* ages ago, after a party, and I mean I think men and women ought to be free to follow their sex-impulses anyway, and not repress them. But I mean I don't think Pilgrim *ever* did because he doesn't seem as if he would somehow, but anyway, I don't see why not, because as Garcia once said, if you're hungry——" Miss Lee, scarlet with determination, shut her eyes and added: "you eat."

"Quite so," said Alleyn, "but you needn't guzzle, of course."

"Oh well—no, I suppose you needn't. But I mean I should think Pilgrim never *did.*"

"The model suggested there had been a definite intimacy between herself and Pilgrim?"

"Yes. She said she could tell Seacliff a thing or two about him, and if he didn't look out she would."

"I see."

"But I don't think there ever was. Truly. It was because she was so furious with Pilgrim for not taking any notice of her."

"You returned in the bus yesterday evening with the model, didn't you?"

"Yes. Watt—I mean Hatchett and me and Ormerin and Malmsley."

"Did you notice anything out of the way about her?"

"No. She was doing a bit of a woo with Ormerin to begin with, but I think she was asleep for the last part of the trip."

"Did she mention what she had done in London?"

"I think she said she'd gone to stay with a friend or something."

"No idea where or with whom?"

"No, Mr. Alleyn."

"Nothing about Mr. Garcia?"

"No."

"Did she ever speak much of Garcia?"

"Not much. But she seemed as if—as if in a sort of way she was *sure* of Garcia. And yet he was tired of her. She'd lost her body-urge for him, if you ask me. But she seemed *sure* of him and yet furious with him. Of course, she wasn't very well."

"Wasn't she?"

"No. I'm sure that was why she did that *terrible* thing to Troy's portrait of Seacliff. She was ill. Only she asked me not to say anything about it, because she said it didn't do a model any good for her to get a reputation of not being able to stand up to the work. I wouldn't have known except that I found her one morning looking absolutely *green*, and I asked her if anything was the matter. She said the pose made her feel sick—it was the twist that did it, she said. She was *honestly* sick, and she felt sort of giddy."

Alleyn looked at Miss Lee's inquisitive, rather pretty, rather commonplace face and realised that her sophistication was more synthetic than even he had supposed. "Bless my soul," he thought, "the creature's a complete baby—an infant that has been taught half a dozen indecorous phrases by older children."

"Well, Miss Lee," he said, "I think that's all we need worry about for the moment. I've got your aunt's address——"

"Yes, but you *will* remember, won't you? I *mean*——"

"I shall be the very soul of tact. I shall say we are looking for a missing heiress believed to be suffering from loss of memory, and last heard of near Bossicote, and she will think me very stupid, and I shall learn that you spent the entire week-end in her company."

"Yes. And Watt—Hatchett, I mean."

"He was there too, was he?"

Again Miss Lee looked self-conscious and maidenly.

"Well, I mean, not *all* the time. I mean he didn't *stay* with us, but he came to lunch and tea—and dinner on Saturday and lunch on Sunday. Of course he *is* rough, and he does speak badly, but I told auntie he can't help that because everybody's like that in Australia. Some of the others were pretty stinking to him too, you know. They made him feel dreadfully out of it. I was sorry for him, and I thought they were such snobs. And anyway, I think his work is frightfully exciting."

"Where did he stay?"

"At a private hotel near us, in the Fulham Road. We went to the flicks on Saturday night. Oh, I told you that, didn't I?"

"Yes, thank you. When you go back to the dining-room, will you ask Mr. Hatchett to come and see me in ten minutes' time?"

"Yes, I will."

She got up and gazed at Alleyn. He saw a sort of corpse-side expression come into her face.

"Oh, Mr. Alleyn," she said, "Isn't it all *awful?*"

"Quite frightful," responded Alleyn cheerfully. "Good evening, Miss Lee."

She walked away with an air of bereavement, and shut the door softly behind her.

"Oy!" said Nigel from the arm-chair.

"Hullo!"

"I'm moving over to the fire till the next one comes along. It's cold in this corner."

"All right."

Fox, who had remained silently at the writing-desk throughout the interview with Miss Lee, joined Alleyn and Nigel at the fire.

"That was a quaint little piece of Staffordshire," said Nigel.

"Little simpleton! All that pseudo-modern nonsense! See here, Bathgate, you're one of the young intelligentsia, aren't you?"

"What do you mean? I'm a pressman."

"That doesn't actually preclude you from the intelligentsia, does it?"

"Of course it doesn't."

"Very well then. Can you tell me how much of this owlishness is based on experience, and how much on handbooks and hearsay?"

"You mean their ideas on sex?"

"I do."

"Have they been shocking you, Inspector?"

"I find their conversation bewildering, I must confess."

"Come off it," said Nigel.

"What do you think, Fox?" asked Alleyn.

"Well, sir, I must say I thought they spoke very free round the dining-room table. All this talk about mistresses and appetites and so forth. Very free. Not much difference between their ways and the sort of folk we used to deal with down in the black divisions if you're to believe what you hear. Only the criminal classes are just promiscuous without being able to make it sound intellectual, if you know what I mean. Though I must say," continued Fox thoughtfully, "I don't fancy this crowd is as free-living as they'd like us to believe. This young lady, now. She seems like a nice little girl from a good home, making out she's something fierce."

"I know," agreed Alleyn. "Little donkey."

"And all the time she was talking about deceased and body-urges and so forth, she never seemed to realise what these sick, giddy turns might mean," concluded Fox.

"Of course the girl was going to have a child," said Nigel complacently.

"It doesn't follow as the night the day," murmured Alleyn. "She may have been liverish or run-down. Nevertheless, it's odd that the little thought never entered Miss Lee's head. You go back to your corner, Bathgate, here's Mr. Watt Hatchett."

Watt Hatchett came in with his hands thrust into his trousers' pockets. Alleyn watched him curiously, thinking what a perfect type he was of the smart Sydney tough about to get on in the world. He was short, with the general appearance of a bad man in a South American movie. His hair resembled a patent-leather cap, his skin was swarthy, he walked with a sort of hard-boiled slouch, and his clothes fitted him rather too sleekly. A cigarette seemed to be perpetually gummed to his under-lip which projected. He had beautiful hands.

"Want me, Inspector?" he inquired. He never opened his lips more than was absolutely necessary, and he scarcely seemed to move his tongue, so that every vowel was strangled at birth, and for preference he spoke entirely through his nose. There was, however, something engaging about him; an aliveness, a raw virility.

"Sit down, Mr. Hatchett," said Alleyn, "I shan't keep you long."

Hatchett slumped into an arm-chair. He moved with the slovenly grace of an underbred bounder, and this in its way was also attractive.

"Good-oh," he said.

"I'm sure you realise yourself the importance of the information we have from you as regards the drape."

"Too right. I reckon it shows that whoever did the dirty stuff with the knife did it after everyone except Garcia and Mr. Highbrow Malmsley had cleared off to London."

"Exactly. You will therefore not think it extraordinary if I ask you to repeat the gist of this information."

Hatchett wanted nothing better. He went over the whole story again. He went down to the studio on Friday afternoon—he remembered now that it was half-past two by the hall clock when he left the house—and noticed the drape lying crumpled on the throne, as Sonia had left it when she got up at noon. It was still undisturbed when he went away to catch the bus.

"And yesterdee evening it was stretched out tight. There you are."

Alleyn said nothing about Troy's discovery of this condition on Saturday afternoon. He asked Hatchett to account for his own movements during the week-end. Hatchett described his Friday evening's entertainment with Phillida Lee and Ormerin.

"We had tea and then we went to a theatre they called the Vortex, and it was just about the lousiest show I've *ever* had to sit through. Gosh! it gave me a pain in the neck, dinkum it did. Three blokes in a sewer magging at each other for two bloody hours, and they called it a play. If that's a play give me the talkies in Aussie. They'll do me. We met the chap that runs the place. One of these die-away queens that likes to kid himself he amounts to something. You won't get me inside a theatre again."

"Have you never seen a flesh-and-blood show before?"

"Naow, and I never will again. The talkies'll do me."

"But I assure you the Vortex is no more like the genuine theatre than, shall we say, Mr. Malmsley's drawings are like Miss Troy's portraits."

"Is that a fact?"

"Certainly. But we're straying a little from the matter in hand. You spent Friday night at the Vortex and returned with Miss Lee to the Fulham Road?"

"Yeah, that's right. I took her home and then I went to my own place close by."

"Anyone see you come in?"

They plodded on. Hatchett could, if necessary, produce

the sort of alibi that might hold together or might not. Alleyn gleaned enough material to enable him to verify the youth's account of himself.

"To return to Garcia," he said at last. "I want you to tell me if you have ever heard Garcia say anything about this warehouse he intends to use as a studio in London."

"I never had much to do with that bloke. I reckon he's queer. If you talk to him, half the time he never seems to listen. I did say once I'd like to have a look when he started in on the marble. I reckon that statue'll be a corker. He's clever all right. D'you know what he said? He said he'd take care nobody knew where it was because he didn't want any of this crowd pushing in when he was working. He did let out that it belonged to a bloke that's gone abroad somewhere. I heard him tell the girl Sonia that much."

"I see. That's no go, then. Now, on your bus trips to and from London, did you sit anywhere near Sonia Gluck?"

"Naow. After the way she mucked up Miss Troy's picture, I didn't want anything to do with her. It's just too bad she's got hers for keeps, but all the same I reckon she was a fair nark, that girl. Always slinging off about Aussie, she was. She'd been out there once with a Vordervill show, and I tipped it was a bum show because she was always shooting off her mouth about the way the Aussies don't know a good thing when they see it. These pommies! She gave me the jitters. Just because I couldn't talk big about my home and how swell my people were, and how we cut a lot of ice in Sydney, she treated me like dirt. I said to her one time, I said: 'I reckon if Miss Troy thought I was good enough to come here, even if my old pot did keep a bottle store on Circular Quay, I reckon if she thought I was O.K. I'm good enough for you.' I went very, very crook at her after she did that to the picture. Miss Troy's been all right to me. She's been swell. Did you know she paid my way in the ship?"

"Did she?"

"Too right she did. She saw me painting in Suva. I worked my way to Suva, yer know, from Aussie, and I got a job there. It was a swell job, too, while it payed. Travelling for Jackson's Confectionary. I bought this suit and some paints with my first cheque, and then I had a row with the boss and walked out on him. I used to paint all the time then. She saw me working and she reckoned I had talent, so she brought me home to England. The girl Sonia seemed to think I was living on charity."

"That was a very unpleasant interpretation to put upon a gracious action."

"Eh? Yeah! Yeah, that's what I told her."

"Since you joined Miss Troy's classes, have you become especially friendly with any one of the other students?"

"Well, the little girl Lee's all right. She treats you as if you were human."

"What about the men?"

"Malmsley makes me tired. He's nothing but a big sissie. The French bloke doesn't seem to know he's born, and Garcia's queer. They don't like me," said Hatchett, with extraordinary aggression, "and I don't like them."

"What about Mr. Pilgrim?"

"Aw, he's different. He's all right. I get on with him good-oh, even if his old pot is one of these lords. Him and me's cobbers."

"Was he on good terms with the model?"

Hatchett looked sulky and uncomfortable.

"I don't know anything about that," he muttered.

"You have never heard either of them mention the other?"

"Naow."

"Nor noticed them speaking to each other?"

"Naow."

"So you can tell us nothing about the model except that you disliked her intensely?"

Hatchett's grey eyes narrowed in an extremely insolent smile.

"That doesn't exactly make me out a murderer though, does it?"

"Not precisely."

"I'd be one big boob to go talking about how I couldn't stick her if I'd had anything to do with it, wouldn't I?"

"Oh, I don't know. You might be sharp enough to suppose that you would convey just that impression."

The olive face turned a little paler.

"Here! You got no call to talk that way to me. What d'you want to pick on me for? I've been straight enough with you. I've given you a square deal right enough, haven't I?"

"I sincerely hope so."

"I reckon this country's crook. You've all got a down on the new chum. It's a blooming nark. Just because I said the girl Sonia made me tired, you got to get leery and make me out a liar. I reckon the wonderful London police don't know they're alive yet. You've as good as called me a murderer."

"My dear Mr. Hatchett, may I suggest that if you go through life looking for insults, you may be comfortably assured of finding them. At no time during our conversation have I called you a murderer."

"I gave you a square deal," repeated Hatchett.

"I'm not absolutely assured of that. I think that a moment ago you deliberately withheld something. I mean, when I asked you if you could tell me anything about the model's relationship with Mr. Pilgrim."

Hatchett was silent. He moved his head slightly from side to side, and ostentatiously inhaled cigarette smoke.

"Very well," said Alleyn. "That will do, I think." But Hatchett did not get up.

"I don't know where you get that idea," he said.

"Don't you? I need keep you no longer, Mr. Hatchett. We shall probably check your alibi, and I shall ask you to sign a written account of our conversation. That is all at the moment."

Hatchett rose, hunched his shoulders and lit a fresh cigarette from the butt of the old one. He was still rather pale.

"I got nothing in for Pilgrim," he said. "I got no call to talk to dicks about my cobbers."

"You prefer to surround them with a dubious atmosphere of uncertainty, and leave us to draw our own conclusions? You are doing Mr. Pilgrim no service by these rather transparent evasions."

"Aw, talk English, can't you!"

"Certainly. Good evening."

"Pilgrim's a straight sort of a bloke. Him do anything like that! It's laughable."

"Look here," said Alleyn wearily. "Are you going to tell me what you know, or are you going away, or am I going to remove you? Upon my word, if we have many more dark allusions to Mr. Pilgrim's purity, I shall feel like clapping both of you in jug."

"By cripey!" cried Hatchett violently. "Aren't I telling you it was nothing at all! And to show you it was nothing at all, I'll bloody well tell you what it was. Now then."

"Good!" said Alleyn. "Speak up!"

"It's only that the girl Sonia was going to have a kid, and Pilgrim's the father. So now what?"

CHAPTER X

Week-end of an Engaged Couple

In the silence that followed Watt Hatchett's announcement Fox was heard to cough discreetly. Alleyn glanced quickly at him, and then contemplated Hatchett. Hatchett glared defiantly round the room rather as if he expected an instant arrest.

"How do you know this, Mr. Hatchett?" asked Alleyn.

"I've seen it in writing."

"Where?"

"It's like this. Me and Basil Pilgrim's got the same kind of paint-smocks, see? When I first come I saw his new one and I thought it was a goody. It's a sort of dark khaki stuff, made like a coat, with corking great big pockets. He told me where he got it, and I sent for one. When I got it, I hung it up with the others in the junk-room. That was last Tuesdee. On Wensdee morning I put it on, and I noticed at the time that his smock wasn't there. He'd taken it up to the house for something, I suppose. Well, when we cleaned up at midday, I put me hand in one of me pockets and I felt a bit of paper. I took it out and had a look at it. Thought it might be the docket from the shop or something, see? When I got it opened up, I see it was a bit of a note scrawled on the back of a bill. It said, as near as I remember: 'Congrats on the engagement, but what if I tell her she's going to have a step-child? I'll be in the studio to-night at ten. Advise you to come.' Something like that it was. I may not have got it just the same as what it was, but that's near enough. It was signed 'S'."

"What did you do with it?"

"Aw, cripey, I didn't know what to do. I didn't feel so good about reading it. Gee, it was a fair cow, me reading it by mistake like that. I just went into the junk-room and I saw he'd put his smock back by then, so I shoved the blooming paper into his pocket. That evening I could see he was feeling pretty crook himself, so I guessed he'd read it."

"I see."

"Look, Mr. Alleyn, I'm sorry I went nasty just now. I'm like that. I go horribly crook, and the next minute I could knock me own block off for what I said. But look, you don't want to think too much about this. Honest! That girl Sonia was easy. Look, she went round asking for it, dinkum she did. Soon as I saw that note I tipped she'd got hold of old Basil some time, and he'd just kind of thought, 'Aw, what the hell' and there you were. Look, he's a decent old sport, dinkum he is. And now he's got a real corking girl like Valmai Seacliff, it'd be a nark if he got in wrong. His old pot's a wowser, too. That makes things worse. Look, Mr. Alleyn, I'd hate him to think I——"

"All right, all right," said Alleyn good-humouredly. "We'll keep your name out of it if we can."

"Good-oh, Mr. Alleyn. And, look, you won't——"

"I won't clap the handcuffs on Mr. Pilgrim just yet."

"Yeah, but——"

"You buzz off. And if you'll take a tip from an effete policeman, just think sometimes, before you label the people you meet! 'No good' or 'standoffish,' or—what is that splendid phrase?—'fair cows.' Have you ever heard of an inferiority complex?"

"Naow."

"Thank the Lord for that. All the same I fancy you suffer from one. Go slow. Think a bit more. Wait for people to like you and they will. And forgive me if you can, for prosing away like a Victorian uncle. Now, off you go."

"Good-oh, Mr. Alleyn."

Hatchett walked to the door. He opened it and then swung round.

"Thanks a lot," he said. "Ta-ta for now."

The door banged, and he was gone. Alleyn leant back in his chair and laughed very heartily.

"Cheeky young fellow, that," said Fox. "Australian. I've come across some of them. Always think you're looking down on them. Funny!"

"He's an appalling specimen," said Nigel from the corner. "Bumptious young larrikin. Even his beastly argot is bogus. Half-American, half-Cockney."

"And pure Australian. The dialect is rapidly becoming Americanised."

"A frightful youth. No wonder they sat on him. He ought to

be told how revolting he is whenever he opens his mouth. Antipodean monster."

"I don't agree with you," said Alleyn. "He's an awkward pup, but he might respond to reason in time. What do you make of this business of the note, Fox?"

"Hard to say," said Fox. "Looks like the beginnings of blackmail."

"Very like, very like."

"From all accounts it wouldn't be very surprising if we found Garcia had set her on to it, would it now?"

"Speculative, but attractive."

"And then murdered her when he'd collared the money," said Nigel.

"You're a fanciful fellow, Bathgate," said Alleyn mildly.

"Well, isn't it possible?"

"Quite possible on what we've got."

"Shall I get Mr. Pilgrim, sir?"

"I think so, Fox. We'll see if he conforms to the Garcia theme or not."

"I'll bet he does," said Nigel. "Is it the Basil Pilgrim who's the eldest son of the Methodist Peer?"

"That's the one. Do you know him?"

"No, but I know of him. I did a story for my paper on his old man. The son's rather a pleasant specimen, I fancy. Cricketer. He was a Blue and looked good enough for an M.C.C. star before he took to this painting."

"And became a little odd?" finished Alleyn with a twinkle.

"I didn't say that, but it was rather a waste. Anyhow I fail to visualise him as a particularly revolting type of murderer. He'll conform to the Garcia theme, you may depend upon it."

"That's because you want things to work out that way."

"Don't you think Garcia's your man?"

"On what we've got I do, certainly, but it's much too early to become wedded to a theory. Back to your corner."

Fox returned with Basil Pilgrim. As Nigel had remarked, Pilgrim was a very pleasant specimen. He was tall with a small head, square shoulders and a narrow waist. His face was rather fine-drawn. He had a curious trick while he talked of turning his head first to one member of his audience and then to another. This habit suggested a nervous restlessness. He had a wide mouth, magnificent teeth and very good manners. Alleyn got him to sit down, gave him a cigarette and began at once to establish his movements after he drove away with

Valmai Seacliff from Tatler's End House on Friday afternoon. Pilgrim said that they motored to some friends of Valmai Seacliff's who lived at Boxover, twelve miles away. They dined with these friends—a Captain and Mrs. Pascoe—spent the evening playing bridge and stayed the night there. The next day they motored to Ankerton Manor, the Oxfordshire seat of Lord Pilgrim, where Basil introduced his fiancée to his father. They spent Saturday night at Ankerton and returned to Tatler's End House on Sunday afternoon.

"At what time did you break up your bridge party on Friday night?" asked Alleyn.

"Fairly early, I think, sir. About elevenish. Valmai had got a snorter of a headache and could hardly see the cards. I gave her some aspirin. She took three tablets, and turned in."

"Did the aspirin do its job?"

"Oh-rather! She said she slept like the dead." He looked from Alleyn to Fox and back again. "She didn't wake till they brought in tea. Her head had quite cleared up."

"Is she subject to these headaches?"

Pilgrim looked surprised.

"Yes, she is rather. At least, she's had one or two lately. I'm a bit worried about them. I want her to see an oculist but she doesn't like the idea of wearing glasses."

"It may not be the eyes."

"Oh, I think it is. Painters often strain their eyes, you know."

"Did you sleep comfortably?"

"Me?" Pilgrim turned to Alleyn with an air of bewilderment. "Oh, I always sleep like a log."

"How far is Ankerton Manor from here, Mr. Pilgrim?"

"Eighty-five miles by my speedometer. I took a note of it."

"So you had a run of seventy-three miles from Boxover on Saturday?"

"That's the idea, sir."

"Right. Now about this unfortunate girl. Can you let any light in on the subject?"

"Afraid I can't. It's a damn' bad show. I feel rotten about it."

"Why?"

"Well, wouldn't anybody? It's a foul thing to happen, isn't it?"

"Oh, yes—perfectly abominable. I meant, had you any personal reason for feeling rotten about it?"

"Not more than any of the others," said Pilgrim after a pause.

"Is that quite true, Mr. Pilgrim?"

"What do you mean?" Again he looked from Alleyn to Fox. He had gone very white.

"I mean this. Had Sonia Gluck no closer link with you than with the rest of the class?"

If Pilgrim had been restless before, he was now very still. He stared straight in front of him, his lips parted, and his brows slightly raised.

"I see I shall have to make a clean breast of it," he said at last.

"I think you would be wise to do so."

"It's got nothing to do with this business," he said. "Unless Garcia knew and was furious about it. My God, I don't know what put you on to this, but I'm not sure it won't be a relief to talk about it. Ever since this morning when she was killed, I've been thinking of it. I'd have told you at once if I'd thought it had any bearing on the case, but I—I didn't want Valmai to know. It happened three months ago. Before I met Valmai. I was at a studio party in Bloomsbury and she—Sonia—was there. Everyone got pretty tight. She asked me to drive her back to her room and then she asked me if I wouldn't come in for a minute. Well—I did. It was the only time. I got a damned unpleasant surprise when I found she was the model here. I didn't say anything to her and she didn't say anything to me. That's all."

"What about the child?" asked Alleyn.

"God! Then she *did* tell somebody?"

"She told you, at all events."

"I don't believe it's true. I don't believe the child was mine. Everybody knows what sort of girl she was. Poor little devil! I don't want to blackguard her after this has happened, but I can see what you're driving at now, and it's a serious business for me. If I'd thought the child was my affair, I'd have looked after Sonia, but everybody knows she's been Garcia's mistress for months. She was poisonously jealous of Valmai, and after our engagement was announced she threatened this as a hit at Valmai."

"How was the matter first broached?"

"She left a note in the pocket of my painting-coat. I don't know how long it had been there. I burnt it. She said she wanted me to meet her somewhere."

"Did you do this?"

"Yes. I met her in the studio one evening. It was pretty ghastly."

"What happened?"

"She said she was going to have a baby. She said I was the father. I said I didn't believe it. I knew she was lying, and I told her I knew. I said I'd tell Valmai the whole story myself and I said I'd go to Garcia and tell him. She seemed frightened. That's all that happened."

"Are you sure of that?"

"Yes. What d'you mean? Of course I'm sure."

"She didn't try blackmail? She didn't say she would go to Miss Seacliff with this story or, if that failed, she didn't threaten to appeal to your father?"

"She said all sorts of things. She was hysterical. I don't remember everything she said. She didn't know what she was talking about."

"Surely you would remember if she threatened to go to your father?"

"I don't think she did say she'd do that. Anyway, if she had it wouldn't have made any difference. He couldn't force me to marry her, I know that sounds pretty low, but, you see, I knew the whole thing was a bluff. It was all so foul and squalid. I was terrified someone would hear her or something. I just walked away."

"Did she carry out any of her threats?"

"No."

"How do you know?"

"Well, I'd have heard pretty soon if she'd said anything to my father."

"Then she *did* threaten to tell your father?"

"God damn you, I tell you I don't remember what she threatened."

"Did you give her any money?"

Pilgrim moved his head restlessly.

"I advise you to answer me, Mr. Pilgrim."

"I needn't answer anything. I can get a lawyer."

"Certainly. Do you wish to do that?"

Pilgrim opened his mouth and shut it again. He frowned to himself as if he thought very deeply, and at last he seemed to come to a decision. He looked from Alleyn to Fox and suddenly he smiled.

"Look here," he said, "I didn't kill that girl. I couldn't have killed her. The Parkers and Valmai will tell you I spent Friday

110

night with them. My father and everyone else at Ankerton knows I was there on Saturday. I hadn't a chance to rig the knife. I suppose there's no reason why I should shy off talking about this business with Sonia except that—well, when there's a crime like this in the air one's apt to get nervous."

"Undoubtedly."

"You know all about my father, I expect. He's been given a good deal of publicity. Some bounder of a journalist wrote a lot of miserable gup in one of the papers the other day. The Methodist Peer and all that. Everyone knows he's a bit fantastic on the subject of morals, and if he ever got to hear of this business there'd be a row of simply devastating magnitude. That's why I didn't want it to leak out. He'd do some tremendous heavy father stuff at me, and have a stroke on top of it as likely as not. That's why I didn't want to say any more about it than I could possibly help. I see now that I've been a fool not to tell you the whole thing."

"Good," said Alleyn.

"As a matter of fact I did give Sonia a cheque for a hundred, and she promised she'd make no more scenes. In the end she practically admitted the child was not mine, but," he smiled ruefully, "as she pointed out, she had a perfectly good story to tell my father or Valmai if she felt inclined to do so."

"Have you made a clean breast of this to Miss Seacliff?"

"No. I—I—couldn't do that. It seems so foul to go to her with a squalid little story when we were just engaged. You see, I happen to feel rather strongly about—well, about some things. I rather disliked myself for what had happened. Valmai's so marvelous." His face lit up with a sudden intensity of emotion. He seemed translated. "She's so far beyond all that kind of thing. She's terribly, terribly attractive—you only had to see how the other men here fell for her—but she remains quite aloof from her own loveliness. Just accepts it as something she can't help and then ignores it. It's amazing that she should care——" He stopped short. "I don't know that we need discuss all this."

"I don't think we need. I shall ask you later on to sign a statement of your own movements from Friday to Sunday."

"Will the Sonia business have to come out, sir?"

"I can promise nothing about that. If it is irrelevant it will not be used. I think it advisable that you should tell Miss Seacliff, but that, of course, is entirely a matter of your own judgment."

"You don't understand."

"Possibly not. There's one other question. Did you return to the studio on Friday before you left for Boxover?"

"No. I packed my suit-case after lunch. Young Hatchett came in and talked to me while I was at it. Then I called Valmai and we set off in the car."

"I see. Thank you. I won't keep you any longer, Mr. Pilgrim."

"Very well, sir. Thank you."

Fox showed Pilgrim out and returned to the fire. He looked dubious. Nigel reappeared and sat on the wide fender.

"Well, Fox," said Alleyn, raising an eyebrow, "what did you think of that?"

"His ideas on the subject of his young lady seem a bit high-flown from what we've seen of her," said Fox.

"What's she like?" asked Nigel.

"She's extremely beautiful," Alleyn said. "Beautiful enough to launch a thousand crimes, perhaps. But I should not have thought the Sonia episode would have caused her to so much as bat an eyelid. She has completely wiped the floor with all the other females, and that, I imagine, is all that matters to Miss Seacliff."

"Of course, the poor fool's besotted on her. You can see that with half an eye," said Nigel. He glanced at his shorthand notes. "What about his alibi?"

"If this place Boxover is only twelve miles away," grunted Fox, "his alibi isn't of much account. Is it, Mr. Alleyn? They went to bed early on Friday night. He could slip out, run over here, rig the knife and get back to Boxover almost within the hour."

"You must remember that Garcia slept in the studio."

"Yes, that's so. But he may not have been there on Friday night. He may have packed up by then and gone off on his tour."

"Pilgrim must have known that, Fox, if he planned to come to the studio."

"Yes. That's so. Mind, I still think Garcia's our man. This Mr. Pilgrim doesn't strike me as the chap for a job of this sort."

"He's a bit too obviously the clean young Englishman, though, isn't he?" said Nigel.

"Hullo," remarked Alleyn, "didn't Pilgrim come up to your high expectations, Bathgate?"

"Well, you were remarkably cold and snorty with him, yourself."

"Because throughout our conversation he so repeatedly shifted ground. That sort of behaviour is always exceedingly tedious. It was only because I was round with him that we got the blackmail story at all."

"He seemed quite an honest-to-God sort of fellow, really," pronounced Nigel. "I think it was that stuff about being ashamed of his affair with the model that put me off him. It sounded spurious. Anyway, it's the sort of thing one doesn't talk about to people one has just met."

"Under rather unusual conditions," Alleyn pointed out.

"Certainly. All the same he talks too much."

"The remark about bounding journalists and miserable gup was perhaps gratuitous."

"I didn't mean that," said Nigel in a hurry.

"I'm inclined to agree with you. Let us see Miss Valmai Seacliff, Brer Fox."

"I wish you wouldn't make me coil up in that chair," complained Nigel when Fox had gone. "It's plaguilly uncomfortable and right in a draught. Can't I just be here, openly? I'd like to have a look at this lovely."

"Very well. I suppose you'll do no harm. The concealment was your own suggestion, if you remember. You may sit at the desk and make an attempt to look like the Yard."

"You don't look much like it yourself in your smart gent's dinner jacket. Tell me, Alleyn, have you fallen in love with Miss Troy?"

"Don't be a fool, Bathgate," said Alleyn, with such unusual warmth that Nigel's eyebrows went up.

"I'm sorry," he said. "Merely a pleasantry. No offence and so on."

"I'm sorry, too. You must forgive me. I'm bothered about this case."

"There, there," said Nigel. "Coom, coom, coom, it's early days yet."

"True enough. But suppose Garcia walks in with a happy smile in answer to our broadcast? That bit of clay in the drape. Acid marks and no acid to make 'em. This legendary warehouse. Clay models of comedy and tragedy melted into the night. Damn, I've got the mumbles."

The door was thrown open, and in came Valmai Seacliff followed by Fox. Miss Seacliff managed to convey by her entrance that she never moved anywhere without a masculine satellite. That Inspector Fox in his double-breasted blue serge was not precisely in the right manner did nothing to unsettle her poise. She was dressed in a silk trousered garment. Her hair was swept off her forehead into a knot on the nape of her neck. Moving her hips voluptuously, she walked rather like a mannequin. When she reached the chair Alleyn had pushed forward, she turned, paused, and then sank into it with the glorious certainty of a well-trained show-girl. She stared languidly at Nigel whose hand had gone automatically to his tie.

"Well, Mr. Alleyn?" said Miss Seacliff.

The three men sat down. Alleyn turned a page of his tiny note-book, appeared to deliberate, and embarked upon the familiar opening.

"Miss Seacliff, my chief concern at the moment is to get a clear account of everybody's movements during the week-end. Mr. Pilgrim has told us of your motor trip with him to Boxover, and then to Ankerton Manor. I should like you to corroborate his statement if you will. Did you return to the studio before you left?"

"No, I was packing. The housemaid helped me and carried my things down to the car."

"You arrived at Captain and Mrs. Pascoe's house in Boxover on Friday afternoon?"

"Yes."

"And spent the afternoon together?"

"Yes. The Pascoes talked about tennis but I didn't feel inclined to play. I rather loathe tennis. So we talked."

Alleyn noticed again her curious little stutter, and the trick she had of letting her voice die and then catching it up on an intake of breath.

"How did you spend the evening?"

"We played bridge for a bit. I had a frightful headache and went to bed early. I felt quite sick with it."

"That was bad luck. Do you often have these headaches?"

"Never until lately. They started about a month ago. It's rather tiresome."

"You should consult an oculist."

"My eyes are perfectly all right. As a matter of fact a rather distinguished oculist once told me that intensely blue eyes like mine usually give no trouble. He said my eyes were the most vivid blue he had ever seen."

"Indeed!" said Alleyn, without looking at them. "How do you explain the headaches, then?"

"I'm perfectly certain the one on Friday night was due to champagne and port. The Pascoes had champagne at dinner to celebrate my engagement, and there was brandy afterwards. I loathe brandy, so Basil made me have a glass of port. I told him it would upset me but he went on and on. The coffee was filthy, too. Bitter and beastly. Sybil Pascoe is one of those plain women whom one expects to be good housekeepers, but I must say she doesn't appear to take the smallest trouble over the coffee. Basil says his was abominable, too."

"When did you give up the bridge?"

"I've no idea, I'm afraid. I simply couldn't go on. Basil got me three aspirin and I went to bed. The others came up soon afterwards, I fancy. I heard Basil go into his room."

"It was next to yours."

"Yes."

"Did you sleep?"

"Like the dead. I didn't wake till they brought my tea at nine o'clock."

"And the headache had cleared up?"

"Yes, quite. I still felt a little unpleasant. It was a sort of carry-over from that damned port, I imagine."

"Were your host and hostess anywhere near you upstairs?"

"Sybil and Ken? Not very. There was Basil and then me, and then I think two spare rooms and a bathroom. Then their room. Why?"

"It sounds rather absurd, I know," said Alleyn, "but you see we've got to find out as closely as possible what everyone did that night."

"Basil didn't come into my room, if that's what you're hinting at," said Miss Seacliff without heat. "It wasn't that sort of party. Anyway, I'm not given to that kind of thing even when I haven't got a headache. I don't believe in it. Sooner or later you lose your glamour. Look at Sonia."

"Quite so. Then as far as you know the household slept without stirring from Friday night to Saturday morning?"

"Yes," said Miss Seacliff, looking at him as if he was slightly demented.

"And on Saturday you went on to Ankerton Manor. When did you start?"

"We had a glass of sherry at about ten, and then pushed off. Basil was in a great state lest we should be late for lunch, and wanted to get away earlier, but I saw no reason why we should go rushing about the countryside before it was necessary. We had plenty of time."

"Why was he so anxious?"

"He kept saying that he was sure Sybil Pascoe wanted to get away. She was going up to London for a week and leaving Ken to look after himself. I pointed out that was no reason why we should bolt off. Then Basil said we mustn't be late at Ankerton. The truth was, the poor lamb wanted me to make a good impression on his extraordinary old father. I told him he needn't worry. Old men always go quite crazy about me. But Basil was absurdly nervous about the meeting and kept fidgeting me to start. We got there early as it was, and by luncheon-time the old person was talking about the family jewels. He's given me some emeralds that I'm going to have reset. They're rather spectacular."

"You left Ankerton yesterday after luncheon, I suppose?"

"Yes. Basil was rather keen to stay on till Monday, but I'd had enough. The old person made me hack round the ancestral acres on a beastly little animal that nearly pulled my arms out. I saw you looking at my hand."

With a slow and beautiful movement she extended her left arm, opened her hand, and held it close to Alleyn's face. It was warmly scented and the palm was rouged. At the base of the little finger were two or three scarlet marks.

"My hands are terribly soft, of course," said Miss Seacliff, advancing it a little closer to his face.

"Yes," said Alleyn. "You are evidently not an experienced horsewoman."

"What makes you say that?"

"Well, you know, these marks have not been made by a rein. I should say, Miss Seacliff, that your pony's mane had been called into service."

She pulled her hand away and turned rather pink.

"I don't pretend to be a horsey woman, thank God! I simply loathe the brutes. I must say I got very bored with the old person. And besides, I didn't want to miss the pose this morning. I'd got a good deal to do to my thing of Sonia. I suppose I'll never get it done now."

Fox coughed and Nigel glanced up at Valmai Seacliff in astonishment.

"I suppose not," agreed Alleyn. "Now, Miss Seacliff, we come to this morning's tragedy. Will you describe to us exactly what happened, please?"

"Have you got a cigarette?"

Alleyn sprang up and offered her his case.

"What are they? Oh, I see. Thank you."

She took one and he lit it for her. She looked into his eyes deliberately but calmly, as if she followed a familiar routine. Alleyn returned her glance gravely and sat down again.

"This morning?" she said. "You mean when Sonia was killed? It was rather ghastly. I felt wretched after it was all over. Ill. I suppose it was shock. I do think it was rather cruel that I should be the one to—to do it—to set the pose. They all knew I always pushed her shoulders down." She caught her breath, and for the first time showed some signs of genuine distress. "I believe Garcia deliberately planned it like that. He loathed the sight of Sonia, and at the same time he wanted to revenge himself on me because I didn't fall for him. It was just like Garcia to do that. He's a spiteful little beast. It was cruel. I—I can't get rid of the remembrance. I'll never be able to get rid of it."

"I'm sorry that I am obliged to ask you to go over it again, but I'm sure you will understand——"

"Oh, yes. And the psycho people say one shouldn't repress things of this sort. I don't want to get nervy and lose my poise. After all, I didn't do it really. I keep telling myself that."

"When did you go down to the studio?"

"Just before class time. Basil and I walked down together. Katti Bostock was there and—let me see—yes, the appalling Hatchett youth, Lee and Ormerin and Malmsley came down afterwards, I think."

"Together?"

"I don't remember. They were not there when I got down."

"I see. Will you go on, Miss Seacliff?"

"Well, we all put up our easels and set our palettes and so on. Sonia came in last and Katti said we'd begin. Sonia went into the junk-room and undressed. She came out in her white kimono and hung about trying to get the men to talk to her. Katti told her to go on to the throne. She got down into the chalkmarks. She always fitted her right thigh into its trace first, with the drape behind her. I don't know if you understand?"

"Yes, I think I do."

And indeed Alleyn suddenly had a very vivid impression of what must have taken place. He saw the model, wrapped in the thin white garment, her warm and vital beauty shining through it. He saw her speak to the men, look at them perhaps with a pathetic attempt to draw their attention to herself.

117

Then the white wrapper would slide to the floor and the nude figure sink gingerly into a half-recumbent posture on the throne.

"She grumbled as usual about the pose and said she was sick of it. I remember now that she asked us if we knew where Garcia had gone on his hiking trip. I suppose he wouldn't tell her. Then she lay down on her side. The drape was still stretched taut behind her. There is generally a sort of key position among the different canvases. When we set the pose we always look at that particular canvas to get it right. My painting was in this position so it was always left to me to push her down into the right position. She could have done it all herself but she always made such a scene. I'd got into the way of taking her shoulders and pressing them over. She wouldn't do it otherwise. So I leant over and gripped them. They felt smooth and alive. She began to make a fuss. She said 'Don't,'and I said 'Don't be such a fool.' Katti said: 'Oh, for Heaven's sake, Sonia!' Something like that. Sonia said: 'Your hands are cold, you're hurting me.' Then she let herself go and I pushed down." Valmai Seacliff raised her hands and pressed them against her face.

"She didn't struggle but I felt her body leap under my hands and then shudder. I can't tell you exactly what it was like. Everything happened at the same moment. I saw her face. She opened her eyes very wide, and wrinkled her forehead as if she was astonished. I think she said 'Don't again, but I'm not sure. I thought—you know how one's thoughts can travel—I thought how silly she looked, and at the same moment I suddenly wondered if she was going to have a baby and the pose really hurt her. I don't know why I thought that. I knew s-something had happened. I didn't know what it was. I just leant over her and looked into her face. I think I said: 'Sonia's ill.' I think Katti or someone said 'Rot.' I still touched her—leant on her. She quivered as if I tickled her and then she was still. Phillida Lee said: 'She's fainted.' Then the others came up. Katti put her arm behind Sonia to raise her. She said: 'I can't move her—she seems stuck.' Then she pulled. There was a queer little n-noise and Sonia came up suddenly. Ormerin cried out loudly: '*Mon Dieu, c'est le poignard.*' At least that's what he told us he said. And the drape stuck to my fingers. It came out of the hole in her back—the blood, I mean. Her back was wet. We moved her a little, and Katti tried to stop the blood with a piece of rag. Troy came. She sent

Basil out to ring up the doctor. She looked at Sonia and said she wasn't dead. Troy put her arms round Sonia. I don't know how long it was before Sonia gave a sort of cough. She opened her eyes very wide. Troy looked up and said: 'She's gone.' Phillida Lee started to cry. Nobody said very much. Basil came back and Troy said n-nobody was to leave the studio. She covered Sonia with a drape. We began to talk about the knife. Lee and Hatchett said G-Garcia had done it. We all thought Garcia had done it. Then the doctor came and when he had seen Sonia he sent for the p-police."

Her voice died away. She had begun her recital calmly enough, but it was strange to see how the memory of the morning grew more vivid and more disquieting as she revived it. The slight hesitation in her speech became more noticeable. When she had finished her hands were trembling.

"I d-didn't know I was so upset," she said. "A doctor once told me my nerves were as sensitive as the strings of a violin."

"It was a horrible experience for all of you," said Alleyn. "Tell me, Miss Seacliff, when did you yourself suspect that Garcia had laid this trap for the model?"

"I thought of Garcia at once. I remembered what Lee had told me about the conversation between Garcia and Sonia. I don't see who else could have done it, and somehow——"

"Yes?"

"Somehow it—it's the sort of thing he might do. There's something very cold-blooded about Garcia. He's quite mad about me, but I simply can't bear him to touch me. Lee says he's got masses of S.A. and he evidently had for Sonia—but I can't see it. I think he's rather repulsive. Women do fall for him, I'm told."

"And the motive?"

"I imagine he was sick of her. She literally hurled herself at him. Always watching him. Men hate women to do that——" She looked directly into Alleyn's eyes. "Don't they, Mr. Alleyn."

"I'm afraid I don't know."

"And of course he was livid when she defaced my portrait. She must have hated me to do that. In a way it was rather interesting, a directly sexual jealousy manifesting itself on the symbol of the hated person."

Alleyn repressed a movement of impatience and said: "No doubt."

"My own idea is that she was going to have a baby and had

119

threatened to sue him for maintenance. I suppose in a way I'm responsible."

She looked grave enough as she made this statement, but Alleyn thought there was more than a hint of complacency in her voice.

"Surely not," he said.

"Oh, yes. In a way. If he hadn't been besotted on me, I dare say he might not have done it."

"I thought," said Alleyn, "that you were worrying about your actual hand in the business."

"What do you mean?"

"I mean," Alleyn's voice was grave, "the circumstance of it being your hands, Miss Seacliff, that thrust her down upon the knife. Tell me, please, did you notice any resistance at first? I should have thought that there might even be a slight sound as the point entered."

"I—don't think——"

"We are considering the actual death throes of a murdered individual," said Alleyn mildly. "I should like a clear picture."

She opened her eyes wide, a look of extreme horror came into her face. She looked wildly round the room, darted a furious glance at Alleyn, and said in a strangled voice: "Let me out. I've got to go out."

Fox rose in consternation, but she pushed him away and ran blindly to the door.

"Never mind, Fox," said Alleyn.

The door banged.

"Here," said Fox, "what's she up to?"

"She's bolted," exclaimed Nigel. "Look out! She's doing a bolt."

"Only as far as the cloak-room," said Alleyn. "The fatal woman is going to be very sick."

CHAPTER XI

Ormerin's Nerves and Sonia's Correspondence

"Well, really, Alleyn," said Nigel, "I consider you were hard on that girl. You deliberately upset her lovely stomach."

"How do you know her stomach's lovely?"

"By inference. What did you do it for?"

"I was sick of that Cleopatra nonsense. She and her catgut nerves!"

"Well, but she *is* terrifically attractive. A really magnificent creature."

"She's as hard as nails. Still," added Alleyn with satisfaction, "I did make her sick. She went through the whole story the first time almost without batting an eyelid. Each time we came back to it she was a little less confident, and the last time when I mentioned the words 'death throes' she turned as green as asparagus."

"Well, wasn't it natural?"

"Quite natural. Served her jolly well right. I dislike fatal women. They reek of mass production."

"I don't think you can say she's as hard as nails. After all, she *did* feel ill. I mean she was upset by it all."

"Only her lovely stomach. She's not in the least sorry for that unfortunate little animal who died under her hands. All that psychological clap-trap! She's probably nosed into a *Freud Without Tears* and picked out a few choice phrases."

"I should say she was extremely intelligent."

"And you'd be right. She's sharp enough. What she said about Garcia rang true, I thought. What d'you say, Brer Fox?"

"You mean when she talked about Garcia's cold-bloodedness, don't you, sir?"

"I do."

"Yes. They all seem to agree about him. I think myself that it doesn't do to ignore other people's impressions. If you find a lot of separate individuals all saying so-and-so is a cold, unscrupulous sort of person, why then," said Fox, "it usually turns out that he is."

"True for you."

"They might all be in collusion," said Nigel.

"Why?" asked Alleyn.

"I don't know."

"'More do I."

"Well," said Fox, "if this Garcia chap doesn't turn up in answer to our broadcast and ads. and so on, it'll look like a true bill."

"He's probably the type that loathes radio and never opens a paper," said Nigel.

"Highly probable," agreed Alleyn.

"You'll have to arrest all hikers within a three-days' tramp from Tatler's End House. What a bevy of shorts and ruck-sacks."

"He'll have his painting gear if he's innocent," said Alleyn. "If he's innocent, he's probably snoring in a pub not twenty miles away. The police stations have all been warned. We'll get him soon enough—if he's innocent."

"And if he's guilty?"

"Then he's thought out the neatest method of murder that I've come across for a very long time," said Fox. "He knew that nobody would meddle with the throne, he knew he'd got two-days' start before the event came off, and he very likely thought we'd have a tough job finding anything to pin on to him."

"Those traces of modelling clay," murmured Alleyn.

"He didn't think of that," said Fox. "If Bailey's right they dropped off his overall while he fixed the knife."

"What's all this?" askd Nigel. Alleyn told him.

"We've got to remember," said Alleyn, "that he'd got the offer of a good job. Marble statues of Comedy and Tragedy are not commissioned for a few pounds. It is possible, Fox, that a guilty Garcia might be so sure of himself that he would turn up in his London warehouse at the end of a week or so's tramp and set to work. When we found him and hauled him up for a statement, he'd be all vague and surprised. When we asked how the traces of clay were to be accounted for, he'd say he didn't know, but that he'd often sat on the throne, or stood on it, or walked across it, and the clay might have dropped off him at any moment. We'll have to find out what sort of state his working smock was in. The bit of clay Bailey found is hardish. Modellers' clay is wettish and kept so. When faced with Phillida Lee's statement he'd say he'd had dozens of rows with Sonia, but hadn't plotted to kill her. If we find she was going to have a child he'd very likely ask what of it?"

"What about the appointment he made with her for Friday night?" asked Fox.

"Did he make an appointment with her for Friday night?"

"Well, sir, you've got it there. Miss Lee said——"

"Yes, I know, Fox. According to Miss Lee, Garcia said: 'All right. On Friday night then.' And Sonia answered: 'Yes, if it's possible.' But that may not have meant that they arranged to meet each other on Friday night. It might have meant a thousand and one things, damn it. Garcia may have talked about leaving on Friday night. Sonia may have said she'd do something for him in London on Friday night. It is true that the young Lee person got the impression that they arranged to meet her, but she may have been mistaken."

"That's so," said Fox heavily. "We'll have to get on to deceased's movements from Friday afternoon till Sunday."

"Did you get anything at all from the maids about Friday night?"

"Not a great deal, sir, and that's a fact. There's three servants living in the house, a Mr. and Mrs. Hipkin who do butler and cook, and a young girl called Sadie Welsh, who's housemaid. They all went to a cinema in Baxtonbridge on Friday night and returned by the front drive. There's another girl—Ethel Jones—who comes in as a daily from Bossicote. She leaves at five o'clock in the afternoon. I'll get on to her tomorrow, but it doesn't look promising. The Hipkins seem a very decent couple. Devoted to Miss Troy. They've not got much to say in favour of this crowd. To Mrs. Hipkin's way of thinking they're all out of the same box. She said she wasn't surprised at the murder and expected worse."

"What? Wholesale slaughter did she mean?"

"I don't think she knew. She's a Presbyterian—Auld Licht—maiden name McQumpha. She says painting from the figure is no better than living in open sin, and she gave it as her opinion that Sonia Gluck was fair soused in wickedness. That kind of thing. Hipkin said he always thought Garcia had bats in the belfry, and Sadie said he once tried to assault her and she gave him a smack in the chops. She's rather a lively girl, Sadie is. They say Miss Seacliff's no lady because of the way she speaks to the servants. The only one they seemed to have

123

much time for was the Honourable Basil Pilgrim."

"Good old snobs. What about Garcia's evening meal on Friday?"

"Well, I did get something there, in a way. Sadie took it on a tray to the studio at seven-thirty. She tapped on the screen inside the door and Mr. Garcia called out to her to leave the tray there. Sadie said she didn't know but what he had naked women exhibiting themselves on the platform, so she put it down. When she went to the studio on Saturday morning the tray was still there, untouched. She looked into the studio but didn't do anything in the way of housework. She's not allowed to touch anything on the throne and didn't notice the drape. Garcia was supposed to make his own bed. Sadie says it's her belief he just pulled the counterpane over it and that's what we found, sir, isn't it?"

"Garcia wasn't there on Saturday morning?"

"No. Sadie says he'd gone and all his stuff as far as she could make out. She said the room smelt funny, so she opened the window. She noticed a queer smell there on Friday night, too. I wondered if it was the acid Bailey found the marks of, but she said no. She's smelt the acid before, when they've been using it for etching, and it wasn't the same."

"Look here, Fox, I think I'd like a word with your Sadie. Be a good fellow and see if she's still up."

Fox went off and was away some minutes.

"He must have broken into the virgin fastness of Sadie's bedroom," said Nigel.

Alleyn wandered round the room and looked at the books. "What's the time?" he said.

"After twelve. Twelve-twenty-five."

"Oh Lord! Here's Fox."

Fox came in shepherding an extraordinary little apparition in curling-pins and red flannel.

"Miss Sadie Welsh," explained Fox, "was a bit uncomfortable about coming down, Mr. Alleyn. She'd gone to bed."

"I'm so sorry to bring you out," said Alleyn pleasantly. "We shan't keep you here very long. Come over to the fire, won't you?"

He threw a couple of logs on the fire and persuaded Miss Welsh to perch on the extreme edge of a chair: with her feet on the fender. She was a girl of perhaps twenty-two, with large brown eyes, a button nose and a mouth that looked as though she constantly said: "Ooo." She gazed at Alleyn as if he was a grand inquisitor."

"You're Miss Troy's housemaid, aren't you?" said Alleyn.

"Yes, sir."

"Been with her long?"

"Ooo, yes, sir. I was a under-housemaid here when the old gentleman was alive; I was sixteen then, sir. And when Miss Troy was mistress I stayed on, sir. Of course, Miss Troy's bin away a lot, sir, but when the house was opened up again this year, Miss Bostock asked me to come with Mr. and Mrs. Hipkin to be housemaid. I never was a real housemaid like before, sir, but Mr. Hipkin he's training me now for parlourmaid. He says I'll be called Welsh then, because Sadie isn't a name for a parlourmaid, Mr. Hipkin says. So I'll be 'Welsh.'"

"Splendid. You like your job?"

"Well, sir," said Sadie primly. "I like Miss Troy very much, sir."

"Not so sure about the rest of the party?"

"No, I am not, sir, and that's a fact. I was telling Mr. Fox, sir. Queer! Well, I mean to say! That Mr. Garcia, sir. Ooo! Well, I dare say Mr. Fox has told you. I complained to Miss Troy, sir. I asked Mrs. Hipkin what would I do and she said: 'Go straight to Miss Troy,' she said, 'I would,' she said. 'I'd go straight to Miss Troy.' Which I did. There was no trouble after that, sir, but I must say I didn't fancy taking his dinner down on Friday."

"As it turned out, you didn't see Mr. Garcia then, did you?"

"No, sir. He calls out in a sort of drawly voice: 'Is that you, Sadistic?' which was what he had the nerve to call me, and Mr. Hipkin says he didn't ought to have because Mr. Hipkin is very well educated, sir."

"Astonishingly," murmured Alleyn.

"And then I said: 'Your dinner, Mr. Garcia,' and he called out—excuse me, sir—he called out: 'Oh Gawd, eat it yourself.' I said: 'Pardon?' and he said 'Put it down there and shove off.' So I said: 'Thank *you*,' I said, 'Mr. Garcia,' I said. And I put down the tray and as I told Mrs. Hipkin, sir, I said: 'There's something peculiar going on down there,' I said, when I got back to the hall."

"What made you think that?"

"Well, sir, he seemed that anxious I wouldn't go in, and what with the queer perfume and one thing and another—well!"

"You noticed an odd smell?"

"Yes, I did that, sir."

"Ever smelt anything like it before?"

"Ooo well, sir, that's funny you should think of that because I said to myself: 'Well, if that isn't what Mr. Marziz's room smells like of a morning sometimes.'"

"Mr. Malmsley?"

"Yes, sir. It's a kind of—well, a kind of a bitterish sort of smell, only sort of thick and sour."

"Not like whisky, for instance?"

"Oh no, sir. I didn't notice the perfume of whisky till I went down next morning."

"Hullo!" said Fox genially, "you never told me it was whisky you smelt on Saturday morning, young lady."

"Didn't I, Mr. Fox? Well, I must of forgotten, because there was the other smell, too, mixed up with it. Anyway, Mr. Fox, it wasn't the first time I've noticed whisky in the studio since Mr. Garcia's been there."

"But you'd never noticed the other smell before?" asked Alleyn.

"Not in the studio, sir. Only in Mr. Marziz's room."

"Did you make the bed on Saturday morning?"

Sadie turned pink.

"Well, no, I didn't, sir. I opened the window to air the room, and thought I'd go back later. Mr. Garcia's supposed to make his own bed. It looked fairly tidy so I left it."

"And on Saturday morning Mr. Garcia's clay model and all his things were gone?"

"That queer-looking mud thing like plasticine? Ooo yes, sir, it was gone on Saturday."

"Right. I think that's all."

"May I go, sir?"

"Yes, off you go. I'll ask you to sign your name to a statement later on. You'll do that, won't you? It will just be what you've told us here?"

"Very good, sir."

"Good night, Welsh," said Alleyn smiling. "Thank you."

"Good night, sir. I'm sure I'm sorry to come in, such a fright. I don't know what Mr. Hipkin would say. It doesn't look very nice for 'Welsh,' the parlourmaid, does it, sir?"

"We think it was quite correct," said Alleyn.

Fox, with a fatherly smile, shepherded Sadie to the door.

"Well, Fox," said Alleyn, "we'd better get on with it. Let's have Mr. Francis Ormerin. How's the French, by the way?"

"I've mastered the radio course, and I'm on to Hugo's

Simplified now. I shouldn't fancy an unsimplified, I must say. I can read it pretty steadily, Mr. Alleyn, and Bob Thompson, the super at number three, has lent me one or two novels he picked up in Paris, on the understanding I translate the bits that would appeal to him. You know Bob." Fox opened his eyes wide and an expression of mild naughtiness stole over his healthy countenance. "I must say some of the passages are well up to expectation. Of course, you don't find all those words in the dictionary, do you?"

"You naughty old scoundrel," said Alleyn. "Go and get M. Ormerin."

"Toot sweet," said Fox. "There you are."

"And you'd better inquire after the Seacliff." Fox went out. "This case seems to be strewn with upheavels," said Alleyn. "Garcia was sick when he saw the defaced portrait. Sonia was sick in the mornings, and Miss Seacliff is heaving away merrily at this very moment, or I'm much mistaken."

"I begin to get an idea of the case," said Nigel, who had gone through his notes. "You're pretty certain it's Garcia, aren't you?"

"Have I said so? All right, then, I do feel tolerably certain he laid the trap for this girl, but it's purely conjectural. I may be quite wrong. If we are to accept the statements of Miss Troy and Watt Hatchett, the knife was pushed through the boards some time after three o'clock on Friday afternoon, and before Saturday afternoon. Personally I am inclined to believe both these statements. That leaves us with Garcia and Malmsley as the most likely fancies."

"There's——"

"Well?"

"Of course if you accept her statement if doesn't arise," said Nigel nervously.

Alleyn did not answer immediately, and for some reason Nigel found that he could not look at him. Nigel ruffled the pages of his notes and heard Alleyn's voice: "I only said I was inclined to believe Hatchett's statement—and hers. I shall not regard them as inviolable."

Fox returned with Francis Ormerin and once again they settled down to routine. Ormerin had attended the private view of the Phoenix Group Show on Friday night, and had spent the week-end with a French family at Hampstead. They had sat up till about two o'clock on both nights and had been together during the day-time.

"I understand that during the bus drive back from London yesterday, the model sat beside you?" said Alleyn.

"Yes. That is so. This poor girl, she must always have her flirt in attendance."

"And you filled the role on this occasion?"

Ormerin pulled a significant grimace.

"Why not? She makes an invitation with every gesture. It is a long and tedious drive. She is not unattractive. After a time I fell asleep."

"Did she say anything about her movements in London?"

"Certainly. She told me that she stayed with another girl who is in the chorus of a vaudeville show at the Chelsea Theatre. It is called 'Snappy.' Sonia shared this girl's room. She went to 'Snappy' on Friday evening, and on Saturday she went to a studio party in Putney where she became exceedingly drunk, and was driven home by a young man, not so drunk, to the room of this girl whose name is—*tiens!*—ah yes—Bobbie is the name of the friend. Bobbie O'Dawne. All this she told me, and for a while I was complacent, and held her hand in the bus. Then after a time I fell asleep."

"Did she say anything at all that could possibly be of any help to us?"

"Ah! Any help? I do not think so. Except one thing, Perhaps. She said that I must not be surprised if I learn soon of another engagement."

"What engagement was that?"

"She would not tell me. She became *retenue—espiegle*—in English, sly-boots. Sonia was very sly-boots on the subject of this engagement. I received the impression, however, that it would be to Garcia."

"I see. She did not talk about Garcia's movements on Friday?"

"But I think she did!" exclaimed Ormerin, after a moment's consideration. "Yes, it is quite true, she did speak of him. It was after I had begun to get sleepy. She said Garcia would start for his promenade through this country on Saturday morning, and return to work in London in a week's time."

"Did she say where his work-room was in London?"

"On the contrary, she asked me if I could tell her this. She said: 'I do not know what his idea is, to make such a mystery of it.' Then she laughed and said: 'But that is Garcia—I shall have to put up with it, I suppose.' She spoke with the air of a woman who has certain rights over a man. It may, of course, have been an assumption. One cannot tell. Very often I have noticed that it is when a woman begins to lose her power with a man that she assumes these little postures of the proprietress."

"What did you think of Sonia Gluck, M. Ormerin?"

Ormerin's sharp black eyes flashed in his sallow face and his thin mouth widened.

"Of Sonia? She was a type, Mr. Alleyn. That is all one can say of her. The *gamine* that so often drifts towards studio doors, and then imperceptibly, naturally, into the protection of some painter. She had beauty, as you have seen. She was very difficult. If she had lived, she would have had little work when her beauty faded. While she was still good for our purpose we endured her temperament, her caprice, for the sake of her lovely body, which we might paint when she was well-behaved."

"Had you so much difficulty with her?"

"It was intolerable. Never for one minute would she remain in the same position. I myself began three separate drawings of the one pose. I cannot paint in such circumstances, my nerves are lacerated and my work is valueless. I had made my resolution that I would leave the studio."

"Really! It was as bad as that?"

"Certainly. If this had not happened, I would have told Troy I must go. I should have been very sorry to do this, because I have a great admiration for Troy. She is most stimulating to my work. In her studio one is at home. But I am very greatly at the mercy of my nerves. I would have returned when Bostock and Pilgrim had completed their large canvases, and Troy had rid herself of Sonia."

"And now, I suppose, you will stay?"

"I do not know." Ormerin moved restlessly in his chair. Alleyn noticed that there was a slight tic in his upper-lip, a busy little cord that flicked under the dark skin. As if aware of Alleyn's scrutiny, Ormerin put a thin crooked hand up to his lip. His fingers were deeply stained by nicotine.

"I do not know," he repeated. "The memory of this morning is very painful. I am *bouleversé*. I do not know what I shall do. I like them all here at Troy's—even this clumsy, shouting Australian. I am *en rapport* with them well enough, but I shall never look towards the throne without seeing there the tableau of this morning. That little unfortunate with her glance of astonishment. And then when they moved her—the knife—wet and red."

"You were the first to notice the knife, I think?"

"Yes. As soon as they moved her I saw it." He looked uneasily at Alleyn.

"I should have thought the body would still have hidden it."

"But no. I knelt on the floor. I saw it. Let us not speak of it. It is enough that I saw it."

"Did you expect to see the blade, Mr. Ormerin?"

Ormerin was on his feet in a flash, his face ashen, his lips drawn back. He looked like a startled animal.

"What do you say? Expect! How should I expect to see the knife? Do you suspect me—*me*—of complicity in this detestable affair?" His violent agitation came upon him so swiftly that Nigel was amazed, and gaped at him, his notes forgotten.

"You are too sensitive," Alleyn said quietly, "and have read a meaning into my words that they were not intended to convey. I wondered if the memory of your experiment with the knife came into your mind before you saw it. I wondered if you guessed that the model had been stabbed."

"Never!" exclaimed Ormerin, with a violent gesture of repudiation. "Never! Why should I think of anything so horrible?"

"Since you helped in the experiment, it would not be so astonishing if you should remember it," said Alleyn. But Ormerin continued to expostulate, his English growing more uncertain as his agitation mounted. At last Alleyn succeeded in calming him a little, and he sat down again.

"I must ask you to pardon my agitation," he said, his stained fingers at his lips. "I am much distressed by this crime."

"That is very natural. I shall not keep you much longer. I spoke just now of the experiment with the dagger. I understand that you and Mr. Hatchett did most of the work on the day you made this experiment?"

"They were all interested to see if it could be done. Each one as much as another."

"Quite so," agreed Alleyn patiently. "Nevertheless you and Mr. Hatchett actually tipped up the throne and drove the dagger through the crack."

"And if we did! Does that prove us to be——"

"It proves nothing at all, M. Ormerin. I was about to ask you if Mr. Garcia had any hand in the experiment?"

"Garcia?" Ormerin looked hard at Alleyn, and then an

expression of great relief came upon him and he relaxed. "No," he said thoughtfully, "I do not believe that he came near us. He stood in the window with Sonia and watched. But I will tell you one more thing, Mr. Alleyn. When it was all over and she went back to the pose, Malmsley began to mock her, pretending the dagger was still there. And Garcia laughed a little to himself. Very quietly. But I noticed him, and I thought to myself that was a very disagreeable little laugh. That is what I thought!" ended Ormerin with an air of great significance.

"You said in the dining-room that we might be sure this was a *crime passionnel*. Why are you so sure of this?"

"But it is apparent—it protrudes a mile. This girl was a type. One had only to see her. It declared itself. She was avid for men."

"Oh dear, oh dear," murmured Alleyn.

"*Pardon?*"

"Nothing. Please go on, M. Ormerin."

"She was not normal. You shall find, I have no doubt, that she was *enciente*. I have been sure of it for some time. Even at the beginning women have an appearance, you understand? Her face was a little"—he made an expressive movement with his hand down his own thin face— "dragged down. And always she was looking at Garcia. Mr. Alleyn, I have seen him return her look, and there was that in his eyes that made one shudder. It was not at all pretty to see him watching her. He is a cold young man. He must have women, but he is quite unable to feel any tenderness for them. It is a type."

Ormerin's distress had apparently evaporated. He had become jauntily knowing.

"In a word," said Alleyn, "you consider he is responsible for this tragedy?"

"One draws one's own conclusions, of necessity, Mr. Alleyn. Who else can it be?"

"She was on rather uncertain terms with most of you, it appears?"

"Ah yes, yes. But one does not perform murders from exasperation. Even Malmsley——"

Ormerin hesitated, grimaced, wagged his head sideways and was silent.

"What about Mr. Malmsley?" asked Alleyn lightly.

"It is nothing."

"By saying it is nothing, you know, you leave me with an

impression of extreme significance. What was there between the model and Mr. Malmsley?"

"I have not been able to discover," said Ormerin rather huffily.

"But you think there was something?"

"She was laughing at him. On the morning of our experiment when Malmsley began to tease Sonia, pretending that the knife was still there, she entreated him to leave her alone, and when he would not she said: 'I wouldn't be too damn' funny. Where is it that you discover your ideas, is it in books or pictures?' He was very disconcerted and allowed his dirty brush to fall on his drawing. That is all. You see, I was right when I said it was nothing. Have you finished with me, Mr. Alleyn?"

"I think so, thank you. There will be a statement later on," said Alleyn vaguely. He looked at Ormerin, as though he wasn't there, seemed to recollect himself, and got to his feet.

"Yes, I think that's all," he repeated.

"I shall wish you good night then, Mr. Alleyn."

"Good night," said Alleyn, coming to himself. "Good night, M. Ormerin."

But when Ormerin had gone, Alleyn wandered about the room, whistled under his breath, and paid no attention at all to Fox or Nigel.

"Look here," said Nigel at last, "I want to use a telephone."

"You?"

"Yes. Don't look at me as though I was a fabulous monster. I want to use the telephone, I say."

"What for?"

"Ring up Angela."

"It's eleven o'clock."

"That's no matter. She'll be up and waiting."

"You're burning to ring up your odious newspaper."

"Well—I thought if I just said——"

"You may say that there has been a fatal accident at Tatler's End House, Bossicote, and that an artist's model has died as the result of this accident. You may add that the authorities are unable to trace the whereabouts of the victim's relatives and are anxious to communicate with Mr. W. Garcia who is believed to be on a walking tour and may be able to give them some information about the model's family. Something on those lines."

"And a fat lot of good——" began Nigel angrily.

"If Garcia is not our man," continued Alleyn to Fox, "and sees that, he may do something about it."

"That's so," said Fox.

"And now we'll deal with the last of this collection, if you please, Fox. The languishing Malmsley."

"I'll go to the telephone," said Nigel.

"Very well. Don't exceed, now. You may tell them that there will be a further instalment to-morrow."

"Too kind," said Nigel haughtily.

"And Bathgate—you might ring my mamma up and say we won't be in until after midnight."

"All right."

Nigel and Fox collided in the doorway with Bailey, who looked cold and disgruntled.

"Hullo," said Alleyn. Wait a moment, Fox. Let's hear what Bailey's been up to."

"I've been over deceased's room," said Bailey.

"Any good?"

"Nothing much, sir. It's an attic-room at the front of the house."

He paused, and Alleyn waited, knowing that "nothing much" from Bailey might mean anything from a vacuum to a phial of cyanide.

"There's deceased's prints," continued Bailey, "and one that looks like this Garcia. It's inside the door where the maid's missed with the duster, and there's another print close beside it that isn't either of 'em. Broad. Man's print, I'd say. And of course there are the maid's all over the show. I've checked those. Nothing much about the clothes. Note from Garcia in the pocket. She was in the family way all right. Here it is."

He opened his case, and from a labelled envelope drew out a piece of paper laid between two slips of glass.

"I've printed it and taken a photo."

Alleyn took the slips delicately in his fingers and laid them on the desk. The creases in the common paper had been smoothed out and the scribbled black pencil lines were easy to read:

Dear S.—What do you expect me to do about it? I've got two quid to last me till I get to Troy's. You asked for it, anyway. Can't you get somebody to fix things? It's not exactly likely that I should want to be saddled with a wife and a kid, is it? I've got a commission for a big thing, and for God's sake don't throw me off my stride. I'm sorry but I can't do anything. See you at Troy's. *Garcia*.

"A charming fellow," said Alleyn.

"That was in a jacket pocket. Here's a letter that was just kicking about at the back of the wardrobe. From somebody called Bobbie. Seems as if this Bobbie's a girl."

This letter was written in an emormous hand on dreadful pink paper:

> The Digs,
> 4, Batchelors Gardens,
> Chelsea.
> Monday.

Dear Sonia,

I'm sorry you're in for it dear I think it's just frightful and I do think men are the limit but of course I never liked the sound of that Garcia too far upstage if you ask me but they're all alike when it comes to a girl. The same to you with bells on and pleased to join in the fun at the start and sorry you've been troubled this takes me off when they know you're growing melons. I've asked Dolores Duval for the address she went to when she had her spot of trouble but she says the police found out about that lady so it's no go. Anyway I think your idea is better and if Mr. Artistic Garcia is willing O.K. and why not dear you might as well get it both ways and I suppose it's all right to be married he sounds a lovely boy but you never know with that sort did I ever tell you about my boy friend who was a Lord he was a scream really but nothing ever came of it thank God. It will be O.K. if you come here on Friday and I might ask Leo Cohen for a brief but you know what managements are like these days dear they sweat the socks off you for the basic salary and when it comes to asking for a brief for a lady friend it's just too bad but they've forgotten how the chorus goes in that number. Thank you very much good morning. I laughed till I sobbed over that story of the Seacliff woman's picture it must have looked a scream when you'd done with it but all the same dear your tempreement will land you well in the consommy one of these days dear if you don't learn to kerb yourself which God knows you haven't done what with one thing and another. What a yell about Marmelade's little bit of dirt. Well so long dear and keep

smiling see you Friday. Hoping this finds you well as I am,
Cheerio. Ever so sincerely,
Your old pal,
BOBBIE.

PS.—You want to be sure B.P. won't turn nasty and say all
right go ahead I've told her the story of my life anyhow so now
what!

CHAPTER **XII**

Malmsley on Pleasure

Nigel returned while Alleyn was still chuckling over Miss O'Dawne's letter.

"What's up?" asked Nigel.

"Bailey has discovered a remarkably rich plum. Come and read it. I fancy it's the sort of thing your paper calls a human document. A gem in its own way." Nigel read over Fox's shoulder.

"I like Dolores Duval and her spot of trouble," he said.

"She got her pass from Leo Cohen for Sonia," said Alleyn. "Sonia told Ormerin she'd seen the show. Fox, what do you make of the passage where she says Sonia might as well get it both ways if Garcia is willing? Then she goes on to say she supposes it's all right to be married and he sounds a lovely boy."

"The lovely boy seems to be the Hon. Pilgrim, judging by the next bit about her boy-friend that was a lord," said Fox. "Do you think Sonia Gluck had an idea she'd get Mr. Pilgrim to marry her?"

"I hardly think so. No, I fancy blackmail was the idea there. Pilgrim confessed as much when he couldn't get out of it. If Mr. Artistic Garcia was willing! Is she driving at the blackmail inspiration there, do you imagine? Her magnificent disregard for the convention that things that are thought of together should be spoken of together, is a bit baffling. I shall have to see Miss Bobbie O'Dawne. She may be the girl we all wait for. Anything else, Bailey?"

"Well," said Bailey grudgingly, "I don't know if there's anything in it but I found this." He took out of his case a shabby blue book and handed it to Alleyn. "It's been printed, Mr. Alleyn. There's several of deceased's prints and a few of the broad one I got off the door. Same party had tried to get into the case where I found the book."

"The Consolations of a Critic," Alleyn muttered, turning the book over in his long hands. "By C. Lewis Hind, 1911. Yes, I see. Gently select. Edwardian manner. Seems to be a mildly ecstatic excursion into aesthetics. Nice reproductions. Hullo! Hullo! Why stap me and sink me, there it is!"

He had turned the pages until he came upon a black and white reproduction of a picture in which three medieval figures mowed a charming field against a background of hayricks, pollard willows and turreted palaces.

"By gum and gosh, Bailey, you've found Mr. Malmsley's secret. I knew I'd met those three nice little men before. Of course I had. Good Lord, what a fool! Yes, here it is. From *Les Très Riches Heures du Duc de Berry*, by Pol de Limbourge and his brothers. The book's in the Musée Condé at Chantilly. I had to blandish for half an hour before the librarian would let me touch it. It's the most exquisite thing. Well, I'll be jiggered, and I can't say fairer than that."

"You can tell us what you're talking about, however," suggested Nigel acidly.

"Fox knows," said Alleyn. "You remember, Fox, don't you?"

"I get you now, Mr. Alleyn," said Fox. "That's what she meant when she sauced him on the day of the experiment."

"Of course. This is the explanation of one of the more obscure passages in the O'Dawne's document. 'What a yell about Marmelade's bit of dirt.' What a yell indeed! Fetch him in, Fox—any nonsense from Master Cedric Malmsley and we have him on the hip." He put the book on the floor beside his chair.

"You might tell me, Alleyn, why you are so maddeningly perky all of a sudden," complained Nigel.

"Wait and see, my dear Bathgate. Bailey, you've done extremely well. Anything else for us in the room?"

"Not that I could make out, Mr. Alleyn. Everything's put back as it was, but I thought there was nothing against taking these things."

"Certainly not. Pack them into my case, please. I want you to wait until I've seen Mr. Malmsley. Here's Fox."

Malmsley drifted in ahead of Fox. Seen across the dining-room table he had looked sufficiently remarkable with his beard divided into two. This beard was fine and straight and had the damp pallor of an infant's crest. Malmsley wore a crimson shirt, a black tie and a corduroy velvet jacket. Indeed he had the uncanny appearance of a person who had come round, full circle, to the Victorian idea of a Bohemian. He was almost an illustration for "Trilby." "Perhaps," thought Alleyn, "there is nothing but that left for them to do." He wore jade rings on his, unfortunately, broad fingers.

"Ah, Mr. Alleyn," he said, "you are painfully industrious."

Alleyn smiled vaguely and invited Malmsley to sit down. Nigel returned to the desk, Bailey walked over to the door, Fox stood in massive silence by the dying fire.

"I want your movements from Friday noon to yesterday evening, if you will be so obliging, Mr. Malmsley," said Alleyn.

"I am afraid that I am not fortunate enough to have a very obliging nature, Mr. Alleyn. And as for my movements, I always move as infrequently as possible, and never in the right direction."

"London was, from your point of view, in the right direction on Friday afternoon."

"You mean that by going to London I avoided any question of complicity in this unpleasant affair."

"Not necessarily," said Alleyn. Malmsley lit a cigarette. "However," continued Alleyn, "you have already told us that you went to London by the six o'clock bus, at the end of an afternoon spent with Mr. Garcia in the studio."

"I am absurdly communicative. It must be because I find my own conversation less tedious, as a rule, than the conversation of other people."

"In that," said Alleyn, "you are singularly fortunate."

Malmsley raised his eyebrows.

"What did Mr. Garcia tell you about Mr. Pilgrim during your conversation in the studio?" asked Alleyn.

"About Pilgrim? Oh, he said that he thought Valmai would find Pilgrim a very boring companion. He was rather ridiculous and said that she would soon grow tired of Pilgrim's good looks. I told him that it was much more likely that she would tire of Pilgrim's virtue. Women dislike virtue in a husband almost as much as they enjoy infidelity."

"Good Lord!" thought Alleyn. "He *is* late Victorian. This is Wilde and Water."

"And then?" he said aloud.

"And then he said that Basil Pilgrim was not as virtuous as I thought. I said that I had not thought about it at all. 'The superficial observer,' I told him, 'is the only observer who ever lights upon a profound truth.' Don't you agree with me, Mr. Alleyn?"

"Being a policeman, I am afraid I don't. Did you pursue this topic?"

"No. I did not find it sufficiently entertaining. Garcia then invited me to speculate upon the chances of Seacliff's virtue saying that he could astonish me on that subject if he had a mind to. I assured him that I was unable to fall into a ecstasy of wonderment on the upshot of what was, as I believe racing enthusiasts would say, a fifty-fifty chance. I found Garcia quite, quite tedious and pedestrian on the subject of Seacliff. He is very much attracted by Seacliff, and men are always more amusing when they praise women they dislike than when they abuse the women to whom they are passionately attracted. I therefore changed the topic of conversation."

"To Sonia Gluck?"

"That would be quite brilliant of you, Inspector, if I had not mentioned previously that we spoke of Sonia Gluck."

"That is almost the only feature of our previous conversation that I do remember, Mr. Malmsley. You told us that Garcia asked you if—" Alleyn consulted his note-book— "if you had ever felt like murdering your mistress just for the horror of doing it. How did you reply?"

"I replied that I had never been long enough attached to a woman for her to claim the title of my mistress. There is something dreadfully permanent in the sound of those two sibilants. However, the theme was a pleasant one and we embroidered it at our leisure. Garcia strolled across to my table and looked at my drawing. 'It wouldn't be worth it,' he said. I disagreed with him. One exquisite pang of horror! 'One has not experienced the full gamut of nervous luxury,' I said, 'until one has taken a life.' He began to laugh and returned to his work."

"Is he at all insane, do you think?"

"Insane? My dear Inspector, who can define the borders of abnormality?"

"That is quite true," said Alleyn patiently. "Would you say that Mr. Garcia is far from being abnormal?"

"Perhaps not."

"Is he in the habit of taking drugs, do you know?"

Malmsley leant forward and dropped his cigarette on an ash-tray. He examined his jade rings and said:

"I really have no idea."

"You have never noticed his eyes, for instance?" continued Alleyn, looking very fixedly into Malmsley's. "One can usually tell, you know, by the eyes."

"Really?"

"Yes. The pupils are contracted. Later on they occasionally become widely dilated. As you must have observed, Mr. Malmsley, when you have looked in a mirror."

"You are wonderfully learned, Mr. Alleyn."

"I ask you if, to your knowledge, Garcia has contracted this habit. I must warn you that a very thorough search will be made of all the rooms in this house. Whether I think it advisable to take further steps in following up evidence that is not relevant to this case, may depend largely upon your answer."

Malmsley looked quickly from Fox to Nigel.

"These gentlemen are with me on this case," said Alleyn. "Come now, Mr. Malmsley, unless you wish to indulge the—what was Mr. Malmsley's remark about nervous enjoyment, Bathgate?"

Nigel looked at his notes.

"The full gamut of nervous luxury?" he said.

"That's it. Unless you feel like experiencing the full gamut of such nervous luxury as police investigations can provide, you will do well to answer my question."

"He could not afford it," said Malmsley. "He is practically living on charity."

"Have you ever treated him to—let us say—to a pipe of opium?"

"I decline to answer this question."

"You are perfectly within your rights. I shall obtain a search-warrant and examine your effects."

Malmsley shrank a little in his chair.

"That would be singularly distasteful to me," he said. "I am fastidious in the matter of guests."

"Was Garcia one of your guests?"

"And if he was? After all, why should I hesitate? Your methods are singularly transparent, Inspector. You wish to know if I have ever amused myself by exploring the pleasures of opium. I have done so. A friend has given me a very beautiful set in jade and ivory, and I have not been so churlish as to neglect its promise of enjoyment. On the other hand, I have not allowed myself to contract a habit. In point of fact, I have not used half the amount that was given to me. I am not a creature of habit."

"Did you invite Garcia to smoke opium?"

"Yes."

"When?"

"Last Friday afternoon."

"At last," said Alleyn. "Where did you smoke your opium?"

"In the studio."

"Where you were safe from interruption?"

"Where we were more comfortable."

"You had the six o'clock bus to catch. Surely you felt disinclined to make the trip up to London?"

Malmsley moved restlessly.

"As a matter of fact," he said, "I did not smoke a full pipe. I did not wish to. I merely started one and gave it to Garcia."

"How many pipes did you give him?"

"Only one."

"Very well. You will now, if you please, give us an exact account of the manner in which you spent your afternoon. You went to the studio immediately after lunch. Was Garcia there?"

"Yes. He had just got there."

"How long was it before you gave him opium?"

"My dear Inspector, how should I know? I should imagine it was round about four o'clock."

"After your conversation about the model and so on?"

"It followed our conversation. We discussed pleasure. That led us to opium."

"So you went to the house and fetched your jade and ivory paraphernalia?"

"Ah—yes."

"In your first account you may remember that you told me you did not leave the studio until it was time to change and catch your bus?"

"Did I? Perhaps I did. I suppose I thought that the opium incident would over-excite you."

"When you finally left the studio," said Alleyn, "what was Mr. Garcia's condition?"

"He was very tranquil."

"Did he speak after he had begun to smoke?"

"Oh, yes. A little."

"What did he say?"

"He said he was happy."

"Anything else?"

"He said that there was a way out of all one's difficulties if one only had the courage to take it. That, I think, was all."

"Did you take your opium and the pipe back to the house?"

"No."

"Why not?"

"The housemaid had said something about changing the sheets on my bed. I didn't particularly want to encounter her."

"Where did you put the things then?"

"In a box under Garcia's bed."

"And collected them?"

"This morning before class."

"Had they been disturbed?"

"I have no idea."

"Are you sure of that?"

Malmsley moved irritably.

"They were in the box. I simply collected them and took them up to the house."

"How much opium should there be?"

"I don't know. I think the jar must be about half full."

"Do you think Garcia may have smoked again, after you left?"

"Again I have no idea. I should not think so. I haven't thought of it."

Alleyn looked curiously at Malmsley.

"I wonder," he said, "if you realize what you may have done?"

"I am afraid I do not understand."

"I think you do. Everything you have told me about Mr. Garcia points, almost too startlingly, to one conclusion."

Malmsley made a sudden and violent gesture of repudiation.

"That is a horrible suggestion," he said. "I have told you the truth—you have no right to suggest that I have—that I had any other motive, but—but——"

"I think I appreciate your motives well enough, Mr. Malmsley. For instance, you realised that I should discover the opium in any case if I searched your room. You realised that if Mr. Garcia makes a statement about Friday, he will probably speak of the opium you gave him. You may even have known that a plea of irresponsibility due to the effect of opium might be made in the event of criminal proceedings."

"Do you mean—if he was tried for murder, that I—I might be implicated? That is monstrous. I refuse to listen to such a suggestion. You must have a very pure mind, Inspector. Only the very pure are capable of such gross conceptions."

"And only the very foolish attitudinise in the sort of

circumstances that have risen round you and what you did on Friday afternoon. Come, Mr. Malmsley, forget your pose for a moment. To my aged perceptions it seems a little as if you were mixing Dorian Grey with one of the second-rate intellectuals of the moment. The result is something that—you must forgive me—does not inspire a policeman with confidence. I tell you quite seriously that you are in a predicament."

"You suspect Garcia?"

"We suspect everyone and no one at the moment. We note what you have told us and we believe that Garcia was alone in the studio in a semi-drugged condition on Friday evening when we suppose the knife was thrust through the throne. We learn that you drugged him."

"At his own suggestion," cried Malmsley.

"Really? Will he agree to that? Or will he say that you persuaded him to smoke opium?"

"He was perfectly ready to do it. He wanted to try. And he only had one pipe. A small amount. He would sleep it off in a few hours. I tell you he was already half asleep when I left."

"When do you think he would wake?"

"I don't know. How should I know? The effect varies very much the first time. It is impossible to say. He would be well enough in five hours at all events."

"Do you think," said Alleyn very deliberately, "that Garcia set this terrible trap for Sonia Gluck?"

Malmsley was white to the lips.

"I don't know. I know nothing about it. I thought he must have done it. You have forced me into an intolerable position. If I say I believe he did it—but not because of the opium—I refuse to accept——"

His voice was shrill, and his lips trembled. He seemed to be near to tears.

"Very well. We shall try to establish your own movements after you left the house. You caught the six o'clock bus?"

Malmsley eagerly gave an account of his week-end. He had attended the private view, had gone on to the Savoy, and to a friend's flat. They had sat up till three o'clock. He had spent the whole of Saturday with this friend, and with him had gone to a theatre in the evening, and again they had not gone to bed until very late. Alleyn took him through the whole business up to his return on Sunday. Malmsley seemed to be very much shaken.

"Excellent, so far," said Alleyn. "We shall, of course, verify your statements. I have looked at your illustrations, Mr. Malmsley. They are charming."

"You shake my pleasure in them," said Malmsley, rallying a little.

"I particularly liked the picture of the three little men with scythes."

Malmsley looked sharply at Alleyn but said nothing.

"Have you ever visited Chantilly?" asked Alleyn.

"Never."

"Then you have not seen *Les Très Riches Heures du Duc de Berry*?"

"Never."

"You have seen reproductions of the illustrations, perhaps?"

"I—I may have."

Nigel, staring at Malmsley, wondered how he could ever have thought him a pale young man.

"Do you remember a book called *The Consolations of a Critic*?"

"I—don't remember—I——"

"Do you own a copy of this book?"

"No—I—I——"

Alleyn picked up the little blue volume from under his chair and laid it on Malmsley's knee.

"Isn't this book your property, Mr. Malmsley?"

"I—I refuse to answer. This is intolerable."

"It has your name on the fly-leaf."

Nigel suddenly felt desperately sorry for Malmsley. He felt as if he himself had done something shameful. He wished ardently that Alleyn would let Malmsley go. Malmsley had embarked on a sort of explanation. Elaborate phrases faltered into lame protestations. The subconscious memory of beautiful things—all art was imitative—to refuse a model was to confess yourself without imagination. On and on he went, and ended in misery.

"All this," said Alleyn, not too unkindly, "is quite unnecessary. I am not here to inquire into the ethics of illustrative painting. The rightness or wrongness of what you have done is between yourself, your publisher, and your conscience, if such a thing exists. All I want to know is how this book came into the possession of Sonia Gluck."

"I don't know. She was odiously inquisitive—I must have left it somewhere—I had it in the studio one afternoon when I—when I was alone. Someone came in and I—I put it aside. I am not in the least ashamed. I consider I had a perfect right. There are many dissimilarities."

"That is what she was driving at when she asked you, on the morning of the experiment, where you got your ideas?"

"Yes. I suppose so. Yes."

"Did you ask her for the book?"

"Yes."

"And she refused to give it up?"

"It was abominable. It was not that I objected to anybody knowing."

"Did you go to her room?"

"I had every right when she refused. It was my property."

"I see. You tried to recover it while she was away. On Friday, perhaps, before you left?"

"If you must know, yes."

"And you couldn't find your book?"

"No."

"Where was this book, Bailey?"

"In a locked suit-case, sir, under deceased's bed. Someone had tried to pick the lock."

"Was that you, Mr. Malmsley?"

"I was entirely justified."

"Was it you?"

"Yes."

"Why did you not tell Miss Troy what had happened?"

"I—Troy might not look at it—Troy is rather British in such matters. She would confess with wonderful enthusiasm that her own work is rooted in the aesthetics of the primitives, but for someone who was courageous enough to use boldly such material from the past as seemed good to him, she would have nothing but abuse. Women—English women especially—are the most marvellous hypocrites."

"That will do," said Alleyn. "What was Sonia's motive in taking this book?"

"She simply wanted to be disagreeable and infuriating."

"Did you offer her anything if she returned it?"

"She was preposterous," muttered Malmsley, "preposterous."

"How much did she ask?"

"I do not admit that she asked anything."

"All right," said Alleyn. "It's your mess. Stay in it if you want to."

"What am I to understand by that?"

"Think it out. I believe I need not keep you any longer, Mr.

Malmsley. I am afraid I cannot return your book just yet. I shall need a specimen of your fingerprints. We can take them from the cigarette-box you picked up when you came in, or from objects in your room which I am afraid I shall have to examine. It would help matters if you allowed Sergeant Bailey to take an official specimen now."

Malmsley consented to this with a very ill grace, and made a great fuss over the printer's ink left on his thick white finger-tips.

"I fail to see," he said, "why I should have been forced to go through this disgusting performance."

"Bailey will give you something to clean up the ink," said Alleyn. "Good evening, Mr. Malmsley."

"One more job for you, Bailey, I'm afraid," said Alleyn, when Malmsley had gone. "We'll have to look through these rooms before we let them go to bed. Are they still boxed up in the dining-room, Fox?"

"They are that," said Fox, "and if that young Australian talks much more, I fancy we'll have a second corpse on our hands."

"I'll start off on Mr. Malmsley's room, will I, sir?" asked Bailey.

"Yes. Then tackle the other men's. We'll be there in a jiffy. I don't expect to find much, but you never know in our game."

"Very good, Mr. Alleyn," said Bailey. He went off with a resigned look.

"What do you make of this dope story, Mr. Alleyn?" said Fox. "We'll have to have a go at tracing the source, won't we?"

"Oh Lord, yes. I suppose so. Malmsley will say he got it from the friend who gave him the pretty little pipe and etceteras, and I don't suppose even Malmsley will give his dope-merchant away. Not that I think he's far gone. I imagine he spoke the truth when he said he'd only experimented—he doesn't look like an advanced addict. I took a pot-shot on his eyes, his breath, and the colour of his beastly face. And I remembered Sadie noticed a smell. Luckily the shot went home."

"Smoking," ruminated Nigel. "That's rather out of the usual in this country, isn't it?"

"Fortunately, yes," agreed Alleyn. "As a matter of fact it's less deadly than the other methods. Much less pernicious than injecting, of course."

"Do you think Garcia may have done his stuff with the knife while he was still dopey?" asked Nigel.

"It would explain his careless ways," said Fox, "dropping clay about the place."

"That's true, Brer Fox. I don't know," said Alleyn, "if, when he woke at, say, seven-thirty, when Sadie banged on the screen, he'd feel like doing the job. We'll have to have expert opinion on the carry-over from opium. I'm inclined to think he might wake feeling damed unpleasant and take a pull at his whisky bottle. Had it been handled recently, Bailey?"

"Yes, sir, I'd say it had. It's very dusty in patches, but there's some prints that were left after the dust had settled. Only a very light film over the prints. Not more than a couple of days' deposit."

"That's fairly conclusive," said Alleyn. "Taken with Sadie's statement it looks as if Garcia's Friday evening dinner was a jorum of whisky."

"What beats me," said Fox, "is when he got his stuff away."

"Some time on Friday night."

"Yes, but *how*? Not by a local carrier. They've all been asked."

"He must have got hold of a vehicle of some sort and driven himself," said Nigel.

"Half doped and three-quarters tight, Mr. Bathgate?"

"He may not have been as tight as all that," said Alleyn. "On the other hand——"

"Well?" asked Nigel impatiently.

"On the other hand he may have," said Alleyn. "Come on, we'll see how Bailey's got on, and then we'll go home."

CHAPTER XIII

Upstairs

When Fox had gone upstairs and Nigel had been left to write a very guarded story for his paper on one of Troy's scribbling-pads, Alleyn went down the hall and into the dining-room. He found Troy and her class in a state of extreme dejection. Phillida Lee, Ormerin and Watt Hatchett were seated at the table and had the look of people who have argued themselves to a standstill. Katti Bostock, hunched on the fender, stared into the fire. Malmsley was stretched out in the only arm-chair. Valmai Seacliff and Basil Pilgrim sat on the floor in a dark corner with their arms round each other. Curled up on a cushion against the wall was Troy—fast asleep. The local constable sat on an upright chair inside the door.

Katti looked up at Alleyn and then across to Troy.

"She's completely done up," said Katti gruffly. "Can't you let her go to bed?"

"Very soon now," said Alleyn.

He walked swiftly across the room and paused, his head bent down, his eyes on Troy.

Her face looked thin. There were small shadows in the hollows of her temples and under her eyes. She frowned, her hands moved, and suddenly she was awake.

"I'm so sorry," said Alleyn.

"Oh, it's you," said Troy. "Do you want me?"

"Please. Only for a moment, and then I shan't bother you again to-night."

Troy sat up, her hands at her hair, pushing it off her face. She rose but lost her balance. Alleyn put his arm out quickly. For a moment he supported her.

"My legs have gone to sleep," said Troy. "Damn!"

Her hand was on his shoulder. He held her firmly by the arms and wondered if it was Troy or he who trembled.

"I'm all right now," she said, after an hour or a second. "Thank you." He let her go and spoke to the others.

"I am very sorry to keep you all up for so long. We have had a good deal to do. Before you go to your rooms we should like to have a glance at them. I hope nobody objects to this."

"Anything, if we can only go to bed," said Katti, and nobody contradicted her.

"Very well, then. If you—" he turned to Troy,—"wouldn't mind coming with me——"

"Yes, of course."

When they were in the hall she said: "Do you want to search our rooms for something? Is that it?"

"Not for anything specific. I feel we should just——" He stopped short. "I detest my job," he said; "for the first time I despise and detest it."

"Come on," said Troy.

They went up to a half-landing where the stairs separated into two short flights going up to their left and right.

"Before I forget," said Alleyn, "do you know what has happened to the bottle of nitric acid that was on the top shelf in the junk-room?"

Troy stared at him.

"The acid? It's there. It was filled up on Friday."

"Bailey must have missed it. Don't worry—we saw the stains and felt we ought to account for them. What about these rooms?"

"All the students' rooms are up there," said Troy, and pointed to the upper landing on the right. "The bathrooms, and mine, are on the other side. Through here"—she pointed to a door on the half-landing—"are the servants' quarters, the back stairs and a little stair up to the attic-room where—where Sonia slept."

Alleyn saw that there were lights under two of the doors on the students' landing.

"Fox and Bailey are up there," he said. "If you don't mind——"

"You'd better do my room," said Troy. "Here it is."

They went into the second room on the left-hand landing. It was a large room, very spacious and well-proportioned. The walls, the carpet, and the narrow bed, were white. He saw only one picture and very few ornaments, but on the mantlepiece sparkled a little glass Christmas tree with fabulous glass flowers growing on it. Troy struck a match and lit the fire.

"I'll leave you to your job," she said.

Alleyn did not answer.

"Is there anything else?" asked Troy.

"Only that I should like to say that if it was possible for me to make an exception——"

"Why should you make any exceptions?" interrupted Troy. "There is no conceivable reason for such a suggestion."

"If you will simply think of me as a ship's steward or—or some other sexless official——"

"How else should I think of you, Mr. Alleyn? I can assure you there is no need for these scruples—if they are scruples."

"They were attempts at an apology. I shall make a third and ask you to forgive me for my impertinence. I shan't keep you long."

Troy turned at the door.

"I didn't mean to be beastly," she said.

"Nor were you. I see now that I made an insufferable assumption."

"—But you can hardly expect me to be genial when you are about to hunt through my under-garments for incriminating letters. The very fact that you suspect——"

Alleyn strode to the door and looked down at her.

"You little fool," he said, "haven't you the common-or-garden gumption to see that I no more suspect you than the girl in the moon?"

Troy stared at him as if he had taken leave of his senses. She opened her mouth to speak, said nothing, turned on her heel and left the room.

"Blast!" said Alleyn. "Oh, blast and hell and bloody stink!"

He stood and looked at the door which Troy had only just not slammed. Then he turned to his job. There was a bow-fronted chest of drawers full of the sorts of garments that Alleyn often before had had to turn over. His thin fastidious hands touched them delicately, laid them in neat heaps on the bed and returned them carefully to their appointed places. There was a little drawer, rather untidy, where Troy kept her oddments. One or two letters. One that began "Troy darling" and was signed "Your foolishly devoted, John." "John," thought Alleyn, "John Bellasca?" He glanced through the letters quickly, was about to return them to the drawer, but on second thoughts laid them in a row on the top of the chest. "An odious trade," he muttered to himself. "A filthy degrading job." Then there were the dresses in the wardrobe, the slim

150

jackets, Troy's smart evening dresses, and her shabby old slacks. All the pockets. Such odd things she kept in her pockets—bits of charcoal, india-rubbers, a handkerchief that had been disgracefully used as a paint-rag, and a sketch-book crammed into a pocket that was too small for it. There was a Harris tweed coat—blue. Suddenly he was back on the wharf at Quebec. The lights of Troy's ship were reflected in the black mirror of the river. Silver-tongued bells rang out from all the grey churches. The tug, with its five globes of yellow light, moved outwards into the night tide of the St. Lawrence, and there on the deck was Troy, her hand raised in farewell, wearing blue Harris tweed. "Good-bye. Thank you for my nice party. Good-bye." He slipped his hand into a pocket of the blue coat and pulled out Katti Bostock's letter. He would have to read this.

. . . You are a gump to collect these blood-suckers . . . he's a nasty little animal . . . that little devil Sonia Gluck . . . behaving abominably . . . funny this 'It' stuff . . . you're different. They'd fall for you if you'd let them, only you're so unprovocative. . . . (Alleyn shook his head at Katti Bostock.) Your allusions to a detective are quite incomprehensible, but if he interrupted you in your work you had every right to bite his head off. What had you been up to anyway? Well, so long until the 3rd. Katti.

The envelope was addressed to Troy at the Chateau Frontenac.

"Evidently," thought Alleyn, "I had begun to make a nuisance of myself on board. Interrupting her work. Oh Lord!"

In a minute or two he had finished. It would have been absolutely all right if he had never asked about her room. No need for that little scene. He hung up the last garment, glanced round the room and looked for the fourth or fifth time at the photograph of a man that stood on the top of the bow-fronted chest. A good-looking man who had signed himself "John." Alleyn, yielding to an unworthy impulse, made a hideous grimace at this photograph, turned to leave the room and saw Troy, amazed, in the doorway. He felt his face burning like a sky sign.

"Have you finished, Mr. Alleyn?"

"Quite finished, thank you."

He knew she had seen him. There was a singular expression in her eyes.

"I have just made a face at the photograph on your tallboy," said Alleyn.

"So I observed."

"I have gone through your clothes, fished in your pockets and read all your letters. You may go to bed. The house will be watched, of course. Good night, Miss Troy."

"Good morning, Mr. Alleyn."

Alleyn went to Katti Bostock's room where he found nothing of note. It was a great deal untidier than Troy's room, and took longer. He found several pairs of paint-stained slacks huddled together on the floor of the wardrobe, an evening dress in close proximity to a painting-smock, and a row of stubborn-looking shoes with no trees in them. There were odds and ends in all the pockets. He plodded through a mass of receipts, colour-men's catalogues, drawings and books. The only personal letter he found was the one Troy had written and posted at Vancouver.* This had to be read. Troy's catalogue of the students was interesting. Then he came to the passages about himself. "... turned out to be intelligent, so I felt the fool.... Looks like a grandee ... on the defensive about this sleuth ... Took it like a gent and made me feel like a bounder." As he read, Alleyn's left eyebrow climbed up his forehead. He folded the letter very carefully, smoothed it out and returned it to its place among a box of half-used oil-colours. He began to whistle under his breath, polished off Katti Bostock's effects, and went in search of Fox and Bailey. They had finished the men's bedrooms.

Fox had found Malmsley's opium-smoking impedimenta and had impounded it. The amount of opium was small. There were signs that the jar had at one time been full.

"Which does not altogether agree with Mr. Malmsley's little story," grunted Alleyn. "Has Bailey tried the thing for prints?"

"Yes. Two sets, Garcia's and Malmsley's on the pipe, the lamp and the jar."

"The jar. That's interesting. Well, let's get on with it."

He sent Bailey into Phillida Lee's room, while he and Fox tackled Valmai Seacliff's. Miss Seacliff's walls were chiefly adorned with pictures of herself. Malmsley and Ormerin had

* See page 13.

each painted her, and Pilgrim had drawn her once and painted her twice.

"The successful nymphomaniac," thought Alleyn, remembering Katti's letter.

A very clever pencil drawing of Pilgrim, signed "Seacliff," stood on the bedside table. The room was extremely tidy and much more obviously feminine than Troy's or Katti's. Seacliff had at least three times as many clothes, and quantities of hats and berets. Alleyn noticed that her slacks were made in Savile Row, and her dresses in Paris. He was amused to find that even the Seacliff painting-bags and smock melt of Worth. Her week-end case had not been completely unpacked. In it he found three evening dresses, a nightdress and bath-gown, shoes, three pairs of coloured gloves, two day dresses, two berets, and an evening bag containing among other things a half-full bottle of aspirin.

"Maybe Pilgrim's," said Alleyn, and put them in his case. "Now for the correspondence."

They found more than enough of that. Two of her dressing-table drawers were filled with neatly tied-up packets of letters.

"Help!" said Alleyn. "We'll have to glance at these, Fox. There might be something. Here, you take this lot. Very special. Red ribbon. Must be Pilgrim's, I imagine. Yes, they are."

Fox put on his spectacles and began impassively to read Basil Pilgrim's love-letters.

"Very gentlemanly," he said, after the first three.

"You're out of luck. I've struck a most impassioned series from a young man, who compares her bitterly and obscurely to a mirage. Golly, here's a sonnet."

For some time there was no sound but the faint crackle of note-paper. Bailey came in and said he had drawn a blank in Phillida Lee's room. Alleyn threw a bundle of letters at him.

"There's something here you might like to see," said Fox. "The last one from the Honourable Mr. Pilgrim."

"What's he say?"

Fox cleared his throat.

"'Darling,'" he began, "'I've got the usual sort of feelings about not being anything like good enough for you. Your last letter telling me you first liked me because I seemed a bit different from other men has made me feel rather bogus. I suppose, without being an insufferable prig, I might agree that I can at any rate bear comparison with the gang we've got to know—the studio lot—like Garcia and Malmsley and Co. But that's not a hell of a compliment to myself, is it? As a matter of fact, I simply loathe seeing you in that setting. Men like Garcia have no right to be in the same room as yourself, my lovely, terrifyingly remote Valmai. I know people scream with mirth at the sound of the word "pure." It's gone all *déclassé* like "genteel." But there is a strange sort of purity about you, Valmai, truly. If I've understood you, you've seen something of —God, this sounds frightful—something of the same sort of quality in me. Oh, darling, don't see *too* much of that in me. Just because I don't get tight and talk bawdy, I'm not a blooming Galahad, you know. This letter's going all the wrong way. Bless you a thousand, thousand——' I think that's the lot, sir," concluded Fox.

"Yes. I see. Any letters in Pilgrim's room?"

"None. He may have taken them to Ankerton Manor, chief."

"So he may. I'd like to see the one where Miss Seacliff praised his purity. By the Lord, Fox, she has without a doubt got a wonderful technique. She's got that not undesirable parti, who'll be a perfectly good peer before very long, if it's true that old Pilgrim is failing; she's got him all besotted and wondering if he's good enough." Alleyn paused and rubbed his nose. "Men turn peculiar when they fall in love, Brer Fox. Sometimes they turn damned peculiar, and that's a fact."

"These letters," said Fox, tapping them with a stubby forefinger, "were all written before they came down here. They've evidently been engaged in a manner of speaking for about a month."

"Very possibly."

"Well," said Fox, "there's nothing in these letters of Mr. Pilgrim's to contradict any ideas we may have about Garcia, is there?"

"Nothing. What about Pilgrim's clothes?"

"Nothing there. Two overcoats, five suits, two pairs of odd trousers and an odd jacket. Nothing much in the pockets. His week-end suit-case hasn't been unpacked. He took a dinner suit, a tweed suit, pyjamas, dressing-gown, and toilet things."

"Any aspirin?"

"No."

"I fancy I found his bottle in one of Miss Seacliff's pockets. Come on. Let's get on with it."

They got on with it. Presently Bailey said: "Here's one from Garcia."

"Let me see, will you?"

Like the note to Sonia, this was written in pencil on an odd scrap of paper. It was not dated or addressed, and the envelope was missing.

Dear Valmai,

I hear you're going to Troy's this term. So am I. I'm broke. I haven't got the price of the fare down, and I want one or two things—paints, mostly. I'm going to paint for a bit. I took the liberty of going into Gibson's, and getting a few things on your account. I told old Gibson it would be all right, and he'd seen me in the shop with you, so it was. Do you think Basil Pilgrim would lend me a fiver? Or would you? I'll be O.K. when Troy gets back, and I've got a good commission, so the money's all right. If I don't hear from you, I'll ask Pilgrim. I can't think of anyone else. Is it true you're going to hitch up with Pilgrim? You'd much better try a spot of free love with me.—G.

"Cool," said Fox.

"Does this bloke live on women?" asked Bailey.

"He lives on anyone that will provide the needful, I'd say," grunted Fox.

"That's about it," said Alleyn. "We'll keep this and any other Garcia letters we find, Fox. Well, that's all, isn't it? Either of you got any more tender missives? All right then, we'll pack up. Fox, you might tell them all they may turn in now. My compliments and so on. Miss Troy has gone to her room. The others, I suppose, will still be in the dining-room. Come on, Bathgate."

A few minutes later they all met in the hall. Tatler's End House was quiet at last. The fires had died down in all the grates, the rooms had grown cold. Up and down the passages the silence was broken only by the secret sounds made by an old house at night, small expanding noises, furtive little creaks, and an occasional slow whisper as though the house sighed at the iniquity of living men. Alleyn had a last look round and spoke to the local man who was to remain on duty in the hall. Bailey opened the door and Fox turned out the last of the lights. Nigel, huddled in an overcoat, stowed his copy away in a pocket and lit a cigarette. Alleyn stood at the foot of the stairs, his face raised, as if he listened for something.

"Right, sir?" asked Fox.

"Coming," said Alleyn. "Good night."

"Good night, sir," said the local man.

"By the way—where's the garage?"

"Round the house to the right, sir."

"Thank you. Good night."

The front door slammed behind them.

"Blast that fellow!" said Alleyn. "Why the devil must he wake the entire household?"

It was a still, cold night, with no moon. The gravel crunched loudly under their feet.

"I'm just going to have a look at the garage," said Alleyn. "I've got the key from a nail in the lobby. I won't be long. Give me my case, Bailey. Bathgate—you drive on."

He switched on his torch and followed the drive round the house to an old stable-yard. The four loose-boxes had been converted into garages, and his key fitted all of them. He found an Austin, and a smart super charged sports car—"Pilgrim's," thought Alleyn—and in the last garage a small motor caravan. Alleyn muttered when he saw this. He examined the tyre-treads, measured the distance between the wheels and took the height from the ground to the rear doorstep. He opened the door and climbed in. He found a small lamp on a battery in the ceiling, and switched it on. It was not an elaborate interior, but it was well planned. There were two bunks, a folding table, a cupboard and plenty of lockers. He looked into the lockers and found painting gear and one or two canvases. He took one out. "Troy's," he said. He began to look very closely at the board floor. On the doorstep he found two dark indentations. They were shiny and looked as though they had been made by small wheels carrying a heavy load. The door opened outwards. Its inner surface had been recently scored across. Alleyn looked through a lens at the scratches. The paint had frilled up a little and the marks were clean. The floor itself bore traces of the shiny tracks, but here they were much fainter. He looked at the petrol gauge and found it registered only two gallons. He returned to the floor and crawled over it with his torch. At last he came upon a few traces of a greenish-grey substance. These he scraped off delicately and put in a small tin. He went into the driver's cabin, taking an insufflator with him, and tested the wheel. It showed no clear prints. On the floor of the cabin Alleyn found several Player's cigarette-butts. These he collected and examined carefully. The ray from his torch showed him a tiny white object that had dropped into the gear-change slot. He fished it out with a pair of tweezers. It was the remains of yet another cigarette and had got jammed and stuck to the inside of the slot. A fragment of red paper was mixed with the flattened wad of tobacco strands. One of Troy's, perhaps. An old one. He had returned to the door with his insufflator, when a deep voice said:

"Have they remembered your hot-water bottle, sir, and what time would you wish to be called?"

"Fox!" said Alleyn, "I am sorry. Have I been very long?"

"Oh no, sir. Bert Bailey's in his beauty sleep in the back of our car, and Mr. Bathgate has gone off in his to her ladyship's. Mr. Bathgate asked me to tell you, sir, that he proposed to make the telephone wires burn while the going was good."

"I'd like to see him try. Fox, we'll seal up this caravan and then we really will go home. Look here, you send Bailey back to London and stay the night with us. My mother will be delighted. I'll lend you some pyjamas, and we'll snatch a few hours' sleep and start early in the morning. Do come."

"Well, sir, that's very kind of you. I'd be very pleased."

"Splendid!"

Alleyn sealed the caravan door with tape, and then the door of the garage. He put the key in his pocket.

"No little jaunts for them to-morrow," he said coolly. "Come along, Fox. Golly, it's cold."

They saw Bailey, arranged to meet him at the Yard in the morning, and drove back to Danes Lodge.

"We'll have a drink before we turn in," said Alleyn softly, when they were indoors. "In here."

Fox tiptoed after him towards Lady Alleyn's boudoir. At the door they paused and looked at each other. A low murmur of voices came from the room beyond.

"Well, I'll be damned," said Alleyn, and walked in. A large fire crackled in the open fireplace. Nigel sat before it cross-legged on the heathrug. Curled up in a wing-backed chair was Lady Alleyn. She wore a blue dressing-gown and a lace cap and her feet were tucked under her.

"Ma'am!" said Alleyn.

"Hullo, darling! Mr. Bathgate's been telling me all about your case. It's wonderfully interesting, and we have already solved it in three separate ways."

She looked round the corner of her chair and saw Fox.

"This is disgraceful," said Alleyn. "A scene of license and depravity. May I introduce Mr. Fox, and will you give him a bed?"

"Of course I will. This is perfectly delightful. How do you do, Mr. Fox?"

Fox made his best bow and took the small, thin hand in his enormous fist.

"How d'you do, my lady?" he said gravely. "It's very kind of you."

"Roderick, bring up some chairs, darling, and get yourselves drinks. Mr. Bathgate is drinking whisky, and I am drinking port. It's not a bit kind of me, Mr. Fox. I have hoped so much that we might meet. Do you know, you look exactly as I have always thought you would look, and that is very flattering to me and to you. Roderick has told me so much about you. You've worked together on very many cases, haven't you?"

"A good many, my lady," said Fox. He sat down and contemplated Lady Alleyn placidly. "It's been a very pleasant association for me. Very pleasant. We're all glad to see Mr. Alleyn back."

"Whisky and soda, Fox?" said Alleyn. "Mamma, what will happen to your bright eyes if you swill port at one a.m.? Bathgate?"

"I've got one, thank you. Alleyn, your mother is quite convinced that Garcia is not the murderer."

"No," said Lady Alleyn. "I don't say he *isn't* the murderer, but I don't think he's the man you're after."

"That's a bit baffling of you," said Alleyn. "How d'you mean?"

"I think he's been made a cat's-paw by somebody. Probably that very disagreeable young man with a beard. From what Mr. Bathgate tells me——"

"I should be interested to know what Bathgate has told you."

"Don't be acid, darling. He's given me a perfectly splendid acount of the whole thing—as lucid as Lucy Lorrimer," said Lady Alleyn.

"Who's Lucy Lorrimer?" asked Nigel.

"She's a prehistoric peep. Old Lord Banff's eldest girl she was, and never known to finish a sentence. She always got lost in the thickets of secondary thoughts that sprang up round her simplest remarks, so everybody used to say 'as lucid as Lucy

Lorrimer.' No, but really, Roderick, Mr. Bathgate was as clear as glass over the whole affair. I am absolutely *au fait*, and I feel convinced that Garcia has been a cat's-paw. He sounds so unattractive, poor fellow."

"Homicides are inclined to be unattractive, darling," said Alleyn.

"What about Mr. Smith? George Joseph? You can't say that of *him* with all those wives. The thing that makes me so cross with Mr. Smith," continued Lady Alleyn, turning to Fox, "is his monotony. Always in the bath and always a pound of tomatoes. In and out of season, one supposes."

"If we consider Mr. Malmsley, Lady Alleyn," said Fox with perfect gravity, "his only motive, as far as we know, would be vanity."

"And a very good motive too, Mr. Fox. Mr. Bathgate tells me Malmsley is an extremely affected and conceited young man. No doubt this poor murdered child threatened him with exposure. No doubt she said she would make a laughing-stock of him by telling everybody that he cribbed his illustration from Pol de Limbourge. I must say, Roderick, he showed exquisite taste. It is the most charming little picture imaginable. Do you remember we saw it at Chantilly?"

"I do, but I'm ashamed to say that I didn't at first spot it when I looked at his drawing."

"That was rather slow of you, darling. Too gay and charming for words. Well, Mr. Fox, suppose this young Malmsley deliberately stayed behind on Friday, deliberately gave Garcia opium, deliberately egged him on to set the trap, and then came away, hoping that Garcia would do it. How about that?"

"You put it very neatly indeed, my lady," said Fox, looking at Lady Alleyn with serious approval. "May I relieve you of your glass?"

"Thank you. Well now, Roderick, what about Basil Pilgrim?"

"What about him, little mum?"

"Of course, *he* might easily be unbalanced. Robert Pilgrim is as mad as a March hare, and I think that unfortunate wife of his was a cousin of sorts, so there you are. And she simply set to work and had baby after baby after baby—all gels, poor thing—until she had this boy Basil, and died of exhaustion. Not a very good beginning. And Robert turned into a Primitive Methodist in the middle of it all, and used to ask everybody the most ill-judged questions about their private lives. I remember quite well when this boy was born, Roderick, your father said Robert's methods had been too primitive for Alberta. Her name was Alberta. Do you think the boy could have had anything to do with this affair?"

"Has Bathgate told you all about our interview with Pilgrim?" asked Alleyn.

"He was in the middle of it when you came in. What sort of boy has he grown into? Not like Robert, I hope?"

"Not very. He's most violently in love."

"With this Seacliff gel. What kind of gel is she, Roderick? Modern and hard? Mr. Bathgate says beautiful."

"She's very good-looking and a bit of a huntress?"

"At all murderish, do you imagine?"

"Darling, I don't know. Do you realise you ought to be in bed, and that you've led Bathgate into the father and mother of a row for talking out of school?"

"Mr. Bathgate knows I'm as safe as the Roman Wall, don't you, Mr. Bathgate?"

"I'm so much in love with you, Lady Alleyn," said Nigel, "that I wouldn't care if you were the soul of indiscretion. I should still open my heart to you."

"There now, Roderick," said his mother, "isn't that charming? I think perhaps I will go to bed."

Ten minutes later, Alleyn tapped on his mother's door. The familiar, high-pitched voice called: "Come in, darling," and he found Lady Alleyn sitting bolt upright in her bed, a book in her hand, and spectacles on her nose.

"You look like a miniature owl," said Alleyn, and sat on the bed.

"Are they tucked away comfortably?"

"They are. Both besotted with adoration of you."

"Darling! Did I show off?"

"Shamelessly."

"I do like your Mr. Fox, Roderick."

"Isn't he splendid? Mum——"

"Yes, darling?"

"This is a tricky business."

"I suppose so. How is she?"

"Who?"

"Don't be affected, Roderick."

"We had two minor rows and one major one. I forgot my manners."

"You shouldn't do that. I don't know, though. Perhaps you should. Who do you think committed this horrible crime, my dear?"

"Garcia."

"Because he was drugged?"

"I don't know. You won't say anything about——"

"Now, Roderick!"

"I know you won't."

"Did you give her my invitation?"

"Unfortunately we were not on them terms. I'll be up betimes in the morning."

"Give me a kiss, Rory. Bless you, dear. Good night."

"Good night, little mum."

Now, the window-sill...
...to their...
...icle...

CHAPTER XIV

Evidence from a Twig

Alleyn and Fox were back at Tatler's End House at seven o'clock in the thin chilly light of dawn. A thread of smoke rose from one of the chimneys. The ground was hard and the naked trees, fast, fast asleep, stretched their lovely arms against an iron sky. The air was cold and smelt of rain. The two men went straight to the studio, where they found a local constable, wrapped in his overcoat, and very glad to see them.

"How long have you been here?" asked Alleyn.

"Since ten o'clock last night, sir. I'll be relieved fairly soon—eight o'clock with any luck."

"You can go off now. We'll be here until then. Tell Superintendent Blackman I said it was all right."

"Thank you very much, sir. I think I'll go straight home. Unless——"

"Yes?"

"Well, sir, if you're going to work here, I'd like to look on—if it's not a liberty, sir."

"Stay, by all means. What's your name?"

"Sligo, sir."

"Right. Keep your counsel about our business. No need to tell you that. Come along."

Alleyn led them to the studio window. He released the blind and opened the window. The ledge outside was rimy with frost.

"Last night," said Alleyn, "we noticed certain marks on this window-sill. Look first of all at the top of the stool here. You see four marks—indentations in the surface?"

"Yes, sir."

"We're going to measure them."

Alleyn produced a thin steel tape and measured the distance between the indentations. Fox wrote the figures in his note-book.

"Now the window-sill. You see these marks?" He pointed to two lateral marks, shiny and well defined, like shallow grooves. Alleyn measured the distance between them and found that it corresponded exactly with the previous figure. The width of the marks, the depth, and the appearance were the same as those on the stool.

"Garcia had his model on a small wheeled platform," said Alleyn. "Now, Malmsley told us that Garcia proposed to wheel the model into the case and then put the whole thing on board whatever vehicle called to collect it. I think he changed his mind. I think he put the empty crate in the vehicle, drew the stool up to the sill, and wheeled the model over the sill into the crate, and aboard the caravan which was backed up to the window in the lane outside."

"The caravan, sir?" asked Sligo. "Was it a caravan?"

"Lock this place up and come along outside. You can get over the sill, but don't touch those two marks just yet. Jump well out to the side and away from the tyre-tracks."

In the lane Alleyn showed them the traces left by the wheels. They had been frozen hard.

"Bailey has taken casts of these, but I want you to note them carefully. You see at once that the driver of the van or whatever it was did a good deal of skirmishing about. If there were any footprints within twelve feet of the window, they've been obliterated. Farther out are the traces of the mortuary van, blast it. The caravan tracks overlap, and there are four sets of them. But if you look carefully, you can pick out the last impression on top of all the others. That's when the van was finally driven away. The next set, overlaid by these, represents the final effort to get in close to the window. Damn! it's beginning to rain. This will be our last chance in the lane, so let's make the most of it. Observe the tread, Sligo. There, you see, is the clear impression of a patch. I'll measure the distance between the wheels and the width of the tyres. There a little oil has dripped on the road. The van or whatever it is has been recently greased. It was backed in and the brakes jammed on suddenly, but not quite suddenly enough. The outer edge of the window-sill has had a knock. The front wheels were turned after the vehicle had stopped. There are the marks. From them we get the approximate length of the wheel-base. Out in the middle of the lane they disappear under the tracks of more recent traffic. Now look at the branches of that elm. They reach across the lane almost to our

163

side, and are very low. I wonder the county councillors have not lopped them down. Do you see that one or two twigs have been snapped off? There's been no wind, and the breaks are quite recent. See here!"

He stooped and picked up a broken twig.

"It is still sappy. There are several. One quite close to the studio wall, and there's another across the lane. If it should happen they were snapped off by the top of a vehicle, it must have moved from one side to the other. It is a fair chance, isn't it, that they were broken by our van, and, if this is so, they give an idea of its height. Right?"

"That's right, sir," said Mr. Sligo, breathing loudly through his nostrils.

"You know all this sort of stuff, of course," said Alleyn, "but it's a characteristic example of outside work. Now come along to the garage."

They walked along the lane through a wide entrance into the garage yard. Alleyn unlocked the garage doors and broke the police tape. It had begun to rain steadily.

"I took some measurements here last night, but it would be as well to verify them. Suppose you have a stab at it, Sligo."

Sligo, intensely gratified, measured the width of the tyres and the wheel-base.

"The tyres are the same, sir. Look here, sir, here's the patch on the rear tyre on the driving side. We found the trace on the left-hand as you faced the window, sir, so she was backed all right."

"Good," said Alleyn. "That's the way, Sligo. Now take a look at the doorstep. Wait a moment. I'll just have a go at the handle for prints."

He opened his bag and got out his insufflator. The grey powder showed no prints on the door or doorknob. Alleyn closely examined the three steps, which were worn and dirty.

"Don't touch these," he said, and opened the door.

"Now then, Sligo——"

"There they are, sir, there they are. Same marks on the top step. That's the marks of them little wheels, sir, isn't it?"

"I think so. Check them to make sure. Here are the measurements of the scars on the window-sill."

Out came Sligo's tape again.

"It's them, for sure," he said.

"Now have a look on the roof. If you climb on that bench, you'll do no harm. Go carefully, though. You never know if you won't spoil a perfectly good bit of evidence in the most unlikely spot."

Sligo mounted the bench like a mammoth Agag, and peered over the roof of the caravan.

"Eh, there's a-plenty of scratches, sir, right enough, and Gor', Mr. Alleyn, there's a bit of a twig jammed between the top roofing and the frame. Dug into the crack. Gor', that's a bit of all right, isn't it, sir?"

"It is indeed. Can you reach it?"

"Yes, sir."

"Take these tweezers and draw it out carefully. That's right. Now you can come down. Let's have an envelope, Fox, may we? We'll put your twig in there, Sligo, and label it. How far is it from here to London?"

"Twenty miles exactly, sir, to the end of the drive from Shepherd's Bush," answered Sligo promptly.

"Right!"

Alleyn packed his case and began with Fox and Sligo to examine the yard and the gateway into the lane.

"Here are the tracks clear enough in the lane," said Fox. "We've got enough here and more to show this caravan was driven into the lane, backed up to the studio window and loaded up through the window. Who does the caravan belong to?"

"Miss Troy, I think," said Alleyn.

"Is that so?" responded Fox, without any particular emphasis.

"We'll find out presently. Seal the garage up again, will you, Fox? Blast this weather. We'd better have a look at Pilgrim's car."

Basil Pilgrim's car was a very smart supercharged two-seater. The upholstery smelt definitely of Valmai Seacliff, and one of the side-pockets contained an elaborate set of cosmetics. "For running repairs," grunted Alleyn. They opened the dicky and found a man's rather shabby raincoat. Pilgrim's. "Also for running repairs, I should think." Alleyn examined it carefully, and sniffed at it. "Very powerful scent that young woman uses. I fancy, Fox, that this is the pure young man's garment for changing wheels and delving in engines. Now then, Sligo, you have a look at this. It's ideal for demonstration purposes—the sort of thing Holmes and Thorndyke read like a book. Do you know Holmes and Thorndyke? You should. How about giving me a running commentary on an old raincoat?"

Sligo, breathing noisily, took the coat in his enormous hands.

"Go on," said Alleyn; "you're a Yard man, and I'm taking notes for you."

"It's a man's mackintosh," began Sligo. "Made by Burberry. Marked 'B. Pilgrim' inside collar. It's mucked up like and stained. Inside of collar a bit greasy, and it's got white marks, too, on it. Grease on one sleeve. That's car grease, I reckon, and there's marks down front. Pockets. Righthand: A pair of old gloves used, likely, for changing tyres. There's other marks, too. Reckon he's done something to battery some time."

"Well done," said Alleyn. "Go on."

Sligo turned the gloves inside out.

"Left hand inside has got small dark stain on edge of palm under base of little finger. Left-hand pocket: Piece of greasy rag. Box of matches." Sligo turned the coat over and over. "I can't see nothing more, sir, except a bit of a hole in right-hand cuff. Burnt by cigarette, likely. That's all, sir."

Alleyn shut his note-book.

"That's the method," he said. "But——" He glanced at his watch. "Good Lord, it is eight o'clock. You'd better cut back to the studio or your relief will be giving you a bad mark."

"Thank you very much, sir. I'm much obliged, sir. It's been a fair treat."

"That's all right. Away you go."

Sligo pounded off.

Leaving Fox at the garage, Alleyn walked round the house and rang the front-door bell. It was answered by a constable.

"Good morning. Do you know if Miss Troy is down yet?"

"She's in the library, sir."

"Ask if I may see her for a moment."

The man came back to say Troy would receive Alleyn, and he went into the library. By daylight it was a pleasant room, and already a fire blazed in the open grate. Troy, in slacks and a pullover, looked so much as she did on that first morning at Suva that Alleyn felt for a moment as if there had been nothing between them but the first little shock of meeting. Then he saw that she looked as if she had not slept.

"You are early at your job," said Troy.

"I'm very sorry, indeed, to worry you at the crack of dawn. I want to ask you if the caravan in the garage belongs to you."

"Yes. Why?"

"When did you last use it, please?"

"About a fortnight ago. We all went out in it to Kattswood for a picnic and a day's sketching."

"Do you know how much petrol there was in the tank when you got back?"

"It must have been more than half full, I should think. I got it filled up when we started, and we only went about forty miles there and back."

"What does she do to the gallon?"

"Twenty."

"And the tank holds——?"

"Eight gallons."

"Yes. It's just over a quarter full this morning."

Troy stared at him.

"There must be a leak in the petrol tank," she said. "I couldn't have used more than five that day—not possibly."

"There isn't a leak," said Alleyn. "I looked."

"Look here, what is all this?"

"You're sure no one else has used the caravan?"

"Of course I am. Not with my permission." Troy seemed puzzled and worried. Then as her eyes widened "Garcia!" she cried out. "You think Garcia took it, don't you?"

"What makes you so sure of that?"

"Why, because I've puzzled my own wits half the night to think how he got his stuff away. The superintendent here told me none of the local carriers knew anything about it. Of course Garcia took it! Just like him. Trust him not to pay a carrier if he could get his stuff there free."

"Can he drive?"

"I really don't know. I shouldn't have thought so, certainly. I suppose he must be able to drive if he took the caravan." She paused and looked steadily at Alleyn.

"I know you think he went in the caravan," she said.

"Yes, I do."

"He must have brought it back that night," said Troy.

"Couldn't have been some time on Saturday before you came back?"

"He didn't know when I was coming back. He wouldn't have risked my arriving early and finding the caravan gone. Besides, anyone might have seen him."

"That's perfectly true," said Alleyn.

"If this warehouse place is somewhere in London, he could

167

do the trip easily if it was late at night, couldn't he?" asked Troy.

"Yes. Dear me, I shall have to do a sum. Wait a moment. Your car does twenty to the gallon, and holds eight gallons. You went forty miles, starting with a full tank. Therefore there should be six gallons, and there are only about three. That leaves a discrepancy of sixty miles or so. How fast can she go?"

"I suppose forty to forty-five or fifty if pressed. She's elderly and not meant for Brooklands."

"I know. I do wish he'd told one of you where this damned warehouse was."

"But he did. At least, Seacliff said this morning she thought she remembered he said something about it being near Holloway."

"Good Lord, why didn't she say so last night?"

"Why does she always behave in the most tiresome manner one could possible conceive? I'm nearly as bad, not to have told you at once."

"You're nothing like as bad. How did Miss Seacliff happen to remember Holloway?"

"It was at breakfast, which, I may tell you, was not a very sparkling event this morning. Phillida Lee would talk about every murder story she has ever read, and Hatchett was more bumptious than words can describe. At last the Lee child remarked that if a woman was convicted of murder, she was hanged at Holloway, and Seacliff suddenly exclaimed: 'Holloway—that's it—that's where Garcia's warehouse is; he said something about it when he first came down.'"

"Is she sure?"

"She seems to be fairly certain. Shall I send for her?"

"Would you?"

Troy rang the bell, which was answered by Hipkin, a large man with a small head and flat feet.

"Ask Miss Seacliff if she'll come and see me."

Seacliff strolled in, dressed in black trousers and a magenta sweater. She looked very lovely.

"Good morning, Miss Seacliff," said Alleyn cheerfully. "Are you recovered?"

"Why, what was the matter with *you*?" Troy asked her.

Seacliff glared at Alleyn with positive hatred.

"Miss Seacliff was indisposed last night," said Alleyn.

"What was the matter?"

"Nerves," said Seacliff.

"Was it *you* who was sick in the downstairs bathroom?" demanded Troy with an air of sudden enlightenment. "Sadie was furious at having to clear up. She said——"

"Need we discuss it, Troy? I'm really terribly upset."

"You must have been," agreed Troy, with a suspicion of a grin. "I must say I think you might have cleared up after yourself. Sadie said she thought at least three men——"

"Troy!"

"All right. Do you want to be alone, Mr. Alleyn?"

"No, no. I just wanted to ask Miss Seacliff about this Holloway business."

"Oh," said Seacliff. "You mean the place where Garcia is going to sculp?"

"Yes. Did he tell you it was somewhere near Holloway?"

"Yes, he did. I'd forgotten. I suppose you are furious with me?" She smiled at Alleyn. Her glance said, very plainly: "After all, you are rather good-looking."

"I'd like to know exactly what he said, if you can remember the conversation."

"I suppose I can remember a good deal of it if I try. It took place during one of his periodical attempts to make a pass or two at me. He asked me if I would come and see him while he was working. I forget what I said. Oh, I think I said I would if it wasn't too drearily far away or something. Then he said it was near Holloway, because I remember I asked him if he thought he'd be safe. I said I knew better than to spend an afternoon with him in a deserted studio, but I might get Basil to drive me there, and, of course, that made him quite livid with rage. However, he told me how to get there and drew a sort of map. I'm afraid I've lost it. As a matter of fact, I would rather like to see that thing, wouldn't you, Troy? Still, as long as he's not arrested or something, I suppose we shall see it in its proper setting. I told Garcia I thought it was a bit of a comedown to take a commission from a flick-shop. I said they'd probably ask him to put touches of gilt on the breasts and flood it with pink lights. He turned as acid as a lemon and said the surroundings were to be appropriate. He's got absolutely no sense of humour, of course."

"Did he tell you exactly where it was?"

"Oh, yes. He drew up the map, but I can't remember anything but Holloway."

"Not even the name of the street?" asked Alleyn resignedly.

"I don't think so. He must have mentioned it and marked it

down, but I don't suppose I'd ever remember it," said Seacliff, with maddening complacency.

"Then I think that's all, thank you, Miss Seacliff."

She got up, frowned, and closed her eyes for a moment.

"What's the matter?" asked Troy.

"I've got another of these filthy headaches."

"Carry-over, perhaps."

"No, it's not. I've been getting them lately."

"You're looking a bit white," said Troy, more kindly. "Why don't you lie down? Would you like some aspirin?"

"Basil gave me his last night, thanks." She took out her mirror and looked at herself with intense concentration.

"I look too bloody," she said, and walked out of the room.

"Is she always like that?" asked Alleyn.

"Pretty much. She's spoilt. She'd have been comparatively easy to live with if she hadn't got that lovely face. She *is* beautiful, you know."

"Oh! magnificent," agreed Alleyn absently.

He was looking at Troy, at the delicate sparseness of her head, the straight line of her brows and the generous width between her grey-green eyes.

"Are you very tired?" he asked gently.

"Who, me? I'm all right." She sat on the fender holding her thin hands to the fire. "Only I can't get it out of my head."

"Small wonder," said Alleyn, and to himself he thought: "She's treating me more like a friend this morning. Touch wood."

"Oddly enough, it's not so much Sonia, poor little thing, but Garcia, that I can't get out of my head. You needn't bother to be mysterious and taciturn. I know you must suspect Garcia after what Phillida Lee and Malmsley said last night. But you see, in a way, Garcia's a sort of protégé of mine. He came to me when he was almost literally starving, and I've tried to look after him a bit. I know he's got no conscience at all in the usual sort of way. He's what they call unmoral. But he has got genius and I never use that word if I can get out of it. He couldn't *do* a shabby thing with clay. Wait a moment."

She went out of the room for a few minutes. When she returned she carried a small bronze head, about half lifesize, of an old woman. Troy put the head on a low table and pulled back the curtains. The cold light flooded the little bronze. It looked very tranquil and pure; its simple forms folded it into a great dignity. The lights shone austerely and the shadows seemed to breathe.

"'All passion spent,'" said Alleyn after a short pause.

"That's it," agreed Troy. She touched it delicately with a long finger. "Garcia gave me this," she said.

"It wouldn't be too florid to say it looked as if it had been done by an inspired saint."

"Well—it wasn't. It was done by a lecherous, thieving little guttersnipe who happens to be a superb craftsman. But——" Troy's voice wavered. "To catch and hang the man who made it——"

"God—yes, I know—I know." He got up and moved restlessly about the room, returning to her.

"Oh, Troy, you mustn't cry," he said.

"What the devil's it got to do with you?"

"Nothing, nothing, nothing, and don't I know it!"

"You'd better get on with your job," said Troy. She looked like a boy with her head turned shamefacedly away. She groped in her trousers pocket and pulled out a handkerchief disgracefully stained with paint. "Oh blast!" she said, and pitched it into the wastepaper basket.

"Have mine."

"Thank you."

Alleyn turned away from her and leant his arms on the mantelpiece. Troy blew her nose violently.

"My mother's so happy about my picture," said Alleyn to the fire. "She says it's the best present she's ever had. She said, if you'll forgive the implication, that you must know all about the subject. I suppose that's the sort of lay remark that is rather irritating to a craftsman for whom the model must be a collection of forms rather than an individual."

"Bosh!" said Troy down her nose and behind his handkerchief.

"Is it? I'm always terrified of being highfalutin' about pictures. The sort of person, you know, who says: 'The eyes follow you all round the room.' It would be so remarkably rum if they didn't when the model has looked into the painter's eyes, wouldn't it? I told my mamma about the thing you did at Suva. She rather fancies her little self about pictures. I think her aesthetic taste is pretty sound. Do you know she remembered the Pol de Limbourge thing that Malmsley cribbed, for one of his illustrations."

"What!" exclaimed Troy loudly.

"Didn't you spot it?" asked Alleyn without turning. "That's one up to the Alleyn family, isn't it? The drawing of the three little medieval reapers in front of the chateau; it's Sainte

171

Chapelle, really, I think—do you remember?"

"Golly, I believe you're right," said Troy. She gave a dry sob, blew her nose again, and said: "Are there any cigarettes on the mantelpiece?"

Alleyn gave her a cigarette and lit it for her. When he saw her face, marred by tears, he wanted almost overwhelmingly to kiss it.

"Little serpent!" said Troy.

"Who—Malmsley?"

"Yes. Malmsley of all people, with his beard and his precicosity."

"There's no such word as precicosity."

"There may be."

"It's preciosity if it's anything."

"Well, don't be a scold," said Troy. "Did you face Malmsley with this?"

"Yes. He turned as red as a rose."

Troy laughed.

"What a doody-flop for Cedric," she said.

"I must get on with my odious job," said Alleyn. "May I use your telephone?"

"Yes, of course. There'll be an inquest, won't there."

"To-morrow, I think. It won't be so bad. Good-bye."

"Good-bye."

He turned at the doorway and said: "Lady Alleyn's compliments to Miss Troy, and if Miss Troy would like to sample the amenities of Danes Lodge, Lady Alleyn will be very happy to offer them."

"Your mother is very kind," said Troy, "but I think it would be better not. Will you thank her from me? Please say I am very grateful indeed."

Alleyn bowed.

"I'm grateful to you, too," said Troy.

"Are you? That is rather dangerously nice of you. Good-bye."

CHAPTER XV

Lady of the Ensemble

Before he left Tatler's End House Alleyn rang up Superintendent Blackman and asked if there was any news of Garcia. There was none. A discreetly-worded notice had appeared in the morning papers and the B.B.C. had instructions to send out a police message. The police, within a fifty-mile radius, had made intensive inquiries.

"It looks as if he didn't want to be found, Mr. Alleyn. The weather's been fine and if he'd sketched as he said he intended to do, he wouldn't have gone far in two days. It looks to me as if the bird had flown."

"It does a bit. Of course he might have changed his plans and taken a train or bus. We'll have to get on to the railway stations. All that deadly game. Thanks so much, Mr. Blackman. I'll let you know if there are any developments. Inquest to-morrow?"

"No, Thursday. Our gentleman's full up to-morrow. Bossicote Town Hall at eleven. He's a sensible sort of chap, our man."

"Good. I'll call on the C.C. this morning, before I go up to London."

"Just as well. He likes to be consulted."

"What about the post-mortem?"

"I wanted to let you know. She was going to have a child. About a month gone, the doctor says."

"I thought as much. Look here, I think I'll get straight up to London. Make my apologies to the Chief Constable, will you? I want to catch a friend of Sonia Gluck's, and I can't risk missing her."

"Right you are. He'll understand. So long. See you on Thursday."

Alleyn found Fox, who had renewed his acquaintance with the Hipkins and Sadie, and drove him back through teeming rain to Danes Lodge for breakfast.

"I've had a bit of a yarn with Ethel Jones," said Fox.

"Ethel? Oh yes, the help from the village. What had she got to say for herself?"

"Quite a bit," said Fox. He opened his note-book and put on his spectacles.

"You're looking very bland, Brer Fox. What have you got on to?"

"Well, sir, it seems that Ethel and her boy took a walk on Friday night down the lane. They passed by the studio window on their way home from the pictures at about eleven-thirty, perhaps a bit later. There were lights going in the studio but the blind was down. They walked straight past, but when they'd gone a piece further down the lane they stopped in the shadow of the trees to have a bit of a cuddle as you might put it. Ethel doesn't know how long it lasted. She says you're apt to lose your idea of time on these occasions, but when they got back to earth and thought about moving on, she glanced down the lane and saw someone outside the studio window."

"Did she, by gum! Go on, Fox!"

"Well, sir, she couldn't see him very distinctly."

"Him?"

"Yes. She says she could just see it was a man, and he seemed to be wearing a raincoat, and a cap or beret of some sort. He was standing quite close to the window, Ethel reckons, and was caught by a streak of light coming through the blind. I asked her about the face, of course, but she says it was in a shadow. She remembers that there was a small patch of light on the cap."

"There's a hole in the blind," said Alleyn.

"Is that so, sir? That might account for it, then. Ethel says the rest of the figure was a shadow. The collar of his raincoat was turned up and she thinks his hands were in his pockets."

"What height?"

"About medium, Ethel thought, but you know how vague they are. She said to her boy: 'Look, there's someone down the lane. They must have seen us,' and I suppose she gave a bit of a giggle, like a girl would."

"You ought to know."

"Why not, sir? Then, she says, the man turned aside and disappeared into the darker shadow and they could just hear his footfall as he walked away. Well, I went into the lane to see if I could pick up his prints, but you've been there and you know there wasn't much to be seen near the window, except the tyre-tracks where the caravan had been manoeuvred about. When you get away from the window and out into the lane there are any number of them, but there's been people and cars up and down during the week-end and there's not much hope of picking up anything definite."

"No."

"I've looked carefully and I can't find anything. It's different with the car traces under the window. They're off the beaten track, but this downpour about finished the lane as far as we're concerned."

"I know."

"Well, we got a description of Garcia last night, of course, but to make sure, I asked the Hipkins and Sadie and Ethel to repeat it. They gave the same story. He always wears a very old mackintosh, whether it's wet or fine, and it's their belief he hasn't got a jacket. Miss Troy gave him a grey sweater and he wears that with a pair of old flannel trousers. Mrs. Hipkin says Miss Troy has given him two shirts and Mr. Pilgrim gave him some underclothes. He doesn't often wear anything on his head, but they have seen him in a black beret. Sadie says he looks as rough as bags. Ethel said straight out that she thought the figure outside the window was Garcia. She said so to her boy. She says it was the dead spit of Garcia, but then, we've got to remember it wasn't at all distinct, and she may think differently now that she knows Garcia has gone. You know how they make up all sorts of things without scarcely knowing what they're up to."

"I do indeed. Had this figure by the window anything on its back—like a rucksack, for instance?"

"They say he hadn't, but of course, if it was Garcia, he might not have picked up his gear when they saw him."

"No."

"I look at it this way. He might have gone through the window to take a short cut to the garage by way of the lane, and he might have stood there, having a last look at the arrangement on the model's throne."

"Through the hole in the blind? Rather a sinister picture, Fox. Wouldn't they have heard him open the window?"

"Um," said Fox.

"It makes a fair amount of noise."

"Yes. Yes, that's so."

175

"Anything else?"

"No. They ambled off home. Hullo, sir, what's up?"

Alleyn had pulled up and now began to turn the car in the narrow lane.

"Sorry, Fox, but we're going back to have a look at the hole in the blind."

And back to the studio they went. Alleyn measured the distance from the window-sill to the hole—a triangular tear, of which the flap had been turned back. He also measured the height of the lamps from the floor. He climbed on Fox's shoulders and tied a thread to the light nearest the window. He stretched the thread to the hole in the blind. Fox stood outside in the pouring rain. Alleyn threw the window up, passed the thread through the hole to Fox, who drew it tight and held it against his diaphragm.

"You see?" said Alleyn.

"Yes," said Fox, "I'm six foot two in my socks and it hits me somewhere—let's see——"

"About the end of the sternum."

"That's right, sir."

"Good enough, but we'll take a look at night. Let's go and have breakfast."

And a few minutes later they joined Nigel Bathgate at breakfast.

"You might have told me you were going out," complained Nigel.

"I wouldn't dream of interrupting your beauty sleep," said Alleyn. "Where's my mamma?"

"She finished her breakfast some minutes ago. She asked me to tell you she would be in her workshop. She's going to weave me some tweed for a shooting jacket."

"Divine creature, isn't she? What have you written for your paper?"

"I'll show you. I've left Miss Troy's name out altogether, Alleyn. They simply appear as a group of artists in a charming old-world house in Buckinghamshire."

"I'll try to be a good godfather," said Alleyn gruffly.

"Good enough," said Nigel. "Can I publish a picture of the girl?"

"Sonia? Yes, if you can rake one up. I can give you one of Garcia. Just talk about him as a very brilliant young sculptor, mention the job for the cinema if you like, and if you can manage it, suggest that we suspect the thing to be the work of some criminal lunatic who had got wind of the way the model was posed. Far-fetched, but I understand the tallest, the most preposterous tarradiddle will be gulped down whole by your public. You may even suggest that we have fears for Garcia's safety. Do anything but cast suspicion on him. Is all this quite impossible, Bathgate?"

"I don't *think* so," said Nigel thoughtfully. "It can be brought out with what I have already written. There's nothing in this morning's paper. That's an almost miraculous bit of luck. Blackman and Co. must have been extraordinarily discreet."

"The hunt will be up and the murder out, at any moment now. Show me your stuff. We're for London in twenty minutes."

"May I come with you? I've telephoned the office. I'll make a bit of an entrance with this story."

Alleyn vetted the story and Nigel made a great to-do at each alteration, but more as a matter of routine than anything else. He then went to the telephone to ring up his office, and his Angela. Alleyn left Fox with the morning paper and ran upstairs to his mother's workshop. This was a large, sunny room, filled with what Lady Alleyn called her insurances against old age. An enormous hand-loom stood in the centre of the room. In the window was a bench for bookbinding. On one wall hung a charming piece of tapestry worked by Lady Alleyn in a bout of enthusiasm for embroidery and on another was an oak shrine executed during a wave of intensive wood-carving. She had made the rugs on the floor, she had woven the curtains on the walls, she had created the petit-point on the backs of the chairs, and she had done all these things extremely and surprisingly well.

At the moment she was seated before her hand-loom, sorting coloured wools. She looked solemn. Tunbridge Tessa, an Alsatian bitch, lay at her feet.

"Hullo, darling," said Lady Alleyn. "Do you think Mr. Bathgate could wear green and red? His eyes are grey, of course. Perhaps grey and purple."

"His eyes!"

"Don't be silly, Roderick. I've promised him some tweed. Yours is finished. It's in the chest over there. Go and look at it."

"But—your dog!"

"What about her? She's obviously taken a fancy to you."

"Do you think so? She certainly has her eye on me."

Alleyn went to the hand-carved chest, closely followed by Tunbridge Tessa. He found his tweed.

"But, darling, it really is quite amazingly good," he said. "I'm delighted with it."

"Are you?" asked his mother a little anxiously.

"Indeed I am."

"Well, your eyes are so blue it was easy for me. Mr. Bathgate has told me all about the baby coming. We've had a lovely talk. How did you get on at Tatler's End House, Roderick?"

"Better, thank you. We're off now, darling. I hope I'm going to spend the rest of the morning in a chorus lady's bed-sit, in Chelsea."

"Are you?" said his mother vaguely. "Why?"

"Routine."

"It seems to lead you into strange places. I'll come downstairs and see you off. You may take the car, Roderick."

"I wouldn't dream of it."

"I've already told French to drive you in. I've got a job for him in Sloane Street."

When they were half-way downstairs she said: "Roderick, shall I ring her up? Would you like me to ring her up?"

"Very much," said Alleyn.

He collected Fox and Nigel. They wrote their names in Lady Alleyn's book.

"And you will come again whenever you like?" she said.

"That will be very soon, I'm afraid," Nigel told her.

"Not too soon. What about Mr. Fox?"

"It has been very pleasant indeed, my lady," said Fox. He straightened up, pen in hand, and gravely unhooked his spectacles. "I shall like to think about it. It's been quite different, you see, from my usual run of things. Quite an experience, you might say, and a very enjoyable one. If I may say so, you have a wonderful way with you, my lady. I felt at home."

Alleyn abruptly took his arm.

"You see, ma'am," he said, "we have courtiers at the Yard."

"Something a little better than that. Good-bye, my dear."

In the car Alleyn and Fox thumbed over their notebooks and occasionally exchanged remarks. Nigel, next the chauffeur, spent the time in pleasurable anticipation of his reception at the office. They cut through from Shepherd's Bush to Holland Road, and thence into Chelsea. Alleyn gave the man directions which finally brought them into a narrow and not very smart cul-de-sac behind Smith Street.

"This is Batchelors Gardens," said Alleyn. "And there's No. 4. You can put me down here. If I don't come out in five minutes take Mr. Fox to the Yard and Mr. Bathgate to his office, will you, French? Good-bye, Bathgate. Meet you at the Yard somewhere round noon, Fox."

He waved his hand and crossed the street to No. 4, a set of flats that only just escaped the appearance of a lodging-house. Alleyn inspected the row of yellowing cards inside the front door. Miss Bobbie O'Dawne's room was up two flights. He passed the inevitable charwoman with her bucket of oil and soot, and her obscene grey wiper so like a drowned rat.

"Good morning," said Alleyn, "is Miss O'Dawne at home," can you tell me?"

"At 'ome," said the charlady, viciously wringing the neck of the rat. "'Er! She won't be out of 'er bed!"

"Thank you," said Alleyn and tapped at Miss O'Dawne's door. He tapped three times, closely watched by the charlady, before a submerged voice called out: "All *right*." There were bumping noises, followed by the sound of bare feet on thin carpet. The voice, now much nearer, asked: "Who is it?"

"May I speak to Miss O'Dawne?" called Alleyn. "I've an important message for her."

"For me?" said the voice in more refined accents. "Wait a moment, please."

He waited while the charlady absently swilled the rat round and round in the oil and soot before slopping it over the top stair. The door opened a few inches and then widely enough to admit the passage of a mop of sulphur-coloured curls and a not unattractive face.

"Oh," said the face, "pardon me, I'm afraid——"

"I'm sorry to disturb you so early," said Alleyn, "but I would be most grateful if you could see me for a moment."

"I don't want anything," said Miss O'Dawne dangerously.

"And I'm not selling anything," smiled Alleyn.

"Sorry, I'm sure, but you never know, these days, do you, with 'vasity boys travelling in anything from vacuums to foundation garments."

"It's about Sonia Gluck," said Alleyn.

"Sonia? Are you a pal of hers? Why didn't you say so at first? Half a tick, and I'll get dressed. Pardon the stage-wait

179

but the lonely west wing's closed on account of the ghost and the rest of the castle's a ruin."

"Don't hurry," said Alleyn, "the morning's before us."

"I'll say! Tell yourself stories and be good!"

The door slammed. Alleyn lit a cigarette. The charlady descended three steps backwards in a toad-like posture.

"Cold morning," she said suddenly.

"Very cold," agreed Alleyn, noticing with a pang that her old hands were purple.

"You a theatrical?"

"No, no. Nothing so interesting, I'm afraid."

"Not a traveller neither?"

"No—not even a traveller."

"You look too classy now I come to look atcher. I was in service for ten years."

"Were you?"

"Yers. In service. Lidy be the name of Wells. Then she died of dibeets and I 'adter come down to daily. It's all right in service, you know. Comferble. Meals and that. Warm."

"It's beastly to be cold," said Alleyn.

"That's right," she said dimly.

Alleyn felt unhappily in his pocket and she watched him. Inside the room Miss O'Dawne began to whistle. On the next landing a door banged, and a young man in a tightfitting royal blue suit tripped lightly downstairs, singing professionally. He had a good stare at Alleyn and said: "'Morning, ma? How's tricks?"

"'Mornin', Mr. Chumley."

"Look out, now, I don't want to kick the bucket just yet." He vaulted neatly over the wet steps and disappeared in full voice.

"'E's in the choreus," said the charlady. "They get a lot of money in the choreus."

She had left her dustpan on the landing. Alleyn dropped his gloves, and as he stooped he put two half-crowns under the dustpan. He did it very neatly and quickly but not neatly enough, it seemed.

"Yer dropped some money, sir," said the charlady avidly.

"That's—that's for you," said Alleyn, and to his relief the door opened.

"Take your place in the queue and don't rush the ushers," said Miss O'Dawne. Alleyn walked in.

Miss O'Dawne's bed-sitting-room looked a little as if it had been suddenly slapped up and bounced into a semblance of tidiness. The cupboard doors had an air of pressure from within, the drawers looked as if they had been rammed home under protest, the divan-bed hunched its shoulders under a magenta artificial-silk counterpane. Two jade green cushions cowered against the wall at the head of the bed, the corner of the suit-case peeped out furtively from underneath. Miss O'Dawne herself was surprisingly neat. Her make-up suggested that she was a quick-change artist.

"Sit down," she said, "and make yourself at our place. It's not Buckingham Palace with knobs on, but you can't do much on chorus work and 'Hullo, girls, have you heard the news?' Seen our show?"

"Not yet," said Alleyn.

"I've got three lines in the last act and a kiss from Mr. Henry Molyneux. His breath smells of whisky, carbide and onions, but it's great to be an actress. Well, how's tricks?"

"Not so wonderful," said Alleyn, feeling for the right language.

"Cheer up, you'll soon be dead. I was going to make a cup of coffee. How does that strike you?"

"It sounds delightful," said Alleyn.

"Well, we strive to please. Service with a smile. No charge and all questions answered by return in plain envelopes."

She lit her gas-ring and clapped a saucepan over it.

"By the way you haven't told me who you are?"

"My name's Roderick Alleyn, I'm afraid——"

"Roderick Alleyn? Sounds pretty good. You're not in the business, are you?"

"No, I'm——"

"Well, if you'll excuse my freshness you look a bit more Eton and Oxford than most of Sonia's boyfriends. Are you an artist?"

"No. I'm a policeman."

"And then he came to. Is this where the big laugh comes, Roddy?"

"Honestly."

"A policeman? Where's your make-up? Pass along there, please, pass along there. Go on, you're kidding."

"Miss O'Dawne, I'm an official of Scotland Yard."

She looked sharply at him.

"Here, what's wrong?" she said.

"Was Miss Gluck a very close friend of yours?" asked Alleyn gently.

"*Was!* What d'you mean? Here, has anything happened to Sonia?"

"I'm afraid so."

"What, God, she's not——!"

"Yes." ·

The coffee-pot bubbled and she automatically turned down the gas. Her pert little face had gone white under the make-up.

"What had she done?" she said.

"She hadn't done anything. I think I know what you mean. She was going to have a child."

"Yes. I know that, all right. Well—what happened?"

Alleyn told her as kindly as possible. She made the coffee as she listened to him, and her distress was so unaffected that he felt himself warm to her.

"You know I can't sort of believe it," she said. "Murder. That seems kind of not real, doesn't it? Know what I mean? Why, it was only Saturday she was sitting where you are now and telling me all her bits and pieces."

"Were you great friends?"

"Well, *you* know. We'd sort of teamed up, in a way. Mind, she's not my real pal like Maudie Lavine or Dolores Duval, but I was quiet matey with her. Here's your coffee. Help yourself to shoog. God, I can't believe it. Murdered!"

She stirred her coffee and stared at Alleyn. Suddenly she made a jab at him with her spoon.

"Garcia!" she said.

Alleyn waited.

"Garcia's done it," said Miss O'Dawne, "you take it from me. I never liked that boy. She brought him up here once or twice and I said to her: 'You watch your business with that gentleman,' I said. 'In my opinion he's a very dirty bit of work and I don't mind who hears me.' Well, I mean to say! Letting a girl as good as keep him. And when the spot of trouble comes along it's 'Thanks for the buggy ride, it was O.K. while it lasted.' Had she tried the funny business with the kid? You know."

"I don't think so." Alleyn took Miss O'Dawne's letter from his pocket and handed it to her.

"We found this in her room. That's what made me come to you."

She looked sharply at him.

"What about it?"

"You can understand that we want to collect any information that is at all likely to lead us to an arrest."

"I can understand that all right, all right."

"Well, Miss O'Dawne, this letter suggests that you may be able to give us this information. It suggests, at all events, that you may know more about the Sonia-Garcia situation than we do."

"I know all there was to know. She was going to have his kid, and he'd got sick of her. Pause for laugh. Laugh over."

"Isn't there a bit more to it than that?"

"How d'you mean?"

"I think I may as well tell you that we know she got a hundred pounds from Mr. Basil Pilgrim."

"Did he tell you?"

"Yes. Was that the plan you refer to in this letter?"

"Since you're asking, Mr. Clever, it was. Pilgrim'd had his fun and Sonia didn't see why he shouldn't pay for it."

"But the child was not Pilgrim's?"

"Oh no, dear, but for all he knew——"

"Yes, I see. She said she'd go to his father if he didn't pay up. Was that it?"

"That was the big idea. Or to his girl. Sonia told me this boy Basil is a bit silly. You know—one of the purity song and dance experts. He must be a bit soft, from what she told me. Said his feeongsay thought he was as pure as her. Soft music and tears in the voice. Sonia said it was a big laugh, anyway, because the girl's not so very very ongenoo either. Anyway, Basil was all worked up and gave Sonia the cheque."

"What did she do with his cheque?"

"Oh, she cashed it and gave the money to Garcia, dear. What do you know about that? Could you beat it? I told her she was crazy. On Saturday when she was here I said: 'Well, did it all go big?' and she said this boy Basil came in on his cue all right, but she'd handed the money to Garcia and asked him if they couldn't get married straight away. And Garcia started his funny business. He said a hundred quid wasn't enough to marry with."

"Hadn't she got anything out of Malmsley?"

"Listen, Mr. Blake, aren't you wonderful? How did you get on to the Marmalade stuff?"

Alleyn folded his arms and raised his eyebrows.

"'I have my methods,' said the great sleuth."

"Well, of course!" exclaimed Miss O'Dawne, greatly diverted. "Aren't you a yell!"

"Please tell me," said Alleyn. "What happened when she offered to sell Malmsley his own book?"

"He wouldn't give more than five pounds, dear, and Sonia stuck out for twenty. Well, I mean to say, what's five pounds to a girl in her condition? So she said she'd give him the week-end to think it over. She didn't mind waiting. It wasn't as if she hadn't got——" Miss O'Dawne stopped short, gave Alleyn another of her sharp glances and lit a cigarette.

"Hadn't got what?" asked Alleyn.

"Look here—you're asking a lot of questions, aren't you, dear? Keep forgetting you're a bobby with all this upstage-and-county manners of yours. What's wrong with a girl getting her own back like Sonia did?"

"Well, it was blackmail, you know."

"Was it? Isn't that a pity, I don't suppose. Have some more coffee?"

"Thank you, it's extremely good."

"That's right. I say, it's all very funny us talking away sort of cosy like this, but when I think of Sonia—honest, I *am* upset, you know. You have to keep on cracking hardy, but just the same it's a swine, isn't it? You know what I mean. Help yourself to shoog. No, reely, I *am* upset."

"I'm quite sure you are."

"Look, Roddy. You don't mind me calling you Roddy, do you?"

"I'm delighted," said Alleyn.

"Well, look, if what Sonia did was blackmail, I don't want to let everybody know the dirt about her after she's gone. Don't sling off at the dead's what I've always said, because they can't come in on the cross-talk and score the laughs where they are. See? You've got on to the Garcia-Pilgrim-Malmsley tale. All right! That's your luck or your great big talent. But I'm not in on this scene. See?"

"Yes, I do see. But you don't want her murderer to get off, do you?"

"Do I look funny?"

"Very well, then. I'm afraid the blackmail is bound to come

out in evidence. You can't stop that, and won't you help us? Won't you tell me anything you know that may throw a little light on the tragedy of her death? There is something more, I'm sure. Isn't there?"

"Do you mean the joke with the picture of Basil's girl?"

"No," said Alleyn.

"D'you know about that?"

"Yes."

"Well, then!"

"Is there anything else about the Pilgrim stunt? Did she threaten to take any further steps?"

"With Pilgrim?" Miss O'Dawne's sharp eyes looked thoughtfully at Alleyn. "No. She didn't. She'd done her stuff with the Hon. Bas. Mine's a Bass, I *don't* suppose."

"Well then, had Garcia any more tricks up his sleeve?"

Miss O'Dawne twisted her fingers together. "She's frightened about something," thought Alleyn.

"If you know anything more about Garcia," he said, "I do beg of you to tell me what it is?"

"Yeah? And get a permanent shop where Sonia's gone? It's no good, dear, I'm not in on this act."

"I promise you that no harm——"

"No, dear, there's nothing doing. I don't know anything that you haven't found out."

"Was Garcia off on a separate line?"

"You go for Garcia," said Miss O'Dawne. "That's all I'm going to say. Go for Garcia. Have you arrested him?"

"No. He's gone on a walking tour."

"Well, that's a scream—I bloody well don't think. Pardon my refinement," said Miss O'Dawne.

CHAPTER XVI

Back to the Yard

Alleyn cursed himself secretly and heartily for that unlucky word "blackmail." Miss Bobbie O'Dawne refused, pointblank, to give him any further information that might possibly come under that heading. He seemed to have come up against a tenet. If Sonia had committed blackmail and Sonia was dead, Bobbie O'Dawne wasn't going to give her away. However, she told him quite willingly how Sonia had spent the week-end, and pretty well proved that Sonia could not possibly have gone down to Tatler's End House between Friday and Monday. With this Alleyn had to be content. He thanked his hostess and promised to go and see her show.

"That's right, dear, you come along. It's a bright show. I don't have much to do, you know. I hope you don't think any the worse of me for minding my own business about Sonia?"

"No. But if it comes to—well—if it comes to the arrest of an innocent person and you know you could save them, what would you do then?"

"Garcia's not innocent, dear, not so's you'd notice it."

"It might not be Garcia."

"Come off it. Listen. Do you know Garcia told the poor kid that if she let on to anybody that the child was his, he'd do for her? Now! She told me that herself. She was dead scared I'd forget and let something out. She made me swear I wouldn't. She said he'd do for both of us if we talked. Isn't that good enough?"

"It's sufficiently startling," said Alleyn. "Well, I suppose I'd better be off. I do ask you, very seriously, Miss O'Dawne, to think over what I have said. There is more than one kind of loyalty, you know."

"I wouldn't have said a thing about the kid if I didn't know you'd find out. Anyway, that's the sort of thing that might happen to any girl. But I'm not going to do the dirty and have

186

them calling her criminal names, and it's no good asking me to. Are you going, dear? Well, so long. See you some more."

"Suppose I sent a man along from one of the evening papers, would you care to give him an interview?"

"Who, me? Well, I don't pretend a bit of publicity doesn't help you in the business," said Miss O'Dawne honestly. "D'you mean the 'Sonia Gluck as I knew her' gag?"

"Something like that."

"With perhaps my picture along of hers? I've got a nice picture of Sonia. You know—wound up in georgette with the light behind her. Very nice. Well, as long as they don't want the dirt about her, I wouldn't mind the ad., dear. You know. It sounds hard, but it's a hard old world."

"I'll come again, if I may."

"Welcome, I'm sure. Be good."

Alleyn went thoughtfully to Scotland Yard. He saw his Assistant Commissioner and went over the case with him. Then he went to his office. He had been for a year in the south of the world and the room looked at once strange and familiar. The respectably worn leather chairs, his desk, the untidy groove where he had once let a cigarette burn itself out, the little dark print of a medieval town above the mantelpiece—there they all were, as it seemed, waiting for him after a period of suspension. He sat at his desk and began to work on the report of this case. Presently Fox came in. Alleyn realised that he had clicked right back into his socket in the vast piece of machinery that was Scotland Yard. New Zealand, the wharf at Suva, the night tide of the St. Lawrence—all had receded into the past. He was back on his job.

He related to Fox the gist of his interview with Miss O'Dawne.

"What about yourself?" he asked when he had finished. "Any news, Brer Fox?"

"The city's been set going on the warehouse business. It's a bit of a job and no mistake. According to Miss Troy's reckoning, we've got sixty miles to account for. That correct, sir?"

"Yes."

"Yes. Well, supposing Garcia didn't tell lies about his warehouse, it's somewhere in London. It's twenty miles to Shepherd's Bush from the house. There and back, forty. Of course, he might not have come in by the Uxbridge Road, but it's by far the most direct route and it would be the one he was familiar with. For the sake of argument say he took it. That leaves us a radius of ten miles, roughly, from Shepherd's Bush to wherever the warehouse is. Twenty, there and back."

"Total, sixty."

"Yes. Of course, if this warehouse is somewhere, west, north-west, or south-west, he might have branched off before he got to Shepherd's Bush, but he said Holloway to Miss Seacliff and if he went to Holloway he'd go by Shepherd's Bush. Then on by way of, say, Albany Street and the Camden Road. As the crow flies, Holloway Prison is only about five miles from Shepherd's Bush, but the shortest way by road would be nearer eight or nine. Holloway fits in all right as far as the petrol consumption goes. Of course, it's all very loose," added Fox, looking over his spectacles at Alleyn, "but so's our information."

"Very loose. Holloway's a large district."

"Yes. Still, it squares up, more or less, with what we've got."

"True enough."

"Well, sir, following out your suggestion we've concentrated on Holloway and we're raking it for warehouses."

"Yes, it's got to be done."

"On the other hand," continued Fox stolidly, "as you pointed out on the trip up, it may not be in Holloway at all. Suppose Garcia lied about the position of the warehouse, having already planned the job when he spoke to Miss Seacliff. Suppose he deliberately misled her, meaning to use this warehouse as a hideout after the job was done?"

"It doesn't look like that, Fox. She says Garcia tried to persuade her to visit him there alone. He actually gave her a sketch-map of how to get to the studio. She's lost it, of course."

"Look here," said Fox. "The idea was that Pilgrim should drive her up. I wonder if there's a chance she handed the sketch-map to Pilgrim and he knows where the place is?"

"Yes. If he does know he didn't bother to mention it when I asked them all about the warehouse. Of course, that might have been bluff, but the whole warehouse story is rather tricky. Suppose Garcia planned this murder in cold blood. He would have to give up all idea of carrying out his commission for the marble group unless he meant to brazen it out, go for his walk, and turn up at the warehouse to get on with his work. If he meant to do this it would be no good to tell preliminary

188

lies about the site, would it? Suppose, on the other hand, he meant to disappear. He wouldn't have mentioned a warehouse at all if he meant to lie doggo in it."

"That's right enough. Well, sir, what if he planned the murder while he was still dopey after the opium?"

"That, to me, seems more probable. Malmsley left the pipe, the jar and the lamp in a box under Garcia's bed because he was afraid of your friend Sadie catching him if he returned them to his bedroom. Bailey found Garcia's as well as Malmsley's prints on the jar. There's less opium than Malmsley said there would be. It's at least possible that Garcia had another go at it after Malmsley had gone. He may have woken up, felt very dreary, and sought to recapture the bliss. He may have smoked another pipe or taken a pull at his whisky. He may have done both. He may even have laid the trap with the dagger while still under the influence of the opium and—or—whisky. This is shamefully conjectural, Fox, but it seems to me that it is not too fantastic. The macabre character of the crime is not inconsistent, I fancy, with the sort of thing one might expect from a man in Garcia's condition. So far—all right. Possible, at any rate. But would he be sensible enough to get Miss Troy's caravan, back it, however clumsily, up to the window, put the empty case on board and wheel the model through the window and into the case? And what's more, my old Foxkin, would he have the gumption to drive to this damnable warehouse, dump his stuff, return the caravan to Tatler's End House, and set out on his walking tour? Would he not rather sink into a drugged and disgusting slumber lasting well into Saturday morning? And having come to himself would he not undo his foul trap for Sonia?"

"But if he *wanted* her out of the way?" persisted Fox.

"I know, I know. But if he was going to bolt he had so much to lose. His first big commission!"

"Well, perhaps he'll turn up and brazen it out. He doesn't know he dropped the pellet of clay with his thumb-print. He doesn't know Miss Lee overheard his conversation with Sonia. He doesn't know Sonia told anyone she was going to have his child. He'll think the motive won't appear."

"He'll know what will appear at the post-mortem. What's worrying me is the double aspect of the crime, if Garcia's the criminal. There's no reason to suppose Malmsley lied about giving Garcia opium. It's the sort of thing he'd suppress if he could. Very well. The planning of the murder and the laying of the trap might have been done under the influence of a pipe or more of opium. The subsequent business with the caravan has every appearance of the work of a cool and clearheaded individual."

"Someone else in it?"

"Who?"

"Gawd knows," said Fox.

"Meanwhile Garcia does not appear."

"Do you think he may have got out of the country?"

"I don't know. He had a hundred pounds."

"Where d'you get that, chief?"

"From Miss Bobbie O'Dawne. Sonia gave him the hundred pounds she got from Basil Pilgrim."

"I've fixed up with the people at the ports," said Fox, "he won't get by, now. But has he already slipped through? That's what's worrying me."

"If he left Tatler's End House on his flat feet in the early hours of Saturday morning," said Alleyn, "we'll pick up his track."

"If?"

"It's the blasted psychology of the brute that's got me down," said Alleyn with unusual violence. "We've got a very fair picture of Garcia from all these people. They all agree that he lives entirely for his work, that he will sacrifice himself and everyone else to his work, that his work is quite remarkably good. I can't see a man of this type deliberately committing a crime that would force him to give up the biggest job he has ever undertaken."

"But if the opium's to blame? Not to mention the whisky?"

"If they're to blame I don't think he's responsible for the rest of the business with the caravan. He'd either sleep it off there in the studio or wander away without taking any particular pains to cover his tracks. In that case we'd have found him by now."

"Then do you think there's any likelihood of someone else driving him up to London and hiding him in this blasted warehouse? What about the man Ethel and her boy saw in the lane? Say it wasn't Garcia but someone else. Could he have found Garcia under the weather and offered to drive him up to London with the stuff and return the caravan?"

"Leaving the knife where it was?" said Alleyn. "Yes, that's possible, of course. He may not have noticed the knife, this lurker in the lane. On the other hand——"

Alleyn and Fox stared thoughtfully at each other.

"As soon as I got here this morning," said Fox at last, "I looked up this Mr. Charleson, the secretary to the board of the New Palace Theatre in Westminster. Had a bit of luck, he was on the premises and answered the telephone. He's coming in at eleven-thirty, but beyond confirming the business about this statue he can't help us. Garcia was to order the marble and start work on next Monday. They offered him two hundred pounds and they were going to pay for the marble after he'd chosen it. Mr. Charleson says they'd never get anyone else at that price whose work is as good as Garcia's."

"Bloodsucker," grunted Alleyn.

"But he's no idea where the work was to be done."

"Helpful fellow. Well, Fox, we'd better get a move on. We're going to spend a jolly day checking up alibis. I'll take Miss Troy's and Miss Bostock's to begin with. You start off with young Hatchett and Phillida Lee. To your lot will fall the breaded intelligentsia of the Vortex Experimental Studio theatre, the Lee aunt, and the Hatchett boardinghouse keeper. To mine Sir Arthur Jaynes, Cattcherley's hairdressing establishment, Mr. Graham Barnes, and the staff of the United Arts Club."

"And this Mr. John Bellasca, sir, Miss Troy's friend."

"Yes," said Alleyn. "Me too."

"And then what?"

"If we get done to-day we'll run down to Boxover in the morning and see the people with whom Pilgrim and Miss Seacliff stayed on Friday night."

He opened a drawer in his desk and took out the photograph of the group at Tatler's End House.

"How tall is Garcia?" he asked. "Five foot nine according to the statement Blackman gave us. Yes. Pilgrim looks about two and a half inches taller in this photograph, doesn't he? You get a very good idea of the comparative heights. Ormerin, Hatchett and Garcia are all within an inch of each other. Miss Bostock, Miss Seacliff and Miss Lee are much shorter. The model is a little taller than Miss Bostock, but not so tall as the others. Miss Troy is taller than the first batch, but about two inches shorter than Pilgrim. Pilgrim is the tallest of the lot. Alas, alas, Fox, how little we know about these people! We interview them under extraordinary circumstances and hope to get a normal view of their characters. We ask them alarming questions and try to draw conclusions from their answers. How can we expect to discover them when each must be secretly afraid that his most innocent remark may cast suspicion upon himself? How would you or I behave if we came within the range of conjecture in a murder case? Well, damn it, let's get on with the job."

The desk telephone rang and he answered it.

"It's me," said Nigel's voice winningly.

"What do you want?"

"I'd like to come and see you, Alleyn."

"Where are you?"

"In a call-box about five minutes away."

"Very well, come up. I've got a job for you."

"I'll be there."

Alleyn hung up the receiver.

"It's Bathgate. I'll send him round to get an exclusive story from Miss Bobbie O'Dawne. There's just a remote hope she may become less discreet under the influence of free publicity. I'm damn' well positive she's keeping something up her sleeve about the blackmailing activities. She's rather an attractive little creature, Fox. Hard as nails and used to the seamy side of life, but a curious mixture of simplicity and astuteness. She knew we'd find out about the child and had no qualms in talking about it, but as soon as the word blackmail cropped up she doubled up like a hedgehog. I don't think it had occurred to her that Sonia's gentle art of extracting money was in any sense criminal. And I—blundering booby that I was—must needs enlighten her. She's terrified of Garcia. She's convinced he murdered Sonia and I honestly think she believes he'd go for her if she informed against him."

He moved restlessly about the room.

"There's something missing," he said. "I'm positive there's something missing."

"Garcia," said Fox. "He's missing all right."

"No, blast you, not Garcia. Though Lord knows, we'll have to get him. No, there was something else that the O'Dawne had on the tip of her tongue. By gum, Fox, I wonder——Look here."

Alleyn was still talking when the telephone rang to say Nigel Bathgate had arrived.

"Send him up," said Alleyn. And when Nigel appeared Alleyn talked about Bobbie O'Dawne and suggested that Nigel should get a special interview.

"This is extraordinarily decent of you, Alleyn," said Nigel.

"It's nothing of the sort. You're the tool of the Yard, my boy, and don't you forget it. Now listen carefully and I'll tell you what line you're to take. You must impress upon her that you are to be trusted. If she thinks you'll publish every word she utters, she'll say nothing to the point. If you can, write the interview there and then and read it to her. Assure her that you will print nothing without her permission. Photograph the lady in every conceivable position. Then get friendly. Let her think you are becoming indiscreet. You may say that you have had instructions from the Yard to publish a story about Sonia's blackmailing activities unless we can hear, privately, exactly what they were. You may say that we think of publishing an appeal through the paper to any of her victims, asking them to come forward and tell us without prejudice what they paid her. We hope that this will lead to the arrest of Garcia. Emphasise this. It's Garcia we're after, but we can't lay it home to him without the evidence of the people Sonia blackmailed. We think Sonia refused to give him any more of the proceeds and he killed her to get them. It's a ridiculous tarradiddle, but I think if you are low and cunning she may believe you. She'll tell you about Pilgrim and Malmsley, I fancy, because she knows we have already got hold of that end of the stick. If, however, she thinks she may save Sonia's name by going a bit farther, there's just a chance she may do it. Do you understand?"

"I think so."

"If you fail, we'll be no worse off than we were before. Off you go."

"Very well," Nigel hesitated, his hand in his coat pocket.

"What is it?" asked Alleyn.

"Do you remember that I made a sort of betting list on the case last time you allowed me to Watson for you?"

"I do."

"Well—I've done it again," said Nigel modestly.

"Let me have a look."

Nigel took a sheet of foolscap from his pocket and laid it before Alleyn with an anxious smile.

"Away you go," said Alleyn. "Collect your cameraman and use your wits."

Nigel went out and Alleyn looked at his analysis of the case.

"I'd half a mind to do something of the sort myself, Fox,"

he said. "Let us see what he makes out."

Fox looked over his shoulder. Nigel had headed his paper: "Murder of an Artist's Model. Possible suspects."

(1) GARCIA.

Opportunity. Was in the studio on Friday after all the others had gone. Knew the throne would not be touched (rule of studio).

Motive. Sonia was going to have a baby. Probably his. He had tired of her and was after Valmai Seacliff (V.S.'s statement). They had quarrelled (Phillida Lee's statement), and he had said he'd kill her if she pestered him. Possibly she threatened to sue him for maintenance. He may have egged her on to blackmail Pilgrim and taken the money. If so, she may have threatened to give him away to Troy. He had taken opium at about four o'clock in the afternoon. How long would he take to get sufficiently over the effect to drive a car to London and back?

(2) AGATHA TROY.

Opportunity. Could have done it on Saturday after she returned from London, or on Sunday. We have only her word for it that the drape was already arranged when she visited the studio on Saturday afternoon.

Motive. Sonia had hopelessly defaced the portrait of Valmai Seacliff—on Troy's own admission the best picture she had painted.

(3) KATTI BOSTOCK.

Same opportunities as Troy.

Motive. Sonia had driven her to breaking-point over the sittings for her large picture.

(4) VALMAI SEACLIFF.

Opportunity. Doubtful, but possibly she could have returned from Boxover after they had all gone to bed. The headache might have been an excuse.

Motive. Unless you count Sonia's defacement of her portrait by Troy, there is no motive. If she had heard of Pilgrim's affair with Sonia, she might be furious, but hardly murderous. Anyway, she had cut Sonia out.

(5) BASIL PILGRIM.

Opportunity. Same as Seacliff. Perhaps more favourable. If she had taken aspirin, she would sleep soundly, and the others were nowhere near his room. He would have slipped out after they had all gone to bed, taken his car, gone to the studio and fixed the knife.

Motive. Sonia had blackmailed him, threatening to tell Seacliff and Lord Pilgrim that the child was Basil's. He seems to have a kink about purity and Seacliff. On the whole, plenty of motive.

N.B. If Seacliff or Pilgrim did it, either Garcia was not at the studio or else he is a confederate. If he was not at the studio, who took the caravan and removed his stuff? Could he have done this before Pilgrim arrived, leaving the coast clear?

(6) CEDRIC MALMSLEY.

Opportunity. He could have fixed the knife after he had knocked Garcia out with opium.

Motive. Sonia was blackmailing him about his illustration. He is the type that would detest an exposure of this sort.

(7) FRANCIS ORMERIN.

Opportunity. If Hatchett and Malmsley are correct in saying the drape was still crumpled on Friday afternoon after Ormerin had left, and if Troy is correct in saying it was stretched out on Saturday before he returned, there seemed to be no opportunity.

Motive. Only the model's persistent refusal to keep still (v. Unlikely).

(8) PHILLIDA LEE.

Opportunity. Accepting above statements—none.
Motive. None.

(9) WATT HATCHETT.

Opportunity. On Malmsley's and Troy's statements —none.

Motive. Appears to have disliked her intensely and quarrelled over the pose. Sonia gibed about Australia. (Poor motive.)

Remarks. It seems to me there is little doubt that Garcia did it. Probably gingered up by his pipe of opium. If he fails to answer advertisements, it will look still more suspicious.

Suggestion. Find the warehouse.

Alleyn pointed a long finger at Nigel's final sentence.

"Mr. Bathgate's bright idea for the day," he said.

"Yes," said Fox. "It looks nice and simple just jotted down like that."

"The thing's quite neat in its way, Fox."

"Yes, sir. And I think he's got the right idea, you know."

"Garcia?"

"Yes. Don't you?"

"Oh Lord, Fox, you've heard my trouble. I don't see how we can be too sure."

"There's that bit of clay with his print on it," said Fox. "On the drape, where it had no business."

"Suppose it was planted? There'd be any number of bits like that lying on the floor by the window. We found some. Let's get Bailey's further report on the prints, shall we?"

Alleyn rang through to Bailey's department and found that Bailey had finished his work and was ready to make a report. In a minute or two he appeared with a quantity of photographs.

"Anything fresh?" asked Alleyn.

"Yes, sir, in a sort of a way there is," said Bailey, with the air of making a reluctant admission.

"Let's have it."

Bailey laid a set of photographs on Alleyn's desk.

"These are from the empty whisky bottle under Garcia's bed. We got them again from different parts of the bed-frame, the box underneath and the stool he used for his work. Some of them cropped up on the window-sill and there's a good thumb and forefinger off the light switch above his bed. These"—he pointed to a second group—"come from bits of clay that were lying about the floor. Some of them were no good, but there's a couple of clear ones. They're made by the same fingers as the first lot. I've marked them 'Garcia.'"

"I think we may take it they are his," said Alleyn.

"Yes. Well then, sir, here's the ones off the opium-box and the pipe. Four of those I've identified as Mr. Malmsley's. The others are Garcia's. Here's a photo of the clay pellet I found in the drape. Garcia again. This set's off the edge of the throne. There were lots of prints there, some of them Mr. Hatchett's some Mr. Pilgrim's and some the French bloke's—this Mr.

Ormerin. They seem to have had blue paint on their fingers, which was useful. But this set is Garcia's again and I found it on top of the others. There were traces of clay in this lot, which helped us a bit."

Alleyn and Fox examined the prints without comment. Bailey produced another photograph and laid it on the desk.

"I got that from the drape. Took a bit of doing. Here's the enlargement."

"Garcia," said Alleyn and Fox together.

"I reckon it is," said Bailey. "We'd never have got it if it hadn't been for the clay. It looks to me, Mr. Alleyn, as if he'd only half done the job. There's no prints on the knife, so I supposed he held that with a cloth or wiped it after he'd only half done the job. There's nothing on the knife but a smudge of blue. You may remember there were the same blue smudges on the throne and the easel-ledge that was used to hammer in the dagger. Now, this print we got from the bit of paint-rag that you suggested was used to wipe off the prints. Some of the paint on the rag was only half dry, and took a good impression. It matches the paint smudges on the knife. Blue."

"Garcia's."

"That's correct, sir."

"This about settles it, Mr. Alleyn," said Fox.

"That Garcia laid the trap? I agree with you."

"We'll have to ask for more men. It's going to be a job getting him, sir. He had such a big start. How about letting these alibis wait for to-day, Mr. Alleyn?"

"I think we'd better get through them, but I tell you what, Fox. I'll ask for another man and leave the alibi game to the pair of you. I'm not pulling out the plums for myself, Foxkin."

"I've never known you to do that, Mr. Alleyn, don't you worry. We'll get through these alibis," said Fox. "I'd like to see what our chaps are doing round the Holloway district."

"And I," said Alleyn, "think of going down to Brixton."

"Is that a joke?" asked Fox suspiciously, after a blank pause.

"No, Fox."

"Brixton? Wh, Brixton?"

"Sit down for a minute," said Alleyn, "and I'll tell you."

"Eet old her words," murmured Alleyn. "The a little.
say we understand. Clever, but doting. Do you think you can help us?"
"I know, let me see. Tha... ... ..."
now it

CHAPTER XVII

The Man at the Table

At four o'clock on the following afternoon, Wednesday, September 21st, Alleyn turned wearily into the last land and estate agents' office in Brixton. A blond young man advanced upon him.

"Yes, sir? What can I have the pleasure of doing for you?"

"It's not much of a pleasure, I'm afraid. If you will, *and* if you can, tell me of any vacant warehouses in this district, or of any warehouses that have let part of themselves to artists, or of any artists who, having rented such premises, have taken themselves off to foreign parts and lent the premises to a young man who sculps. As you will probably have guessed, I am an officer of Scotland Yard. Here's my card. Do you mind awfully if I sit down?"

"Er—yes. Of course not. Do," said the young man in some surprise.

"It's a weary world," said Alleyn. "The room would be well lit. I'd better show you my list of all the places I have already inspected."

The list was a long one. Alleyn had continued his search at eleven o'clock that morning.

The blond young man ran through it, muttering to himself. Occasionally he cast a glance at his immaculately dressed visitor.

"I suppose," he said at last, with an avid look towards an evening paper on the corner of his desk, "I suppose this wouldn't happen to have any connection with the missing gentleman from Bucks?"

"It would," said Alleyn.

"By the name of Garcia?"

"Yes. We believe him to be ill and suffering from loss of memory. It is thought he may have wandered in this direction, poor fellow."

"What an extraordinary thing!" exclaimed the young man.

"Too odd for words," mummured Alleyn. "He's a little bit ga-ga, we understand. Clever, but dottyish. Do you think you can help us?"

"Well now, let me see. This list is pretty comprehensive. I don't know if——"

He bit his finger and opened a large book. Alleyn closed his eyes.

"It's not exactly in our line, really," said the young man. "I mean to say, any of the warehouses round here might have a room to let and we'd never hear of it. See what I mean?"

"Alas, yes," said Alleyn.

"Now there's Solly and Perkins. Big place. Business not too good, they tell me. And there's Anderson's shirt factory, and Lacker and Lampton's used-car depot. That's in Gulper Row, off Cornwall Street. Just by the waterworks. Opposite the prison. Quite in your line, Inspector."

He laughed shrilly.

"Damn' funny," agreed Alleyn.

"Lacker and Lampton's foreman was in here the other day. He's taken a house from us. Now, he did say something about there being a lot of room round at their place. He said something about being able to store his furniture there if they went into furnished rooms. Yes. Now, I wonder. How about Lacker and Lampton's?"

"I'll try it. Could you give me the foreman's name?"

"McCully's the name. Ted McCully. He's quite a pal of mine. Tell him I sent you. James is my name. Look here, I'll come round with you, if you like."

"I wouldn't dream of troubling you," said Alleyn firmly. "Thank you very much indeed. Good-bye."

He departed hurriedly, before Mr. James could press his offer home. A fine drizzle had set in, the sky was leaden, and already the light had begun to fade. Alleyn turned up the collar of his raincoat, pulled down the brim of his hat and strode off in the direction of Brixton Prison. Cornwall Street ran along one side of the waterworks and Gulper Row was a grim and deadly little alley off Cornwall Street. Lacker and Lampton's was at the far end. It was a barn of a place and evidently combined wrecking activities with the trade in used cars. The ground floor was half full of spare parts, chassis without wheels, engines without chassis, and bodies without either.

Alleyn asked for Mr. Ted McCully, and in a minute or two a giant in oil-soaked dungarees came out of a smaller workshop, wiping his hands on a piece of waste.

"Yes, sir?" he asked cheerfully.

"I'm looking for an empty room with a good light to use as a painting-studio," Alleyn began. "I called in at the estate agents, behind the prison, and Mr. James, there, said he thought you might have something."

"Bert James?" said Mr. McCully with a wide grin. "What's he know about it? Looking for a commission as per usual, I'll bet."

"Have a cigarette. Will that thing stand my weight?"

"Thank you, sir. I wouldn't sit there; it's a bit greasy. Take the box."

Alleyn sat on a packing-case.

"Have you any vacant rooms that would do to paint in?"

"Not here, we haven't, but it's a funny thing you should ask."

"Why's that?"

"Well, it's a bit of a coincidence," said Mr. McCully maddeningly.

"Oh?"

"Yes. The world's a small place, you know, sir. Isn't it, now?"

"No bigger than a button," agreed Alleyn.

"That's right. Look at this little coincidence, now. I dare say you've had quite a ramble looking for this room you want."

"I have rambled since eleven o'clock this morning."

"Is that a fact? And then you look in on Bert James and he sends you round here. And I'll swear Bert knows nothing about it, either. Which makes it all the more of a coincidence."

"Makes what, though?" asked Alleyn, breathing through his nostrils.

"I was just going to tell you," said Mr. McCully. "You see, although we haven't got the sort of thing you'd be wanting, on the premises, there's a bit of a storehouse round the corner that would do you down to the ground. Skylight. Paraffin heater. Electric light. Plenty of room. Just the thing."

"May I——"

"Ah! Wait a bit, though. It's taken. It's in use in a sort of way."

"What sort of way?"

"That's the funny thing. It was taken by an artist like yourself."

Alleyn flicked the ash off his cigarette.

"Really?" he said.

"Yes. Gentleman by the name of Gregory. He used to look in here pretty often. He once took a picture of this show. What a thing to want to take a photo of, I said, but he seemed to enjoy it. I wouldn't have the patience myself."

"Is he in his studio this afternoon?"

"Hasn't been there for three months. He's in Hong Kong."

"Indeed," murmured Alleyn, and he thought: "Easy now. Don't flutter the brute."

"Yes. In Hong Kong taking pictures of the Chinks."

"Would he sublet, do you know?"

"I don't know whether he *would* but he *can't*."

"Why not?"

"Because he promised the loan of it to someone else."

"I see. Then somebody else is using it?"

"That's where the funny part comes in. He isn't. Never turned up."

"Gosh!" thought Alleyn.

"Never turned up," repeated Mr. McCully. "As a matter of fact I asked the boss only yesterday if I might store some bits of furniture there during Christmas because the wife and I are moving and it's a bit awkward what with this and that and the other thing——"

He rambled on. Alleyn listened with an air of sympathetic attention.

"... so the boss said it would be all right if this other chap didn't turn up, but all Mr. Gregory said was that he'd offered the room to this other chap and given him his key, and he'd just come in when he wanted it. So that's how it stands."

"What was this other man's name, do you know?"

"Have I heard it now?" ruminated Mr. McCully, absently accepting another of Alleyn's cigarettes. "Wait a bit now. It was a funny sort of name. Reminded me of something. What was it? By crikey, I remember. It reminded me of the rubbish van—you know—the chaps that come round for the garbage tins."

"Garbage?"

"Garbage—that's the name. Or nearly."

"Something like Garcia, perhaps." And Alleyn thought: "Has he read the evening paper or hasn't he?"

"That's it! Garcia! Well, fancy you getting it. Garcia! That's the chap. Garcia." Mr. McCully laughed delightedly.

Alleyn stood up.

"Look here," he said, "I wish you'd just let me have a look at this place, will you? In case there is a chance of my getting it."

"Well, I suppose there's nothing against that. The boss is away just now, but I don't see how he could object. Not that there's anything to see. We don't go near it from one week to another. I'll just get our key and take you along. Fred!"

"Hooray?" said a voice in the workshop.

"I'm going round to the shed. Back before knock-off."

"Right-oh."

Mr. McCully got a key from behind a door, hooked an old tarpaulin over his shoulders and, talking incessantly, led the way out of the garage by a side door into a narrow alley.

It was now raining heavily. The alley smelt of soot, grease, and stagnant drainage. Water streamed down from defective gutters and splashed about their feet. The deadliness and squalor of the place seemed to close about them. Their footsteps echoed at the far end of the alley.

"Nasty weather," said Mr. McCully. "It's only a step."

They turned to the left into a wider lane that led back towards Cornwall Street. McCully stopped in front of a pair of rickety double-doors fastened with a padlock and chain.

"Here we are, sir. Just half a tick and I'll have her opened. She's a bit stiff."

While he fitted the key in the padlock Alleyn looked up the lane. He thought how like this was to a scene in a modern talking-picture of the realistic school. The sound of the rain, the grime streaked with running trickles, the distant mutter of traffic, and their own figures, black against grey—it was almost a Dostoievsky setting. The key grated in the lock, the chain rattled and McCully dragged the reluctant doors back in their grooves.

"Darkish," he said. "I'll turn up the light."

It was very dark inside the place they had come to. A greyness filtered through dirty skylights. The open doors left a patch of light on a wooden floor, but the far end was quite lost in shadow. McCully's boots clumped over the boards.

"I don't just remember where the switch is," he said, and his voice echoed away into the shadows. Alleyn stood like a figure of stone in the entrance, waiting for the light. McCully's hand fumbled along the wall. There was a click and a dull yellow globe, thick with dust, came to life just inside the door.

"There we are, sir."

Alleyn walked in.

The place at first looked almost empty. A few canvases stood at intervals with their faces to the wall. Half-way down there was a large studio easel, and beyond it, far away from the light, stood a packing-case with a few old chairs and some shadowy bundles. Beyond that again, deep in shadow, Alleyn could distinguish the corner of a table. An acrid smell hung on the air. McCully walked on towards the dark.

"Kind of lonesome, isn't it?" he said. "Not much comfort about it. Bit of a smell, too? There was some storage batteries in here. Wonder if he broke one of them."

"Wait a moment," said Alleyn, but McCully did not hear him.

"There's another light at this end. I'll find the switch in a minute," he said. "It's very dark, isn't it, sir? Cripes, what a stink. You'd think he'd——"

His voice stopped as if someone had gagged him. He stood still. The place was filled with the sound of rain and with an appalling stench.

"What's the matter?" asked Alleyn sharply.

There was no answer.

"McCully! Don't move."

"Who's that!" said McCully violently.

"Where? Where are you?"

"Here—who—*Christ*!"

Alleyn strode swiftly down the room.

"Stay where you are," he said.

"There's someone sitting at the table," McCully whispered.

Alleyn came up with him and caught him by the arm. McCully was trembling like a dog.

"Look! Look there!"

In the shadow cast by the packing-case Alleyn saw the table. The man who sat at it leant across the top and stared at them. His chin seemed to be on the surface of the table. His arms were stretched so far that his hands reached the opposite edge. It was an uncouth posture, the attitude of a scarecrow. They could see the lighter disc that was his face and the faint glint of his eyeballs. Alleyn had a torch in his pocket. He groped for it with one hand and held McCully's arm with the other. McCully swore endlessly in a whisper.

The sharp beam of light ran from the torch to the table. It

ended in the man's face. It was the face of a gargoyle. The eyeballs started from their sockets, the protruding tongue was sulphur yellow. The face was yellow and blue. McCully wrenched his arm from Alleyn's grasp and flung it across his eyes.

Alleyn walked slowly towards the table. The area of light widened to take in an overturned cup and a bottle. There was a silence of a minute broken by McCully.

"Oh, God!" said McCully. "Oh, God, help me! Oh, God!"

"Go back to your office," said Alleyn. "Telephone Scotland Yard. Give this address. Say the message is from Inspector Alleyn. Ask them to send Fox, Bailey, and the divisional surgeon. Here!"

He turned McCully round, marched him towards the door and propped him against the wall.

"I'll write it down." He took out his note-book wrote rapidly and then looked at McCully. The large common face was sheet-white and the lips were trembling.

"Can you pull yourself together?" asked Alleyn. "Or had I better come with you? It would help if you could do it. I'm a C.I.D. officer. We're looking for this man. Come now, can you help me?"

McCully drew the back of his hand across his mouth.

"He's dead," he said.

"Bless my soul, of course he is. Will you take this message? I don't want to bully you. I just want you to tell me if you can do it."

"Give us a moment, will you?"

"Of course."

Alleyn looked up and down the alley.

"Wait here a minute," he said.

He ran through the pelting rain to the top of the alley and looked into Cornwall Street. About two hundred yards away he saw a constable, walking along the pavement towards him. Alleyn waited for him, made himself known, and sent the man off to the nearest telephone. Then he returned to McCully.

"It's all right, McCully, I've found a P.C. Sit down on this box. Here." He pulled a flask from his pocket and made McCully drink. "Sorry I let you in for this," he said. "Now wait here and don't admit anyone. When I've turned up the light at the back of this place, close the doors. You needn't look round."

"If it's all the same to you, sir, I'll wait outside."

"All right. Don't speak to anyone unless they say they're from the Yard."

Using his torch, Alleyn went back to the far end of the room. He found the light switch, turned it on, and heard McCully drag the doors together.

The lamp at this end of the room was much more brilliant. By its light Alleyn examined the man at the table. The body was flaccid. Alleyn touched it, once. The man was dressed in an old mackintosh and a pair of shabby grey trousers. The hands were relaxed, but their position suggested that they had clutched the edge of the table. They were long, the square fingertips were lightly crusted with dry clay and the right thumb and forefinger were streaked with blue. On the backs of the hands Alleyn saw sulphur-coloured patches. Not without an effort he examined the terrible face. There were yellow spots on the jaw amongst the half-grown beard. The mouth was torn, and a glance at the finger-nails showed by what means. On the chin, the table and the floor Alleyn found further ghastly evidence of what had happened before the man died.

Alleyn dropped his silk handkerchief over the head.

He looked at the overturned bottle and cup. The bottle was marked clearly with a label bearing a scarlet cross. It was almost empty and from its neck a corroded patch spread over the table. The same marks appeared on the table round the cup. The table had been heavily coated with dust when the man sat at it. His arms had swept violently across the surface. The floor was littered with broken china and with curiously shaped wooden tools, rather like enormous orange-sticks. Alleyn looked at the feet. The shoes, though shabby and unpolished, had no mud on them. One foot was twisted round the chair-leg, the other had been jammed against the leg of the table. The whole posture suggested unspeakable torture.

Alleyn turned to the packing-case. It was five feet square and well made. One side was hinged and fastened with a bolt. It was not locked. He pulled on his gloves and, touching it very delicately, drew the bolt. The door opened smoothly. Inside the case, on a wheeled platform, was an irregularly shaped object that seemed to be swathed in clothes. Alleyn touched it. The cloths were still damp. "Comedy and Tragedy," he murmured. He began to go over the floor. McCully's and his own wet prints were clear enough, but as far as he could see, with the exception of the area round the table, the wooden boards held no other evidence. He turned his torch on the border where the floor met the wall. There he found a thick deposit of dust down the entire length of the room. In a corner there was a large soft broom. Alleyn looked at this closely, shook the dust from the bristles on to a sheet of paper and then emptied it into an envelope. He returned to the area of floor round the table and inspected every inch of it. He did not disturb the pieces of broken china there, nor the wooden tools, but he found at last one or two strands of dark-brown hair and these he put in an envelope. Then he looked again at the head of the dead man.

Voices sounded, the doors rattled open. Outside in the pouring rain was a police car and a mortuary van. Fox and Bailey stood in the doorway with McCully. Alleyn walked quickly towards them.

"Hullo, Fox."

"Hullo, sir. What's up?"

"Come in. Is Curtis there?"

"Yes. Ready, doctor?"

Dr. Curtis, Alleyn's divisional surgeon, dived out of the car into shelter.

"What the devil have you found, Alleyn?"

"Garcia," said Alleyn.

"Here!" ejaculated Fox.

"Dead?" asked Curtis.

"Very." Alleyn laid his hand on Fox's arm. "Wait a moment. McCully, you can sit in the police car if you like. We shan't be long."

McCully, who still looked very shaken, got into the car. A constable and the man off the local beat joined the group in the doorway.

"I think," said Alleyn, "that before you see the body I had better warn you that it is not a pleasant sight."

"Us?" asked Fox, surprised. "Warn us?"

"Yes, I know. We're pretty well seasoned, aren't we? I've never seen anything quite so beastly as this—not even in Flanders. I think he's taken nitric acid."

"Good God!" said Curtis.

"Come along," said Alleyn.

He led them to the far end of the room, where the man at the table still sat with a coloured handkerchief over his face. Fox, Bailey and Curtis stood and looked at the body.

"What's the stench?" asked Fox. "It's bad, isn't it?"

"Nitric acid?" suggested Bailey.

"And other vomited matter," said Curtis.

"You may smoke, all of you," said Alleyn, and they lit cigarettes.

"Well," said Curtis, "I'd better look at him."

He put out his well-kept doctor's hand and drew away the handkerchief from the face.

"Christ!" said Bailey.

"Get on with it," said Alleyn harshly. "Bailey, I want you to take his prints first. It's Garcia all right. Then compare them with anything you can get from the bottle and cup. Before you touch the bottle we'll take a photograph. Where's Thompson?"

Thompson came in from the car with his camera and flashlight. The usual routine began. Alleyn, looking on, was filled with a violent loathing of the whole scene. Thompson took six photographs of the body and then they covered it. Alleyn began to talk.

"You'd better hear what I make of all this on the face of the information we've already got. Bailey, you carry on while I'm talking. Go over every inch of the table and surrounding area. You've got my case? Good. We'll want specimens of this unspeakable muck on the floor. I'll do that."

"Let me fix it, sir," said Fox. "I'm out of a job, and we'd like to hear your reconstruction of this business."

"You'd better rig something over your nose and mouth. Nitric acid fumes are no more wholesome than they are pleasant, are they, Curtis?"

"Not too good," grunted Curtis. "May as well be careful."

The doors at the end opened to admit the P.C. whom Alleyn had left on guard.

"What is it?" asked Alleyn.

"Gentleman to see you, sir."

"Is his name Bathgate?"

"Yes, sir."

"Miserable young perisher," muttered Alleyn. "Tell him to wait. No. Half a minute. Send him in."

When Nigel appeared Alleyn asked fiercely: "How did you get wind of this?"

"I was down at the Yard. They'd told me you were out. I saw Fox and the old gang tootle away in a car, then the mortuary van popped out. I followed in a taxi. What's up? There's a hell of a stink in here."

"The only reason I've let you in is to stop you pitching some cock-and-bull story to your filthy paper. Sit down in a far corner and be silent."

"All right, all right."

Alleyn turned to the others.

"We'll get on. Don't move the body just yet, Curtis."

"Very good," said Dr. Curtis, who was cleaning his hands with ether. "Speak up, Alleyn. Are you going to tell us this fellow's swallowed nitric acid?"

"I think so."

"Bloody loathsome way of committing suicide."

"He didn't know it was nitric acid."

"Accident?"

"No. Murder."

CHAPTER **XVIII**

One of Five

"I think," said Alleyn, "that we'll start off with the packing-case."

He walked over to it and flashed his torch on the swathed shape inside.

"That, I believe, is Garcia's clay model of the Comedy and Tragedy for the cinema at Westminster. We'll have a look at it when Bailey has dealt with the case and the wet cloths. The point with which I think we should concern ourselves now is this. How did it get here?"

He lit a cigarette from the stump of his old one.

"In the caravan we looked at this morning?" suggested Fox from behind a white handkerchief he had tied across the lower half of his face. He was doing hideous things on the floor with a small trowel and a glass bottle.

"It would seem so, Brer Fox. We found pretty sound evidence that the caravan had been backed up to the window. Twig on the roof, tyre-tracks under the sill, traces of the little wheeled platform on the ledge and the step and floor of the caravan. The discrepancy in the petrol fits in with this place quite comfortably, I think. Very well. That was all fine and dandy as long as Garcia was supposed to have driven himself and his gear up to London, and himself back to Tatler's End House. Now we've got a different story. Someone returned the caravan to Tatler's End House, and that person has kept quiet about it."

"Is it possible," asked Fox, "that Garcia drove the car back and returned here by some other means?"

"Hardly, Fox, I think. On Friday night Garcia was recovering from a pipe or more of opium, and possibly a jorum of whisky. He was in no condition to get his stuff aboard a caravan, drive it thirty miles, open this place up, manoeuvre the caravan inside, unload it, drive it back, and then start off again to tramp back to London or catch a train or bus. But suppose somebody arrived at the studio on Friday night and found Garcia in a state of semi-recovery. Suppose this person offered to drive Garcia up to London and return the caravan. Does that quarrel with anything we have found? I don't think it does. Can we find anything here to support such a theory? I think we can. The front part of the floor has been swept. Why the devil should Garcia sweep the floor of this place at midnight while he was in the condition we suppose him to have been in? Bailey, have you dealt with the bottle on the table?"

"Yes, sir. We've got a fairly good impression of the deceased's left thumb, forefinger and second finger."

"Very good. Will you all look now at the hands?"

Alleyn turned to the shrouded figure. The arms projected from under the sheet. The hands at the far edge of the table were uncovered.

"Rigor mortis," said Alleyn, "has disappeared. The body is flaccid. But notice the difference between the right hand and the left. The fingers of the right are still curved slightly. If I flash this light on the under-surface of the table, you can see the prints left by the fingers when they clutched it. Bailey has brought them up with powder. You took a shot of these, Thompson, didn't you? Good. As rigor wore off, you see, the fingers slackened. Now look at the left hand. It is completely relaxed and the fingers are straight. On the under-surface of the table edge, about three inches to the right of the left hand, are four marks made by the fingers. They are blurred, but the impression was originally a strong one, made with considerable pressure. Notice that the blurs do not seem to have been caused by any relaxation of the fingers. It looks rather as if the pressure had not been relaxed at all, but the fingers dragged up the edge while they still clutched it. Notice that the present position of the hand bears no sort of relation to the prints—it is three inches away from them. Did you find any left-hand prints on the top of the table, Bailey?"

"No, sir."

"No. Now, taking into consideration the nature and direction of the blurs and all the rest of it, in my opinion there is a strong assumption that this hand was forcibly dragged from the edge of the table, possibly while in a condition of cadaveric spasm. At all events, there is nothing here to contradict such an assumption. Now have a look at this cup. It contains dregs of what we believe to be nitric acid and is standing in a stain made, presumably, by nitric acid. It is on the extreme right hand of the body. You've tried it for prints, Thompson, and found——?"

"Four left-hand fingerprints and the thumb."

"Yes, by Jove!" Alleyn bent over the cup. "There's a good impression of the left hand. Now see here. You notice these marks across the table. It was thickly covered in dust when this man sat down at it. Dust on the under-surface of his sleeves—lots of it. If we measure these areas where the dust has been removed and compare it with the length of the sleeve, we find pretty good evidence that he must have swept his arms across the surface of the table. Something like this."

Alleyn took the dead arms and moved them across the table. "You see, they follow the marks exactly. Here on the floor are the things he knocked off. Modeller's tools. A plate—smashed in four pieces. Two dishes that were probably intended for use as etching-baths. There's almost as much dust under them as there is on the rest of the floor, so they haven't been there more than a day or two. They themselves are not very dusty—he brushed them with his sleeves. Agreed that there's a strong likelihood he swept them off?"

"Certainly," said Fox.

"All right. Now look again at the table. This bottle which held the nitric acid and this cup into which it was poured—these two objects we find bang in the middle of the area he swept with his arms in the violent spasm that followed the moment when he drank. Why were they not hurled to the floor with the plate and the modeller's tools?"

"By God, because they were put there afterwards," said Curtis.

"Yes, and why was the cup which he held with his left hand put down on the right of the table with the prints on the far side. To put the cup down where we found it he must have stood where I am now—or here—or perhaps here. Well, say he drank the stuff while he was in such a position. After taking it he put the cup at this end of the table and the bottle, which has a left-hand print, beside it. He then moved to the chair, swept away the other stuff in his death throes, but replaced the bottle and the cup."

"Which is absurd," said Thompson solemnly.

"Ugh," said Bailey.

"I think it is," said Alleyn. He glanced at Curtis. "What would happen when he drank nitric acid?"

"Undiluted?"

"I think so."

"Very quick and remarkably horrible." Curtis gave a rapid description of what would happen. "He wouldn't perform any intelligent action. The initial shock would be terrific, and intense spasms would follow immediately. It's quite beyond the bounds of possibility that he would replace the cup, seat himself, or do anything but make some uncontrolled and violent movements such as you've described in reference to the arms. But I cannot believe, Alleyn, that anybody in his senses could ever take nitric acid without knowing what he was doing."

"If he was not in his senses, but half doped with opium, and very thirsty? If he asked for a drink and it was put beside him?"

"That's more likely, certainly, but still——"

"If he was asleep in this chair with his mouth open, and it was poured into his mouth," said Alleyn. "What about that?"

"Well then—of course"—Curtis shrugged—"that would explain everything."

"It may be the explanation," said Alleyn. "The stuff had spilled over the face very freely. I want you now to look at the back of the head." With his long, fastidious fingers he uncovered the hair, leaving the face·veiled.

"He wore his hair long, you see. Now look here. Look. Do you see these tufts of hair that are shorter? They seem to have been broken, don't they? And see this. Hold your torch down and use a lens. The scalp is slightly torn as though a strand of hair has actually been wrenched away. On the floor behind this chair I found several hairs, and some of them have little flakes of scalp on the ends. Notice how the hair round the torn scalp is tangled. What's the explanation? Doesn't it suggest that a hand has been twisted in this hair? Now see the back of the chair. I think we shall find that these stains were make by nitric acid, and the floor beneath is stained in the same way. These are nitric stains—I'm afraid I'll have to uncover the face—yes—you see, running from the corners of the mouth down the line of the jaw to the ears and the neck. Notice the direction. It's important. It suggests strongly that the head was leaning back, far back, when the stuff was taken. Now if we lean him back in the chair—God, this is a filthy business! All right Bathgate, damn you, get out. Now, Curtis, and you, Fox. Look how the head fits between the acid stains on the back of the chair, and how the stains carry on from the jaw to the chair as if the stuff had run down. Would a man ever drink in this attitude with his face to the ceiling? Don't you get a picture of someone standing behind him and pouring something into his mouth? He gasps and makes a violent spasmodic movement. A hand is wound in his hair and holds back his head. And still nitric acid is poured between his lips. God! Cover it up again. Now, let's go to the door."

They walked in silence down the place, opened the door, and were joined by a very green Nigel. Alleyn filled his pipe and lit it. "To sum up," he said, "and for Heaven's sake, all of you, check me if I go too far—we have difficulty in fitting the evidence of the hands, the table, the position of the body, the cup and the bottle, with any theory of suicide. On the other hand, we find nothing to contradict the suggestion that this man sat at this table, was given a dose of nitric acid, made a series of violent and convulsive movements, vomited, clutched the edge of the table and died. We find nothing to contradict the theory that his murderer dragged the left hand away from the ledge of the table and used it to print the bottle and the cup, and then left them on the table. I don't for a moment suggest there is a good case for us here, but at least there is a better case for murder than for suicide." He looked from one dubious face to another.

"I know it's tricky," he said. "Curtis—how long would he take to die?"

"Difficult to say. Fourteen hours. Might be more, might be less."

"Fourteen hours! Damn and blast! That blows the whole thing sky-high."

"Wait a moment, Alleyn. Have we any idea how much of the stuff he took?"

"The bottle was full. Miss Troy and Miss Bostock said it was full on Friday morning. Allowing for the amount that splashed over, it must have been quite a cupful."

"This is the most shocking affair," said little Curtis. "I—never in the whole course of my experience have I—however. My dear chap, if a stream of the stuff was poured into his mouth while his head was held back, he may have died in a few minutes of a particularly unspeakable form of asphyxiation. Actually, we may find he got some of it down his larynx, in which case death would be essentially from obstruction to breathing and would take place very quickly unless relieved by tracheotomy. You notice that the portions of the face that are not discoloured by acid are bluish. That bears out this theory. If you are right, I suppose that's what we shall find. We'd better clear up here and get the body away. We'll have the autopsy as soon as possible."

It was almost dark when they got back to the Yard. Alleyn went straight to his room, followed by Fox and by a completely silent Nigel. Alleyn dropped into an arm-chair. Fox switched on the light.

"You want a drink, sir," he said, with a look at Alleyn.

"We all do. Bathgate, I don't know what the hell you're doing here, but if you are going to be ill, you can get out. We've had enough of that sort of thing."

"I'm all right now," said Nigel. "What shall I do about this? The late edition——"

"A hideous curse on the late edition! All right. Tell them we've found him and where, and suggest suicide. That's all. Go away, there's a good chap."

Nigel went.

"For pity's sake, Fox," said Alleyn violently, "why do you stand there staring at me like a benevolent bullock? Is my face dirty?"

"No, sir, but it's a bit white. Now, you have that drink, Mr. Alleyn, before we go any further. I've got my emergency flask here."

"I poured most of mine down McCully's gullet," said Alleyn. "Very well, Fox. Thank you. Have one yourself and let's be little devils together. Now then, where do we stand? You were very silent in that place of horror. Do you agree with my theory?"

"Yes, sir, I do. I've been turning it over in my mind and I don't see how any other theory will fit all the facts, more especially the tuft of hair torn from the scalp and found, as you might say, for the greater part on the floor."

Fox briefly sucked in his short moustache and wiped his hand across his mouth.

"He must have jerked about very considerably," he said, "and have been held on to very determinedly."

"Very."

"Yes. Now, sir, as we know only too well, it's one thing to have a lot of circumstantial evidence and another to tie somebody up in it. As far as times go, we're all over the shop here, aren't we? Some time late Friday night or early Saturday morning's the nearest we can get to when Garcia left Tatler's End House. All we can say about the time the caravan was returned is that it was probably before it was light on Saturday morning. Now, which of this crowd could have got away for at least two hours——"

"At the very least."

"Yes. Two hours between seven-thirty on Friday evening, when Sadie Welsh heard Garcia speak, and before anybody was about—say, five o'clock—on Saturday morning. Do you reckon any of the lot that were up in London may have met him here?"

"Murdered him, taken the caravan to Tatler's End House and returned here—how?"

"That's true."

"And I repeat, Fox, that I cannot believe a man in Garcia's condition could have gone through all the game with the caravan and the transport. We don't even know if he could drive and I should not be at all surprised if we find he couldn't. It would take a tolerably good driver to do all this. If it was one of the London lot, he went to Tatler's End House by means unknown, brought Garcia here and murdered him, returned the caravan and came back here, again by means unknown. You've seen the alibis. Pretty hopeless to fit anything on to any single one of them, isn't it?"

"I suppose so."

"Except, perhaps, Malmsley. Could Malmsley have stayed behind and not caught the six o'clock bus? Where's the stuff about Malmsley?"

Fox got a file from the desk and thumbed it over.

"Here we are, sir. I saw the conductor of the six o'clock this morning. He says four people got on at Bossicote corner on Friday evening. One woman and three men. He's a dull sort of chap. I asked him if any of the men had beards and he said he couldn't rightly remember, but he thinks one had a very wide-brimmed hat and wore a muffler, so he might have had a beard. Silly sort of chap. We did see a wide-brimmed affair in Malmsley's wardrobe, too, but we'll have to try and get closer to it than that."

"Yes. If Malmsley did it, what about his dinner at the Savoy and his late night with his friend? I suppose he could have driven the caravan, killed Garcia and left the body here at about seven to eight-thirty, come back after he'd seen his friend to bed, and done all the rest of it. But how the devil did he get back from the studio to London after returning the caravan?"

"That's right." Fox licked his thumb and turned a page. "Now, here's Miss Troy and Miss Bostock. Their alibis are the only ones we seem to have a chance of breaking among the London push. They've been checked up all right and were both seen by the club night porter when they came in, Miss Bostock at about one o'clock and Miss Troy at two-twenty. I've seen Miss Troy's friend, Mr. Bellasca, and he says he took her back to the club at two-twenty or thereabouts. So that fits."

"Is he a reliable sort of fellow?"

"I think so, sir. He's very concerned on Miss Troy's behalf. He's been ringing her up, but apparently she didn't exactly encourage him to go down there. He's a very open sort of young gentleman and said she always treated him as if he was a schoolboy. However, the time at the club's all right. The porter says definitely he let Miss Troy in at two-twenty. She exclaimed at the time, he says, so he remembered that. He says neither she nor Miss Bostock came out again, but he sits in a little cubby-hole by the lift, and may have dozed off. The garage is open all night. Their car was by the door. The chap there admits he slipped out to the coffee stall at about three o'clock." Fox glanced up from the notes, looked fixedly at Alleyn's white face, and then cleared his throat. "Not that I'm suggesting there's anything in that," he said.

"Go on," said Alleyn.

"Well, sir, we may still admit there's a possibility in the cases of these two ladies and Malmsley. On the evidence in this file I'd say all the others are wash-outs. That leaves us with what you might call a narrowed field. The Hon. Basil Pilgrim, Miss Seacliff, Miss Troy, Miss Bostock, and Mr. Malmsley."

"Yes. Oh Lord, Fox, I forgot to ask Bathgate if he had any success with Miss Bobbie O'Dawne. I must be sinking into a detective's dotage. I'd better go along and tell the A.C. about this afternoon. Then I'll write up my report and I think this evening we'd better go broody on the case."

Alleyn had a long interview with his Assistant Commissioner, a dry man with whom he got on very well. He then wrote up his report and took Fox off to dine at his own flat in a cul-de-sac off Coventry Street. After dinner they settled down over the fire to a systematic review of the whole case.

At eleven o'clock, while they were still at it, Nigel turned up.

"Hullo," said Alleyn, "I rather wanted to see you."

"I guessed as much," said Nigel complacently.

"Get yourself a drink. How did you hit it off with Bobbie O'Dawne? I see your extraordinary paper has come out strong with a simpering portrait."

"Good, isn't it? She liked me awfully. We clicked."

"Anything to the purpose?"

"Ah, ah, ah! *Wouldn't* you like to know!"

"We are not in the mood," said Alleyn, "for comedy."

"All right. As a matter of fact, I'm afraid from your point of view the visit was not a howling success. She said she wouldn't have Sonia's name blackened in print and gave me a lot of stuff about how Sonia was the greatest little pal and a real sport. I took her out to lunch and gave her champagne, for which I expect the Yard to reimburse me. She got fairly chatty, but nothing much to the purpose. I told her I knew all about Sonia's little blackmailing games with Pilgrim and Malmsley, and she said that was just a bit of fun. I asked her if Sonia had the same kind of fun with anybody else, and she told me, with a jolly laugh, to mind my own business. I filled up her glass and she did get a bit unreserved. She said Garcia found out Sonia had told her about the Pilgrim game. Garcia was absolutely livid and said he'd do Sonia in if she couldn't hold her tongue. Of course, Sonia told Bobbie all this and made her swear on a Bible and a rosary that she wouldn't split to anyone. It was at this stage, Alleyn that Bobbie took another pull at her champagne and then said—I memorised her actual words—'So you see, dear, with an oath like that on my conscience I couldn't say anything about Friday night, could I?' I said: 'How d'you mean?' and she said: 'Never mind, dear. She oughtn't to have told me. Now I'm scared. If he knows she told me, as sure as God's above us he'll do for me, too.' And then, as there was no more champagne, the party broke up."

"Well—I'll pay for the champagne," said Alleyn. "Damn this girl, Fox, she's tiresome. Sink me if I don't believe she knows who had the date with Garcia on Friday night. She's proved that it wasn't Sonia. Sonia spent the week-end with her. Well—who was it?"

The telephone rang. Alleyn picked up the receiver. "Hullo. Yes, Bailey? I see. He's sure of that? Yes. Yes, I see. Thank you."

He put down the receiver and looked at Fox.

"The hole on the cuff of Pilgrims' coat was made by an acid. Probably nitric acid."

"Is that so?" said Fox. He rose slowly to his feet.

"There's your answer!" cried Nigel. "I don't see how you can get away from it, Alleyn. You've got motive and opportunity. You've got evidence of a man who stood in the lane and looked in at the studio window. It might just have been Malmsley, but by God, I think it was Pilgrim."

"In that case," said Alleyn, "we'll call on Captain and Mrs. Pascoe at Boxover, where Pilgrim and Miss Seacliff spent the night. Run along, Bathgate. I want to talk to Inspector Fox. I'm most grateful for your work with Bobbie O'Dawne, and I won't tell your wife you spend your days with ladies of the chorus. Good evening."

CHAPTER **XIX**

Alleyn Makes a Pilgrimage

The inquest on the body of Sonia Gluck was held at Bossicote on the morning of Thursday, September 22nd. The court, as might have been expected, was jammed to the doors; otherwise the proceedings were as colourless as the coroner, a gentleman with an air of irritated incredulity, could make them. He dealt roundly with the witnesses and with the evidence, reducing everything by a sort of sleight-of-hand to a dead norm. One would have thought that models impaled on the points of poignards were a commonplace of police investigation. Only once did he appear to be at all startled and that was when Cedric Malmsley gave evidence. The coroner eyed Malmsley's beard as if he thought it must be detachable, abruptly changed his own glasses, and never removed his outraged gaze from the witness throughout his evidence. The barest outline of the tragedy was brought out. Alleyn gave formal evidence on the finding of Garcia's body, and the court was fraught with an unspoken inference that it was a case of murder and suicide. Alleyn asked for an adjournment, and the whole thing was over by eleven o'clock.

In the corridor Alleyn caught Fox by the arm.

"Come on, Brer Fox. We're for Boxover. The first stop in the pilgrimage. I've got my mother's car— looks less official. It's over there—wait for me, will you?"

He watched Fox walk away and then turned quickly into a side lane where Troy sat in her three-seater. Alleyn came up to her from behind, and she did not see him. She was staring straight in front of her. He stood there with his hat in his hands, waiting for her to turn her head. When at last she woke from her meditation and saw him, her eyes widened. She looked at him gravely and then smiled.

"Hullo. It's you," said Troy. "I'm waiting for Katti."

"I had to say a word to you," said Alleyn.

"What is it?"

"I don't know. Any word. Are you all right?"

"Yes, thank you."

"I'm afraid it's difficult for you," said Alleyn, "having all these people still in the house. This second case made it necessary. We can't let them go."

"It's all right. We're doing some work out of doors when it's fine, and I've moved everything round in the studio and got a man from the village to sit. Katti's doing a life-size thing of the policeman at the front gate. It's a bit—difficult—at times, but they seem to have made up their minds Garcia did it."

"This last thing—about Garcia. It's been a pretty bad shock to you."

"In a way—yes," said Troy. "It was kind of you to send me a telegram."

"Kind! Oh, well, if it broke the news a bit, that's something. You had no particular feeling about him, had you? It was his work, wasn't it?"

"True enough. His work. That clay group was really good, you know. I think it would have been the best thing he ever did. Somebody will do the marble from the model, I suppose." She looked directly into Alleyn's eyes. "I'm—I'm horrified," she whispered.

"I know."

"Nitric acid! It's so beyond the bounds of one's imagination that anyone could possibly——Please tell me—they seemed to suggest that Garcia himself——I *must* know. Did he kill her and then himself? I can't believe he did. He would never do that. The first—all that business with the knife—I *can* imagine him suddenly deciding to kill Sonia like that. In a ghastly sort of way it might appeal to his imagination, but it's just because his imagination was so vivid that I am sure he wouldn't kill himself so horribly. Why—why, Ormerin once spilt acid from that bottle on his hand—Garcia was there. He knew. He saw the burn."

"He was drugged at the time he died. He'd been smoking opium."

"Garcia! But——All right. It's not fair to ask you questions."

"I'm so sorry. I think we're nearly at an end. Tomorrow, perhaps, we shall know."

"Don't look so—so worried," said Troy suddenly.

"I wonder if it has ever entered your head," said Alleyn, "that it is only by wrenching my thoughts round with a remarkable effort that I can keep them on my job and not on you."

She looked at him without speaking.

"Well," he said. "What have you got to say to that, Troy?"

"Nothing. I'm sorry. I'd better go."

"A woman never actually objects to a man getting into this state of mind about her, does she? I mean—as long as he behaves himself?"

"No. I don't think she does."

"Unless she happens to associate him with something particularly unpleasant. As you must me. Good God, I'm a pretty sort of fellow to shove my damned attentions on a lady in the middle of a job like this."

"You're saying too much," said Troy. "You must stop. Please."

"I'm extremely sorry. You're perfectly right—it was unpardonable. Good-bye."

He stood back. Troy made a swift movement with her hands and leant towards him.

"Don't be so 'pukka sahib,'" she said. "It is quite true—a woman doesn't mind."

"Troy!"

"Now I'm saying too much. It's her vanity. Even mixed up with horrors like these she rather likes it."

"We seem to be an odd pair," said Alleyn. "I haven't the smallest idea of what you think of me. No, truly, not the smallest idea. But even in the middle of police investigations we appear to finish our thoughts. Troy, have you ever thought of me when you were alone?"

"Naturally."

"Do you dislike me?"

"No."

"That will do to go on with," said Alleyn. "Good morning."

With his hat still in his hand he turned and walked away quickly to his mother's car.

"Off we go, Fox," he said. "Alley houp! The day is ours."

He slipped in the clutch and in a very few minutes they were travelling down a fortunately deserted road at fifty miles an hour. Fox cleared his throat.

"What's that, Brer Fox?" asked Alleyn cheerfully.

"I didn't speak, Mr. Alleyn. Are we in a hurry?"

"Not particularly. I have a disposition of speed come upon me."

"I see," said Fox dryly.

Alleyn began to sing.

> *"Au claire de la lune*
> *Mon ami, Pierrot."*

Trees and hedges flew past in a grey blur. From the back of the car a muffled voice suddenly chanted:

> "I thought I saw Inspector Alleyn hunting for a clue.
> I looked again and saw it was an inmate of the Zoo.
> 'Good God,' I said, 'it's very hard to judge between
> these two.'"

Alleyn took his foot off the accelerator. Fox slewed round and stared into the back of the car. From an unheaval of rugs Nigel's head emerged.

> "I thought," he continued, "I saw Gargantua in fancy
> worsted socks.
> I looked again and saw it was a mammoth picking locks.
> 'Good God,' I said, 'it might have been my friend
> Inspector Fox.'"

"Rude is never funny," said Alleyn. "When did you hide in my mother's car?"

"Immediately after the old gentleman pronounced the word 'adjournment.' Where are we bound for?"

"I shan't tell you. Alley houp! Away we go again."

"Mr. Fox," said Nigel, "what has overtaken your chief? Is he mad, drunk, or in love?"

"Don't answer the fellow, Brer Fox," said Alleyn. "Let him burst in ignorance. Sit down, behind, there."

They arrived at Boxover and drew up outside a rather charming Georgian house on the outskirts of the village.

"Twenty minutes," said Alleyn, looking from his watch to the speedometer. "Twenty minutes from Bossicote and twelve miles. It's two miles from the studio to Bossicote. Fourteen miles and a straightish road. We slowed down once on Bathgate's account and once to ask the way. At night you could do the whole trip in a quarter of an hour or less. Now then. A certain amount and yet not too much finesse is indicated. Come on, Fox."

"May I come?" asked Nigel.

"You? You have got the most colossal, the most incredible, the most appalling cheek. Your hide! Your effrontery! Well, well, well. Come along. You are a Yard typist. Wait by the car until I give you a leery nod, both of you."

He rang the front-door bell and whistled very sweetly and shrilly.

"What *is* the matter with him, Fox?" asked Nigel.

"Search me, Mr. Bathgate. He's been that worried over this case ever since we found Garcia, you'd think he'd never crack a joke again, and then he comes out from this inquest, crosses the road to have a word with Miss Troy and comes back, as you might say, with bells on."

"Oh ho!" said Nigel. "Say you so, Fox. By gum, Fox, do you suppose——"

The door was opened by a manservant. Alleyn spoke to him and gave him a card. The man stood back and Alleyn, with a grimace at them over his shoulder, stepped inside, leaving the door open.

"Come on, Mr. Bathgate," said Fox. "That means us."

They joined Alleyn in a little hall that was rather overwhelmed with the horns, masks, and hides of dead animals.

"Mrs. Pascoe is away," whispered Alleyn, "but the gallant captain is within. Here he comes."

Captain Pascoe was short, plump and vague-looking. He had prominent light blue eyes and a red face. He smelt of whisky. He looked doubtfully from Alleyn to Fox.

"I'm sorry to bother you, Captain Pascoe," said Alleyn.

"That's all right. You're from Scotland Yard, aren't you? This business over at Bossicote, what?"

"That's it. We're checking up everybody's movements on the night in question—you'll understand it has to be done."

"Oh quite. Routine, what?"

"Exactly. Inspector Fox and Mr. Bathgate are with me."

"Oh ya'," said Captain Pascoe. "H' are y'. H' are y'. Have a drink."

"Thank you so much, but I think we'll get on with the job."

"Oh. Right-ho. I suppose it's about Valmai—Miss Seacliff—and Pilgrim, isn't it? I've been followin' the case. Damn' funny, isn't it? They're all right. Spent Friday here with us. Slept here and went on to old Pilgrim's place next day."

"So they told us. I'm just going to ask you to check up the

times. It won't take a moment."

"Oh, quite. Right-ho. Sit down."

Alleyn led him through the week-end from the moment when Valmai Seacliff and Pilgrim arrived, up to the time they all sat down to dinner. Captain Pascoe said nothing to contradict the information given by the other two. Alleyn complimented him on his memory and on the crispness of his recital, which was anything but crisp. The little man expanded gratefully.

"And now," said Alleyn, "we come to the important period between ten o'clock on Friday night and five the following morning. You are a soldier, sir, and you understand the difficulties of this sort of thing. One has to be very discreet——" Alleyn waved his hands and looked respectfully at Captain Pascoe.

"By Jove, ya'. I 'member there was a feller in my reg'ment"—the anecdote wound itself up into an impenetrable tangle—"and, by Jove, we nearly had a court martial over it."

"Exactly. Just the sort of thing we want to avoid. So you see, if we can account, now, for every second of their time during Friday evening they will be saved a lot of unpleasantness later on. You know yourself, sir——"

"Oh, quite. All for it. Damned unpleasant. Always flatter myself I've got the faculty of observing detail."

"Yes. Now, I understand that during dinner Miss Seacliff complained of a headache?"

"No, no. Not till after dinner. Minor point, but we may's well be accurate, Inspector."

"Certainly, sir. Stupid of me. Was it about the time you had coffee that she first spoke of it?"

"No. Wait a bit, though. Tell you what—just to show you—what I was saying about my faculty for tabulatin' detail——"

"Yes."

"I 'member Valmai made a face over her coffee. Took a swig at it and then did a sort of shudder and m'wife said: 'What's up?' or words to the same effect, and Val said the coffee was bitter, and then Pilgrim looked a bit sheepish and I said: 'Was yours bitter?' and he said: 'Matter of fact it was!' Funny—mine was all right. But my idea is that Val was feeling a bit off colour then, and he just agreed the coffee was bitter to keep her in countenance. In my opinion the girl had a liver.

224

Pilgrim persuaded her to have a glass of port after champagne, and she said at the time it would upset her. Damn' bad show. She's a lovely thing. Damn' good rider to hounds. Lovely hands. Goes as straight and as well as the best of 'em. Look at that." He fumbled in a drawer of his writing-desk and produced a press photograph of Valmai Seacliff looking magnificent on a hunter. Captain Pascoe gloated over it, handed it to Alleyn, and flung himself back in his chair. He appeared to collect his thoughts. "But to show you how one notices little things," he resumed. "Not till after dinner that she talked about feeling under the weather. Matter of fact, it was when I took her empty cup. Precise moment. There you are." And he laughed triumphantly.

"Splendid, sir. I wish everyone was as clear-minded. I remember a case where the whole thing hinged on just such an incident. It was a question of who put sugar in a cup of tea, and do you think we could get anyone who remembered? Not a bit of it. It's only one witness in a hundred who can give us that sort of thing."

"Really? Well, I'll lay you a tenner, Inspector, I can tell you about the coffee on Friday night. Just for the sake of argument."

"I'm not betting, sir."

"Ha, ha, ha. Now then. M'wife poured out our coffee at that table over there. Pilgrim handed it round for her. He put Val's down beside her with his own, told her he'd put sugar in it, and went back to the table for mine. There you are, Inspector. Val complained her coffee was bitter. She asked Pilgrim if his tasted funny and he said it did, and——" He stopped short and his eyes bulged. "Look here," he said, "'way I'm talking anybody might think this was a case of hanky-panky with the coffee. Good Lord, Inspector. Here! I say, I hope you don't——"

"Don't let that bother you, sir. We're only taking a sample case and I congratulate you. We don't get our information as lucidly as that very often, do we, Fox?"

"Very nice, indeed, sir," agreed Fox, wagging his head.

"And then," said Alleyn, "I believe you played bridge?"

"Yes. That's right. But by that time Val was looking very seedy and said her head was splitting, so after two or three hands we chucked it up and m'wife took Val up to her room."

"Gave her some aspirin perhaps?"

"No. Pilgrim rushed off and got some aspirin for her.

Anxious about her as an old hen. Engaged couples, what? Ha! She took the bottle up with her. M'wife tucked her up and went to her own room. Pilgrim said he was sleepy—I must say he's a dreary young blighter. Not nearly good enough for Val. Said he felt like bed and a long sleep. Dull chap. So we had a whisky and soda and turned in. That was at half-past ten. I wound up the clocks, and we went and had a look at Val and found she was in bed. Very attractive creature, Val. Naughty little thing hadn't taken the aspirin. Said it made her sick trying to swallow. So Pilgrim dissolved three in water and she promised she'd take 'em. M'wife looked in later and found her sound sleep. We were all tucked up and snoozing by eleven, I should think. And now let's see. Following morning——"

Captain Pascoe described the following morning with a wealth of detail to which Alleyn listened with every sign of respect and appreciation. Drinks were again suggested. "Well, if you won't, I will," said Captain Pascoe, and did, twice. Alleyn asked to see the bedrooms. Captain Pascoe mixed himself a third drink, and somewhat noisily escorted them over the house. The guest-rooms were at the top of the stairs.

"Val had this one, and that fellow was next door. What! Felt like a good long sleep! My God." Here the captain laughed uproariously and pulled himself together. "Not that Val'd stand any nonsense. Thoroughly nice gal. Looks very cometoish, but b'lieve me—na poo. I know. Too much other way 'fanything. I mean, give you ninstance. Following morning took her round rose garden. Looking lovely. Little purple cap and little purple gloves. Lovely. Just in friendly spirit I said, ''ffected little thing, wearing little purple gloves,' and gave little left-hand purple glove little squeeze. Just like that. Purely platonicalistic. Jumped as if I'd bitten her and snatched away. Pooff!"

Captain Pascoe sat on the edge of Valmai's bed and finished his drink. He glared round the room, sucking his upper lip.

"Tchah!" he said suddenly. "Look 't that. Disgraceful. Staff work in this house is abominable. M'wife's away. Maid's away. Only that feller to look after me. Meals at club. Nothing to do, and look at that."

He pointed unsteadily to the mantelpiece.

"'Bominable. Never been touched. Look at this!"

He turned his eye on the bedside table. Upon it stood a row of books. A dirty table-napkin lay on top of the books.

Captain Pascoe snatched it up. Underneath it was a tumbler holding three fingers of murky fluid.

"D'yer know what that is? That's been there since Friday night. I mean!" He lurched again towards the bedside table. Alleyn slipped in front of him.

"Maddening, that sort of thing. I wonder if we might see Mr. Pilgrim's room, sir."

"By George, we'll see every room in this house," shouted Captain Pascoe. "By God, we'll catch them red-handed."

With this remarkable pronouncement he turned about and made for the door. Alleyn followed him, looked over his shoulder at Fox, raised his left eyebrow, and disappeared.

To Nigel's surprise, Fox said: "Wait here, Mr. Bathgate, please," darted out of the room and reappeared in about a minute.

"Stand by that door if you please, Mr. Bathgate," whispered Fox. "Keep the room clear."

Nigel stood by the door and Fox, with surprising dexterity and speed, whipped a small wide-necked bottle from his pocket, poured the contents of the tumbler into it, corked it, and wrapped the tumbler in his handkerchief.

"Now, sir. If you'll take those down to the car and put them in the chief's case—thank you very much. Quickly does it."

When Nigel got back he found that Captain Pascoe, accompanied by Alleyn, had returned to the hall and was yelling for his servant. The servant arrived and was damned to heaps. Fox came down. Captain Pascoe suddenly collapsed into an arm-chair, showed signs of drowsiness, and appeared to lose all interest in his visitors. Alleyn spoke to the servant.

"We are police officers and are making a few inquiries about the affair at Bossicote. Will you show us the garage, please?"

"Very good, sir," said the man stolidly.

"It's nothing whatever to do with your employer, personally, by the way."

Captain Pascoe's servant bestowed a disappointed glance upon his master and led his visitors out by the front door.

"The garage is a step or two down the lane, sir. The house, being old and what they call restored, hasn't many conveniences."

"Do you keep early hours here? What time do you get up in the mornings?"

"Breakfast is not till ten, sir. The maids are supposed to get up at seven. It's more like half-past. The Captain and Mrs.

Pascoe breakfast in their rooms, you see, and so do most guests."

"Did Mr. Pilgrim and Miss Seacliff breakfast in their rooms?"

"Oh yes, sir. There's the garage, sir."

He showed them a double garage about two hundred yards down the lane. Captain Pascoe's Morris Cowley occupied less than half the floor space.

"Ah yes," said Alleyn. "Plenty of room here. I suppose, now, that Mr. Pilgrim's car fitted in very comfortably?"

"Oh yes, sir."

"Nice car, isn't it?"

"Very nice job, sir. Tiger on petrol, sir."

"Really? What makes you think that?"

"Well, sir, I asked the gentleman on Saturday morning was she all right for petrol—I'm butler-chauffeur, sir—and he said yes, she was filled up as full as she'd go in Bossicote. Well, sir, I looked at the gauge and she'd eaten up two gallons coming over here. Twelve miles, sir, no more. I looked to see if she was leaking but she wasn't. Something wrong there, sir, isn't there?"

"I agree with you," said Alleyn. "Thank you very much, I think that's all."

"Thank you very much indeed, sir," said the butler-chauffeur, closing his hand gratefully.

Alleyn, Fox and Nigel returned to their car and drove away.

"Get that tumbler, Fox?" asked Alleyn.

"Yes, sir. And the liquid. Had to go down to the car for a bottle."

"Good enough. What a bit of luck, Fox! You remember the Seacliff told us Mrs. Pascoe was leaving on Saturday and giving the maids a holiday? My golly, *what* a bit of luck."

"Do you think that stuff was the melted aspirin Pilgrim doled out for her on Friday night?" asked Nigel.

"That's my clever little man," said Alleyn. "I do think so. And if the tumbler has Pilgrim's prints, and only his, we'll know."

"Are you going to have the stuff analysed?"

"Yes. Damn' quick about it, too, if possible."

"And what then?"

"Why then," said Alleyn, "we'll be within sight of an arrest."

CHAPTER XX

Arrest

The analysts' report on the contents of the tumbler came through at nine-thirty that evening. The fluid contained a solution of Bayer's Aspirin—approximately three tablets. The glass bore a clear imprint of Basil Pilgrim's fingers and thumb. When Alleyn had read the analysts' report he rang up his Assistant Commissioner, had a long talk with him, and then sent for Fox.

"There's one thing we must make sure of," he said wearily, "and that's the position of the light on the figure outside the studio window. Our game with the string wasn't good enough. We'll have to get something a bit more positive, Brer Fox."

"Meaning, sir?"

"Meaning, alas, a trip to Tatler's End."

"Now?"

"I'm afraid so. We'll have a Yard car. It'll be needed in the morning. Come on."

So for the last time Alleyn and Fox drove through the night to Tatler's End House. The Bossicote church clock struck midnight as Fox took up his old position outside the studio window. A fine drizzle was falling, and the lane smelt of leaf-mould and wet grass. The studio lights were on and the blind was drawn down.

"I shall now retire to the shady spot where Ethel and her boy lost themselves in an interlude of modified rapture," said Alleyn.

He walked down the lane and returned in a few minutes.

"Fox," he said, "the ray of light that comes through the hole in the blind alights upon your bosom. I think we are on the right track."

"Looks like it," Fox agreed. "What do we do now?"

"We spend the rest of the night with my mamma. I'll ring

up the Yard and get the official party to pick us up at Danes Lodge in the morning. Come on."

"Very good, Mr. Alleyn. Er——"

"What's the matter?"

"Well, sir, I was thinking of Miss Troy. It's going to be a bit unpleasant for her, isn't it? I was wondering if we couldn't do something to make it a bit easier."

"Yes, Fox. That's rather my idea, too. I think—damn it all, it's too late to bother her now. Or is it? I'll ring up from Danes Lodge. Come on."

They got to Danes Lodge at twelve-thirty, and found Lady Alleyn reading D. H. Lawrence before a roaring fire in her little sitting-room.

"Good evening," said Lady Alleyn. "I got your message, Roderick. How nice to see you again, Mr. Fox. Come and sit down."

"I'm just going to the telephone," said Alleyn. "Won't be long."

"All right, darling. Mr. Fox, help yourself to a drink and come and tell me if you have read any of this unhappy fellow's books."

Fox put on his spectacles and gravely inspected the outside of *The Letters of D. H. Lawrence*.

"I can't say I have, my lady," he said, "but I seem to remember we cleaned up an exhibition of this Mr. Lawrence's pictures a year or two ago. Very fashionable show it was."

"Ah yes. Those pictures. What did you think of them?"

"I don't exactly know," said Fox. "They seemed well within the meaning of the act, I must say, but the colours were pretty. You wouldn't have cared for the subjects, my lady."

"Shouldn't I? He seems never to have found his own centre of gravity, poor fellow. Some of these letters are wise and some are charming, and some are really rather tedious. All these negroid deities growling in his interior! One feels sorry for his wife, but she seems to have had the right touch with him. Have you got your drink? That's right. Are you pleased with your progress in this case?"

"Yes, thank you. It's coming on nicely."

"And so you are going to arrest somebody tomorrow morning? I thought as much. One can always tell by my son's manner when he is going to make an arrest. He gets a pinched look."

"So does his prisoner, my lady," said Fox, and was so enraptured with his own pun that he shook from head to foot with amazed chuckles.

"Roderick!" cried Lady Alleyn as her son came in, "Mr. Fox is making nonsense of your mother."

"He's a wise old bird if he can do that," said Alleyn. "Mamma, I've asked Miss Agatha Troy if she will lunch here with you to-morrow. She says she will. Do you mind? I shan't be here."

"But I'm delighted, darling. She will be charming company for me and for Mr. Bathgate."

"What the devil——!"

"Mr. Bathgate is motoring down to-morrow to their cottage to see his wife. He asked if he might call in."

"It's forty miles off his course, the little tripe-hound."

"Is it, darling? When I told him you would be here he said he'd arrive soon after breakfast."

"Really, mum! Oh well, I suppose it's all right. He's well trained. But I'm afraid he's diddled you."

"He thinks he has, at all events," said Lady Alleyn. "And now, darling, as you are going to make an arrest in the morning, don't you think you ought to get a good night's sleep?"

"Fox!"

"Mr. Fox has been fabulously discreet, Roderick."

"Then how did you know we were going to arrest anybody?"

"You have just told me, my poor baby. Now run along to bed."

At ten o'clock the next morning two police cars drove up to Tatler's End House. They were followed by Nigel in a baby Austin. He noted, with unworthy satisfaction, that one or two young men in flannel trousers and tweed coats hung about the gate and had evidently been refused admittance by the constable on duty. Nigel himself had been given a card by Alleyn on the strict understanding that he behaved himself and brought no camera with him. He was not allowed to enter the house. He had, he considered, only a minor advantage over his brother journalists.

The three cars drew up in the drive. Alleyn, Fox, and two plain-clothes men went up the steps to the front door. Nigel manoeuvred his baby Austin into a position of vantage. Alleyn glanced down at him and then turned away as Troy's butler opened the front door.

"Will you come in, please?" said the butler nervously. He showed them into Troy's library. A fire had been lit and the room would now have seemed pleasantly familiar to Alleyn if he had been there on any other errand.

"Will you tell Miss Troy of our arrival, please?"

The butler went out.

"I think, Fox, if you don't mind——" said Alleyn.

"Certainly, sir. We'll wait in the hall."

Troy came in.

"Good morning," said Alleyn, and his smile contradicted the formality of his words. "I thought you might prefer to see us before we go any further."

"Yes."

"You've realised from what I said last night on the telephone that as far as the police are concerned the first stage of this business may come to an end this morning?"

"Yes. You are going to make an arrest, aren't you?"

"I think we shall probably do so. It depends a little on the interview we hope to have in a minute or two. This has been an abominable week for you. I'm sorry I had to keep all these people together here and station bluebottles at your doors and before your gates and so on. It was partly in your own interest. You would have been overrun with pressmen."

"I know."

"Do you want me to tell you——?"

"I think I know."

"You *know*?"

"I think I do. Last night I said to myself: 'Which of these people do I feel in my own bones is capable of this crime?' There was only one—only one of whom it did not seem quite preposterous to think: 'It might—it just *might* be you!' I don't know why—there seems to be no motive, but I believe I am right. I suppose woman's instinct is the sort of phrase you particularly abominate."

"That depends a little on the woman," said Alleyn gravely.

"I suppose it does," said Troy and flushed unexpectedly.

"I'll tell you who it is," he said after a moment. And he told her. "I can see that this time the woman's instinct was not at fault."

"It's—so awful," whispered Troy.

"I'm glad you decided to lunch with my mother," said Alleyn. "It will be easier for you to get right away from everything. She asked me to say that she would be delighted if you would come early. I suggest that you drive over there now."

Troy's chin went up.

"Thank you," she said, "but I'm not going to rat."

"There's no question of ratting——"

"After all, this is *my* ship."

"Of course it is. But it's not sinking and, unfortunately, you can't do anything about this miserable business. It may be rather particularly unpleasant. I should take a trip ashore."

"It's very kind of you to think of me, but, however illogically, I would feel as if I was funking something if I went away before—before you did. I've got my students to think of. You must see that. And even—even Pilgrim——"

"You can do nothing about him——"

"Very well," said Troy angrily, "I shall stay and do nothing."

"Don't, please, be furious with me. Stay, then, but stay with your students."

"I shan't make a nuisance of myself."

"You know perfectly well that ever since I met you, you have made a nuisance of yourself. You've made my job one hundred per cent more difficult, because you've taken possession of my thoughts as well as my heart. And now, you go off to your students and think that over. I want to speak to Pilgrim, if you please."

Troy gazed bleakly at him. Then she bit her lips and Alleyn saw that her eyes were full of tears.

"Oh, hell and damnation, darling," he said.

"It's all right. I'm going. Shut up," mumbled Troy, and went.

Fox came in.

"All right," said Alleyn. "Tell them to get Pilgrim, and come in."

Fox spoke to someone outside and joined Alleyn at the fire.

"We'll have to go warily, Fox. He may give a bit of trouble."

"That's so, sir."

They waited in silence until Basil Pilgrim came in with one of the Yard men. The second man walked in after them and stood inside the door.

"Good morning," said Pilgrim.

"Good morning, Mr. Pilgrim. We would like to clear up one or two points relating to your former statement and to our subsequent investigations."

"Certainly."

Alleyn consulted his note-book.

"What does your car do to the gallon?" he asked.

"Sixteen."

"Sure of that?"

"Yes. She may do a bit more on long runs."

"Right. Now, if you please. We'll go back to Friday evening during your visit to Captain and Mrs. Pascoe. Do you remember the procedure when coffee was brought in?"

"I suppose so. It was in the hall."

He looked, with that curiously restless turn of his head. From Alleyn to Fox and back again.

"Can you tell us who poured out and who handed round the coffee?"

"I suppose so. Though what it can have to do with Sonia—or Garcia——Do you mean about Val's coffee being bitter? Mine was bitter, too. Beastly."

"We should like to know who poured the coffee out."

"Mrs. Pascoe."

"And who handed it round?"

"Well—I did."

"Splendid. Can you remember the order in which you took it round?"

"I'm not sure. Yes, I think so. I took mine over with Val's to where she was sitting, and then I saw Pascoe hadn't got his, and I got it for him. Mrs. Pascoe had poured out her own. Then I went back and sat with Val and I had my coffee."

"You both took black coffee?"

"Yes."

"And sugar?"

"And sugar."

"Who put the sugar in the coffee?"

"Good Lord! I don't know. I believe I did."

"You didn't say anything about your coffee being bitter?"

"I didn't like to. I gave Val a look and made a face and she nodded. She said: 'Sybil, darling, your coffee is perfectly frightful.' Mrs. Pascoe was—" he laughed—"well, she was a bit huffy, I think. Val is always terribly direct. They both appealed to me and I—well, I just said I thought the coffee

234

wasn't quite what one usually expects of coffee, or something. It was dashed awkward."

"It must have been. Later on, when Miss Seacliff complained of feeling unwell, you gave her some aspirin, didn't you?"

"Yes. Why?" asked Pilgrim, looking surprised.

"Was the bottle of aspirins in your pocket?"

"What do you mean? I went upstairs and got it out of my suit-case. Look here, what are you driving at?"

"Please, Mr. Pilgrim, let us get this tidied up. When did you actually give Miss Seacliff the aspirins?"

"When she went to bed. I tell you I got them from my suit-case and took them downstairs and gave her three."

"Did she take them?"

"Not then. We looked in after she was in bed and she said she could never swallow aspirins, and so I dissolved three in water and left the tumbler by her bedside."

"Did you see her drink this solution?"

"No. I think I said, Inspector, that I left it at her bedside."

"Yes," said Alleyn, "I've got that. Where's the bottle?"

"What bottle? Oh, the aspirin. I don't know. I suppose it's in my room upstairs."

"After you left Miss Seacliff's room on Friday night where did you go?"

"I had a drink with Pascoe and went to bed."

"Did you get up at all during the night?"

"No."

"You slept straight through the night?"

"Like the dead," said Pilgrim. He was no longer restless. He looked steadily at Alleyn and he was extremely pale.

"It is strange you should have slept so soundly. There was a very severe thunderstorm that night," lied Alleyn. "Lightning. Doors banging. Maids bustling about. Didn't you hear it?"

"As a matter of fact," said Pilgrim, after a pause, "it's a funny thing, but I slept extraordinarily soundly that night. I'm always pretty good, but that night I seemed to be fathoms deep. I suppose I'd had a bit too much of Pascoe's 1875 courvoisier."

"I see. Now, Mr. Pilgrim, I want you to look at this, if you please."

He nodded to one of his men, who came forward with a brown-paper parcel. He opened it and took out a most disreputable garment.

"Why," said Pilgrim, "that's my old car coat."

"Yes."

"What on earth do you want with that, Mr. Alleyn?"

"I want you to tell me when you burnt this little hole in the cuff. There, do you see."

"I don't know. How the devil should I know! I've had the thing for donkey's years. It never comes out of the car. I've crawled under the car in it. It's obviously a cigarette burn."

"It's an acid burn."

"Acid? Rot! I mean, how could it be acid?"

"Well, I'm afraid I can't tell you. Considering the use the thing's had, I suppose it might have come in contact with acid some time or another."

"This is a recent stain."

"Is it? Well then, it is. So what?"

"Might it be nitric acid?"

"Why?"

"Do you do any etching, Mr. Pilgrim?"

"Yes. But not in my garage coat. Look here, Mr. Alleyn——"

"Will you feel in the pockets?"

Pilgrim thrust a hand into one of the pockets and pulled out a pair of gloves.

"If you look on the back of the right-hand glove," said Alleyn, "you will see among all the greasy stains and worn patches another very small mark. Look at it, please. There. It is exceedingly small, but it, too, was made by an acid. Can you account for it?"

"Quite frankly, I can't. The gloves are always left in the pocket. Anything might happen to them."

"I see. Have you ever lent this coat to anyone else? Has anyone else ever worn the gloves?"

"I don't know. They may have." He looked up quickly and his eyes were suddenly bright with terror. "I think it's quite likely I've lent it," he said. "Or a garage hand might have put it on some time—easily. It may be acid from a battery."

"Have you ever lent it to Miss Seacliff, for instance?"

"Never."

"It's an old riding burberry, isn't it?"

"Yes."

"You didn't lend it to her to hack in at your father's house—Ankerton—during the week-end?"

"Good Lord, no! Valami has got very smart riding clothes of her own."

"Not even the gloves?"

Pilgrim achieved a laugh. "Those gloves! I had just given Valmai six pairs of coloured gloves which she tells me are fashionable. She was so thrilled she even lunched in purple gloves and dined in scarlet ones."

"I mean to ride in?"

"She had her own hunting gloves. What *is* all this?"

"She goes well to hounds, doesn't she?"

"Straight as the best."

"Yes. What sort of horse did you mount her on?"

"A hunter—one of mine."

"Clubbed mane and tail?"

"Yes."

"Look inside the right-hand glove—at the base of the little finger. Do you see that bloodstain?"

"I see a small stain."

"It has been analysed. It is a bloodstain. Do you remember recently cutting or scratching the base of your little finger?"

"I—yes—I think I do."

"How did it happen?"

"I forgot. I think it was at Ankerton—on a bramble or something."

"And you had these gloves with you at the time?"

"I suppose so. Yes."

"I thought you said the gloves and coat always lived in the car?"

"It is rather absurd to go on with this," Pilgrim said. "I'm afraid I must refuse to answer any more questions."

"You are perfectly within your rights. Fox, ask Miss Seacliff if she will be good enough to come in. Thank you, Mr. Pilgrim; will you wait outside?"

"No," said Pilgrim. "I'm going to hear what you say to her. Alleyn hesitated.

"Very well," he said at last. He dropped the coat and gloves behind the desk.

Valmai Seacliff arrived in her black slacks and magenta pullover. She made, as usual, a good entrance, shutting the door behind her and leaning against it for a moment to survey the men.

"Hallo," she said. "More investigations? What's the matter with you, Basil, you look as if you'd murdered somebody?"

Pilgrim didn't answer.

Alleyn said: "I have sent for you, Miss Seacliff, to know if you can help us."

"But I should adore to help you, Mr. Alleyn."

"Did you drink the solution of aspirin that Mr. Pilgrim prepared for you on Friday night?"

"Not all of it. It was too bitter."

"But you said, before, that you drank it."

"Well, I did have a sip. I slept all right without it."

"How is your cut hand?"

"My——? Oh, it's quite recovered."

"May I see it, please?"

She held it out with the same gesture that she had used on Monday night, but this time the fingers trembled. Below the base of the little finger there was still a very thin reddish scar.

"What's this?" said Pilgrim violently. "Valmai—don't answer any of their questions. Don't answer!"

"But, why not, Basil?"

"You told me that you cut your hand on your horse's mane," said Alleyn.

"No. You told me that, Mr. Alleyn."

"You accepted the explanation."

"Did I?"

"How do you say, now, that you cut your hand?"

"I did it on the reins."

"Mr. Pilgrim, did you see this cut on Saturday evening? It must have been quite sore then. A sharp, thin cut."

"I didn't see her hand. She wore gloves."

"All through dinner?"

"Scarlet gloves. They looked lovely," she said, "didn't they, Basil?"

"Do you remember that on Monday night you told me you had no pretensions of being a good horsewoman?"

"Modesty, Mr. Alleyn."

Alleyn turned aside. He moved behind the desk, stooped, and in a second the old raincoat and the gloves were lying on the top of the desk.

"Have you ever seen those before?" asked Alleyn.

"I—don't know. Oh yes. It's Basil's, isn't it?"

"Come and look at it."

She walked slowly across the desk and looked at the coat and gloves. Alleyn picked up the sleeve and without speaking pointed a long forefinger to the acid hole in the cuff. He lifted the collar and turned it back, and pointed to a whitish stain. He dropped the coat, took up the left-hand glove and turned it inside out. He pointed to a small stain under the base of the little finger. And still he did not speak. It was Basil Pilgrim who broke the silence.

"I don't know what he's driving at, Val, but you've never worn the things. I know you haven't. I've told him so. I'll swear it—I'll swear you've never worn them. I *know* you haven't."

"You bloody fool," she screamed. "You bloody fool!"

"Valmai Seacliff," began Alleyn, "I arrest you for the murder of Wolf Garcia on——"

CHAPTER **XXI**

Epilogue in a Garden

Troy sat on a rug in the central grass plot of Lady Alleyn's rose garden. Alleyn stood and looked down at her.

"You see," he said, "it was a very clumsy, messy, and ill-planned murder. It seemed the most awful muddle, but it boils down to a fairly simple narrative. We hadn't much doubt after Monday night that Garcia had set the trap for Sonia. He left his prints on the opium jar and, as Malmsley had prepared the first pipe, Garcia evidently gave himself another. He must have been in a state of partial recovery with a sort of exalted carry-over, when he got the idea of jamming the knife through the floor of the throne. Motive—Sonia had been badgering him to marry her. She was going to have his child and wouldn't let him alone. He had exhausted her charms and her possibilities as a blackmailing off-sider, and he was nauseated by her persistence. She came between him and his work. She probably threatened to sue him for maintenance, to make a full-sized scandal, to raise hell with a big stick in a bucket. The opium suggested a beautifully simple and macabre way out of it all. I saw Sonia's friend in the chorus—Miss O'Dawne—again this morning from the arrest. I got a rather fuller account of the blackmailing game. Sonia and Garcia were both in it. Sonia had tackled Pilgrim and threatened to tell the Methodist peer that Basil was the father of her child. He wasn't, but that made no odds. Basil stumped up and Sonia handed the cash to Garcia. We found a note from Garcia to Valmai Seacliff in which he coolly said he'd bought painting-materials at her shop and put them down to her. The wordings of the letter suggested that he had some sort of upper hand over her, and when I first saw Bobbie O'Dawne she obviously had information up her sleeve and admitted as much. She told Bathgate that Sonia had said Garcia would kill both of them if they babbled. When Sonia died Bobbie O'Dawne was certain

Garcia had done it, and that she'd be the next victim if she didn't keep quiet. Now he's dead, and we've got Valmai Seacliff, Miss O'Dawne is all for a bit of front-page publicity, and told me this morning that Sonia had kept her *au fait* with the whole story. Garcia blackmailed Valmai Seacliff. He said he'd tell Basil Pilgrim that she'd been his—Garcia's—mistress. He said he'd go to the Methodist peer with a story of studio parties that would throw the old boy into a righteous fury, and completely cook Seacliff's goose. Garcia worked the whole thing out with Sonia. She was to tackle Pilgrim while he went for Valmai Seacliff. Garcia had started to work with Seacliff, who at first wouldn't rise. But he'd done some drawings of Seacliff in the nude which he said he'd send to old Pilgrim with a suitable letter, and he told her that Sonia was also prepared to do her bit of blackmail as well. At last, Valmai Seacliff—terrified of losing Pilgrim—said she'd meet Garcia on Friday night in the studio, when they were all safely away, and discuss payment. All this Garcia told Sonia, and Sonia told Bobbie O'Dawne, swearing her to secrecy. O'Dawne was too frightened of Garcia to tell me the Seacliff side, and I also think she honestly felt she couldn't break her word. She's got a sort of code, that funny hard little baggage, and she's stuck to it. But, of course, without her evidence we'd got no motive as far as Seacliff was concerned."

"When did you suspect Valmai?"

"I wasn't very certain until I saw that the person, who murdered Garcia had held his head back by the hair, and that he had struggled so hard that—well, that he had struggled. I then remembered the cut on Seacliff's hand, and how she had showed it to me only when she saw me looking at it, and how she had said it had been made by her horse's reins, when it had obviously been made by something much finer. I remembered how, when I suggested it was not the reins, but the horse's mane, she had agreed. But to go back a bit. From the moment we learned that it was Seacliff who posed the model I felt that we must watch her pretty closely."

"I don't understand that. You say Garcia set the trap with the knife."

"Yes, but I believe Seacliff watched him through a hole in the studio window-blind."

"Seacliff!"

"Yes. She had put three aspirins in Pilgrim's coffee to ensure his sleeping soundly. When she realised he had noticed the coffee tasted odd—he made a face at her—she quickly raised an outcry about her own. She pretended to have a headache in order to get them all to bed early. She slipped out to the garage, wearing slacks and a sweater, put on Pilgrim's old coat and gloves, and drove back to the studio, getting there about midnight, with the intention of arguing about blackmail with Garcia. This was the meeting Miss Phillida Lee overheard Sonia discussing with Garcia. Sonia told Miss Bobbie O'Dawne all about it, and Miss O'Dawne told me, this morning. But you should remember that until this morning Miss O'Dawne had only elaborated what we already knew—the Pilgrim-Sonia side. However, I give you the whole thing as completely as I can. Valmai Seacliff arrived at the studio in a desperate attempt to placate Garcia. She must have left the car somewhere in the lane and walked down, meaning to come in at the side gate. Your maid Ethel and her boy, returning from the flicks, saw the figure of a shortish man standing outside the studio window, apparently looking through the hole in the blind. He wore a mackintosh with the collar turned up. The ray of light caught his beret, which was pulled down on one side, hiding his face. Both Garcia and Pilgrim were too tall for the light to get them anywhere above the chest. So was Malmsley. Seacliff seemed to be the only one about the right height. When we saw Pilgrim's old coat in his car we noticed whitish marks on the collar that suggested face- or neck-powder, and they smelt of Seacliff. It was so dirty it didn't seem likely she would let him embrace her while he was wearing it. When we looked inside the left-hand glove we noticed a bloodstain that corresponded with the cut on her hand. That, of course, came into the picture after the Garcia affair. I believe that she actually watched Garcia set his trap for Sonia and decided to say nothing about it. I believe she went in, probably got him to drink a good deal more whisky, and offered to drive him up to London. You told me he did a little etching."

"Yes. He'd prepared a plate a few days before he went."

"Then perhaps he said he'd take the acid to bite it. Is that the right word? Anyway, she got out your caravan and backed it up to the window. There's a slope down from the garage—enough to free-wheel into the lane and start on compression. The servants wouldn't think anything odd if they heard a car in the lane. Malmsley had helped Garcia get everything ready. All she had to do was open the window, wheel the clay model over the sill into the caravan, get Garcia aboard and start off. The packing-case had already been addressed by Garcia. So she knew the address, even if he was incapable of directing her. I think myself that he had told her exactly where the warehouse was when he asked her to go there to see him, and she has admitted that he gave her a sketch-map. Probably his idea was that she should pay blackmail to him while he was there. She made another rather interesting slip over that. Do you remember how she said she was reminded of the warehouse address by a remark someone made at breakfast about Holloway? She told me—and, I think, you—that as soon as she heard the word Holloway she remembered that Garcia had said his warehouse was near the prison, and she had told him to be careful he didn't get locked up. Holloway is a woman's prison. Her very feeble joke would have been a little less feeble if he was blackmailing her, and the place of assignation was not Holloway, but Brixton. By giving us Holloway as the district, she was sending us off in exactly the opposite direction to the right one. We might have hunted round Holloway for weeks. I wondered if she had been the victim of a sort of word-association and I decided to go for Brixton. Luckily enough, as it turned out. As a matter of fact, she has twice fallen into the trap of substituting for the truth something that is linked with it in her mind. The first time was over the cut on her hand. It had been made when she was standing above Garcia with her hand wound in his hair. She saw me looking at the scar, decided to speak of it before I did, was, perhaps, reminded subsconciously of horses' hair, a mane gripped in the hand, rejected the idea of hair altogether and substituted reins. Have you had enough of this, Troy?"

"No. I want to know about it."

"There's not much more. She drove Garcia to his warehouse. He'd got the keys. She murdered him there, because she was hell-bent on marrying Pilgrim, and becoming a very rich peeress, and because it was in Garcia's power to stop her. She's an egomaniac. She drove the caravan back to your garage and drove herself back to the Pascoes' house in Pilgrim's car. The distance to the warehouse is thirty miles. At that time of night she'd do it easily in an hour and a half. She must have been back at the studio by three and probably got to the Pascoes' by half-past. Even supposing she lost her way—and I don't think she would, because there's a good map in the caravan—she'd a margin of two hours before there was a chance of the servants being about."

"Why didn't you think it was Pilgrim?"

"I wondered if it was Pilgrim, of course. After we had checked all the alibis, it seemed to me that Pilgrim and Valmai Seacliff were by far the most likely. I even wondered if Pilgrim had drugged Seacliff with aspirin instead of Seacliff drugging Pilgrim—until she lied about her cut hand, her horsemanship and the address of the warehouse. On top of that there was the glove and the smell of the raincoat. She said she had taken the aspirins Pilgrim gave her. We found that she hadn't. We found that she had aspirins of her own in the evening bag she had taken to Boxover. Why should she pretend she had none? And why, after all, should Pilgrim kill Garcia? He had paid Sonia off, but as far as we know, Garcia had kept out of the picture where Pilgrim was concerned. Garcia was tackling Valmai Seacliff, not Pilgrim. No, the weight of evidence was against her. She lied where an innocent woman would not have lied. And—I'm finishing up where I began—I think that an innocent person would not have pressed Sonia down upon the point of that knife after she had cried out. She would not have disregarded that first convulsive start. She murdered Sonia, knowing the knife was there, as deliberately as she murdered Garcia."

"Will they find her guilty?"

"I don't know, Troy. Her behaviour when we arrested her was pretty damning. She turned on Pilgrim like a wild cat because he kept saying he'd swear she'd never worn the coat. If he'd said she had often worn it, half our case would have gone up in smoke."

Alleyn was silent for a moment, and then knelt down on the rug beside Troy.

"Has this all made a great difference to you?" he said. "Is it going to take you a long time to put it behind you?"

"I don't know. It's been a bit of a shock for all of us."

"For Pilgrim—yes. The others will be dining out on it in no time. Not you."

"I think I'm sort of stunned. It's not that I liked any of them much. It's just the feeling of all the vindictiveness in the house. It's so disquieting to remember what Seacliff's thoughts must have been during the last week. I almost feel I ought to have a priest in with bell and book to purify the house. And now—the thought of the trial is unspeakably shocking. I don't know where I am—I——"

She turned helplessly towards Alleyn and in a moment she was in his arms.

"No, no," said Troy. "I mustn't. You mustn't think——"

"I know." Alleyn held her strongly. He could feel her beating secretly against his own. Everything about trees, the ground beneath him, and the clouds in the still autumn sky, rose like bright images in his mind and vanished on a wave of exultation. He was alone in the world with her. And with that moment of supremacy before him came the full assurance that he must not take it. He knew quite certainly that he must let his moment go by. He heard Troy's voice and bent his head down.

"—you mustn't think because I turn to you——"

"It's all right," said Alleyn. "I love you, and I know. Don't worry."

They were both silent for a little while.

"Shall I tell you," said Alleyn at last, "what I think? I think that if we had met again in a different way you might have loved me. But because of all that has happened your thoughts of me are spoiled. There's an association of cold and rather horrible officiousness. Well, perhaps it's not quite as bad as all that, but my job has come between us. You know, at first I thought you disliked me very much. You were so prickly. Then I began to hope a little. Don't cry, dear Troy. It's a great moment for me, this. Don't think I misunderstand. You so nearly love me, don't you?" For the first time his voice shook.

"So nearly."

"Then," said Alleyn, "I shall still allow myself to hope a little."

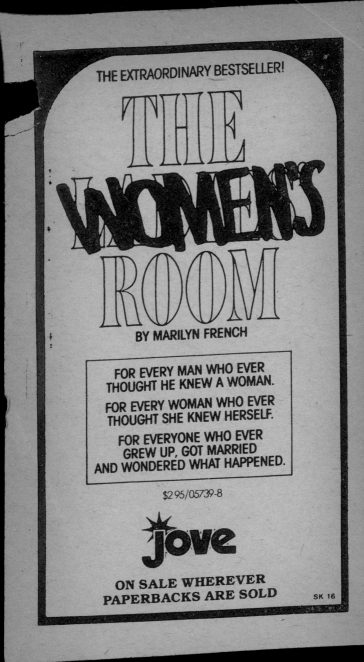